Praise for Before the Swallows Come Back

This is total immersion in the natural world. An absolutely heart-filling and lyrical novel. Fiona Curnow has crafted an immense story, and an incredibly rich one. *Carol McKay*

It is impossible to avoid falling under the spell of Before the Swallows Come Back. *K Bookish Life*

An engaging and a powerful story. *Echoes in an Empty Room*

I absolutely LOVED this book. I was mesmerised by all the beautiful and vivid descriptions. I was rooting for the two main characters: they were quite innocent (and slightly naive) young people who lived on the outskirts of society, a bit different from the others. A beautifully written book with lyrical and poetic passages. *Monika Reads*

I absolutely loved it. The writing was beautiful, vivid and the descriptions of the Scottish Highlands was magical. *Glasgow Book Addict*

It is so beautifully written and full of description you felt like you were in the book yourself. *Leah Mae Reads*

This book is gorgeous. It is poignant, emotional. It definitely gave me major Where the Crawdads Sing vibes... only this one was based in Scotland! BONUS. *Sambooka23*

This story of love and found family and redemption is one I won't soon forget. *Loopy Knot*

Fiona's lyrical writing showcases the beauty and demands of the natural world. *Liz Humphreys*

As an animal lover, I found the relationship Tommy had with his animal family beautiful. *Andrew Lees*

This was a story that really moved me. From the get-go I was so devoted to the main characters and their journey through hell and back and the hardships they had to endure!!...I absolutely loved it. It's so beautifully written and I was completely invested in it! It felt like I was there in Scotland amongst the countryside and surrounded by nature!! Perfect escapism!! *Jade Nomura*

It's very rare that I would reread a book but this is one I can imagine doing so. I adored this book! It was lyrically beautiful with its lush descriptions of nature but it was the characters that make it stand out. *Books By Bindu*

Before
the Swallows
Come Back
by
Fiona Curnow

Before the Swallows Come Back is a work of fiction

For Morag Brownlie
A truly special person

Chapter 1

A knock at the door. 'On you go, sweetheart. It's for you.' His words, slow, breathy, like they had been pushed from somewhere very deep, very narrow. Charlotte grinned at her father, tip-toed to the door, let out a deep sigh, and pulled it open. The delivery man stood there with her birthday present. There was only one thing it could possibly be. The size of it. The shape of it.

She glanced back at her father. 'Dad, you didn't?' The grin so big now it seemed to split her face in two. Her blue eyes twinkled with a happiness not seen for too long.

Her dad just smiled. The pleasure this gave him. To see her so full of joy. There was nothing on this planet that he could want more than this.

She turned her attention back to the delivery, jiggling from one foot to the other as she did so.

'Delivery for...' The driver looked at his note.

'Charlotte. Charlotte Desson.' Looked back up with a smile. 'Would that be you then?'

'Yes,' she whispered and reached gingerly for the package as if it might disappear if she actually touched it. Her hands were shaking. 'I'll need a signature.'

'Mine?'

'Yours'll do just fine.'

She scribbled something illegible that she thought looked grown-up. Like her dad would do.

'Enjoy!'

'Thank you.'

She hurried into the kitchen, grabbed the scissors and attacked the packaging. No shaking now. No hesitation. So many bits. Sticky annoying bits that just didn't want to come off. Finally the bike was clean and clear and glowing in the most perfect deep crimson. The lettering gold. It was simply beautiful. Not some little girly thing. Not a little child's thing. This was the real deal. Her very own perfect big-person's bike. A basket up front for her bag, jacket – whatever – a speedometer, a bell, and everything! She pulled it and it jangled through the house, a statement. This is me! I have arrived!

'Dad! It's just. Oh thank you!'

Her dad had shuffled across to the door. She hugged him with one arm, the other holding tightly onto the handlebars.

'Go on then. Take it for a spin.'

She glanced out of the door at the disappearing road, the woods, the beckoning hills in the distance. All waiting just for her. 'Are you sure? Will you be okay?'

'Yes, yes. Off you go now. I didn't buy it so as you could just stare at it. Not too far though!' he added, balancing himself against the door-frame, trying his hardest to look casual. Capable.

She waved as she wheeled it down the path and onto the road.

He watched intently as she straddled it, secured her

balance and cycled off into the countryside. Once she had disappeared he closed his eyes, blew out a tired, tense breath, before sliding his way back to his seat. *How on earth had that happened? Twelve years old in a whisper.* He wouldn't worry, wouldn't fret. She was such a sensible wee thing. She would be just fine.

She held her head high, the wind flying past. This was the very best kind of freedom. A far-from-anyone kind of freedom. An I-can-just-be kind of freedom. Her heart swelled with her lungs and if she had been a different person she might have called out some ecstatic whoops or cheers, but she just whispered, *yes!* to herself, to the skies, to the wind. She would keep to the back road, as promised. Of course she would. The whole point of this – of wanting her very own bicycle – was so that she could disappear into new, quiet places. Explore the world away from buildings and people and noise and intrusions.

She couldn't go too far, be out for too long. Her father would worry and that would be wrong. Her legs soon began to get a bit achy. A bit tired. She glanced down at the speedometer. Five miles. That was quite far. Probably too far, but far was such an objective word. How far is far, really?

To her left she peered into a forest crawling down the hill. Dense and green and crackling and buzzing. Light dancing on the leaves, trickling through the needles, settling on bracken, twitching and swaying and mesmerising. She wheeled her bike into the dense bracken, the trees. Stopped. Sighed. She wanted to explore but was worried she might scratch her bike. Damage it. She stared all around, listened, before laying it carefully down amongst the bracken. There was no one here, but it was best to be careful. Satisfied that it couldn't easily be seen. Not by some stranger. Not unless you knew it was there. So, not unless it was her. She edged her way further downhill, wary at first. This was all new and she was alone, far from home. If anything happened all the way out here who would know? Who could help her? She decided that was silly. There was nothing to worry about.

Suddenly she stopped. Held her breath. There, some distance from where she stood hidden amongst the tall, tall pines, someone was in the river. Something odd about the curl of his body as he stared beneath the water, bent over like some wild creature waiting to pounce on its prey, one hand holding a long knobbly stick, the other a peculiar tin cone through which he peered.

The swell of the river cascading through the deep valley swept away any need for silence. She doubted that he would hear even a scream from up here, let alone her breath, but she kept it low and still nevertheless. Well, as low and still as she could considering the circumstances. Considering the fear, the excitement and whatever else this feeling was that was threatening to take her over. *Silly, silly. It's just some boy!*

It felt like she had reached a different world. There were hills and forests, and the river, and she wanted to spend as much time as she could grab hold of exploring, clambering through deserted places, inventing games, adventures. And the sighting of this boy – or was he a young man? – wasn't about to spoil it all for her. As long as he didn't see her; didn't know of her presence, she was fine. As she watched she allowed her imagination to fly far away. He became a villain. A vagabond. An escaped convict! Her heart raced in splendid fear with thoughts of what he might do if he caught sight of her. There would be a chase, of course, but she was nimble and fast. In her story this was her land and she knew every inch. She would scamper up a tree, stifling a giggle as he searched in vain, confused at her inexplicable disappearance. Eventually he would give up. She would be victorious!

As she stared, mulling over what to do, she decided she could risk getting just a little bit closer. She began to edge her way further down the steep slope, from one moss encrusted boulder to the next, her body swishing through the ferns that stood almost as tall as her shoulder. It felt as if they were speaking to her; whispering secrets of the forest that only she could hear. She crept down further still, enjoying that sense of invisibility. Of being silent and secretive. Of spying on some poor unsuspecting boy who was blissfully unaware of her presence.

She froze. Fear bolted up her spine, snatched at her breath, as he suddenly stood straight, stretching his back, twisting his shoulders in a peculiar jiggly spin. He stared up the hillside as he waded back to the riverbank and clambered out, his eyes still fixed on where she crouched. She had been quite sure that he couldn't see her. The trees, the ferns, the boulders. So much all around her. But the boy was still staring. She didn't dare move. She narrowed her eyes, straining to see better, to focus in like the stare of a wild cat, the lens of a camera.

He lifted his hand to his brow to cut off the glare of the sun and cast a shadow over his eyes. It had to be her that he was staring at. A gulp. Wide eyes. Thumping heart.

Chapter 2

No. A soft exhalation. No it wasn't her at all. She could see now that his gaze appeared to be caught just beyond her, higher up the slope.

She turned her head slowly and almost let out a giggle, slapping her hand on her mouth to smother it. A deer, two, three, more, all staring back at her. A moment of magic. In a shiver they were off, darting as one into the darkness of the woods. She peered through the trees but could see nothing other than trunks and branches, as if they had never been there at all. They had done that in a breath. Just disappeared. She wondered if they were even of this earth. Spectral creatures paying a visit and retreating back into their own world. She could relate to that. Would sometimes like to be that.

The boy's attention had been drawn back to the river again and she took the chance to creep closer. Closer still. She lay on her front staring through the bracken and the ferns. She was near enough now to make out his face when he looked up from whatever it was he was doing. Young, she guessed – older than her but not by much, perhaps thirteen or fourteen – quite handsome really, but in an odd kind of a way. His dark shoulder length hair was messy, tangled. Not quite black, but near enough, and in the sunlight a bright red, like copper seemed to spin through it. His eyes looked dark too, but she couldn't quite make out their colour. Not from this far away. His lips curled up at the edges like he was smiling at something.

His clothes were ragged. Perhaps he had dressed for adventure, for not having to care about getting muddy, or tangled in brambles, or some such thing. A jumper with catches and loose threads. Trousers that had seen better days. He seemed to be talking to something, to someone she couldn't see, chatting away to absolutely nothing.

As she stared she felt a tickle in her nose. Oh no! A sneeze was building. She squeezed her nose to try and stifle it. It built some more. She shook her head trying to shake it out, away. Still there and building to that point. That point when there was absolutely nothing she could do. The loudest, most awful sneeze exploded from her and filled all of the spaces around her.

He didn't flinch. Didn't turn towards her. That was just odd. Perhaps he was deaf. Perhaps he was just plain crazy. Perhaps he just didn't bother about such things.

There was nothing for it now, she decided, but to stand up. To show herself. And do what? Smile? Say hello? Just walk on by? Head back up the hill and into the forest? How on earth could she explain why she had been there, crouching down in the undergrowth? Did she even need to? Life was just so complicated.

She stood up, brushed herself down. Told herself to

push some words out. 'Hello,' she said, trying to sound normal, wondering what on earth she was doing. 'I was just–' She was just what? Nothing feasible came to her mind. She found herself blurting out an unexpected apology. 'Well, you see, um, I'm sorry. I didn't mean anything. I. It was rude. Sorry.'

He simply stood there, staring, almost smiling but not quite, a sort of curl at the edges of his lips, lopsided, a bit odd.

'I was just.' She looked down at her feet. 'Oh, I was watching. Watching you. What is it you're doing anyway?'

He didn't reply, just crooked his finger and beckoned her closer.

She paused, hesitated, felt foolish and unsure. She took a deep breath and held her head high before stepping forward so that she was within touching distance of him. A thrill tingled through her, quite unlike anything she had felt before.

But he was just plain peculiar. No acknowledgement. No greeting. He sat down on the riverbank, his bare feet dangling in the frothing water, and patted the grass beside him. She slipped out of her trainers, tugged her socks off and rolled up her jeans before sitting down beside him. The water was freezing, but the day hot, so it wasn't an unpleasant feeling. Her toes tingled. Of course, this was forbidden on so many levels. Being this far away. Forbidden. The river. Forbidden. Talking to strangers. Forbidden. Her father would be so disappointed if he knew, but he didn't and he wouldn't. Not if she could help it.

'R-right, well,' the boy sort of whispered. 'This here.' He paused, took a deep breath. 'Is so that I can see what's going on, um.' Another pause. Another breath. It was like he didn't really know how to speak, how to say a whole sentence without having to stop. He shook his head as if a wasp, or an insect of some sort had settled on him, then closed his eyes tight, squeezing them. Another big breath. 'D-down, down there.' He held the metal cone up, showed her the glass bottom, dipped it into the water. 'Come, come close now or, or you-you'll not see.' His voice was slow and careful with a precision, a gentleness to it that she hadn't been expecting. Really not very boy-like at all. In fact nothing about him was very boy-like. He was odd! Different.

She inched her way along the bank until their bodies were almost touching. He took her hand. She didn't wince, didn't pull away, as he wrapped her fingers around the handle of the canister.

'F-forward now and, and under. Under the water, like this, see?'

She copied his actions.

'Oh. Oh!' The pebbles, a multitude of colours, stilled beneath the gurgling of the water. And the silver flash of tiny fish. And the weeds swishing, and swaying and jiggling in the water. It was like they were dancing. 'Oh, it's so, so pretty!'

He smiled. Her joy trickled between them like the best music. It was a good thing to make someone happy. To have them see what he saw; love what he loved. He felt himself relax a little. Strengthen a little. His words strung themselves together more easily now. Something about this girl eased him 'Now what you're looking for is, is mussels. Black shells.'

'Okay.'

He stared for far too long, like he wasn't looking at her at all; like he couldn't see her. His eyes, dark brown with flecks of gold and purple – extraordinary. She couldn't help but stare back, get drawn in.

Then he shrugged and turned his attention back to the water. The spell, or whatever it was, broken.

'You'll need to come d-deeper if you want to do it p-proper, like.'

'But I'll get soaked.'

'But it's hot! A w-wee bit water isn't going to bother you, is it?'

Challenge given, she wasn't about to refuse. To seem like a weak girl. 'Right. Okay then.'

They slid off the bank and into the knee-deep water, wading out to thigh-deep, to waist-deep. She refused to wince at the cold, as her feet tentatively curled their way around the pebbles, the stones, feeling for a grip, security. He was ahead of her now on the edge of a pool where the water was still and dark and deep.

Just as she had relaxed into it all, felt like she knew what she was doing, she slipped, her feet giving way, and she fell backwards, tumbling towards the water. He lunged at her. Tried to grab hold of her, keep her upright, but the water took both of them. Swept them downriver. He was swimming, she floundering. Her head bobbing up and down, disappearing and rising again as she snatched at desperate gulps of air.

'You need to be like the water. F-flow. Flow with it,' he

called, fearing that she was going to stay under next time. He took one last desperate lunge. Caught her arm. Held tight.

The water swirled around them. The sound of it, strong and sweeping, rushing through their ears. She was gasping desperately for breath. Her lungs burning. Under the water. Above it again. Under again. Her legs were hitting against nothing but water. She could feel nothing solid. Nothing safe. This was it. She was going to drown. This was the end of her life.

He fought to keep a hold of her, his fingers now tightly gripping on to her T-shirt. He battled against the force of the water, his eyes flicking from her to the bank, from her to the bank. They would make it. They had to make it. The water wouldn't take him as it had his grandpa. Panic. *No, don't do that. Don't do that.*

At last he felt control. He was winning. Overpowering the water. He pulled her back towards the bank, to shallower water. She spluttered and gasped as her feet took hold once more. Held her upright once more.

She coughed, cleared her lungs, snatched desperately at the air, fighting for her breath, slowly straightening up. Standing tall. She splashed at him. Angry. Embarrassed. Humiliated.

Chapter 3

He watched as she ran back up the hill, through the bracken and on into the woods, until he couldn't see her any more. But the image of her stayed. He thought she looked like a faerie; pale skin and long dark hair that curled all the way down her back, black like the raven. Her eyes were a bright blue, but dark too. Deep like the ocean. A wee bit magic. A wee bit unreal. That was what she seemed to him.

'I'm sorry,' he whispered into the air. 'I didn't mean nothing. I didn't mean. I didn't.'

He turned despondently back to the river, intending to carry on checking the pearl shells, but his heart wasn't in the right place and he couldn't focus. He didn't like this feeling. It hurt him. Stabbed at his chest. Buzzed through his head like angry wasps. Instead he swam back across to his side of the river, the current pulling him down with it, but he knew how to ride it, go with it. That girl, she didn't. She hadn't known the way of things. He could see that now.

Why had he even gone over to the other side? That was foolish behaviour. No good could come of it and he knew well enough. There had been stories aplenty, warnings from his family. You keep to places you know; people you know. That's best. A boy like you has to stay safe.

He knew he was just that wee bit different. Not quite the same as other folk. His world was a stranger to them. But it didn't really matter as long as he was careful. As long as he listened.

But that girl. He had thought she understood. He had talked to her and that wasn't normal. And she had talked back and sat beside him and followed him and he wished he hadn't gone and spoiled it all. He gathered his things – his can, his pole, and his bag – and followed the twist of the river. He caught the silver flash of a salmon leaping up out of the river and he smiled and stared and tried to track it through the water, but it disappeared soon enough into the blackness of the deep.

His mind was in a better place again. A softer place. He ran across the field, his arms wide, flying like the swallows that swept through the sky above him. By the time he got back to the camp the smell of the fire and the cooking of the fish bit at his hunger. His dog, Rona – a scruffy wee Jack Russell cross – came running to meet him, all waggy-tailed and joyous panting.

He bent down and scratched her head. 'Hi there, wee one,' he whispered.

His ma beckoned him over. Always a comfort in seeing her. Red hair tied back. Purple eyes sparkling in a ruddy face that looked like nature itself. The glow of the fire lighting her up, bringing beads of sweat to her brow. The smile that said everything is okay. The world is okay.

'Where have you been, Tommy lad? Checking on the

pearls again, aye?' she asked.

'Aye, Ma. Checking,' Tommy answered.

'And how are they the day, then?'

'I'm still waiting on them. They're not quite ready. Not yet.'

A chuckle broke from his brothers. His mother stared them down, knowing that a wise crack was about to fly out of one of their mouths.

'Hold your tongues!' she warned in a powerful whisper.

She turned her attention back to the pot that stood on its stand in the fire. Fried salmon fresh out of the river. The river was the boundary between the two estates. It was a free place, flowing water like that, free and wild and that had always been the way of things. Anyway it was just one fish. Food was food, and this was right good! Another pot of *skirlie* – oatmeal and onions – sat to the side.

Tommy, his parents, and his two brothers sat around the fire and ate their dinner. Stories were shared about the day's work, about berries picked (it was raspberry season and all of them had fingers stained red with the juice) about other Tinkers they had met at the picking. Who was doing what and where they were headed. There weren't so many of them now. Not like the old days.

There was hardly a tent like theirs to be seen any more. Their way of life was fast disappearing, but they wouldn't give up on it. The tent, how it encouraged them to live, the quietness and the slowness. It was as if they lived in a different time to the rest of the world. They could still touch their history, their ancient relatives. The tracks they had trodden were now theirs. Their stories were shared, kept alive, night after night, around the fire.

After dinner Tommy fetched some white milk – oats steeped in milk then mixed with hot water. The best thing for the horses – and slipped silently over to where they were tethered.

'Here you are my lovelies,' he said, setting the pails of white milk at their feet, stroking their manes, their backs, their flanks, their thighs. Boy and beast both enjoying the touch, the connection.

'He'll make a fine horseman yet,' Jeannie, his mother said proudly.

'Aye, well, let's hope so. Like father, like son, eh?' Robbie, his father replied.

'Ma, he's no got the sense for looking after himself, let alone any other creatures!'

'Nonsense! He's got *the way* right enough, of that there's no doubt. And that's more precious than anything. Just you remember that.'

'Ma, he's touched!'

'I'll not hear you speak like that of your own brother!' She stretched across and slapped him, good and hard.

'Ooch ya! Ma!'

'I'll ooch ya, you, so I will! There's more wisdom in that laddie than the pair of you put together, so there is. You mark my words!'

Tommy heard none of this. There was no other world but the one he was in. Him and his horses. He listened to the sound of them eating, to the swish of their tails, to the gentle stamping of their hooves, to the contented snuffles of their satisfied breathing. He snuffled back at them, speaking in horse, staying with them until the shadows lengthened and the sun began to slip behind the mountains.

He knew that his family were sat around their fire, telling stories, laughing. His father playing his chanter, his mother singing along. A lifetime of harmonies drifting up into the night air mingling with all of the others. Skyward. His brothers would be joking around. Tonight wasn't a night for being a part of that.

He looked up at the perfectly blue sky impossible for any human to replicate, to describe even, such was its beauty. It was as clear as he had ever seen it, and soon it would be sprinkled with stars. First one or two twinkling like beacons – he wondered what they were signalling to; who else could see them as he did? – then, in the breath of a sigh, there would be a multitude of them. All different, all unique lights in the night sky. All shining for him.

Tonight he would sleep right under the stars. There wouldn't even be canvas between them. Those were the best nights. He would lie there, staring up at the endlessness of the stars and feel free and safe and special.

Chapter 4

Charlotte reached her bicycle, breathless and exasperated, pulled it out from under the bracken, swiped it free of bits of leaf and twig, wheeled it back up to the road, leapt on and cycled off. She was cold. The wet of her clothes uncomfortable. She pedalled as fast as she could, not looking back, not looking down, her head high, her blood pumping, her clothes drying, her anger softening.

As she rode along the single-track road she played the events over in her mind. Had he really done that on purpose? Led her to a place so deep, with such a strong undertow, that she could no longer stand up? What was he trying to do? Frighten her? Harm her? She didn't really know. He had seemed nice, friendly, even sweet, but he was a boy, and boys, well, they could be such idiots.

She decided that it didn't matter one way or the other. Chances were that she would never see him again anyway. She turned off the single-track road onto the path which led to the back of her house. The garden was a mess. Not like it should be. Weeds had long since taken dominance over what had once been flowerbeds. The grass was overgrown and calling out for a mow. She had to do something about that. Make it at least a wee bit nice for her dad. They had had such plans for it when they moved in last year. Soft chats on warm days about the flowers they would grow. The tree swing, maybe even a tree-house, or had she grown out of such things?

'No, of course not! We could make it a sort of grown-up tree-house.'

He had smiled at her, pulled her close and hugged her tight. 'My big wee girl.'

It was only a couple of months after that he had got sick. Really sick. On nice days, on good days, she could help him out here. Set his chair in the shade of the big old oak tree, sheltered. Sometimes they would stay out all day. Those were the best days. Almost normal days.

She told herself off for not having been better at making the garden nice. It made him happy and she should be better. A better daughter. But it was quite hard to be that person all of the time.

She set her bike against the little wooden garden shed, its roof giving off the smell of a hot summer's day. Softly melting tar. She checked for any damage, wiped the chassis clean and dry with an old tea towel that hung above her dad's tools. Polished the seat, though there wasn't really the need. 'Okay.' She stepped back to admire it once more. 'As good as new!' She swiped at a couple of dandelions as she crossed what should have been a lawn and opened the back door. The sound of the radio trickled over the floorboards, dust motes dancing.

'It's just me, Dad,' she called out softly, half-heartedly. He might be sleeping, dozing, best left that way. She was quite sure that she had stayed out for far too long. Guiltily she looked across at his chair, his head slouched. A slight panic. 'Dad?' whispered this time. She leaned in close so that she could feel his breath. Soft and steady. Okay. He was okay.

She tiptoed back out of the room. Changed into dry clothes. Did a quick tidy. Washed the dishes. Made the beds. Opened the windows. Checked the cupboards for tea. There was bread and cheese. That would do her. She fed the cat. Prepared her dad's food. He could only eat mush just now. Mashed up mush like baby food.

She glanced up at the kitchen clock. Not quite dinnertime. Should she attack the garden? At least do a bit? Yes. It would make them both feel better. She wheeled the lawnmower out of the shed but decided against it. The noise. There would be too much noise. Instead she rummaged through the box that held the garden equipment. Found the shears and clattered the blades open and shut. A sharp scratchy sound. Fierce. She swiped at the overgrowth. The weeds fell. The grass would have to wait though. There was no time for that. Not today.

She raked the weeds up, flat and dead, and piled them onto the compost heap. Stabs on her fingers, scratches on her knees, but it didn't matter. Sometimes working hard was good. That free place it took you to. That other space where there was nothing else.

Her back was hurting, her fingers blistered, her stomach grumbling. Enough for today. She walked back in, washed her hands, scrubbing and scrubbing at them until they shone, red raw. She heated his food, set his tray up and carried it into the sitting room. He hadn't moved at all. Panic. Always panic. She squeezed his shoulder gently. 'Dad! Dinner!'

His eyes opened. A weak smile. 'What would I do without you, Princess? A wee cuddle for your dad?' he asked, stretching his arms out.

'Of course,' she said with a smile. In truth, she hated it. The wheeze to his breath, the stab of his bones where flesh should be, the confirmation that he was very, very ill. But she smiled and hugged anyway.

'Can I show you something?' she asked after dinner. After tidying up. After giving him his pills with a glass of water.

'What is it?'

'A wee surprise.'

She helped him out to the back garden. Little things that were once unnoticed, just normal everyday things, had become so big. The effort of getting to the back door. Who'd have thought that would even be a *thing*, a consequential challenge? From A to B in your own house. But here it was.

The sun was sinking now. Long shadows slipped across the grass, but you could see. You could see the difference. At least she hoped so. Hoped that he would see it too. A moment of doubt. She should have waited. Got the lawn done. Got it looking just so. Got it perfect. But these days she had learned that sometimes life wouldn't wait, wouldn't always be there, wouldn't be kind. If there was goodness to be shared, a smile to be brought, it had to be done right then. Right at that very moment.

He lifted his head, breathed the fresh air. The hint of a smile. He scanned the garden slowly, carefully. A tear escaped. 'You're a wee star, so you are. Just look at that.'

'I'm sorry it's not, well, you know. Better.' She shrugged apologetically.

'Princess, it's perfect.' He slapped his forehead. 'How could I forget that?'

'What?'

'In the kitchen, top cupboard. A wee birthday cake for you.'

They sat on the back step, a blanket draped over their shoulders, Charlotte eating cake, him watching, smiling, but wishing for more. For a bit of normality. Just a bit. They stayed out until the nip in the air was too strong. Her dad had grown tired and needed his bed.

As the house stood silently behind her she sat on the back step, looking out at the nothingness of the night, thinking about her day; mostly about that boy.

Why had he done that though?

Chapter 5

The next morning they were to be off picking berries again, but Tommy had set himself a mission to complete before that. He had taken one of the little baskets he had made as he sat and worked alongside his ma. That was what he did. He watched and he copied and he learned before going off and making his own creations.

He watched as his pa and his brothers worked with tin to make pots and the likes. He twisted the metal and twirled it and made his own designs. There was no use to them, no function. He just liked them. Odd shapes, curls and twists and beauty.

It was the same with the baskets. His ma's were large and plain and sturdy, made for carrying laundry or logs or some such thing. Functional. His were delicate and threaded with intricate little patterns; designs that took his fancy.

They were meant to be for the selling, for making a bit of money when the picking had all finished, the work dried up and the harsh dark winter stood there waiting. There were a couple of older folk who took to his wee creations and always bought one when their doors were chapped on.

He stood back, let his ma do the talking and the selling, but the smile the old folk gave was for him. It made him happy to think of the wee things he had made sitting in their houses with maybe some flowers or some shells or some stones sitting in them. Pretty things that made the world a lighter place.

It wasn't just the mussels with their pearls that the river held. Nurtured. It was also jewels. Garnets and pyrite like rubies and gold slipped amongst the rocks at the bottom of the river. Sometimes the odd fleck of real gold itself! He would check on his pearl-bed then scan around for other treasures. Sparkles of beauty hiding in the cold grey of the stone.

He filled his little basket with the best stone he had found that held garnets – dark blood red – and sprigs of the sweetest heather that he and his ma would sell on to the tourists in the nearby town. They twisted them up with dried bracken, or twigs, or moss, making little bouquets that could dangle from a rear-view mirror, or clip to a lapel, or even sit in a girl's hair. His ma wouldn't miss a few sprigs and he would replace them soon enough. It was him that had picked most of them anyway. He had an eye for things like that. A sense of where the best were to be found. The brightest colours, the sweetest scent.

He crept away from the camp with the first calls of the birds and ran across the field, a carpet of early morning mist covering everything, his bare feet feeling the ground, knowing it. He ran with the dogs bounding alongside him. When he came to the river, a heavier, more dense mist curled up from the water, clinging to the overhang of trees. It made him stop, look around, breathe in the magic he could feel all around him.

Remembering that he was in a hurry he snapped himself back out of his reverie and ran ahead, following the river's curves, until he came to the place where he had met the girl.

It was still cold, the sun not yet high enough to warm the air, the dampness of the mist making it colder still. He quickly tossed his clothes to the ground.

'You two stay here now,' he told the dogs. 'Sit and wait and I'll not be two minutes.'

He stepped into the water with the basket held high above his head, waded, then swam across the river. The cold of it stung, but in a good way. In an exciting life-affirming way. His teeth were now chattering, his fingers and toes turning numb. It felt colder still as he clambered out of the river and onto the opposite bank.

He looked back at his dogs who were sat there, their eyes trained on him, both desperate to join him, trembling in anticipation, waiting for that call, but knowing that it wasn't coming. They had to wait. He smiled at them.

'Good dogs,' he whispered.

Treading lightly on the soft grass he sought out the very same spot where they had sat together – him and the girl. He knew because of the patch of wild garlic that he had seen by his side, by the twist of the long grass, the reeds, the nest of the water vole. Things that others might not notice, but he saw them all; held them all in his memory. He drew them in his head, exactly as they had been. Every tiny detail.

He set the basket down. It was so early that no one

would be around, but he checked anyway. He knew he wouldn't be able to hear much above the swell of birdsong dancing with the heavy sound of the river, but he closed his eyes, strained through it, above it. Nothing. Then he stared through the trees, up the hill. Beyond the hill was where the big house stood. He had never seen it. Only heard stories. Imagined it.

His grandma had told of the days when the rivers were full of pearls. When their main income was fishing for them. Her job was to sell the best ones on to the people of the big houses. Oh aye. They were happy enough to see his people at those times. She told of taking a drink with them. Actually being invited in! Those were the days, eh? Those were the days.

He hoped that she would come back. The girl from the big house. At least that was where he guessed she had come from. The way she looked. You could tell, couldn't you? Folk with money and all of the things that went with it. He didn't envy them that way of life. No. He had everything he needed. Everything he wanted. What could be better than to live free and wild and happy?

He hoped that the girl would find his gift. That she would understand. That she would know he was very, very sorry. He hadn't meant for anything to happen. For her to be frightened. Not like that. Sometimes he just forgot that not everyone knew what he knew. Could do what he could do.

Satisfied, he hurried back into the water and swam across. The dogs barked their excitement. Made little circles around him. He pulled his clothes back on and they ran back to the camp. That would warm him up soon enough. None of his family would be bothered if they saw him. He was always first up, and running with the dogs was just something he liked to do. It was all normal.

Chapter 6

Charlotte did all of her chores. It was second nature to her now. Feed dad, help him to the bathroom, wait outside while he washed and showered, just in case he fell or couldn't manage, help him back to his chair, make sure he was comfy and had everything close to hand. A selection of things to read, water, his paper, a pen.

He did his best to keep up with the news, to finish the crossword, but more often than not his brain became fogged. Muddled. And he had to give up, close his eyes, rest. Sometimes he pretended just for her, for Charlotte. Pretended that he was coping. It was okay. He doubted that he was fooling her because she was always there for him. That closeness. Always checking. What a rubbish father. What a rubbish life he had forced on her.

She set to on the garden again, this time meticulously. Edges were clipped, weeds were pulled, and the grass was mown. She had found some packets of seeds in the shed. The packets said they should have been sown by now, but maybe it would be okay. Maybe they would just flower a little bit late. She looked at her bike sitting there calling to her.

'Dad? Can I go out for a while. On my bike? Is that okay? Will you be okay?'

'Yes, away you go. Feeling good today. I'll be just fine.'

'I'll be back for dinnertime.'

'Right you are. Have fun. And be careful!'

As she pedalled off into the countryside her thoughts drifted away and she found herself wondering about what she would be if she could choose absolutely anything. Nothing as silly as a pop-star or a famous actress. It might be nice to be a writer. Of course one of note, but mysterious, reclusive. She would live high up on a hill in India, surrounded by exotic plants and secret, ancient places, like a mystic, or a monk. Or maybe in a hidden valley deep in the Andes with the sound of pan-pipes in the air, and llamas trotting around, and condors swirling overhead, and the cry of wild beasts creeping out of the forests, or was it jungle out there? She would have to check before she could really choose. It was important to know these things. Note to self; *find out about Peru and Argentina and all of those sorts of places.*

Her mind had been so full of pictures and thoughts of her imagined future that she was surprised to suddenly find herself back at that forest. In the distance she could hear the river tumbling its way through the valley. She wondered at the age of it. The strength of it. Something so very ancient. Would it be wise? Could something inanimate be wise? She decided it could. Imagine what it might have seen. Great battles between the clans, between the Scots and the English. A million love affairs. A billion birds.

The ground levelled out beneath her and there she was at the water's edge. She looked all around, half hoping that the boy would be there, half hoping that he wouldn't. Why was life so very complicated? But then, it would be boring if it wasn't; if everything was just as expected, and simple and predictable, and there were no surprises. No delicious dilemmas. Of course the nasty ones, well they could just stay away.

What would she do if the boy was actually there? If he was just standing in the water peering through that peculiar spying thing, fishing for pearls. That was what he had said. Fishing for pearls. Well, she would pretend that the incident had never happened, of course. She would be calm and courteous and chat politely about this and that. It wouldn't do to let him know that he had upset her. That he had triumphed. In truth she knew that she would just be quiet and awkward, as always, but she could imagine. Pretend. It was easier to get past things like that, to pretend and become something else.

She needn't have worried because he wasn't there anyway and actually she was just a little bit disappointed. As she stood, hands on hips, glancing along the bank of the river, she noticed something out of place. She stopped and stared at it for a moment, unsure of what she was seeing. Tentatively she edged towards it, looking around as she did so. When she reached it she checked all around once more, but couldn't see anyone.

At her feet was a peculiar little basket full of sprigs of heather with a stone set in amongst them. How very strange! She looked around again, just to make sure that she truly was alone, before sitting down on the grass. It had been raining and the ground was damp, but she didn't care. The damp brought with it a freshness, as if the whole world had been cleansed and sprinkled with perfume. She put the basket on her lap and pulled one of the sprigs to her nose. The scent was simply heavenly. She put it in her hair so that its perfume clung to her, wrapped itself around her.

As she looked more closely at the rock, rolling it around in her fingers, she noticed some peculiar lumps of a dull red peeking through the grey of the stone. She rubbed at them, scratched at them and they began to glint, to shine, to sparkle! She was sure they were something precious. *I need to investigate you as well!*

She carefully placed the stone back in the little basket, which was unlike anything she had ever seen before. It certainly hadn't been bought in a shop. She was quite sure of that. It was very pretty, and had more curls and twists than a basket should have, but there was a pattern to them. Like vines twisting around bark.

Chapter 7

As she sat there wondering, it dawned on her that this was the exact same spot that she had sat down on with that boy. He must have left it that day. She hadn't noticed it at the time, but there had been so much else to focus on. Mostly just getting away from being so horribly cruelly tricked by a complete stranger!

In the distance a trail of smoke snaked into the sky above the trees. She stared, sniffed at it. A bonfire of some sort. Drifting up with the smoke she could hear voices carried to her on the breeze, a snatch of laughter, the whinnie of horses. This was more than curiosity. She just had to know what was going on over there.

She clambered further up the hill hoping to find out, to see what was making the noise. Who was making it. The trees forbade her a clear view and she climbed all the way back to the road. Still the trees.

Across the road there was a sort of cliff. A jumble of jaggy grey rocks flecked with crunchy yellow and green lichen. She scampered up, turned around and stood up on her tiptoes. At last! There in the valley, beyond the trees, a funny looking round tent. A few people were sitting around a fire. A couple of big horses. An old van. Tinkers? That boy! So he was a Tinker! Of course he was.

She had heard about them. Tales of stolen children, of thievery, of misdoings. These peculiar people who had chosen something different. Something so alien to normal. To most people. "Stay away from the Tinkers!"

Her granny had told her tales of when she was a child and some of them had come to the local primary school. She told her of the taunts, the smell.

"Tinkie, Tinkie, tarry bags.
Go to the well and wash your rags!"

Her granny had laughed and squealed with the rest of the schoolchildren. Before summer the Tinkers had left the school. No one had minded. Quite the opposite. Best left well alone, that lot. Yes! Lock your doors and watch your children.

"Tinkie, Tinkie, stink bags.
Father drunk and mother a hag!"

They had always held a strange fascination for her.

*

She decided that the basket was something like a present. The Tinker boy had felt really badly about what he had done and it was a gift. An apology of sorts. Yes. That was it. He was sorry and he wanted to make her feel better. It had worked and she held a big smile as she slipped back down the rocks, ignoring scratches and scrapes. She uncovered her bicycle and headed home.

As she cycled along she found herself imagining her life as a Tinker, a Gypsy, a Nomad. Of course she would have a beautiful wooden caravan, brightly painted with flowers and birds and it would be the envy of everyone! Her horse would be as black as ebony with a pure white mane. She would dress in flowing reds and greens and have an exquisite shawl draped around her beautiful long curls. Would she have a husband? Yes, she decided, she would, and he would be the most dashing of Gypsy men and he would simply adore her. Life would be just like one very long holiday. Yes. Life would be quite splendid!

Chapter 8

The berry season was over now and it was time to move on. Tommy had been back to see if the basket had been found. He was so happy that morning when he looked and it was gone. There was a chance it had been found by someone else, even picked up by a crow or a magpie, stolen by a fox. But he just knew that it had been her. He could feel her in the air. And he smiled.

It was to be a busy morning, and they were all up and at it with the rising of the sun. The camp had to be packed up. The four overlapping canvasses pulled off the bender, dried and folded. The supports from the wood of the hazel tree, which had been carefully moulded into just the right shape so that they slotted together and took the weight of the canvas, packed away into the van. They worked like clockwork, each knowing exactly what was to be done; where everything belonged.

Once the ground had been cleared and checked, the turf that they had cut to make a place for their fire was laid back down. Nothing was to be left to show that they had been here. No permanent stain would remain on the land. No damage done. The yellowed grass would turn back to green soon enough. The worn down patches would fill again. When they returned next year it would be pristine and welcoming, as always.

Now they were heading to the coast to gather shellfish. It was hard work. Backbreaking work. But it brought in good money if they all played their part. Pulled their weight. Tommy's pa and brothers headed off first in the van. He and his ma followed with the horses. They took their time, enjoying each others quiet company. Truth be told Tommy and his ma were very much alike. A mother shouldn't have such things as favourites, but it was Tommy who pulled the hardest at her heart-strings. She understood him and he her. And this was their special time.

The van would reach the coast in a matter of hours, but the horses had to travel on into the following day and the one after that. Tommy and his ma knew the route well enough; knew where there was fresh water to be had; knew where it was safe to stop for the night. A friendly farmer, a hidden spot in a quiet wood.

They pulled off the road at a small, barely visible track made by themselves over the previous years. If you didn't know it was there you would never see it. They pushed aside the overgrowth – tall grasses, thistles, and wild daisies from below; sweeping fluttering foliage of rowan, oak, and ash from above – and headed into the seclusion of the trees. A burn babbled its way through the rocks and opened itself up into a small, clear pool.

They lay on their stomachs, their hands scooping up the peaty water. Its taste was like the essence of life. They glanced across at one another and grinned. The horses stood beside them drinking, gently swishing their tails.

They set what they needed for the night against a tree. The sky above them was clear, the first stars beginning to glint through the deepening turquoise.

'We'll not be needing the canvas tonight I don't reckon. What do you think, Tommy son? A night with us and the stars?'

Tommy smiled broadly, looking up at the sky then across at his ma. 'Us and the stars,' he confirmed.

They secured the horses to a tree, with fodder at their feet, and stroked them goodnight. Then they lay down some sheeting and their blankets and settled themselves side by side, heads touching.

'What is it's been on your mind, son?' she asked, knowing that something was up. Something distracting him.

He took a deep breath. 'A girl,' he said so quietly it was barely a whisper.

'Oh, a girl is it now?' A slight panic.

'Aye.'

'And where did you come across this girl?'

'Up at the pool for the pearls. I was looking up the hill at some deer and there she was. Sneaking about in the bracken, she was.'

'A Tinker girl up there?' she asked, surprised, knowing that there were no other Tinker families staying thereabouts.

'No. Not a Tinker. She was from the big house, I think. Right pretty too, she was.'

'And what did she have to say for herself?'

'Nothing. We didn't really...she didn't really say

anything. There was an accident, see. It all went wrong.'

His mother sat up, alarmed. 'What do you mean by an accident? What happened?'

'N-nothing. N-nothing at all. It just went all wrong.'

'You haven't gone and got yourself in trouble, have you? Like that other girl?'

'That other girl was just full of lies. She was m–mean and wicked and a liar!'

'I know that, but other folk, well. You know.'

'N-nothing happened, Ma. I just liked her, was all, and I wanted to say sorry, but she was gone and I left her a wee gift instead of words. That's all.'

He was getting upset, his voice rising. She knew to stop this now or he might lose himself. Disappear into that dark place in his mind where no one could reach him. Not even her. Change the topic. Take him to somewhere beautiful.

'And did you see any pearl-shells ready for the picking?'

He smiled. 'Oh aye. I think maybe next year, or the year after that.'

He had never actually pulled one out of the river. They were so rare now, and the fishing for them wasn't meant to be done, but he was only looking. And waiting. He would wait for that one. That one special shell that held a beautiful pearl. It was like a thing of magic. A pearl. A piece of beauty made by dirt and a wee shellfish. You could tell when one was ready if you knew the way of things. The way of the pearls. An uneven shape. A swelling caused by the birth of a pearl, just like the swell of a woman's belly. His father had taught him, as had his father before him. Pearl fishers they had been, for many a generation, but no more. Not for real. Like so much of their history, it had gone.

Chapter 9

When she got home her father was awake, sitting tall, watching a film on the television. Something else to make her heart leap. Every good day was a blessing, the road to recovery, a hint at a future. He turned around at the sound of her footsteps on the floor, a smile on his face.

'Dad! How are you feeling?'

'Brand new, Princess. Brand new.' He patted the arm of his chair. 'Come away and tell me all about your travels.'

'Actually, I found something. And I think. I don't know. But I was wondering...do you know if...' She paused, took a deep breath, felt a bit silly. 'Are there any precious stones, jewels, around here?'

He smiled. 'And why would you be asking that, then?'

'I found...I found something!' she exclaimed, unable to disguise her excitement. She ran back out to the bike, slipped the basket off the handlebars, gently plucked out the stone and hurried back inside. As she held it out to him she took a deep breath. 'I found this and I thought, perhaps it was something special.'

'Let me see now.' He turned the stone over in his hand, rubbed at one of the ruby-red crystals. 'Well now. We'll need to investigate this, right enough.' He walked slowly out to his shed, using his stick to keep his balance, not leaning on Charlotte. Feeling better. Stronger. She pulled a stool across to his workbench and he sat with a sigh. Little things. Little things were so very big these days.

He ran his eye across the row of tools that were lined up along the wall, each hanging from its own special hook, picked up a sharp little hammer, then a thin chisel. He nodded to himself. 'This'll do the trick.' He settled the rock on his workbench and began to chip away at it. 'Come away and have a go yourself, why don't you? Nice and gentle, though. Nothing good ever comes of rushing at things, especially not precious things like this!' He beamed, his blue eyes twinkled. This was what she did for him. Lit his days. Lit his life.

She took the hammer and gripped it tightly in her left hand, her right hand holding the chisel, and began to chip away. Nothing seemed to be happening. She looked up at her dad, her face showing her doubt, her frustration.

'Nice and gentle, but firm. A little bit of force behind the gentleness, okay? Like it's being hit by a girl, but a big strong one!' He grinned at her.

She returned to her task, her eyes squinting in determined concentration, her tongue poking out between her lips. As if by magic the rock snapped open, split in two, revealing ten, perhaps twelve, beautiful sparkling jewels. She squealed in excitement. 'Oh, oh! Are they rubies?'

'No Princess, they're not rubies, but what they are is garnets! Highland rubies! Just as special and twice as beautiful!'

'Oh my word!' She grinned up at him. 'Garnets!'

They worked on for an hour or more, carefully gouging out the garnets. Rubbing at them. Polishing them.

'Right. Bath and bed for you. First day at big school tomorrow! Have you got everything ready? Your uniform, your bag?'

'Yes Dad!'

In truth she had completely forgotten. Lost in a world of forests and rivers and Tinkers and jewels, the thought of school had completely deserted her. She kissed her dad goodnight and went upstairs.

As quietly as she could she checked that she had everything she needed for her first day at big school, not feeling like it at all. Strangers. So many people. So much noise. And it was all completely new and unknown and she really didn't want to face it. Like always she would put on a brave face. She would smile for him and tell him everything was just fine.

*

Her dad was up and dressed before her, which hadn't happened for weeks. She beamed at the sight of him.

'Let me see you then?'

She twirled and curtsied.

'Well, I never. Look at you! Quite the young lady.'

'Oh Dad, don't be silly.'

'Seriously, you look great.'

'Have you got everything sorted, for you I mean?'

'Don't you be worrying about me. I've got the nurse coming in and Martha, from next door, nice woman, said she'd pop by. Apart from that, I'm feeling just fine. You enjoy yourself.'

She hugged him and hurried off to catch the bus.

He watched the bus disappear before slouching, exhaling, taking himself back to his chair. The day would tick by, and he would do his best not to fret. Not to worry about her. He tried to kick away the guilt. The frustration. The fear. There was no point in that. This illness had taught him many things, but mostly that you had to grab every moment. Every precious moment.

*

It was all just as awful as she had imagined. Everyone introducing themselves, describing themselves. Although it seemed, to her, very silly as most of them knew each other anyway. The first task of the day was to write about their summer. What could she say? Her life was secret and private and she didn't want anyone knowing anything about her and her dad and the way things were.

Instead she wrote about the mysterious stranger who had nearly caused her to drown. Of course it was embellished, as all good stories should be. He was older and dashing and quite grumpy. As her imagination flew and her world lifted into a place of her making it was heavenly. The problem was that she had no control over it. Once started it had a life of its own. The clang of the bell, desks and chairs scraped. Break time.

'Right, we'll share some after break,' the teacher called in their wake.

Absolute terror slapped her. There was no way she could possibly do that. No way at all! Thankfully there wasn't time.

'Leave your jotters on my desk as you go.'

They all trailed out, chatting away to their friends.

Laughter and whispers. Nudges and smirks. She held back, watched them thread off into different directions, some in cars and buses, others on foot. As she walked down to the bus stop she wondered about their lives. Their families. What was normal? What would that be like?

*

'The Desson child wrote quite a story today about some stranger nearly drowning her. I don't know, it sounded, well, off. Perhaps something should be asked of the parents?' her teacher reported to the headmistress at the end of the school day.

'Lives with her father, that one. That's a challenge enough in itself! Perhaps she's trying to mask it, make light of it. Anyway, make a note of it. Perhaps raise it at "Pupils of concern" at the end of the week. Keep an eye on her. Poor thing.'

The teacher smiled and nodded.

*

'Well? How did it go?' her dad asked.

'It was okay. It was school, you know.' She raised her eyebrows in a dismissive way. She sniffed at the air. 'Do I smell food?'

'Yes! Martha from next door, bless her. Didn't want you coming back to chores.'

'I don't mind, you know. I can manage.'

'No one's saying you can't, Princess. It's just a nice neighbourly gesture that's all.'

It was a strange mixture of emotions. The food was great. Mince and tatties. Easy enough for her dad to eat and tasty too. But it made her feel like she wasn't up to the mark. She couldn't do *this*. Make *this*. Be *this*.

43

Chapter 10

Winter time. Tommy and his family spent these long, dark months in the shelter of a small, narrow glen whose particular direction kept the worst of the North winds at bay. Scots pine, birch, and oak clad the mountains on both sides, weathered and worn by time but standing strong nonetheless. Centuries of growth crept from root to root, branch to branch. Stories wider than the sky. A deep lochan sat in the middle, drifting from rich turquoise to ebony black depending on the mood of the skies, the height of the sun, the weight of the weather. It was inaccessible from three sides, but the southernmost tip lay open. A small beach of pebbles and sand sprinkled its edge.

Those that knew, and there were few, could wend their way through the seemingly impenetrable forest left to nature and her ways. Wild and full of life. There was no road, no space for a vehicle, and Tommy's family would leave their van with a nearby sympathetic crofter. From there they would make their way on horseback and by foot, travelling all day to reach the safety of the lochan.

Its remoteness coated it with a feeling of foreboding for most. A sense of security for the family.

Even now they were at risk of attack from the disapprovers. Sometimes locals. Sometimes folk from the town, from the city. At least, nasty words would be cast that cut through them, at worst, a destroyed campsite. Stories of generations of hardship were shared around the fire at night. Generations of bigotry and hatred. It was a part of their history and it was important that it be kept alive. Here though, in this desolate place, they knew that they were safe.

They pitched their tent just beyond the beach of the lochan, in the shelter of one of the old abandoned cottages. Four walls with empty holes for windows, no roof, the remains of a chimney, weeds and moss tangling their way through everything. There were many such places across the Highlands. Scatterings of lives once lived and homes stolen. A sadness that sat deep in the land and would never leave. You could always feel it in places such as these if you listened, if you opened yourself to it. The cry of The Clearances.

They all worked as one as the bowed hazel sticks were slotted together to make the dome. The canvasses were stretched across it like the skin of a beast. Winter securing was done with large stones placed all around the edge of the canvas. Not a gap could be left. Rope was strung across and hammered into the ground as defence against any gales that might fight their way through the glen. A ditch was dug all the way around as run-off for excess water. When everything was as it should be they all sat down around the fire and listened. The same story began their wintering every year.

'It all kicked off that spring,' Robbie began, though it could have been any one of them that did the telling, they all knew the story so well. Each word. Each turn of events. 'The spring o the great change. The spring o such dreadful sorrow. Jack and Mary met in the wee gulley, like always. It was sheltered and quiet and, most important, hidden frae all around. At least, so they thought. Jack, our young hero, set his tartan blanket on the ground and gestured for his beautiful Mary to sit. She smiled at him, for he was a kind man, an honest man, the man she loved. The man she was not allowed to be with.'

Robbie glanced from one to the next, briefly holding eye contact, drawing them in. Dark brown eyes that knew so much. Said so much.

'It had been that way for a long time. Since they were wee. No more than bairns. They had played together, running wild through the heather, across the hungry hills, swimming in the cold, cold waters o loch and river, splashing through burns and boggy land. They had been ruffians at war wi enemy soldiers, sailors adrift on a treacherous sea. Two souls that couldnae be separated. Two young folk whose friendship was forbidden. And now two lovers who could never be together. No if they were discovered.

'Jack had lived in this wee village all o his life. No a part o it exactly because his family kept themselves to themselves. They were a wee bit posh, like. His da was the minister. His ma a proper lady. His life was laid right out there afore him. He would be well-to-do, marry the right young lady, have comfort and security and respect.

'Our young heroine, though, she wasna a person for him to talk to. No at all. Oh no! That would never do. She was a Tinker girl, see. Travelling stock. Aye. A fine young woman o travelling stock wi eyes the colour o heather, sprinkled wi gold, and hair as red as copper. You can see it in your ma still.'

He winked across at Jeannie, who smiled back, a flutter of pink washing her cheeks.

'And oh, she loved him so. And he her. Each year, when she left wi the swallows, he would stand on the hilltop and watch as the horses and their cart shrunk into the distance, until they were quite gone. But for a few years now they had stayed. Her Tinker family. For there was an evil spreading across this Highland soil. Good families, simple families, whose people had stayed in the same wee cottages for more generations than could be remembered, toiling at their patch o land, making it work. This was their land and they loved it.

'Now, our young Tinker lass had seen wi her own eyes what was coming. Aye, she knew, as did her family, that this village would soon be gone. It was a place they liked well. It had been kind enough to them, as had its folk. There weren't so many that accepted their way o life, but these folk did. They were grateful for what the Tinkers did; for the mending o pots, for the shoring up o falling buildings. There was nothing that they couldnae turn their hands to. That's where it came from, see? Tinkers. Folk that could tinker away wi anything.

'They told the villagers of what they had seen. How the factors had come and ordered the people to leave. Cowardly men on their big horses that rode through village after village, croft after croft.

'"Be off with you!" they called, as they set fire to the wee houses wi evil grins on their faces. And what could the people do? Well, some fled south to work in the dirt and the smoke o Glasgow. Others were pushed on to the coast to work as fishermen. Some stayed put till the very end.

'"But we are folk o this land. These are our homes. Ours!"

'"The land and all upon it is the laird's. Be gone!"

'Women wept as their children clung to their skirts, their bare feet losing that connection wi their earth. They were like plants, see, and if uprooted they would wither and die. But the man on the horse had descended. He had told them clear as day. Their time was up; their days were numbered. Best leave now afore he returned wi his men. Afore their houses were torn down. Their thatched roofs set alight.

'It was the sheep that were coming in their place, see? That was where the money was. Wi the sheep. Hundreds o them, thousands, sweeping across the hillsides, bleating out their warning. *We're coming and there'll be no stopping us now!*

'Now these Highlanders had survived the very worst that nature could throw at them. They had stood proud and strong. The blizzards, the gales, the whipping rain, and last year, the famine. They had survived all o that and now there was this? How could they give up now?

'But what of our young lovers? I hear you ask. Well, from high on the hill they saw the laird's men coming, heard the gallop o their horses.

'"I have to do something," Young Jack said, turning to Mary, clutching her hands, drawing them to his face and kissing them. "I have to help."

'And with that he was gone, running down the hill to the village. To the vicarage. "Father!" he called. "Father, you can't allow this! You know the laird and his men. You can help."

'"The laird is our superior and, like the Lord, he must be obeyed. It is not my place, nor is it theirs, to be disobedient."

'"Father?" he pleaded. But he could see in his da's eyes and feel in his heart that there was no way to change his mind. What more could he do? He would join them. If need be he would take arms and fight, for this, in his mind, was not the way of any Lord he cared to worship.

'Now Mary had stood on that hill, watching. It was coming now. The end. She could feel it. For she had that power too. She just knew.

'Young Jack mounted his da's horse and galloped through the village, calling out to all who would listen, "They're coming! Be ready. They're coming!"

'Men took up axes, branches. Women clattered pots and pans. They all ran at the men like they were mad. Taken over by a power so strong. So wild!'

He caught his family's eyes again, long and slow, from one to the other. 'Can you imagine it?

'The men on horseback stared for a bit. Nervous. Their horses twitching and stamping and wanting to gallop away. But they pushed the horses forward, charged through the poor folk, striking at will at men, women, and children. It made no difference to them, see? Jack's horse bucked at the awful noise o it all. The crash o something struck his head.

'Now, from up on high Mary could see all o this. "No!" she screamed, running down the hill towards him.

'He was scooped up, along wi many others, and herded through the valley and beyond. She ran after them, calling out his name but it was no use, her calls were drowned by the screams and the cries o the people and the howling o the wind. Her way was blocked by a stranger on horseback brandishing a whip. Aye! A whip to a lassie! He grinned as he jumped off the horse and chased her wi evil on his mind. But she was quick o foot and thought, and made her escape, twisting into places that were secret and hidden.

'When our young Jack woke up he was at the docks. There was an awful kerfuffle "This one's a troublemaker. Get him on board and away." And that was that. Our young hero was on a ship bound for distant lands.

'Now that ship was chock full o people. Below deck they were packed so tight, like fish in a net. Some were there of their own choosing. Seven guineas for a ticket and fortunes to be made for the devils that owned the ship. Lies were told of great promise in these foreign lands. Lands o plenty. Lands o prosperity and beauty. Poor fools had believed it and signed up. Others, like our Jack, well, they had been taken by force. America, some guessed. Canada, said others. Australia was even suggested.

'Rations were less than nothing. Scraps that wouldnae feed a mouse, let alone a man! Some died soon enough o starvation, or a terrible sickness. Scurvy and cholera spread through the passengers. Bodies were tossed overboard one after the other. It was a terrible time, so it was. Darkness and a foul stench, and death. Like holding hands wi the very Devil himself!

'Now, of course, on top o all o this our young Jack was heartbroken. Not a day went by when he didna think o his Mary, there on that hill, watching after him. It had been weeks at least, maybe months, he wasna sure. At last land. Nova Scotia it was. But this was no new Scotland! There was no heather here. It was rocky and cruel and life had to be fought for. Now, I know you're thinking, what's our boy to do in such a foreign land? Well. What he could do was write and there were many others there that couldna. He wrote letters for them. Many said just "Don't Come!" or "This place is hell!" Others wrote long love letters which he helped to make beautiful, for his way was the way wi the words. Those who could pay him did. Maybe a meal. Maybe a penny. Maybe nothing more than a smile. At least it was enough to keep him going.

'He wrote letter after letter to his Mary. Of course, she had no address and the village that had been his would be gone now. But he wrote anyway. "One day. One day," he told himself. "One day I will find her again."'

'And did he? Did he make it back?' Tommy asked. He knew, of course, because the story had been told so many times, but it had become a part of the ritual. A part of the story.

'Well, if he hadna none o you would be here the now, would you? And could you imagine a world that hadna been blessed wi your ma? I couldn't.' He pulled Jeannie to him and squeezed her tight. 'What an awful place that would be, eh?'

Chapter 11

Charlotte had had little time for anything other than doing her schoolwork, keeping the housework up to scratch, and looking after her dad. She was determined to keep it all going. To put busy minds to rest. Have them focus on someone else who needed their words and their questions and their concerned glances. It was fine. They were coping. She was coping. They didn't need anyone else. Go away. Look away. It's all good here! The best way to do that was to make sure her homework was always done and done well, her clothes were clean and ironed, her hair, her nails, everything that she showed to the world was exactly as it should be. Prying eyes turned away. It was exhausting. The pressure of it. The worry of it. The smile for the teachers, for her dad, even when she felt like crying. The smile.

It was Saturday. A chance to switch off. Her dad was still improving. Coping better with each day. The house had been cleaned, the washing done and pegged out on the line. She had sat quietly with her dad in the garden. Just breathing. Just resting.

'How are you coping with it all?' he asked.

She leaned her head against his shoulder.

'School and everything?' he added.

'It's fine, Dad. All good.'

'Have you made any new friends?'

She sighed, wishing she had kept it in. 'Not really, not yet. I don't really, you know, have much in common with them.'

Sometimes he hated himself. Hated his choices. Hated what had been forced upon them. Hated this illness. He shook it off. Tried to offer some encouragement. 'Oh, you'll get used to them soon enough. Early days yet.'

'Honestly Dad, I'm not bothered at all.'

He coughed. Wheezed. Coughed some more.

'Dad?'

He held his hand up to show he was fine. It would settle. And it did.

'Why don't you go off for one of your cycles? No point in having the thing if you don't use it.'

She had, in truth, been quite desperate to head off, back into the hills and the forest and the river – places of absolute freedom – but hadn't wanted to ask. To leave her dad. 'Are you sure?'

'Absolutely. Off you go now.'

He smiled at her back as she pedalled off, looking more like a young girl again. Such precious times that slip away far too quickly. He felt guilty at what he had taken from her. She should be carefree, off enjoying the simple things while she still could.

*

She stood high on her bike, freewheeling along the

53

gentle decline. Up the next hill and she would be at that place again. A trickle of expectation ran along her spine. She could feel the excitement rising as the sound of the river curled through the trees and stroked her senses. Treading as lightly as she could she edged her way down. Closer.

It had been ages since she had last seen that boy and chances were that he would never come back. She knew nothing of their lives other than that they were travellers. Did that mean they always travelled? Never returning to the same place? It wasn't as if it mattered. They were strangers and she didn't think she really cared about whether she saw him again or not. Why would she?

Someone was there. She could feel it in the tingle of her skin, the shiver that ran down her back. There was no doubt at all. But she couldn't see anyone anywhere. She strained to peer through the trees, up the hill behind her, across the river in front. Nothing. It had set her a little bit on edge. An unwelcome nervousness. Nevertheless, she carried on down to the river, her head held high, a not unpleasant flutter in her chest.

She chose a spot on the riverbank where the water had created a small beach of pebbles and sand, and sat on the grass, dipping her feet in the cool, cool water. It tingled and made her giggle. Tiny fish darted around the pebbles. She leaned forward, so that the overhang no longer blocked her view, and looked up and down the river. There was nothing untoward to be seen. Nothing out of the ordinary.

She guddled about in the water for a while, picking up rocks and inspecting them, but no garnets showed themselves to her. Perhaps there was more to it than simply looking? Perhaps there were secret signs that she just didn't know about? She would ask. If she ever saw the boy again, she would ask.

An eel slithered out from under the bank, brushed against her ankles. She squealed, jumped backwards, almost losing her balance. Keeping her eyes trained on it she followed its eerie wriggling form – snake-like but not quite – until it disappeared into the dark of the muddy riverbank again. Unsettled, she clambered back onto the safety of dry land.

As she sat in the lush grass, crows cawed, smaller birds she couldn't recognise the call of sang out, filling the air with twitters and chirrups and songs so complex they seemed impossibly beautiful. Here, far from anywhere, anyone, the silence was anything but! The quiet of the countryside had its own special meaning. Perhaps its silence just meant something that was made by nature, something that occurred without the intervention of man. Whatever, it was beautiful and she was very glad of it.

She splashed at a cloud of midges that had swarmed around her and watched them disperse and reform their cloud in a matter of seconds. On a still day such as this there was no point in trying to defeat them. Attempting to ignore them instead she lay back on the grass, her hands behind her head, and closed her eyes, relieved that the boy wasn't there. Relieved that it was just her and this magic. What had she been thinking?

Chapter 12

There was no work to be found at their winter stopping-place and Tommy and his family had to make sure that they had earned enough earlier in the year to buy sufficient supplies to see them through to the spring, and to leave a pot for emergencies. Mostly they lived off the land. There was fishing and hunting, but little else.

Long, dark nights meant times of storytelling, of reminiscing. Times of reflection. Of deep thought. The history Tommy learned was that of his people, their ways. Of survival. What this earth was made of he knew more than most anyway. He could identify flora and fauna; imitate the call of many a bird, the sound of the fox, the wild cat; explain habitats, food chains, look after the place he had been given to walk upon. And as for horses, it was as if he could speak with them. Share their secrets.

When spring finally crept back in and nature woke up from its deep slumber, they were off again. They called in at the crofter's house. Shared a cup of tea and a blether. The old man lived alone now, seldom seeing another soul. He looked forward to his time with these Tinkers and was always sad to see them move off, but that was their way and he knew it. Sometimes he wondered if it would be easier to just never see anyone; never talk to anyone. That way there was nothing to miss. Ach well, it would be his time soon enough and he could be with his Morag again. Aye, soon enough.

It was Tommy and his mother taking their time with the horses as always. A slow, gentle, incremental slip back into the world again. This time he felt himself strangely restless as they made their way from farm to farm, camp to camp, working the crops – planting, tending, and picking.

He and his ma spent more time hawking, going from door to door selling their wares. They had regular customers. Folk that liked their things handmade. Others that slammed doors in their faces, hid behind twitching curtains whispering. It would have been easier to stay with the ones they knew, the ones that smiled, but Tommy's ma wouldn't be deterred.

'You just never know who you might be missing Tommy, son. You just never know. If you don't show yourself to the world, how's it going to show itself to you?' She had a lot of sayings like that. A string of words that she liked to share when the time was right. 'Aye, the smile from a stranger can brighten up the darkest day.'

Despite his ma's encouragement, Tommy would hang back at the doors of strangers, more fearful of cruel words or sneers. There was no hurrying it. A right time for everything. Places they were expected. Work to be done. And after it all, as dusk fell and fires sparked, stories to be told. Other Tinkers would sometimes join them, talking of the old ways, laughing at shared memories. Tommy preferred to sit back and watch, a part of it all but separate at the same time. He crouched like a shadow on the periphery.

'Yer lad's no coming tae the fire, then?'

'Naw, he likes it just fine where he is.'

And he did. It suited him. Sometimes he listened to every word. Sang quietly along to the songs, for there was always singing and music. His da showing off on the pipes, auld Sandy with his squeeze box, everybody else keeping the beat with whatever was to hand: pans, sticks, a slap on their thighs.

Sometimes he would catch the rustle of a night creature or the beat of a bird's wing and he would be gone with them. Caught up in it until something drew him back. But this time he was itching for time to pass, for it to be high summer again so that he could get back to the camp by the river with the pearl-pool, and the big house, and the girl.

He wanted to see the girl.

Chapter 13

Her dad had grown stronger over the dark days of winter. He was still poorly, but not so much that he needed her help all of the time. It made him happy to send her off with some sandwiches and a smile and not expect her return until dinner time.

Over the course of spring, weather permitting, she had explored that one area over and over again, as if it were her own back garden. She learned the lean of the trees, watched the sprouting of the bracken, wondered at its unfurling, clambered up the largest of the boulders to sit atop and view what she felt was hers. Followed the trail of the birds, dipping in the river and swooping up to settle in the trees.

And now it was summer again. The magic of school holidays; weeks and weeks of them. The forest, the river, the little beach, had become close acquaintances, and despite the apparent solitude of it all she was content with just this. Nature was pure and comforting and trustworthy, and here she felt completely safe. No pretence to call on, no fake smile to hide behind. Here she could breathe. Simply be herself.

As she lay on the riverbank, nibbling absent-mindedly on a blade of fresh summer grass, thinking of nothing but this place, its murmurs and sighs filling her brain, she felt a shadow drift across the sun and her skin began to prickle with goosebumps. Something more than a breeze had suddenly begun to stretch across the land, whistle through the trees. Opening one eye she could see a swell of dark clouds that had sneakily built up and almost taken over the sky.

Even now it took her by surprise how quickly the weather could turn. This looked and felt ominous! One huge drop of rain, another. She sprang to her feet and ran up the hill as the rain began to splatter all around. If she were to cycle all the way home she would get drenched, but this looked horribly like it was on for the long haul. Huddling in the trees she looked skyward. Dark and brooding. The rain was now so heavy that it was forcing itself through the leaves, swelling in great big drops and falling on her.

A crackle in the forest above her. A voice? Was that really a voice? All the way out here? She stared through the mass of trunks, alarmed.

A man slipped out of the trees, dressed in forest camouflage. Trees and leaves and twigs swirling all over his arms and chest. His trousers the colour of the bark of the trees. A Deerhunter cap pulled down low so that it hid his eyes. A gun slung over his shoulder.

If he hadn't spoken, stepped out, she would never have known he was there. An unsettling feeling crept through her. Set her on edge. She didn't like it at all!

'You'll catch your death away out here, lass. Come

away and shelter.' He waved his arm at her, sweeping it to the left. To a part of the land she hadn't explored before where the trees thickened and the ground darkened. It had felt somehow forbidden and she had treated it as such. But what to do now?

'On you come. Hurry now!'

He headed off, striding through the woods as if they were a part of him. No need to watch his step, take his time. He just knew.

She waited, staring after him, trying to size things up. She took a few steps, paused again. A crack of thunder. The rain in torrents. Her mind made up. Despite being a bit on edge, she felt somehow drawn to him. There was something nice about him. A gentleness, even though he had a gun. He didn't look back, didn't wait for her and she had to run to catch up. Her mind was set at ease by the spaniel which happily trotted along at his heels, its tail swishing. That was a good sign. Nice people had friendly dogs. A few minutes later and they came to a small wooden bothy.

All these months of exploring and she had had no idea that this place was here. Its walls were made of the same wood as the forest, the logs left natural, bark and moss stretching across. Tumbling down from the roof, a twist of vines that had to be swept aside to allow entrance. She couldn't be sure if the purpose had been one of camouflage, but it had certainly had that effect. If you didn't know it was here; hadn't walked right up to it, if you weren't actually expecting this, you would most likely walk on by.

Surely he didn't live here? No. That was silly. He was

some kind of warden, gamekeeper, something like that. His clothes suggested that, as did his gun. This was just his hut. Like her dad's garden shed only for the wild. For people who worked the forest.

She paused for a moment. Hesitated. Licked at a raindrop on her lip. Shivered as another trickled its way down her back. She could just turn around and run, but if he had bad intentions he would catch her anyway. There was nothing for it but to trust him.

He swung the door open and ushered her in.

Chapter 14

At last they were nearly back at their summer stopping-place and would be settled right through the season. By the time Tommy and his ma arrived the camp was ready and waiting for them. The tent was pitched, the three legged stove perched above the fire, everything in its place.

The men were playing a game of football. Loud shrieks of laughter, curses, accusations of foul play, fake fights, grins on faces. Pa stopped, hands on hips, panting at his exertions. That tingle across his skin that told him they were back. He turned around and beamed as he saw the horses plodding slowly across the field towards him. Fine big beasts they were. Black and white Vanners with flowing tails that almost reached the ground, thick feathers trimming their fetlocks. Manes that danced like flowing water. They'd had many an offer for them, and healthy ones at that. But they weren't for sale nor exchange. Offspring would be traded for a good price, but not this pair. They were family and family was everything.

Jeannie, Tommy and the horses had returned safely to the fold and all was well with Robbie's world again. His family complete. He ran his fingers through his greying hair in an attempt to smarten himself up a bit, but there was little point. His jeans were stained with grass and mud, his face smudged with dirt, his sweatshirt likewise. He glanced at himself, shrugged, grinned, raised his arm in a grand sweep of a welcome.

'Well now, aren't you just a sight for sore eyes!' he called. How did she do that? Always look so perfect to him? Just jeans tucked into her trusty old cowboy boots, a well-worn plaid shirt, curls of red hair twirling over her shoulder. To him she was the most beautiful creature in the world. Always had been. Always would be. Of that he had no doubt. The years of travel, of hardship and struggle, of love and laughter, shone out of every wrinkle, every imperfection perfect.

He strode across the grass to meet them, wanting to break into a run, but controlling it, keeping his manliness to the fore. He helped first his wife, then his youngest son, down off their horses. Of course there was no need for the helping, but it felt like the right thing to do. Just a wee ritual that they all appreciated. He was a proud man who believed in the old ways. A man has his place and he would never forget that. Never let them down.

Tommy quietly tied the horses up, whispering softly to them. 'You just settle down now. Time for you to rest. That's it.' He stroked their manes and looked deep into those wise, gentle eyes. That connection. Behind him his parents shared tales of each other's journeys, husband and wife hand in hand, full of smiles and love.

'I'll not be long, Ma,' Tommy whispered in the wind as he headed off across the field towards the river.

'You'll be needing dinner, Tommy son, and there's a storm coming. Look!' She gestured up at the darkening sky, but he wasn't taking any heed. 'I don't know what's got into the laddie. Even more quiet than usual the last day or so, and no matter how hard I tried there was nothing forthcoming.'

'Aye, well, he's growing into a man. Mind how moody this pair were?' He nodded at their other sons who had continued their game.

She smiled at his reassurance, but something deeper than that was going on. She was quite sure. A mother knew; saw what others couldn't. He hadn't even taken his dog with him. That wasn't right. Wee Rona sat there and whimpered at being left behind until Jeannie called her over and invited her to jump onto her lap. Gentle strokes calmed her, but her eyes remained fixed on the place across the field and beyond the trees where Tommy had slipped from sight.

The rain started before Tommy had even reached the river. He didn't mind. Quite the opposite. He loved the feel of it on his skin. The sound of it in his head drowning out everything else. It was like this was all there was in the world. Him and the rain. He stood there for a while just enjoying it all. Just being a part of it. Licking at drips as they fell down his face. The flicker of an image broke through the rain and reminded him that he had a different purpose today. The girl.

When he reached the river there was no sign of her. Of course there wouldn't be. Not in this weather. But he could feel her. She had been here. He crossed the river to the side belonging to the big house, although in his mind

65

land wasn't for the owning. He knew this place so intimately, cared for it so deeply, felt such a part of it that, if anything, it owned him.

There, the shadow of her footsteps in the wet grass filled his breath. He walked beside them to the place on the bank where she had sat down. He knelt down and stroked the ground. Brought his hand to his face. Breathed in the essence of her. He was soaked through now; water streaming from his hair, but he was smiling a deep joyous smile. Retracing his steps he found the spot where he had left his last gift for her.

'This is for you,' he whispered, as he placed another delicate little basket on the grass, secured this time by the weight of a glimmering piece of fool's gold. A scattering of little dog roses had been laid around it, their blossom pink and white, their sweet perfume seeping out with the rain.

He didn't linger. His task was complete and now he should to be in the company of his family. The fire would be lit, though because of the rain it would be inside the tent, smoke twirling up through the iron chimney in the roof. There would be songs and stories seeping though the canvas, drifting off into the night air. There would be a celebration of all that was right with this world.

Chapter 15

Inside the bothy the clatter of the rain was all consuming. Charlotte glanced around. It was dark and smelled of oil and tools and fire. Things that reminded her of her dad. Things that put her mind a little bit more at ease. There was a tiny window, but the blackness of the storm rendered it useless, other than confirming that the rain was coming down in a torrent that made it feel like they were underwater.

The man lit a paraffin lamp and hung it on a hook in the ceiling, smiling all the while. The dog was rubbing itself against his legs. A shake, a rub, repeat. She laughed. The man shrugged and laughed in reply. *Dogs eh?*

'There now. That's a bit better, aye?' he shouted above the storm. 'We'll hang on a bit, wait for a lull, and make a dash up to the jeep. Then we can pick your bike up and get you home. How does that sound?'

She squinted at him. 'Um. Yes, but–'

He held his hand up as if he had read her thoughts. 'There's nothing happens on this land that I don't know about. Dougie's the name.' He held out a hand, asking for hers in return.

She giggled. This was a first! A grown-up shaking her hand.

'You're meant to respond, like for like.' He grinned.

The glow of the lamp reflected in his eyes. Brown with flecks of green. Gentle. Yes. She was quite sure he was gentle. Any trepidation she had felt dripped onto the floor along with the drops of rain.

'Oh, yes, sorry. Charlotte. I'm Charlotte.'

'Charlotte, aye? Pretty name, that. Suits you.' He smiled at her, the edges of his eyes wrinkling. 'Seen you up here a lot.'

It felt like she had been spied on and she was suddenly uncomfortable. 'Oh, I'm sorry. Is it not allowed?'

'It's fine by me just so long as you treat the place with respect, like.'

'Oh, of course. I love it here.'

'Aye, seems so. Right now, this might well be on for the rest of the day. Best get a move on if we're to get you home before tea time.' He took a couple of big green umbrellas down from a peg on the wall. 'Prepared for it all up here!' he laughed. 'Ready?'

'Ready!'

*

The drive home only took ten minutes, during which time he told her that he was the manager of the estate. He was always there or thereabouts, checking on the place, on the animals. She could call in any time she wanted. It was good to have young folk around. Decent young folk.

He pulled up at the semi-detached cottage, old-stone with a traditional wooden porch, steep tiled roof, and gabled window, behind which sat her bedroom. When they had moved in she had assumed that it would become her dad's room. The biggest, with the best views of the valley and the mountains beyond, but no, he had insisted it should be hers. What a view to wake up to!

'Um. Thank you,' she said.

'Aye, nae bother!' He reached behind the front seats for one of the umbrellas.

'No, it's okay. Look, it's hardly raining here yet.' She was about to ask how he knew where she lived. She was quite sure she hadn't told him. Instead she pulled at the handle of the door and slipped out. 'Thank you!' She pushed the door to.

'Your bike, lass! Hold on a minute!' He jumped out, unloaded the bike, wheeled it across to the shed for her, despite her protestations. He watched her open her back door before hurrying back and driving off with a wave.

Her dad was watching the television in the front room, oblivious to his daughter's arrival. She decided not to tell him about the man, and the little shed, and the lift home. It would have meant a whole bunch of lectures that she didn't feel it warranted. Besides, he didn't need the worry.

'Hi Dad!'

Chapter 16

The following day, chores done, her dad settled, she returned to the estate. The earth was still wet but the sun shining. Steam rising. A glint to everything. Tiny rainbows caught in the drops of rain that still clung to the trees. The track caught in the shade of the forest was slick, the descent slippery and she took her time, almost tiptoeing her way down, despite her want to hurry. To get to that special place. When at last she did she smiled a soft, satisfied smile as her heart lifted. That boy had been here again and left another gift.

She looked around, wondering if he was nearby, or if Dougie was. It gave the place a different feel. Not quite the same. Not quite as peaceful, even though nothing had actually changed. Not really, apart from in her own mind. Still, the thought of someone being nearby. Watching. Knowing what she was doing. It was a bit unsettling. A bit not-so-perfect.

She sighed as she sat on the bank and placed the little basket on her lap. This one was of a different material and in the shape of a leaf with a nest of tiny roses at its centre. She stroked the petals before picking up the stone that was hidden amongst them. It was a piece of gold. A beautiful piece of gold just for her.

It was late afternoon and the day now hot. Hot enough, she decided, to test the efficacy of the swimming lessons she had taken over the school year, with this river, this spot, uppermost in her mind. Now she would put her newfound skills to good use. She laid her towel on the grass, stripped off down to her swimsuit, and took a last thorough look around to make sure that there were no onlookers. At least, none that she could see. Satisfied, she dipped her toes into the river, watching the little streams of water that parted and stretched around her feet. The pull of the water was strong enough to sweep her feet downstream. She hurriedly sank them to the riverbed, wobbling slightly before securing herself. Straightening up.

As the water rose up her legs, over her bottom, her waist, her blood pulsed like mercury, thick and tremulous. *Okay. This is it!* She took a deep breath and dived down beneath the water, her head exploding into a million sparkles. She resurfaced with a glorious screech of celebration, tossed her head back. Laughed. Was this the best moment in her life? Possibly! Confident now, she swam with the current, floating with it then swimming against it, again and again, until she was quite exhausted.

She swam back to shore, dried herself and lay in the warmth of the sun, before repeating the process over and over again until afternoon was slipping towards evening. The sun would be weakening soon, the birdsong rising.

She felt him before she saw him. She sat up, dangled her feet in the water, trying desperately to appear cool and calm and nonchalant, ignoring him.

Soundlessly he sat down beside her, not looking at her.

'Oh! Hello!' she said. 'I–

'Did–

They both laughed at their simultaneous struggles at conversation.

'You first,' she said.

'Did you like the baskets?' he asked timidly, his voice drifting across the water, barely above a whisper, but flowing. No stutter. No fear.

She smiled. 'Yes! Yes I did! They're just gorgeous. Thank you.'

'I'm glad. You-you've been swimming?'

'Yes. I'm a lot better now.'

He peeled off his clothes and dived in. She followed. They splashed and squealed. He disappeared. She searched the water and panicked slightly.

'Hey! Where are you?'

She felt something brush past her leg, thought at once of that eel. Smothered a squeal. He was there swimming around under the water like an otter. She dived under and chased him, both twirling like a pair of water creatures. Spent, they sat and dried off in the sun, both shivering until its warmth stretched through them.

'Where do you go when you leave here?' she asked, feeling the touch of his hand against hers. She didn't know if the touch was accidental or not, but neither moved away. Neither broke it. A connection, a spark of something unidentifiable flowed from one to the other.

'Oh, all over. We travel all over,' he answered, not meeting her gaze but staring across the river, above the trees and beyond.

'All over where?'

'I don't know, just places.'

She sighed. 'So, you're...you're a Tinker then?'

'I am that.'

'That must be *so* romantic!' She clutched her arms to her chest.

He shrugged, looked back at her, met her eyes. 'I like it.'

'But you have a house for winter? I've heard that your, um, people quite often stay in houses for the winter. Or, or lovely big caravans.'

'No. We have a secret place where we winter.'

A secret place. Imagine!

'But, isn't it freezing, and wet and just quite miserable sometimes?'

He wrinkled his nose. 'You don't feel the harshness of the weather when you live with it, when you love it.'

She cocked her head. 'Gosh!'

'And where do you winter?'

She laughed. 'Oh, I just stay here. In my house.'

But he wasn't listening. His attention had drifted elsewhere. 'Shh.' He put his finger across her lips and pointed to the trees across the river. 'Do you see?' he whispered in her ear.

'See what?'

'There, in the tree, a pine marten. See? Sitting there, staring at us. Having a right good look, so he is!'

She squinted through the leaves, trying to follow exactly the direction he was pointing in. 'I can't...' She shook her head.

'Look closely now. The wee white chest and the pointy ears poking out between the branches. See?'

She squeezed her eyes, focussed, stared through the silent noise, frustrated at her inability to see anything beyond trunks and branches and leaves until finally, there it was. Staring right back at her. A pine marten. Sharp little eyes as black as night, gleaming from the nook of two entwined branches.

'Oh my days! Is it watching us?'

'Aye, it is that.'

They watched in silence until it scampered out of sight.

'I think we should give it a name of our own.'

He smiled. 'And what would that be then?'

'Um, maybe, maybe a pine cat? I mean what is a marten anyway?'

He laughed. 'A pine cat. Aye. Okay. A pine cat it is.'

*

She suddenly jumped up. 'I need to go now. My dad! He'll be getting worried soon.' She tossed her head back in admonishment and sighed. 'I'll be here tomorrow though. Probably,' she added as a defence. It wouldn't do to appear too keen.

He watched her disappear back into the woods and found himself wondering if perhaps this were a dream. If she were a figment of his imagination. This didn't happen to him. He didn't make friends. He didn't chat away to people. He didn't play with other people. He didn't really like them. But this girl? This girl did something to him. Made him someone else and he was very confused. His body tingled, his thoughts raced. He had never felt anything like this before and, truthfully, it frightened him.

Chapter 17

The following day they met up again, and the day after that. On the third day he waited there, in their place, not so worried that she wouldn't show. Not like before. But something didn't feel quite right. As he sat watching the glint of the summer sun slip behind the trees, he knew. The sun fell, and the shadows stretched, and a chill set in, and she wasn't there. He wanted to stay and wait until nightfall, just in case he had read this wrong, but he couldn't. His family would worry. They might even come searching, and this, this had to be kept a secret. This place. Them. A sadness clawed at him. He felt dizzy as he stood up, gathered his things – his pearl-fishing jug, his stick, the sprig of wildflowers he had gathered for her. He paused. No. He would leave the flowers here. They belonged here. He carefully chose which spot they should be left in. A dip in the grass to keep them safe. A circle of pebbles to protect them.

*

'Dad? Dad, what's up?'

He had been doing so well, looking so much better, but today it was like he had slipped right back again. His eyes

75

had lost their sparkle. His skin looked almost grey.

'Should I call someone? The doctors? The ambulance?'

'No, no.' He clutched at her arm. 'I'll be fine. Maybe been doing a bit too much. A day of rest and I'll be just grand again. You'll see.'

'Are you sure?'

These were becoming uncomfortably regular. Relapses. Times when he drifted back into being helpless and sad and it seemed as if the treatment just wasn't working. That he was slipping away and it was altogether terrifying. Sometimes he found himself thinking about her mother. Would there be any point in trying to find her again? Trying to reform that connection? It was always there, wasn't it? Between mother and daughter. At least it was meant to be. He would dismiss it soon enough. There was a reason it was just them. Here. Living a different life. It had been him and his daughter since she was just a scrap of a thing. The move here had felt right. The locals were kind. Helpful. *Poor man.*

*

Charlotte spent the day with her father, making sure he ate, he rested; tried to occupy him, amuse him.

'Shall I turn the telly on?'

He shook his head.

'Maybe a cup of tea?'

A soft smile.

She went through to the kitchen, filled the kettle, turned it on, stretched across to the cupboard and set two mugs down, dropping a teabag into each. Waiting for the water to boil she glanced out of the kitchen window, her eyes fixing on her bike. She sighed softly. By now she should have been down at the river, maybe swimming, maybe resting, maybe exploring the woods, learning new things about the creatures that lived there. The plants that grew all around, secretly spreading and feeding and nourishing. So much that she hadn't known before; hadn't even imagined. It was as if Tommy had unlocked this secret world and invited her in. Now she was a part of it too and that was very special.

Tommy loved sharing what he knew with her. Watching her eyes light up at some new spectacle; scuttling insects gifted with a wash of iridescent colours that only showed themselves to the keenest eyes; a fluttering leaf drifting from silver to green with the stroke of the wind; the opening of a bud from brown to blossom; the mew of a buzzard pealing through the sky; the shrill song of a robin bursting through the trees. All things that she had seen and heard before but not looked at, not listened to. Not noticed. Not really. Not like this.

The kettle clicked off and snapped her attention back. She carried the two steaming mugs through and set them down on the coffee table.

'Thanks, Princess. You're a sweetheart.' He smiled but it was weak and sad. This wasn't what he had wanted for her, but he was mighty grateful that she was here, by his side. Caring.

'How about I read the papers to you?'

'You know, that would be just grand.'

She had always been a precocious wee thing, his daughter, especially with her reading. Her nose stuck in some book or other since the age of five, novels since the age of eight, and now, classics, literature. She would hide under the covers at night, reading books by torchlight, disappearing into other lives. It was magical, life-saving. Of course he knew, but that wasn't a habit to frown upon. Quite the opposite. It brought a smile to him.

They sat there until her father became weary and had to be helped to bed.

'Tomorrow will be a better day.'

She kissed his forehead. 'Night Dad.'

He had had his medication, his pain-killers, and would sleep now until she woke him in the morning. It wasn't properly dark. That half-light of mid-summer evenings. The day not left, the night not fallen. There, sitting in the shadow, her bike called to her. That escape. That freedom. That being someone else. She listened at her father's door. Gentle snoring. She tiptoed down the stairs, pulled on her jacket, dipped into her trainers, clicked open the door, slipped through it, pulled it to.

Shadows stretched after her as she cycled away. So quiet. So very quiet. Nothing but the scuff of her wheels on the track, the puff of her breath. No other traffic. No one else around. She knew this route so well now that little thought was required, no concentration. Suddenly she was there. It was dark now. Properly dark. Made so by the stretch of the trees, the density of their leaves. She ditched her bike in the usual place and headed down the hill, tentatively but still sure of the way, the path she had made welcoming her back.

Overhead the flap of wings, the cawing of disturbed crows. The silent sweep of the owl. The scurry underfoot of night creatures. She had lost her footing a few times and picked up a collection of scratches and bruises but that didn't matter. In a peculiar way it made it all the more exciting. She squealed a couple of times, but there would be nothing to hear her other than wild things.

At last the weight of the trees was behind her and she stood at the riverbank. The clouds had broken sufficiently enough for the moon to streak silver across the valley. It felt as if this were for her alone. The lighting. The magic that was swept across the river, glistening like stars on the black of the water. Her eyes settled with the earth. Breathing it all in.

She glanced back and forth along the bank unsure what she was looking for. A sign. Another gift. Something to say, "I was here. I waited for you." She was searching with the speed of her heart, the pump of her breath. *Slow down. Slow down.* Another slow sweep of the bank, and there it was. His gift. Her heart swelled. A smile stretched across her face. She tiptoed towards the little dip in the land and sat down in the damp grass.

She picked up the flowers, inhaled their scent: soft, sweet, and heady, and held them to her chest. She looked to the sky. 'Thank you,' she whispered. A shiver crept through her. The cold of the night reminding her that she should move. Reluctantly she got to her feet and turned her back on the river. *I need to leave something. I need to let him know!* She gathered some pebbles and placed them in a small circle where the flowers had been. He would understand.

As she meandered her way back up the hill and along the little track, her thoughts were full of what she would do with her flowers. They were too precious to just be left to wither and die. She decided that she would press them and keep them forever. Yes. Forever!

The clouds had all drifted away allowing the half moon to clearly light up the way. Infinite stars kept it company. When she reached the top of the hill she pedalled off along the deserted little road that led home. She was cut in two. The delight of having come here and the guilt at having left her dad. It would be all right. She hadn't been gone for so long.

She crept back up to her room and spread the flowers out along her window-seat so that they could dry. She had read that somewhere; flowers should always be dried before pressing. She stared out of her window and imagined what it might be like to be sleeping out there, amongst the stars, like he did. The Tinker boy. It must be quite magical.

Perhaps he would allow her, her dad, to sleep outside. She didn't know if they had a tent. Probably not, but she could make one. Fashion something out of blankets or curtains or sheets or some such thing. Her mind was so full of the making of her tent, of exactly which materials to use in its creation, precisely where to place it, that sleep didn't come easily.

Chapter 18

A sliver of harsh morning sun broke through a crack in Charlotte's curtains. She could tell by the strength of it that it was early morning. Despite being short on sleep her mind was buzzing, or perhaps because of it. Everything depended on her dad. Was he well enough to be left alone so that she could cycle off to her place by the river? She had so much explaining to do to the boy. Why she hadn't shown up. What bound her to her house sometimes. Her dad. But should she tell him about that? Did he count as one of the people to keep the truth from? She didn't think so. It would be okay.

First things first. Nothing could happen if her dad was still feeling poorly. She slipped on her jeans and a T-shirt, washed her face, brushed her teeth, ran a brush through her hair until it hit a tangle and she gave up, before quietly, slowly, opening her dad's door. Dust motes danced in front of the window. A spider froze on its web in the corner of the ceiling, as if startled by her. She stood there quietly watching her father sleep, the rise and fall of the covers with his heavy breath, a slight whistle to it.

It seemed like only yesterday that he had been her

dependable, funny father, always cracking jokes, making her laugh, making life softer and easier and fun. It also felt like such a very long time ago. A different life. She closed the door again and got everything ready for breakfast as quietly as she could. It was best to let him sleep. Let his body heal. That was what she had decided.

When he finally surfaced he carried a smile on his face for the breakfast she had laid out for him. It wasn't the food itself, as that was minimal, his appetite barely anything at all, but the way she had made it look as appealing as possible. A fresh tablecloth, two small bowls of wild flowers – dandelions, daisies, dog roses – at either side of his cereal bowl. Porridge decorated with raspberries in a smiley face.

'Come. Sit,' she said, pulling out a chair that she had placed a cushion on.

He was a little bit stooped, a little bit slow, and he accepted the seat gratefully, a grunt escaping as he sat down.

She patted his shoulder and it hit him again how this was all the wrong way round. Being cared for by his child, comforted by his child. The gesture was lovely, but the feelings mixed. He swallowed his misgivings and squeezed her hand in thanks. 'You needn't have, but I'm mighty glad you did.' Now he would have to eat every last drop. If that had been its purpose it had worked.

*

'Dad?'

'Yes, Princess?'

'Do we have a tent?'

'No.' He paused, stretched back into his memory. 'No

we don't. Why are you asking?'

She sighed. 'I just thought it would be nice, you know? To maybe camp out in the garden.'

'We could make something if you want. You're not too big for that are you? A wee home-made affair?'

She squealed, clapped her hands. 'That would be great! Do you know how? I mean could you? Could I? Could we really make something?'

'You'd have to do all the work, but I could direct you. Would that do?'

'That would be just great. I love you, Dad.' She threw her arms around his neck and kissed his cheek.

'And I love you too.'

He sat on the back porch suggesting this and that, tutting, shaking his head. 'Not quite right.'

'It doesn't really matter. I mean. It's fine. Just so long as it covers me and doesn't fall down, it's fine.'

'It's important to make something the very best it can be, and don't you forget that. Besides which, what good is a man if he can't help his daughter build a house, eh?'

They both laughed.

Finally, as the sun slipped across the sky and the shadows changed direction they decided it was as good as it was going to get. It was a bit ramshackle, propped up against the shed, sagging and drooping, but it stood nonetheless. Well, sort of.

'Why don't you go off for your bike-ride before it gets too late.'

'Are you sure?'

'Yes. A bit of shut-eye for me and some exercise for you and we'll be right as rain. Off you go now.' He watched as she cycled off, disappearing into the trees, the curve of the lane, and was gone.

Chapter 19

She hurried down to the river. The boy was already there. She smiled.

'Where...I...you weren't here yesterday...I'

'I'm SO sorry. It was my dad. Sometimes he...well, he doesn't feel too good and I have to help him a bit. Look after him. You know, stuff like that.' She shrugged dismissively, grinned at him, hoping there would be no further questions.

'I was just...I don't...I don't. Your name?'

She laughed. 'Charlotte. I'm Charlotte.' She held out her hand. 'Pleased to meet you, um, Boy, well that's who you are in my head.'

He laughed in return. 'Tommy, and I'm mighty pleased to meet you too!'

'There. Now we know each other properly.'

They lay on their stomachs in the soft moss of the upper bank. A chill stepped into the air, but that didn't matter.

'It's like a wee forest, isn't it?' Tommy said.

'And there, see, the castle,' she said. It was a piece of quartz nestled deep in the thickest patch of moss, but to them it was something far more.

She smiled as thoughts of what might live there flitted through her mind. Tiny creatures that kept themselves hidden from human eyes.

'It's the Faeries,' he whispered, as if reading her mind.

'Do you think so? That would be so cool, if they were real, you know?'

'Oh but they are. The Faeries.'

She nudged him. 'You're teasing me!'

'No!' His face turned scarlet. 'Not at all. The Faeries step through all of these places.'

She stared at him. 'Are you really, really telling me that you believe in faeries?'

'Oh, not just faeries. The Faeries. These Faeries. How could some place so perfect not be lived in by The Faeries?'

She turned her gaze back to the moss, the tiny shapes and shadows. 'But that would mean we stand on them, crush them when we walk.'

'Not when you have the magic, like they do. When you can make things un-be and un-see and it's only you in your world.'

'Have you actually seen them then?'

'I have that.'

'No!'

'It's no good just looking. They have to want to show themselves. They have to choose you, see?'

The temperature dropped further, afternoon slipping into evening. She jumped up. 'I have to go. My Dad. Tomorrow. I'll see you tomorrow!' she called as she ran up the hill, trying to push thoughts of trampled faeries out of her mind.

That night she made a bed up in the tent-like structure.

'Are you sure you'll be all right?'

'I'll be fine, Dad.'

'I could keep you company, if you like.'

'You need your bed and I'll be just fine!'

As lights flicked off and darkness took over, the noises changed. Things that she hadn't heard before. Night creatures rustling and flapping and squeaking. Strange sounds that she couldn't identify. She comforted herself by confirming that nothing she could hear sounded human. No strangers lurking with bad intentions. Things like that didn't happen here anyway. She had finally drifted off when a wind picked up, a gust tugging at the curtain stretched above her. Another gust and it flew off. Rain splattered. She squealed, scooped her covers up and ran into the house.

Chapter 20

The next day, as they sat side by side, feet dangling in the water, gazes held by the gentle sway of the trees beyond the river, Tommy laughed as she told him the story of her camping disaster.

'It's not as easy as I thought!' She nudged him gently, took a deep breath. 'I was wondering if you could, you know, show me how to make a real, proper, Tinker tent like the one that you have?'

He grinned at her. 'Aye, I can do that, right enough.'

'Excellent!' She jumped up, cocked her head at him in expectation.

'Now?'

'Well, yes!'

He showed her the best kind of sticks to use, the right size, how to gently bend them and slot them together. He showed her how to secure them with ivy. How to fix them to the ground. And there it was, in less than a quarter of an hour, the skeleton of a tent!

'This is just a wee one, like, but it'll work just fine once there's a canvas on it, or some such. Have you got such a thing? To cover it like?'

'Oh, this is great.' She clapped, grinned up at him. 'I've got curtains that'll do. I think. Sort of. Just so long as it doesn't rain, or get really super windy like it did last night, or, or something.' She ran her fingers over the arch of the frame.

'Well, if it's wind you're worried about you can cast a rope over it and hold it down with stones, or even ivy will do.'

'Okay. I could use the washing line, maybe, if Dad lets me. Or, or maybe we've got some spare somewhere.'

'Be careful, mind, there's beasties that'll crawl in for a wee bit shelter too.'

She laughed. 'I don't think I'm scared of beasties! There aren't any poisonous, dangerous ones here, are there?'

'Naw. Are you not from hereabouts then?'

'Not really. We, um, we used to live in Edinburgh until...well, we're here now.' She changed the subject. 'Can I take these? Untie them and take them?'

'Aye, nae bother. Course you can. Will you mind it all? All that you have to do.'

'Yes, I think so. I'm pretty good at remembering if it's something important to me.'

'Shall I help you up to the big house with them, then?'

She stared, quizzically.

'Your home, up yonder?'

'Oh! No, I don't live anywhere near here. It's quite far really and...' Her shoulders slumped. 'I hadn't even thought about just how I was going to get them home.'

'How far is it then?'

'Five miles.'

'That's quite a way. How do you get here then?'

'I cycle. On my bike.'

'Oh! Do you now? Where is it then?'

'I hide it away up there.'

He gave her some leaves from the hazel trees so that she would know what to build her frame with. She would be able to find the same kind from the small wood that ran just beyond her garden. She was quite sure she had seen them over there. He walked up the hill with her, held the handlebars of her bike as he pushed it up to the road for her. Wiped the seat down, pulled a couple of leaves off. Smiled at her.

*

Her dad watched from behind his bedroom window, lights off, as she crawled into her tent. He had to admit it was a lot better than their previous attempt. She seemed to know just what to do, as if someone else had shown her. He had wanted to ask, but swallowed the question back down. There was a trust between them and that was precious. He decided to let this be. She would tell him in her own time.

It set his mind to wondering though. There had been a change in her. She had become happier and chattier and, well, more like a girl of her age should be. More smiles and fewer frowns. Less of the seriousness that had been forced on her by this damned illness. If he questioned, probed, it might slip away and he didn't want that to happen. But what if? Was there a what-if here? Should he be concerned? He just didn't know. Perhaps he should run it by Martha, next door. A woman's point of view could only help here and he was floundering.

Chapter 21

Tommy and his family moved off again as summer began to slip behind colder weather and lengthening nights. As the seasons turned Charlotte snatched at the chances she got to cycle out to the river. She found herself missing Tommy more than she thought she would. The place just didn't feel quite right without his presence. Emptier somehow. She had spent more time with Dougie who, instead of keeping himself at a discreet distance, showed himself, sat beside her, chatted to her about his estate. He didn't ask too many questions of her, which she liked. It made her feel more grown-up somehow. More of an equal.

The leaves turned and fell. Glowing golds and crimsons curled and died on the ground; the forest stripped bare, skeletons scrambling up the hill, huddling against the cruel winds of winter. Discarding their clothes to allow them to fight against the cold, to stand tall against the onset of snow. Bands of green still marched with the pines. Needles that didn't need to fall away.

Charlotte's father still clung on. Still fought. That cycle of seeming recovery, getting better, slipping into illness again, suffering under treatment. It seemed interminable. In the darkest days of winter she worried most. When he seemed thinner and paler and frailer. But still he pulled through. Snow fell and washed their world white. Spirits rising with the fluttering flakes. There was even time and energy for laughter. For a snowball fight. For the building of a snowman. In between the exertion, the escape, worried glances flicked from daughter to father. *Are you okay, Dad?* Thought, not said, but he knew. He read those thoughts and wished that he couldn't. Didn't need to. Everything upside down in this world of theirs.

The dark nights shrank back and it was spring again and the world seemed to smile. At least for a while. He insisted that Charlotte went off on her bike every weekend and on the odd school day, weather permitting. She went without argument now. He would insist anyway and it was better that he didn't feel guilty, she didn't feel neglectful.

It was one of those glorious spring days when the world was exploding with blossom and new growth and the sun had strength enough to lift the temperature to almost warm, almost summer. Sometimes that was best. The anticipation.

She was quite sure Tommy wouldn't be here yet, but she clambered up the rock face beside the road so that she could cast her eyes across the valley looking for that tent. That oddity that belonged in another age but was so perfectly right. She was quite desperate to get close enough to see their way of life for herself. She would ask him one day. Maybe.

No, it wasn't there, but she could see Dougie standing in amongst the trees, his binoculars trained on something across the water. She crept up.

'Hello,' she whispered.

'Oh, it's yourself, is it?' he whispered back.

'What can you see? Is it something exciting?'

'Well now, creep up in front of me and slip in behind the glasses. That's it. Now, do you see him?'

'No. I. Oh gosh! Yes! Is he a poacher? An actual poacher?'

'Eh, no! I had my eyes on an osprey. Is there a man there too?'

'Yes! Look!'

He took the binoculars back, focused in on the trees where the osprey had been sitting. It had taken off, was swirling around, calling in alarm. There! Making his way up the incline of the slope, creeping into the forest, a figure. A man.

'Right. Well done you! I was so taken by the bird I didn't even see him.'

'So, is he a poacher then?'

'Could well be. Maybe after the osprey's eggs. Just need to keep an eye on him to make sure. I wouldn't want to be frightening the life out of some innocent wee tourist, now would I?'

'But he's got a gun!'

'Och, there's many folk round this way with guns.'

'Really? Why's that? I mean, isn't it against the law?'

'Not if they've got a license, for hunting and the likes, aye? And that they're not poaching, of course!'

'So, what should we do? Oh! This is so exciting!' She clapped her hands together in glee.

'That, over there,' he said, pointing across the river.

'That is part of Craigdour, Campbell land. Not ours. I'll just report it and let them take over.'

'Oh. That's a shame. I mean, that would have been such a thrill! Hunting a dangerous criminal! Imagine!'

He had taken a liking to this girl. A spark about her. Such an imagination. He bit back a laugh.

The stranger disappeared amongst the trees. Dougie called Craigdour estate on his radio and that was that. No chase. No surreptitious creeping through the woods. No citizen's arrest. Of course, she wouldn't have been allowed to be a part of it all anyway, but at least she could have imagined; been there by proxy.

Chapter 22

At last it was summer holiday time again. Charlotte had her tent built and ready before Tommy arrived that evening and waited excitedly. Unable to sit still she tweaked and checked and adjusted. It had to be perfect. Just so! At last the call of the peewit, *pee – ee – wit.* She could differentiate his call from the real thing now, but only just. She grinned and replied. Her call was nowhere near as good as his, but that didn't matter. She crawled out of the tent and stared across the river, through the trees, waiting for a sight of him. His grin arrived first.

He inspected the tent, nodding his head in appreciation as he did so. 'Aye. You've done a grand job, for a scaldie.'

She frowned, stood tall with her hands on her hips. 'And just what is a scaldie?'

'Folk that live in houses, like you.'

'Hmm.'

'Can I come inside, like?'

'Only if you promise to say really nice things about it.'

'I think it's the bonniest wee tent ever, okay?'

'That'll do.'

He poked her in the ribs. She giggled and retaliated.

They fell to the ground and rolled about, tickling each other, play wrestling. He had her pinned down, staring at her, looking into her eyes. A feeling that confused him, frightened him. He let her go. Sat upright. Tense. The feeling was broken by a noise. Something. Someone.

'Shh.'

'What is it? What's wrong?'

He cupped his ear, meaning listen.

There were steps close by. Twigs snapping. He crawled out and stared through the bracken, the ferns, the trees. Shrubs quivered more than by the effect of the wind which was picking up in erratic gusts. Deer. The kicking of hooves as they scampered off.

'Well?'

'Nothing. Just the deer.'

'You frightened me!'

'Aye, well. You just need to be careful. That's what my da says. Listen out for strangers and be ready, just in case.'

'In case of what?'

'There's some folk that don't like us so much; cause trouble, move us on.'

'Oh, that's just horrible.' She shook her head. Mulled things over. 'Not here though. I mean, you've been coming here for years and years, haven't you?'

'Aye, right enough. But scaldie folk are scaldie folk. And, well...' He shrugged. Looked beyond the trees. 'When they've got a drink in them, or a mood on. Well. There's just folk that don't like us.'

They sat in an unusual silence, slightly awkward, until the river called them in. They swam, like always, messing about, splashing and diving and chasing one another. He caught a fish and flipped it at her. She squealed and tried to do the same but couldn't get close enough to one.

'You need to teach me. That would be so cool. To be able to catch my own food!'

'Och, it's easy enough. You just need to have the way.'

'And I don't have *the way* because I'm a scaldie, I suppose.'

'Aye. Something like that!'

They dried off, huddled together under her towel, her head on his shoulder, his arm around her back.

'I wish I wasn't a scaldie.'

He laughed. 'Oh, you might not like the life so much.'

*

After he had gone she followed in the direction he had taken. She wanted to see for real, for herself. Staying close to the river, the trees, she kept herself far enough away. Hidden. Breath held. Eyes wild. She barely dared to look. A stolen glance at a life that didn't belong any more. Slow and secret and somehow quite magical. A part of her felt as if she were committing a crime. Invading someone else's memories. She wanted them to become hers. To be a part of that twist of smoke snaking into the evening sky; to be the laughter, the music, the tangle of voices as deep and secret as the woods themselves. The spell was snatched away from her by the crackle of a twig behind her. She turned, alarmed. There was nothing there, but time had switched and she was back again. Just as well. She had been out too long and should be well on her way home by now.

As she lay in her bed, the window open wide to the

cool night air, the sound of the river crept in, the rustle of the woods drifting around her, stretching through her, she wondered what it would be like. A life like that. A life like theirs. It would be peaceful and magical and she was quite sure that, despite what he had said, she would like it. As sleep wrapped her up and took her away, her thoughts lay with next year. Perhaps she could stay in her tent by the river overnight.

Any pretence of there not being a spark – something special between them – had fallen away over those long days of summer. They both knew that this was more than just a friendship. They both knew that it should never have happened, but were powerless to stop it. This feeling had swept over them and bound them together and when they were apart it felt as if something integral were missing. That stolen hour or two every afternoon was the most precious of gifts.

Chapter 23

Like always, Robbie and the older boys headed off in the van and Jeannie and Tommy followed in their slow, quiet journey through valley and forest, across river and around loch. As they set up camp both felt a pain. Something dark and awful. They looked to each other.

'Are you picking that up too?' Tommy asked.

She was silent for too long. 'Aye son, aye. Probably nothing. An ancient one or...or something. Best get a sleep now. Head off early.' Sleep wasn't coming for either of them. With the first chatter of the dawn they headed off again. Both quiet. Both holding back on what they felt. They followed a steep little dirt-track road, barely a road at all, as it twisted and turned up and down the mountainside. They passed no one, saw no one. This track had been used by them and their family for generations. It would barely exist any more if it weren't for their use of it.

As they drew closer to their next stopping-place signs of an accident lay scattered in the ditch and tumbled down the steep gorge. Part of the cliff had crumbled away settling with the wreckage far below in the river at its base.

Mother and son stared, dismounted, clutched tightly on to one another, both holding their breath, both knowing. Fragments of blue. The blue of their van. They had spoken of this, Jeannie and Robbie, about the dangers, about maybe using the new road like everyone else. "Maybe next year," Robbie had said, with a grin. Both of them knowing full well that he didn't mean it. He loved this old track and the memories it held. The connection with his parents, grandparents; with his people. He had nudged her in the ribs. "We'll be fine, like always. You'll see. Asides from which, I ken this place like the back o my hand. That new road? Now that's the dangerous one and no mistaking. Folk driving so fast, some wi the drink in them, some wi no mind for anything but themselves! Naw, We'll keep on doing what we do and come to no harm."

Jeannie clasped Tommy's arm, stared into his eyes, her face soaked through with tears. She couldn't speak. Couldn't move. The world had frozen around them.

'Mam,' Tommy finally whispered, gathering his strength. 'We need to get down there. Maybe...We need to...to see.'

The way down was almost vertical, mostly rock, slick with the early evening mist. Stunted shrubs – gorse and heather – and gnarled old Scots pines interspersed the rock and scree. A trail worn by mountain goats snaked its treacherous way down, disappearing amidst the scree and reappearing when the ground became more solid again. Tommy began to inch his way down, little by little, more of a slide than a step, his hands clutching on to anything near that felt stable enough to give him the confidence to carry on.

His mouth was dry, his heart thumping. This was the most terrifying thing that he had ever attempted, made even more so by the visions that filled his head of what he might find at the bottom. He tried to throw them away, focus only on this, on what had to be done, but his brain didn't work like that. Every possible image of what lay there waiting for them swarmed his thoughts, buzzing like demented hornets. A mass of terrible wickedness.

His mother followed close behind, her eyes flicking from where to place her feet, what to grasp with her hands, to the progress of her son, the twisting roar of the river, and back again, over and over. They were almost half way down now. She knew they should have taken the horses; found a safer descent, but how could they? How could they possibly wait any longer than this? They couldn't.

Tommy felt some scree tumble down past him. He looked up. His mother's step had faltered, her foot slipping on the rock, into the scree. He watched as she snatched at the roots of some heather. They were loose, working themselves free of the ground. 'Mam!'

She looked down at him, her eyes terrified and staring, as she slipped backwards. She screamed. It seemed to take forever. As if the world had changed. Time had changed. The roots broke free. Her arms were flailing now as she fought for balance. She fell past Tommy. He stretched out and snatched at her arm, just managing to clasp a piece of the sleeve of her sweater. The weight of her stretched him away from the mountainside, one hand grasping the heather, the other his mother. His feet were scrambling in the scree. No purchase being offered. He was losing her in the tiniest of pieces. The slowest of moments. The sweater was stretched to its fullest; his mother's face in torment. Her eyes staring wide.

'You need to let me go, Tommy. Let me go.'

He shook his head.

'Aye!'

The decision was snatched from him as her body slipped its way out of the sweater. She was going and there was nothing he could do about it. He watched as her body tumbled, slipping from taut to soft. From here to gone. His fingers opened and the sweater drifted down after her, his eyes following every ripple of the fabric, every cruel bend. He could see the twist of what had been her, lying bent and broken, on an outcrop of rocks that jutted into the river. He should join her. Join them. Just let go and allow nature to bring them all together once more.

Above him he could hear the whinny of Seil. He closed his eyes and pushed himself into the rock; into the heather, calling on everything he had to help him do what was right. He was weeping as he began to edge his way down again. His vision blurred. He had to pull himself together if he was going to make it down. His mother was gone – that was plain by the twist of her body – but someone might have survived. Something might have protected one of them. Kept them safe and alive. The packs in the van. Clothing. Bedding. Something might have just been enough to save someone. He clung on to that thought, that tiny bit of hope, until at last he reached the bottom of the gorge and safe ground.

There was barely anything left of the van other than

pieces. Broken pieces scattered all around. Remnants of his life. The curved sticks of the bender, the iron chittie, pots and plates. He heard a crack and jumped, part in fear, part in expectation. In desperate hope he turned to face whatever was making the noise; breaking the silence. It was only the flapping of the canvas that had wrapped itself around some elder, catching in the wind, making that familiar sound. The flick of canvas in wind. Protection from the harshness of the weather. Seclusion as they hunkered down for the night, telling stories and dreams as the wind told her own outside. The soft laughter of his ma, the chuckle of his da. "Hush now."

His eyes scanned the river, her banks, the rocks, the reeds that stood tall in tranquil pools carved into the bank. The shrubbery and trees that clambered back up the sides of the gorge, breaking through the scree and beyond. There was birdsong, but he couldn't hear it today. His head buzzed so loudly that it was deafening. Nothing broke through it. Caught in the strangest, darkest place he had ever known he combed every inch, picking up every scrap he could find. Every piece of twisted metal, broken glass, sliver of memory. That was all he had now. Slivers. Disjointed scraps of a distant life. There were pieces of wreckage shouting at him from all around. From high in the scree, from the copse, from the river itself.

And the bodies. He had found them all now; lain them beside each other on the slab of rock where his ma had landed.

He didn't know what to do with everything he had found, gathered together. It was wrong to leave waste, to leave a stain on the land, but he could find no answer to this. Tradition said that everything belonging to the dead should be taken by fire, and he would do his best. He piled everything up amongst dry sticks and logs. Set it alight. Prayed that it would catch; that the flames would be bold enough to eat what they were offered. Send them to be with the souls of his family. He stood and watched as solidity contorted, shrivelled, and shrank; stacking up the fire over and over again until what was left bore no resemblance to its origins.

The bodies had to be buried. He had to give them that grace. Set them at one with the earth. One by one he hoisted each body onto a stretch of the land where the earth was soft and he could dig deep enough down into the soil to give them a decent covering. It was far enough from the river to keep them from being washed away. It was the best he could do.

He had retrieved their shovel, keeping it aside for this very purpose. The light was all but gone now. His hands were raw, his face scratched and torn, his body ached, but he worked on into the night. A full moon rose above the mountain and lit up the river like a piece of molten silver. He felt sick as he untied his da's money-belt and strapped it around himself. Then he rolled the body into the grave with that of his ma and his brothers and covered them all with dark heavy earth. The belt and the money should have gone with his da, but Tommy needed it. He needed to survive. So too the section of canvas he had kept. Just enough to cover himself. His da would understand. The spirits would understand. Would want him to do just this.

His ears caught a sound. The sound of something alive. A creature perhaps. One of the wild goats that lived hereabouts: a hare, a fox. Something at one with the night. He stood tall and listened. There. To the right of him. Something in the bushes. Whimpering. A sad, lonely whimpering. He peered through the darkness. There. On her belly, quivering in terror, was his little dog. How could he have forgotten about her?

'Rona lass. Come here,' he called softly.

She inched across to him, still on her belly, her ears clipped tight against her head, the tip of her tail twitching a timid greeting.

'Aw, lass.'

He sat down and called her onto his lap, stroking her soft head, calming her, easing her pain. His fingers travelled tenderly across every inch of her body, checking for injuries, for sore spots. Somehow she had survived seemingly unscathed. He knew that Swift hadn't. His body was already in the ground beside those of the rest of the family. Everyone accounted for. Everyone gone. The world felt so very big. Just him and his wee dog left alone in it. Tiny specks of insignificance. The weight of it fell on him, pushed him down. Rona snuffled at his face, licked his nose, forced something good to spread through him. He could do this. He had to do this for his family.

As he sat with Rona, waiting for dawn to break and show him the way out, he called to the horses. 'Wait there. We'll be up to get you. Wait there.' They were smart beasts. They would know. They would wait. His only worry was that some stranger would have come along and taken them away, although he knew that was as close to impossible as you could get without actually saying it, being it. This road was barely a road at all and never saw any traffic other than theirs. That was why they liked it. It was like their own private route to the coast. How he loathed it now.

With the rising of the sun he checked over the grave he had made. He stamped the earth down, rolled rocks over – as large as he could manage – so that it was all covered. He dug out the roots of wildflowers and sunk them into the freshly lain soil, securing them with more stones. Finally he knelt and said a prayer for each of them. And that was that. It was all gone. It was all over. He had to become someone else. He had to survive.

He climbed back up the side of the gorge, this time traversing in a slow tedious ascent, but it was safer. Much safer. Why hadn't they done this on the way down? Why? Of course he knew. That desperation. That chance that time might save a life. Instead it took one more. His mam smiling down at him as she whispered goodnight. The stroke of her hand floating across his face. The smell of her: of softness and strength, of earth and air, of cooking and washing and laughing and loving; of all that was right about his world. Her twisted face, grimaced in fear, as she fell away from him. He threw it away. That image wouldn't be what defined her, what was left of her. He found her smile again and held on tight.

Rona was sticking so close to his heels it was almost dangerous. Each foot placed had to be carefully checked for fear of hurting her, trampling on her wee paws. No matter how he encouraged her to go on ahead – to lead the way, even to come beside him – she wouldn't. She stuck by her master's heels as if a shadow. At last he reached the top, fingers grasping at the rough vegetation of the roadside, sliding himself onto something safe, something solid.

He lay on his back, breathless through both exertion and anxiety. Rona slithered onto his chest, her tiny tongue licked softly at his tears. The soft snuffling of the horses pulled him back, made him sit up and take stock. A toss of their heads in gentle acknowledgement as they stood over him. He managed a smile, stroked their muzzles. The only thing he could do now was find a place of safety for all of them. Where was that? This safe place.

Chapter 24

Those last two weeks of summer, after Tommy had gone, were a peculiar concoction of emotions. She was sad at his leaving, but her dad hadn't been this well since the illness began stealing little pieces of him. Over the summer he'd put some weight back on, straightened up, as if his world had become lighter. They laughed and messed about like they had before. He played tricks on her; hid and jumped out; put on silly voices; did his infamously bad dad-dance with exaggerated gusto. The house echoed with laughter. And it felt strange. Wonderful but strange. As if an old friend, presumed dead, had strolled back into their lives.

'I've got a surprise for you!' he said one morning as he walked to join her at the kitchen table, his hands behind his back, a twinkle in his eye. 'Drum roll please!'

She obliged, slapping her hands against the wood of the table, faster and faster, until she couldn't do any more. The cat ran off into the back garden, disgusted.

'Sorry Kittie!' Charlotte called after him.

'Ta-dah!' Her dad slapped an envelope in front of her.

She stared. Looked up at him.

'Go on then. Open it!'

Inside was a booking confirmation. Ten days in Rhodes.

'We fly out tomorrow?' she asked.

'No time like the present, eh? What do you think?'

She stood up, stretched her arms around his neck. 'I think it's brilliant. Thank you!'

He fought back a tear. Finally, something good for her. For them. He felt like a dad again.

'What about Kittie?'

'All sorted. Martha's going to pop in and keep him company, feed him. He'll be fine. He'll probably end up just staying in her house, the amount of spoiling he gets from her!'

She laughed, checked the dates. 'You realise I'm going to miss the beginning of school?'

'You don't mind, do you? I mean, I don't mind if you don't mind.'

'No. Not at all!'

'Great! Splendid! Sometimes you just have to break the rules!' He grinned sheepishly, raised his eyebrows, shrugged. Her father who was such a stickler for rules, for education, for not missing a day, irrespective of what else was going on. 'Meanwhile, you and I are off to the shops. We need to look like proper tourists!'

Twenty four hours later they were sitting on the beach under a baking sun. He hadn't really noticed the change in her. The slip from girl to young woman. Others had. He frowned at the appreciative stares of strangers. A gaggle of teenage boys nudged each other as she sauntered past. She lifted her hair from her back, shook it free. *Please let that have been accidental. Innocent.* He wanted to run across with a towel and wrap her up. Hide her. Protect her from all that was coming her way. But he wouldn't be that man who embarrassed her. Who stopped her from growing up. God, how he wished he could.

The harbour held a semi-circle of tavernas, some for the full-English-breakfast tourists. Others were more traditional, the smell of souvlaki and grilled fish mixing with the night air. Sea, thyme, and jasmine. The clink of metal on mast echoing up from the harbour walls, the insidious thump of Europop drifting out of the tavernas.

After that first night they decided to venture deeper into the town. Twisty little cobbled streets coated with old white-washed walls, behind which people's lives played out: more locals, fewer tourists. A different air to the place. The further up the hill they walked the quieter it became. The screech of crickets louder than human interference.

'What do you think? Somewhere up here, or do you want to go back down to the front? I don't mind.'

'This is fine, Dad. I'm not really into the whole noisy touristy thing either.'

'You sure?'

'Sure.'

She would say that anyway because that was who she was. Who she had become. He wondered if he truly knew her any more. The real her. Not the carer, the girl who has had to grow up too quickly, the girl who puts her father before her. So many things that this illness had taken from them. So many layers.

'You okay there, Dad?'

He shook himself out of his reverie. 'Fine. Sorry. Just drifted off for a minute.'

'Maybe you should pull back on the old Ouzo!'

They both laughed.

'If anything happens–' He stared at her in a way that made her shiver. Suddenly so serious.

'Dad, nothing's going to happen. Look at you!'

'But if it does, I mean, I could get hit by a bus.'

A donkey and trap trundled past.

'Or a donkey?' She grinned.

'Or even a donkey.' He grinned back. 'Seriously though, there's a bit, well quite a lot, put aside for you. You'll be fine.'

'Dad!'

The ten days had suddenly passed and they touched down in Glasgow. Chilly and grey and damp.

'Home sweet home, eh?' Charlotte joked.

Her dad squeezed his eyes shut. Pulled his hands to his forehead. 'Jesus!' he mumbled.

'Dad?'

Chapter 25

Tommy had to think now; to clear his muddled thoughts. He couldn't face travelling on to where his family would have made their camp; their next stopping-place. That would be normality, the way things ought to be, used to be but weren't any more. There might well be others. People who knew him, knew his family. There would be questions that he couldn't answer. That he didn't want to think about. And despite the fact that he was quite sure he had done nothing wrong he felt dirtily guilty. He felt bruised and battered inside and out and was sure that everyone would see. Would know.

Winter would be here soon enough and he needed to be ready for it. At least he knew where he was. This land was like an old friend, although for now she was more of an enemy. The coast was near enough. They had almost made it. His family had only been a whisper away from resting. From chatter, and craic, and fellowship.

He decided he would take the high road, skirt the stopping-place, and head on up to the silver caves. There was shelter, driftwood for the fire, fish for catching, shellfish for gathering, seaweed too. Crofter's land stood about half a morning's ride away – far enough away for him to feel safe, stay hidden, but close enough for him to forage from. If he was lucky there would be some leftover tatties, neeps, barley, straw for the horses, even some fruit. Folk left a lot behind them. Even poor folk. Wasteful. Careless.

The cave with the silver walls and the little cove that stretched out from it – it too seemingly silver, glowing, in the late evening sunlight – stood below him. It couldn't be seen from up here and that was a major part of the attraction, but he could feel it, sense it, picture it in his mind. He would have to walk the long way round so that the horses could manage the descent. There was a good couple of miles to trek around in a big circle, but that kept the place well hidden. Secret.

He tried to keep his thoughts away from what had happened; away from why he was here, like this. Alone. He was good at that. Always had been. He dreamed and thought of other things, of other places, of his own world. This was it now. This was his world and he had to make it good, make it work. He knew that they would want that. *Time to stand up son. Time to be a man now.*

That first night he stayed up. Sleep wouldn't pay him a visit anyway. He knew that well enough. He galloped along the small beach with the horses, riding bareback, feeling like a part of them. Skin on skin. They trotted through the waves, Rona barking from the shore. As the sunlight heralded dawn he settled down in the cave. He built a fire, using straw as tinder, dried out driftwood washed up on the shore as fuel. Some were flat sturdy pieces with the remains of rusted nails protruding from them. He found himself wondering about what they had belonged to. Something from a boat, a shipwreck? Perhaps far out there, at the bottom of the sea, other lives rested. Lives ended by the power of the ocean. The weight of the water. He found himself pondering which he would prefer. To be taken by the land, as his family had been, or by water. He imagined water would be more gentle, life floating away. A softer, kinder parting.

Rona snuffled at his arm, dunting it with her nose, as if to say, "Enough of that. Come back now." He smiled down at her and ruffled her head.

'Aye, right you are, wee one!'

He focused back on his task and struck two flints together as ignition, as his da had taught him. They sparked with not so much bother, the tiny pieces of fire leaping into the straw. A crackle as it caught. Soon enough the timber was ablaze and the warmth crept through his bones. He stretched out beside the horses and Rona, exhaustion taking over and was soon asleep.

Although he had money, it wasn't for the using. Not yet. He would stay hidden for as long as he could. Stay in his own world. As daylight faded he ventured out, Rona settling herself in between his legs on the horse, as she always did. They trotted back along the coast and inland towards the crofts. Tonight it was straw he was after for bedding and food. He was in luck. A bale had tumbled down from its stack and just lay there. Not theft, just picking up something that had fallen.

He slipped down from Seil and hoisted it onto the back of Coll, his mother's horse, securing it with rope. A dog started to bark, alerting its owner of their presence.

Tommy's heart quickened as he leapt back up, Rona doing likewise. A beam of light spread across the land. A door creaked.

'That was a close one,' he whispered into the night, confident enough that he hadn't been spotted, but aware of the need to be more vigilant next time.

The next night it was food that he was after. He and the horses were fine with what he found lying around, but Rona needed something more.

He waded out into the cold salty water, waves breaking against him, while there was still enough light to catch the glimmer of a fish streaking through the darkening blue. Guddling in a river was easy enough for him. He had learned the art as a wee boy copying his brothers; waiting patiently for the feel of the fish, a soft tickle then a sharp snatch.

They preferred to use a line now. Now? No. Not now. Then. It was all then. But he stuck with the guddle. This evening though, he wished for a line. He wished for his brothers. Standing tall he stretched his aching back, closed his eyes and screamed. Again and again. The sound bounced back off the cliffs of the cove and floated out on the water, far, far away, until they were nothing. Rona ran out to him, barking from the edge of the rocks.

'Aw, lass,' he whispered. 'I'm sorry.'

He clambered back up the rock, chastising himself for losing it like that; for being so self-absorbed. It wouldn't do. He ruffled Rona's head. 'I'm going back in now. You just wait here. Be a good girl, aye?'

She cocked her head from one side to the other and waited patiently, her eyes not leaving him.

Finally something swam close enough for him to wheech out of the water. It was a fair size too! A mackerel landed on the rocks, wriggling and squirming. Rona pounced, snapping it tightly in her jaws. Tommy rushed out of the water and took its life with a rock. 'Good girl!'

*

Rona sat drooling as the fish was being grilled on the fire in the cave. Smoke curled along the walls and crept upwards, where it hung on the roof of the cave before creeping out into the night sky and disappearing into nothing.

'You need to wait now, Rona lass,' Tommy whispered to the dog as he sat beside her, his hand on her back. 'It's right hot and it'll burn the skin off of you, so it will! Patience lass. Patience.'

He stretched forward and pressed his finger to the fish. Still a bit too warm for the dog. It would be about perfect for him, but he wouldn't eat until his dog could too. Fair's fair. He picked the fish up by the tail and blew on it, swung it to and fro. Checked the temperature again.

'That'll do just fine!' he said, flaking half the fish and laying it on a piece of flat rock. 'Come on, Rona lass,' he called.

He sat at the mouth of the cave, Rona across his feet as if she were holding him; binding him to her, and watched the sun rise, lighting up the water in pinks and blues and golds. It was breathtaking and in different times he would have felt perfect. But now his heart ached. The weight of his loss choked at him and he cried silently, staring out at the place where the water met the sky and bled into one. Where this world slipped into the next.

116

Chapter 26

Roger sat quietly behind the wheel, taking deep breaths, calming his head, his daughter.

'Are you sure you're okay to drive, Dad?'

'I'm fine.' He turned to her and smiled. 'I'd forgotten how air travel and me are a bad mix! Just give me a minute.'

It was late. The roads were quiet. Home welcomed them in the depth of the night. Kitty greeted their arrival with pleading meows, as if he hadn't been fed for the entire time. Shouting at them. Twisting himself around them.

'Sorry Princess. School tomorrow. You'd best grab as much sleep as you can. On you go.'

'Night Dad. And thank you.' She hugged him tight. 'It was lovely.'

'It was, wasn't it. Good night.'

*

She was supposed to have been off sick, but the patently un-Scottish suntan wasn't going to fool anyone. What the hell? It wasn't as if it mattered anyway. She'd work hard, catch up. Quality time like that, spent with her dad, was worth so much more than they could ever imagine. She just prayed that this "good spell" would carry on, grow and stretch and become their new reality.

She hurried home from school because that was the way of things. Always that slight trepidation as she opened the door.

'It's just me, Dad,' she called. She knew right away that everything was fine. Music was playing softly in the background. Her dad was on the phone to someone. A serious conversation. That was good. A client. More work for him. He'd taken on a few more jobs designing extensions, drawn up plans for a couple of chalets. Soon, he hoped, the bigger work would come again and he could call himself an architect once more. An office, staff, a future.

He raised a just-a-minute finger at her, smiled. She smiled back, waved, and went into the kitchen. The table was set, food ready and waiting: a Greek salad, pastitsio, home-made lemonade. A cookbook lay on the counter, still open, stained with tomato sauce. The sight of it all made her suddenly very hungry. She hurried upstairs; changed out of her uniform.

'Dinner awaits, madame,' he said, a tea-towel draped over his arm, gesturing to the table as he pulled out her chair.

'I could get used to this!'

'That's the plan.'

*

The grass was damp, the air chilled with the onset of autumn. A scattering of leaves slipped down from their branches and tumbled across the forest floor. She walked

118

on, deeper into the woods. That mustiness. A peculiar blend of life and death. An intensity that could only belong to this time of year.

A burst of fungi swelled from the base of a tree. Charlotte bent down and trailed her fingers across them, imagining the messages being carried from tree to tree by these little mushrooms. Underneath the ground a different world. A place of magic and secret whispers and untold stories. The miles and miles of twists and turns and tangles and spirals, and each tiny tendril carrying a message from root to root, fungi to fungi, tree to tree. Whispers in the underworld. You can hear them, you know. If you listen hard enough with an open mind and a purity of thought.

And she was back. Back in these woods with Tommy in the days before she knew anything of this underworld. This magic. He was lying on the ground, his ear to the roots of a giant oak.

'What are you doing?' Charlotte said.

'Listening to the forest.'

'And what's the forest saying to you?' she asked with a giggle to her voice, not expecting a serious response.

'Come and sit by me and I'll tell you.'

If this had been anyone else she would have thought they were having her on, making fun of her. But not him. He never did things like that. That gentle seriousness was one of the things that made him so special. He knew things. Things that nobody else seemed to know. He heard things and saw things in such a way that made them unique. Everything. The trees, the birds, the deer, the pine martens, the water voles, the weather. Everything.

119

Everything spoke with him and he with it.

He showed her how to cup her hands against the trunk of a tree, press her ear to it, and hear the pulse of its heart beat, its breath. Gurgles and sighs. He told her about the web of life underground. How the trees spoke. The forests connected.

'How do you know all of this stuff?'

'It's just the way of things. The way it is. We just know, and now you do too.' His smile slipped into seriousness. A narrowing of his eyes. A frown. 'But be careful with it.'

'Oh, I will. I will.'

They sat in silence that wasn't silence at all, listening to different heartbeats. Different sighs.

*

'It's just...magic...pure magic,' she whispered up into the trees.

'Is that you talking to the trees, lass?'

'Dougie! You frightened me! I wasn't expecting...well. Yes, I was. Talking to the trees that is.'

120

Chapter 27

Tommy had survived well enough. His family had taught him how to do that; how to find what nature had to share; how to protect himself from the harshest of her elements, to keep him and his animals safe, sheltered, and fed. He took satisfaction in how he had coped, putting into practise what he had witnessed, been told about, now proving that he *knew*. It was as if he had been legitimised as a McPhee; a real Tinker; a man of the earth.

The cave had only been good for a few days. It became apparent soon enough that the horses would need somewhere to graze – this wasn't fair on them; sand and salt water. The cave was also too open for the coming winter. Winds would howl, rain would lash, a particularly high tide might even flood him out. No. He had to move. He travelled further north and inland, not sure what he was looking for but relying on instinct that he would find the right place. With each day the weather worsened. Winds picked up, rain blew in with them, fierce and stinging. Amongst the raindrops flecks of frozen water, of hail, of snow, began to show themselves. To find shelter was becoming more and more urgent.

He should have stuck to where he knew; familiar places with soft, welcoming soil where he could pitch his tent, secure it for the winter, knowing that once pitched it would hold firm. The valley. Their winter stopping-place. But he didn't even know where he was now. He was lost and anxious, scanning the harsh treeless landscape, when in the distance something caught his eye. He kept his sight trained on it, patted Seil's neck, whispered in her ear. 'What do you think now?' As he drew closer the valley narrowed and he finally arrived at a lonely collection of ruins.

Ancient stones stood in the shape of old dwellings; walls, spaces where doors had once been secured. There were perhaps six or seven ruins standing well enough to show themselves as dwelling places. More scatterings of stone – perhaps houses, perhaps something else – lay sinking into the grass, moss, and tangled wildness. Unidentifiable but there nonetheless.

He sat tall, breathing in this new land, feeling safer now. The air was so pure and clear that distance was hard to judge, but as far as he could tell he was alone. No. This wasn't a place of people any more.

He slid off Seil with Rona under one arm. 'Off you go lass,' he said, as he put her down on the rough grass. She stood still, looking up at him, unsure. 'Go on! Away and explore!'

She sniffed the ground, not venturing further than a few feet from her master's feet until her nose picked up a scent and she was off, running, yipping as she went.

Tommy laughed, knowing full well what that meant. She would be off hunting for an hour or two, chasing rabbits, or grouse, or whatever it was that she was on the trail of, and she would come back with something for the pot. He unloaded the horses and set them free with a gentle slap. They would stay close.

One of the old dwellings stood almost to its full height. Ancient stone smoothed and beaten by time, encrusted with lichen and tough grasses. The walls were double rows of stone, the windows tiny, the door low and tight. Centuries ago this place had offered shelter. It would do so for him now. Even some of the turf roof was intact, rotting wood uncovered in places like the skeleton of some wild beast.

The remains of a barn stood attached to the little house. It was an easier space to create a shelter in until he had made safe the house itself, if indeed that was what he would do. For now he wasn't sure. The urgency was to create a shelter before darkness fell and the growing storm smothered him. He spent what was left of the day building up the fallen spaces, securing loose stones. He unravelled his canvas and stretched it over the walls of the barn, securing it with heavy stones. Close to a tent, but not quite. Close to familiar.

He whistled for Rona and stared out across the darkening valley, straining for a sight of the flash of white as her little body came bounding back. Sure enough, within minutes, there it was. There she was. She was very pleased with herself, panting heavily, her tongue lolling, looking far too big for her mouth. Her jowls were bloodstained, as were her paws.

'You'll not be needing any dinner then,' he said with a soft laugh, rubbing at her head. 'Now you should have brought some of that back for me!'

She knew that she had broken the rules of her training – catch, kill, return, leave – but this was too much, too exciting, too new. He smiled at her. 'Nae bother, lass. Nae bother.'

He didn't know if it was ghosts, or if it was just knowing that this had once been a village; a place of life and families now gone, but there was a feeling. An air about the place that was unsettling. Something wicked had happened here. He dismissed the thought. Sometimes it didn't do to think too deeply. This would be his safe place for now.

The storm unleashed itself in full as night fell. Wind whipped through the buildings with a howl. Rain clattered against the canvas, falling like a stream into the ditch he had cleared for that purpose. The sound was comforting. Nature breathing all around him. It lulled him to sleep soon enough. The following day he worked on the roof, cutting turf as best he could and laying it on the wooden beams, praying that it would hold. It was peculiar, building a house like this, a home like the scaldies had, a place of stone that had stood for centuries, and might well stand for centuries more.

The day after he explored further afield, looking for trees, for food, for water, for danger. Within a week he was confident of their survival. The building would protect them from the worst that winter would throw their way. The burn he had found ran fresh and clear. The nearby lochan was heavy with fish. Rona was happy hunting every day. The horses would need catered for though and he cut and stored as much grass as he could to help feed them through the snows.

Still there was that feeling. That distant sadness.

Chapter 28

Dougie's winters were quieter times. There was little to do until the return of spring and nesting birds, calving deer, awakening burrowers, and stretching undergrowth. He walked the river most days, watching the leap of the spawning salmon. Prime targets for poachers even though the season didn't start until mid-January. It wasn't so much the theft, the fishing without a license. They were expensive and out of the reach of most of the locals. No. It was the lack of respect. Without laws being adhered to the fish would suffer in the long term. The odd local catching a fish for himself would warrant nothing more than a quiet word, a telling off, perhaps even the turn of a blind eye. But out of season, with no regard for the well-being of the river, the future, well, that was a different matter.

And it wasn't just the salmon. It was everything. A lack of respect for nature and her success, her survival, was what made his blood boil. Man trampling on things so delicate, so precarious, so essential. Didn't they even care? He knew the answer. Had been given it often enough. No. Plain and simple. No. For the life of him he couldn't understand it. Wouldn't tolerate it.

Then there was the stripping of the land for the "sport" of the wealthy. Scotland's barren land, made so by careless thoughtless humans and their lust for money, for glory. For the sheep, for the deer, for the grouse. Centuries now of theft, of lost ancient forest, of disappearing wildlife. He imagined a life in the days when lynx and wolf roamed these woods. That would be something. To see that. To protect that.

He was thankful that he had this job. Durnoch was an estate well managed. No sport here other than licensed fishing. At least not for now. He was a guardian, not an intruder, not an overlord with ideas different to those of nature. If you listened to her she told you. Trouble was most didn't. That Tinker family that camped across the river every year. They knew. They listened. And it seemed young Charlottte did too. Her and that Tinker boy sitting here, soft and gentle. It was like something from a different time. An innocence about them too.

He didn't really have time for people. Didn't care for them too much, but those two, well, he enjoyed them being around, watching them. He loved this place, these woods, this river, but without them around it was that wee bit colder.

He looked to the sky, leaden and swollen. It was getting dark already. Barely daylight at all in the middle of winter. He hardly used his hut at this time of year. A quick check every now and again was enough. The long walk back up the hill, through the forest and home.

His little cottage, ancient, thick, thick walls, tiny windows. It had been built to keep out the weather and that was what it did. A log fire, his comfy old armchair, a blanket and his dog, and all was well with the world. Storms clattering outside, wind howling, rain lashing, and for a short while, snow. He didn't envy folk with their fancy this and their fancy that and their central heating and gadgets and dependencies. No. He had everything he needed and it was quite fine. Quite a fine life.

The rain had begun to fall in earnest. Master and dog both dripping with it. He clicked the front door open; a stoop to get through it without bumping his head.

'It's just me, Sarah love.'

He sat at the old milking stool by the door, slipped off his wellies, pulled on his slippers.

Gypsy shook himself, spraying water over everything.

Dougie laughed. 'Thanks for that, lad!'

The dog crept off, as if on tiptoes, looking back surreptitiously. He was making for the bedroom. Soft, warm bedding, begging for a roll.

'Don't you even think about it! Bed. Your bed! Now!' He slunk unhappily off. Lay there as Dougie towelled him dry. 'Stay!'

'It's turning pretty nasty out there, Sarah, and that's for sure.' He smiled at the thought, the memory. Even now, after all these years he still kept a quiet word for her. Sarah. Long gone, but here in spirit. Here in this wee house. Here deep inside of him.

Chapter 29

Christmas. Charlotte was tidying up in the kitchen, her dad nursing a Scotch. He had never been much of a drinking man, but the occasional decent whisky was something to be savoured. Christmas, Hogmanay, birthdays, and that was about it.

At last he felt as if a corner truly had been turned. He really had beaten this thing. Sometimes you just know, you can feel it. A body free of illness. A future. Normal. Carefree. He smiled at the thought of it. Of this new lightness in the world. In his world. Of his release from some of the guilt. Him and Charlotte behaving like a normal family, doing normal things, normally. That was it. All he wanted. No big dreams now. Just health.

Charlotte flopped down on the settee. 'Penny for them?'

'Nothing really. Just the future, you know, what to do with it.'

'I think you should do whatever makes you happy.'

'And there it is. The wisdom of my daughter. How old are you exactly?'

*

Boxing day tradition had become a walk along the river bank, irrespective of the weather. Today they were blessed by a sparklingly clear winter's day. Everything still, as if frozen in time. A light dusting of frost making the world sparkle. Kittie joined them, running ahead with his tail proud and tall and trembling with excitement. Father and daughter smiled.

'Hard to believe he's a serial killer!' Charlotte said.

'Too darned cute by half.'

'Death comes wrapped in the most beautiful of guises.'

Her dad laughed. 'And where did you get that one from?'

She exhaled heavily, looked skyward as if something up there held the answer. 'Some book or other. Not sure which.'

He crooked his arm for her to take and squeezed her hand against his body. 'You know how proud I am of you?'

She smiled.

'Always remember that. You made your daddy a very, very proud man and I love you more than anything.'

'Is there something you're not telling me?' That unwelcome twist of concern that had been their bedfellow for so long now shadowed her brow.

He squeezed her arm reassuringly 'No, no. Far from it. It's just important to say these things, don't you think? Let people know how special they are to you.'

'People? You mean there's someone else in your life?'

He laughed. 'No! I was just, well, just making a point.'

'I wouldn't mind, you know. I sometimes wonder if Martha has a thing for you. The way she looks at you. The

130

excuses to call in.'

He smiled at her, shook his head. 'She's just a kind woman being neighbourly. Mind you, I've had my chances. This whole single dad thing is quite the lady-puller.'

'Seriously? You old dog, you!'

He held his hands up. 'May I just say that I never took anyone up on it. Being father to you has been all consuming.' He paused. 'In the very best of ways. Then the illness consumed even more. And now, well, I'm too content with my lot to want to mess it up.'

'Hmm.'

They had turned back, both squinting through the glare of the blindingly bright sun.

'And talk of the devil...' he said quietly.

Martha was waving at them from her window. She hurried out. 'I was just thinking about you,' she called as she crossed her back garden. She twisted her pony tail into a knot, smiled. Her jeans and Aran jumper were covered by a flour spattered apron.

'See?' Charlotte whispered.

Her dad suppressed a laugh, turning it into a smile.

'Martha! How are you this beautiful day?'

'Oh fine, just fine.' She glanced down at herself. 'Excuse the state of me! Doing some baking. Listen, I was wondering if you'll be up for a wee first-foot come Hogmanay?'

'Absolutely! You to us or us to you?'

'I was thinking you to me. It seems I'm always round at your place and you've barely set foot in mine.'

'True! We'll see you at the bells then, coal, black bread

and whisky in hand.'

She grinned. 'Right you are, then. You can pretend to be my handsome dark stranger.'

'Pretend eh?' He winked.

She blushed. 'Pretend as in not a stranger! Your handsomeness is, of course, without question!'

A shared laugh.

'You see?' Charlotte whispered as they walked away.

He nudged her, chuckled softly.

Chapter 30

There had been no interlopers, at least none that Tommy had seen, and he felt confident that he would have been aware of anyone. Of anything. Certainly Rona would have alerted him. It was a relief to know that he now had a place of his own in which to winter. A place of seclusion and safety which was his and his alone. No memories. No strangers.

Winter had crawled back, the days stretching themselves open like the arousal of a hibernating animal, and as they did, so his waking hours shifted alongside. His soul was crying out for something else. He was rising with the sun and settling down with it; a seamless part of nature; of the world around him. He was beginning to feel more like himself again. Less afraid. Less alone. He knew it was time to be moving on. That was what they did; travelled with the seasons, with work. He was growing restless having been stationary for so many months. His blood was calling for movement, for fresh sights and a different air.

He had trepidations; of course he did. Everything had changed and he didn't rightly know what to do, where to go. If he found his way back to the old stopping-places – the farms where his family had always been welcomed, the work that his people had done – others would ask why he was on his own, where his family had gone. He knew that he wouldn't be able to lie. It wasn't simply that he had been taught not to, it was also that mentally he found it impossible. If you get asked a question you answer it as best you can. That was what he did. And he really didn't want that. He didn't want to revisit it. He didn't want to share his story. He didn't know if he had done something wrong. Something very wrong. It didn't feel like it. What he had done had felt right and good and true, but he knew that his ways could be misunderstood. He knew that sometimes they brought a whole heap of trouble and he had no one left to protect him from it. To keep him safe and right.

Even the other travellers were different from them with their caravans and trailers and houses. Sure, they were his people, but they weren't like him. Not really. They didn't understand him. No one really understood him apart from his family, his ma. He felt tears fall unbidden down his cheeks at the thought of her. All of the memories of their quiet times trotting across the land with whispers of shared thoughts. Tales of her parents, her grandparents, and those before.

*

"Now, as soon as the good Highland folk left their homes the wicked laird's men with their axes and their crowbars and their hammers, well, they followed behind them, destroying each house they came to. They pulled the timbers down, burned the thatch. Rafters and walls

134

collapsed with such a terrible noise that it could be heard all the way along the valley and the one beyond. Clouds of dust and smoke crawled over the hills. It had all gone.

"Our Mary stood high on that hill, watching in horror, a picture of her sweetheart, her Jack, fixed in her mind. She just stood and stared like there was nothing else that she could do. Like she might even forget how to breathe. A love like that. Well. It can break you in pieces, so it can.

"Her da came to fetch her. It was time to be moving on. There was nothing to keep the family here now. The danger wasn't the same for them. They had no land to lose; no house to be thrown out of. It was a different beast that stalked them. Men like that, who'd lost all of what made a human being something decent, well, with that power and that evil, no one could be sure they were safe. Not any more.

"So they packed up and rode off with their horses and their few possessions. Mary's eyes couldn't be drawn from what they were leaving behind. She watched as the laird's men made their way up the hills, outwards, destroying more. She wished that it had just been a nightmare. Nothing real in this. A nightmare. But, oh it was real. And it hurt something awful.

"When night-time came and darkness fell all around they could see the lick of flames taking everything. Down in the glen, up in the hills. Flames everywhere. They travelled on and as they did so they came upon poor souls traipsing across the land with nothing but the look of loss on their faces. Some tagged along, nothing said, just a knowing that they were welcome. Their lives too became travelling lives. And they were grateful for it. Some

families even mixed. Love between different folk. Because you can't chose that, Tommy son. You can't chose who's been given to you.

"Now, life for the Tinkers had also changed with the Clearances. The villages where they had sold their wares – their tin pots and baskets and brushes – had gone. The crofts where they had worked building up dry stone walls, doing repairs, they had gone too. Now it was just sheep. And the land was dirty. It was a place of cruelty and sadness and that sadness had crept into the earth and stayed there. It wasn't a place for people who could feel such things. Not any more."

*

Her stories held him close, her song that carried on the breeze. It would always be there. That song. He took a deep breath. It would always be there.

Yes, he would leave this place. He would head back to the land of the summer-camp. He would see her again. The other person he shared himself with. The girl. Charlotte. He could feel her skin, smell her hair, see her smile. He would go back for her.

'Come on, Rona!' he called, as he stripped off and ran into the icy cold waters of the lochan. He dived under and swam along the lochan-bed, picking up tiny pebbles. When he resurfaced he laughed at Rona who stood at the water's edge barking and crouching, barking and crouching, calling for his return. She was loathe to get more than her wee paws wet.

'Hush now, wee one.'

He threw the pebbles high up into the air behind him, listening to the sprinkle of soft sound as they landed on the water and twisted their way down to the bed again, watching the ripples spread and dissipate until all was still once more.

'Okay lass. Let's go then.'

Her tail beat its pleasure as they scampered back to the winter-house together.

There was barely anything to pack away, to clear, as he had arrived with so little and had been keeping the place as pristine as was possible. He stripped off the canvas and rolled it up so that it would fit easily across Coll's back. He ran his fingers over the wall of the cottage as he left.

'Rona, up you come, lass.' He patted his thigh and Rona leapt up, settling herself between his legs, eyes alert, tail twitching in excitement.

'Thank you,' he whispered up into the sky as they trotted off. 'Till next year then.'

The sun was glinting off the lochan, turning it into shimmering turquoise and silver, as they walked on around its edges that they now knew so well. This place had become a new friend and that was a good thing. They twisted up through the wild grasses and heather that was beginning to sprout with fresh life.

At the end of the valley he paused, turned around, and took one last look at the sky, the water, the swooping birds, before clicking his tongue, gently squeezing his knees around Seil's body and moving on. This was a strange moving on. His mind was filling with the trepidation of the unknown. But there was Charlotte. He could do this for her. The thought of her surprise at seeing him. It would be very special.

Chapter 31

Spring. New foliage rustled against her bedroom window. She usually slept through this. Nature sounds. Rustles and creaks. But something had woken her. She sat up. A strange feeling about her. An uncommon fear. It wasn't the leaves. It was something else. A crash. Breaking glass. A shout.

She froze. Heart pounding, breath caught, she tiptoed soundlessly across the welcome pile of the carpet. Pulled her door open. The night splintered by sounds of fighting. The house was in darkness, but she could make out two figures. Her dad and one other.

Panic. Confusion. The phone in her dad's room. 999. Whispers. 'Help. Help us.'

'I can't hear you, love. What's the emergency?'

'Briar Cottage. A man attacking my dad.' She left the call open, hoping she had done enough. They could trace the call. Find them. They would respond. Help would be here. But she couldn't wait. Back out to the stairs. She stretched her arm to the wall, fumbled for the light-switch. Flicked it on.

'Charlotte! No!'

There was a moment of peculiar stillness. Both men disorientated. Then the tussle continued. The intruder was on her dad. Both of them on the floor. A sound. Soft. Thick. Sickening. A grunt, almost silent but so violent that everything changed. The world stopped.

The intruder jumped back up. Looked from the body at his feet to the ashen-faced girl. Charlotte stared. Not at him but at her dad lying in an expanding pool of blood. She wanted to run down but couldn't move. It was like a film. It was all happening to someone else. Someone fictional.

The intruder disappeared out of the back door.

Now she ran down the stairs. Fell on her dad. Felt the life creep out of him.

Sirens. Flashing lights.

*

Her world sealed up. She was something else. Somewhere else. They were taking her away. No choice. A blanket wrapped around her shoulders. One of those smiles that is only given to the bereaved. A smile that shouldn't be there at all because the situation could never warrant such a thing.

Martha stood on her doorstep. Her hand on her mouth. 'Did you see anything ma'am?'

'It was so dark. I'm not sure...I.' She closed her eyes, shook her head, tears fell.

'I know this is hard, ma'am, but anything at all might help us catch whoever did this.'

She swiped at her face. Sniffed. Tried to pull herself together. 'A figure. No, two figures. Men, I think. Running off towards the river.' She pointed downhill.

'Right. Anything about them? Size? Age? Anything at all?'

'I...I really can't...I don't know.' She broke down, was helped back inside. A blanket draped across her shoulders.

'If you remember anything else, anything at all, you give us a call now.'

'Yes. Yes, of course.'

Charlotte was taken to the station. Her dad's blood washed off her. Clothes put on her. Social workers came. A doctor.

'I'm Susan. Susan Jamieson. What's your name, love? Can you tell me that?'

No response. Not a flicker.

'Has she spoken at all?'

A shake of the head. 'Nothing. Not a word. Not a sound. The girl hasn't even cried.'

'Poor soul.'

Phone calls, hurried conversations. Nods of heads.

'Okay then. Good.'

Martha had offered to look after her, but they had said no. It was too close. Too traumatic. It wouldn't be good for her. She was placed with foster parents until after the funeral. Still not a word. Still no tears. Not even as the coffin was lowered.

*

They traced her mother. She didn't understand how. Understand why. Her mother was a stranger. Something unknown and never talked of, thought of. She was nothing.

'Your mother sounds lovely and she's really looking forward to seeing you again.'

140

Still nothing. No shadow of recognition.

'Can you just let us know that you understand?'

They didn't know if she wouldn't or couldn't, but nothing was forthcoming.

*

They shuffled her into a car as if a prisoner under arrest. Hand on head. Not in actuality, but that was what it felt like. That was what was happening in her head. Miles ticked away in a hazy blur. Tick, tick, tick, further away. Tick, tick, tick. She felt hollow and alone like a cast off husk. The shell of something that once held life but now lay dying in the mulch of nothingness.

And suddenly it was all too fast, the whir of a life she used to live. A person she used to be. Trees massed as one. A green cloak slipping off the hillside. She stared at the distance. It was just that now. Distance.

The woman driving her barely stopped talking. Chitter chatter this. Chitter chatter that. Incessant nonsense. Until eventually she realised the futility of it and gave up.

Charlotte's stomach lurched as they finally drove into London. The vast inevitability of the place stood cold and treacherous. She had settled into such a dark world and it felt interminable.

The noise of the place. A thick swell of unfamiliarity. Shouts, screeches of horns, clogged angry traffic that seemed to echo between the mass of buildings; no escape, nowhere for it to go. No air to breathe. Then there was the immensity of the place. Buildings that stretched to the sky. People so busy, so intense. A lump snatched at her throat. A deeper darkness that she couldn't shift.

They pulled up alongside a canal. People busying

themselves. Ducks fussing about. A string of houseboats moored along the wharf. The woman scanned the names painted on the side of the boats. Dancing Maiden, Moonlight, NotAHouse, Gypsy Traveller. Charlotte slowed, stopped, stared.

'All right there, love?' They walked on by, stopping at a traditional narrow boat. Midnight blue with a trail of flowers and leaves painted brightly along its sides, up and over its door. On the roof rows of pot-plants fought for space. Flowers, vegetables and some things unidentifiable.

'It's charming, isn't it?' the woman said with a sickly false smile.

A man dressed in overalls, dreadlocks dangling from his head, stood up, stretched, nodded towards them. 'Well fuck me, you're the double of your mum and no mistaking!' He jumped from the boat, wiped his hands on an oil cloth before holding one out. 'Bobby, or you can call me Dad, if that suits.'

He shrugged.

She glared.

'Right, well, that's that then.' He scratched his head. 'Bit new to this. Sorry.' He grinned at her. 'Kids, well, not my scene really, but it'll be cool. We'll be cool. Your mum's just at the shops. Won't be long. Come in?' He jumped back onto the boat and disappeared through the door.

He left a smell trailing in his wake. Maybe petrol, maybe alcohol, whatever, it made her wince.

The woman smiled, ushered Charlotte on board. 'It'll be fine, you'll see.'

It won't. It won't be FINE. How could you even think it

will be FINE?

Chapter 32

Tommy kept close to the tracks that he knew but away from places where others might be. It was easy enough to begin with. Wild places where few ventured. He took his time, walking more often than riding. As night fell he slept on the ground, the canvas over him like a blanket. There was no need to form a tent, and as the earth warmed and the buds opened and birdsong swelled the air it was preferable anyway.

The mountains had drifted into hills, the terrain easier to cover. Swirling through the valley the wind picked up, carrying with it the scent of rain on its shoulders. Not of drizzle or something light and manageable. The animals were alert first to the onset of possible danger, their noses raised and ears pricked. A slight shrink of their bodies. Tommy stopped. Breathed in the surroundings. A storm was definitely close. Nothing gentle or easy. Not something to stand up in; to be a part of. It felt like this would need shelter from. Something more than a canvas. Something more than what he had.

He leapt up on Seil, clicked, and galloped over the crest of the hill. Swell upon swell of hill. Thick forest intermittently climbed their sides. Manufactured. He rode between row upon row of pines. Some mature, others young, barely trees at all. Muddy tracks in between. He paused under a swathe of mature spruce, looked up through the branches and needles. Would that do? Be shelter enough? No. No, he needed more. They needed more. In the distance a small building showed itself in a barely perceptible clearing of the trees. A hut of some kind.

By the time they drew close to the shack the rain had started in earnest. A fierce wind brought with it the feel of winter, not spring. He was desperately hoping that this would be both vacant and open. They circled the building, first from a distance, then close up. It was a peculiar looking place. Not like a scaldie house at all. Wood for the walls and corrugated iron for the roof, covered with branches of pine and bracken, as if someone were trying to hide its presence.

There was no sign of life. No light in the now swallowing darkness, a broken window – glass spreading across the ground, hidden amongst weeds and moss. An old breakage? This must be empty.

He jumped down and tentatively pushed the door. It squeaked, swung open. The horses stood back. Not keen on going in. He pulled them on with a click and a tug.

'No choice. Come on.'

Rona stayed back, hackles raised, a warning growl. 'Come on, wee one.' Reluctantly she followed, sticking by her master's heels, still growling.

In here the dark was so total that there was nothing to see. The wind shrieked. The rain now a torrent. Tommy could hear no sound through it or above it. A totality of storm. Of the wildness of nature. It felt like she was angry. He pulled the door tight behind them. Something scuttled nearby.

'Tch! Who the devil's there?' a hoarse voice called from somewhere in the dark. The words barely audible in the maelstrom of the storm. The strike of a match. The flicker of a flame held out at arm's length. 'Well?'

'It's just m-me. Me and and m-my–'

'Christ, can ye no talk any louder? Cannae hear a thing, son. Out with it now. D'ye have a name on ye?'

'Tommy. N-name's Tommy.'

'Away an come closer now so as I can hear you right, an maybe get a proper look at you. Slowly but. Slow an easy. Aye?'

The figure placed a match to a candle, and another, to expose an old man, wild and dishevelled, long white hair with a beard to match. A frown across his brow. Skin the colour of the bark of the trees. A piece of wood clenched in one hand, held high, ready to strike.

'Aye, an I'll use it too. You mark my words. I've no lived this long without being able to battle. Aye.' He drew the stick back. Aimed. Ready. He stared beyond Tommy. 'Am I seeing this right? Horses? You've come in here wi horses. An a wee dug? Jings son. Who the devil are you? Speak up now so as I can hear you.'

Rona inched forward, her hackles softening, a low growl, barely a growl at all, a twitch of her tail. Sniffing.

'On you come wee one,' the old man called, patting his thigh.

Rona looked back to Tommy before taking full stock of

this stranger. Apparently he met with her approval as she dropped her hackles and padded close enough for a stroke.

'Well, I like yer wee dug, right enough.'

'She's R-Rona.'

'Whit? You'll need to come right close. Cannae hear a word son.'

Tommy had little choice. It was either get uncomfortably close to a stranger or leave, and he wasn't sure of their survival out there. The wind tearing at the roof. Threatening to peel it away any moment now.

The old man gestured to the floor beside him, patted it.

Tommy took a deep breath and joined him.

'Sandy. The name. Sandy.'

'Tommy.'

'Aye, you said.'

The old man squinted, peered deep into Tommy's face. So deep it made a panic rise. A fear. Too close. Then, a recognition. The old squeeze box by his side. Sandy!

'I've met you afore, aye?' Sandy said.

'Aye. Aye you have. S-sat around the fire. Music. Stories. Aye.' *Please don't ask me. Please don't ask.*

'Aye, right enough. Never forget a face, me.'

As the storm raged outside and night fell, Sandy told story after story of his life on the road. The people he had met. 'You'll ken them, aye?' The places he had been to. 'Och, you must have been there an aw.' Thankfully, it seemed that no answer was necessary. He played some tunes, sang some songs. There was barely a tune left in his gravely old voice but that didn't matter. The meaning was there, and Tommy could imagine well enough what the voice would have been like when it held. When it was younger.

Tommy just sat and listened, hummed along to a tune, laughed at some silly adventure. Gasped at near misses. It was like being home. Like belonging. Stories were like that. They held you. Wrapped you up in them. Took you with them. Kept you alive.

When he awoke in the morning all was quiet. The storm had passed on by. The forest around sighing. Dappled sunlight playing with the window, flickering against the wall, dancing on the floor. But he was alone. No old man. No candles. Nothing but him and his animals. He felt a peculiar sadness. Emptiness.

Chapter 33

They were sitting awkwardly on the deck, Bobby not knowing what to say. Charlotte wanting it to stay that way.

Bobby jumped up, waved. 'Here she is now. Your mum. Jasmine.'

Charlotte didn't want to look, stared down at the murky water, petrol glimmering on its surface. Her glance followed the trail of a cigarette butt.

Her mother squealed. 'Charlie, baby!' She dropped her bags at her feet and stood there, grinning, her arms outstretched, as if they knew each other. Cared about each other.

Charlotte dragged her eyes away from the water. There was no doubt that this was her mother. The face, the gait, everything. The soft curl of her black hair fell down to her waist, just like Charlotte's.

Bobby tugged at Jasmine's sleeve, nodded towards the back of the boat. Whispered. 'She doesn't speak. Hasn't said a word.'

'Yeah. I told you, didn't I? Selective muteness, they said, just since the um accident, you know. She just can't find her words any more, poor baby.'

'Yeah, yeah, right. So you did. Sorry. Forgot. I thought she'd be, well, better by now. I wish I knew what I was doing here. Kids are enough of a challenge, never on my radar, you know? But this. Wow! Clueless doesn't even cover it!'

'Time. She just needs time.'

'But how much? I mean, this is difficult, right? Even for child-loving, two-point-four kids people, with the house and the job and all of that shit, this would be difficult.'

She narrowed her eyes, stared. 'You're with me, though? We talked about this.'

He hadn't really listened. Hadn't really thought it through. Processed it. Back then it had just been a conversation. No picture to it. No reality. Right now it frightened him. What they'd taken on. What he'd taken on. Someone else's kid who was so messed up that she couldn't even speak. Jesus! And he was meant to deal with it. Change his life. Everything about it. Yeah, he knew he was being incredibly selfish, but it was his life. And this? This was so much not what he wanted. What he could cope with. It was Jasmine. Just her and him pottering about, taking things real slow. Real easy. Hell, just enjoying life. Living it.

'Bobby?'

'Sorry. Lost in thought.' He shrugged, looked away.

'Come on. Don't be like that. We'll get through this. You and me, like always.'

'Exactly. You and me. And now?'

'Come here.' She held her arms open.

He smiled, accepted, squeezed her tight.

150

'Charlie baby, I know it's all shit and you're hurting, but life goes on. You just have to grab it, and live it and make it beautiful. No one else can do that for you, baby. Just you.'

Bobby put his arms around his partner. Squeezed her to him. 'God, I love this woman! So wise, man. So wise.'

Charlotte just wanted this to be over. This day, this arrangement. All of this. She held on until it was late enough to feign the need to go to bed. As she walked past the kitchen counter she slipped a pair of scissors into her hand.

She stood in front of the mirror-tile that had been stuck at an odd angle to the wall of her bedroom, hacking away at her hair. Shorter. Shorter still. She stared at her reflection. A different person. A stranger. As she lay in her bed she could hear them. Muffled grunts and sighs. The gentle creak of the boat. She pulled the pillow over her head, smothered the sounds, the world, out. Finally sleep.

*

Deep in a dream Charlotte was sitting on a riverbank, her arms stretched out behind her, her hands flat out on the fresh new grass, her head flopped back so that she faced the sky. The heaviness of the river filled the air with its song, drowning out everything else. She could feel him, Tommy, sit behind her, back to back, fingers locked, heads touching.

'Tommy,' she whispered.

'Charlotte,' he whispered back.

They sat, not moving, not speaking, just touching.

He led her deep into the forest and beyond. He held her

151

hand as they crossed a fast-flowing burn by stepping on large rocks that seemed to have been left there for that very purpose. She was lost, with no idea of where they were; of how to get home, but she felt safe. The trust that bound them felt unbreakable. Invincible.

'You need to be very, very quiet now,' he whispered. 'Not even the tiniest wee sound, okay?'

'Okay,' she replied, wondering what this was all about, but so excited; the feeling being picked up from him. This was going to be something beyond special. She just knew it would be. There were birds chattering away in the trees. Nothing unusual. They sat down silently against the moss encrusted trunk of an ancient oak and waited. Nothing.

She turned to face him, her brow furrowed in question. He smiled, put his index finger to his lips. She shrugged and returned her gaze to the trees, hearing the gentle flutter of leaves amongst the birdsong. Just when she thought she couldn't hold her silence any longer the sounds began to swell and suddenly they were sitting in the midst of a great cacophony. From everywhere the most beautiful birdsong rang out. It sounded as if there were thousand upon thousand of them. She was dumbfounded. He squeezed her hand and although she couldn't see, she could feel him smile.

They sat and listened, their bodies becoming stiff with their inability to move, to break the spell, until eventually the singing slipped back into silence.

'That was the most beautiful experience I have ever had!' she said with a breathy whisper. 'Thank you.'

'It is right special, isn't it? You must never tell or it will be lost. It shouldn't happen. Not here. Not like this. But it does. Every year they gather and they sing like this, but only if there's silence. If you make a noise, or you move, they will stop. Never, ever tell.'

'I won't. I promise.'

*

Morning. Light flickering through the porthole. As she woke to it, just for a moment, she forgot where she was. What had happened. She closed her eyes as her new reality began to creep back in. The pain of it all returned, washed over her. No matter how hard she tried to fight with it, push it away again, it smothered her like an awful weight bearing down on her chest. She called on the dream to linger, to come back to her, but it stretched and faded. Tiny snippets of it stayed and she kept them tight, locked away in that special place in her brain. Fractured pieces that wouldn't join. Wouldn't connect. But they were there. This was a memory. This had been real. She was sure of it.

*

'Well, fuck me, that's quite a change!'

'Language, Bobby!' Jasmine scowled at Bobby, turned and smiled at Charlotte. 'Sorry Charlie.'

Charlotte didn't respond. Didn't look their way.

Jasmine stared. 'What have you?...' She stepped towards her. 'Let me sort it for you.'

Fuck off! In her head it spoke the anger she felt. Her contempt at the world that had done this to her. She hated it. Hated them. Hated everything.

Chapter 34

Tommy made his camp where they had always stayed. Their own special stopping-place. He set it up in the same way as they had always done. Everything just so. Just right. He would wake to the same view. The valley, the woods, and beyond, the hill that led to the big house. Only it would be different. He was earlier than usual. He didn't know by how much. He didn't know what month it was, but he could see that the leaves were softer, paler. It felt like early summer and different colours hung in the trees, different scents blew in the breeze. He couldn't see the river for the foliage that hugged it, but he could hear it. It prickled his skin and set his senses alight.

It was late evening. Too late to visit the river. She wouldn't be there now anyway. Perhaps she wouldn't be there for a long time yet, until high summer, like usual. It would be so very hard to wait, to be patient, as both his body and mind were screeching for her. The only person left who understood, who could calm him with her smile like a gentle breeze on a summer's day. He turned his attention to the animals. To food. To making everything right. As it should be. He fed the horses before making a fire and cooking up some fish and oats for himself and Rona.

'There you go, lass,' he said, placing the food in her dish on the ground. He sat on the grass beside her and ate his dinner, watching the flicker of the flames, the smoke disappearing into the sky. It was at moments like this that he hurt the most. This was when his family visited him in memories and longing. And it all felt so real, as if he could touch them, chat with them, laugh with them. Listen to stories. Part of him wanted to cast these moments aside, but the rest of him wanted desperately to cling on to the memories he had. To build them and polish them and make them last forever.

He looked up at the sky, heavy with cloud, and he guessed rain would soon be with him, perhaps even a bit of a storm, as the wind was picking up and whistling its way through the trees. The horses whinnied and stamped, giving him their warning. He led them to a place of shelter in the trees.

'Now you stay there. That's it now.'

Next he secured the base of the tent with heavy boulders and dug a ditch for the rainfall. There was nothing to do now but wait. Settle himself and Rona in the tent and wait.

Despite his pain there was something beautiful about the clatter of rain on canvas; the screech of wind as it broke its way around the tent. Rona had now crept under his legs, fearful of the wildness outside. He smiled at her, called her up to settle on his lap, her head tucked under his arm. She was soon asleep. He couldn't do likewise. There was no point in even trying. Such a wash of contrary emotions churned through him. He brought Charlotte to the fore. Happiness and comfort. His excitement – that wonderful anticipation of seeing her again – was overpowering in the very best of ways. He sat and listened as the storm reached its climax and then began to slow. The wind became a breeze, the rain a soft drizzle.

Daylight crept in and he flipped open the door of the tent. The earth was sweet with the scent of summer rain. He breathed it in and held it deep in his lungs. Birdsong drifted from the woods. A celebration of the new day. He glanced at the sky, still heavy with cloud, disappointed that the signs were of a dull and damp day ahead.

His first sighting of her this year should be in sunlight, beams dancing on her hair, lighting up her face. The river sparkling just for them. Perhaps it would clear. The twisting of seasons wasn't unusual at this time of year. Then he reminded himself that it was too early. He was worrying for nothing. She wouldn't even be here.

He crawled out onto the mulchy, wet grass, Rona stretching beside him before running off in search of a smell that had caught her attention. He wiped down the horses before jumping up and taking them for a gallop. Rona realised soon enough that she was missing out on some excitement and came bounding after them barking her delight.

His intention had been to stay away from their place until it was the right time to meet her, but somehow he had ended up there anyway. The weight of the rain gathered on leaf and branch had left the trees drooping down to the water, switching in the swirl of it. He led the horses in for a drink and a walk through the water. It was fast-flowing, the current strong, the pull at their legs heavy, but they were sturdy beasts, confident and foot-sure.

Tales of the great horse fair filled his mind. Appleby. His father and brothers had gone and come back with stories of hundreds of Travellers – folk from all over, Tinkers and Gypsies, horse traders and dealers. They told of riding their horses through the river. Of races and deals, of nights of drinking and parading and showing off. Of fights and brawls that would end with a hand-shake more often than not. A dispute solved, an old rivalry beaten away with fists.

This was where his family would sell on their foals. Where they would be more like the others for a while. Tommy thought he would like to see it, but from a distance. His ma said, *"Not yet son. Not yet."* She was right. All of those people. All of that noise. It would be too much.

He glanced across at the bank on the other side, at the wee curl of beach. Its pull was strong but he wouldn't go. Not now. This wasn't the time. Instead he turned back, much to Rona's delight, and they trotted home to the camp.

After a day spent foraging through the woods, gathering early fruit, wild garlic, and sorrel, the light in the sky finally told him the time of day was right and the river was calling out to him. There was always that possibility, wasn't there? Maybe he had misread the time of year. Maybe she had come back early. Of course he knew it was beyond far-fetched. Nature was his calendar and he never misread it. And as for Charlotte, she had

157

been as constant as nature.

As if on cue a small patch of blue broke up the grey, a shaft of sunlight splintered the gloom. It brought a smile. Deciding to leave the horses, he and Rona set off to the river again. There was a strength to the sun as it lifted the dampness and warmed the air.

He stripped down to his underpants and slipped into the water. It was icy cold; the tips of the mountains at its source still held snow. The pull was too strong for Rona so he scooped her up and wrapped her around his neck.

'Now you keep your wee claws to yourself.'

Carrying his clothes aloft he waded across to the other side. Despite having had all day to prepare, to anticipate, he had forgotten to bring his pearl-fishing can. He cursed himself. That one he had been watching for so long, waiting for, might have been ready for cultivation this year. What he was going to do with it – how he was going to twist it in threads of the gold he had been panning since they had first met – had been growing in his mind. The picture so strong that it felt real.

'Tomorrow, eh lass? Tomorrow'll do just fine.'

He scooped Rona off his shoulder and she ran up and down the bank as if she had been held captive for days. She stopped and scratched at the ground, digging away.

'Is that wee earth-dwellers you've got the scent of? Come away now. Leave them be.'

She stopped and looked at him then returned to her task.

'Now!'

Her tail dropped and she trotted across to him.

'Good girl.'

He sat down by the riverside, thinking of days long past. The last time he had seen Charlotte. But he couldn't imagine what she might be doing now. Where she was. He knew so little of her life. They had barely mentioned such things. They had talked about where they were, what was around them. The forest and the sky-dwellers, the bracken and earth-creepers, the witchery of the white-chests, how to track the horned-ones, how to follow the trail of the bushy-tails. Where the night-hunters hid. Where the great-sky-dwellers flew. All the names he and his ma had invented for the creatures they watched and loved. It didn't matter that he was grown and knew the real names well enough. Some things were best kept as magical. As a special secret. Some things kept his ma alive. And he was glad to have shared them with Charlotte. She had laughed but in a soft, excited way. In a good way.

He had said he'd take Charlotte up to the loch where the great sky-dwellers nested. He told her of the huge nests they built, of the majestic swoop down to the water, the stretch of lethal talons, the snatch of a twisting salmon, silver and pink and blue. The beauty of it all. It was too far to make it there and back in a day so they would have to wait until she was able to get away for long enough. To stay the night. At least he had been able to take her to the forest of the night-singers. At least they had stolen enough time for that. At least he had that.

Amongst his thoughts, his memories, a darkness hung. Something felt wrong. Very wrong. It clawed at his stomach. He prayed that he was mistaken. That he was somehow misreading this. But deep inside he knew different. It was such a strong feeling. An empty hollow feeling. He stayed until the light began to fall into the trees, before accepting it was time to head on back to the camp. There was an awful fog wrapping around his brain that threatened that the trip would never happen. That was telling him she was gone from his life.

As he rounded the bend of the river, a familiar twist of smoke rose from where the camp was. He smiled thinking family, closeness, familiarity. His chest thumped as he remembered, there was no family. Not any more. There shouldn't be any smoke. Rona barked and ran towards the camp. He followed, terror filling his body, every sinew screaming fear.

The horses had been untied and were bolting off across the grassland. Three men were laughing as the flames leapt higher, as his world was engulfed in them. He screamed. Stood and screamed. Rona froze, frightened by the change in her master. Not knowing what to do.

'Why?' he managed to call out.

'You,' one of the men hissed, pointing at him. 'You stay off this land. You and your type aren't welcome here.' A slow menacing look of distaste travelled from the stranger to Tommy's head, down to his feet and back up again. A sneer. 'Off with you!'

Tommy drew on the strength he had found from a place deep within. 'We...we've stopped here for years. Forever. You c-can't–'

'Not any more you don't.'

Tommy stepped forward, opened his mouth to speak, but was met with the crack of a whip that sliced at his cheek. He fell to the ground, his hands to his burning face, blood spilling between his fingers.

'You saw that boys, didn't you? The dirty Tinker left me with no choice, coming in to attack like that. The man's wild. An absolute nutter!'

'Should be locked up.'

'If I see you here, or anywhere else on my land tomorrow, or any other day of the year, there'll be trouble. And I'll make damned sure they lock you away as well. You got that?'

With that they turned and rode off on their horses.

He watched them, cursing at them. 'Your land. There is no such thing,' he spat.

Chapter 35

Charlotte still didn't speak, just stared blankly through them. The effort that they were making, the annoying false cheerfulness, fake smiles, trying to be like some long lost friends. Trying to be cool. It was just awful.

'Look Charlie, here's the deal. You know this is hard for everyone, right? But, well, if you could just try. Just a little bit. It would make life a whole lot easier for all of us. You know?' Jasmine said, her tone strained.

She and Bobby were sitting there on the deck, cross-legged, holding hands.

Bobby leaned forward. Rested his chin on his clasped hands. 'Yeah, you know...'

No. No, I don't know.

The next time they came back from the shops they had a bag of clothes for her. Flowing things, pretty things, skirts and blouses, velvets and silks rummaged from second-hand shops, market stalls. It felt like they were trying to turn her into someone else – a younger version of Jasmine – cast aside all that she was.

'There now, don't you look gorgeous?'

No! I hate them. I hate this. I hate you. I hate

everything.

That evening her old clothes had been surreptitiously dumped in the refuse sack. Charlotte had noticed, waited until it was safe, rescued them; secreted them under her bed.

*

A woman came towards them, walking along the towpath. She waved, smiled.

'Hey! Great to see you. Come away on board!' Bobby called, ushering her his way with a wave of his hand.

Charlotte disappeared into her room. She sat silently on her bed, the sounds, the voices from outside carried on the canal. A strange buzz of unfamiliarity. Conversations slipping into one another. She strained to tune in. Pick up what was relevant to her.

'So how are things going?'

'Fine.' Jasmine smiled.

'Really?'

'Okay, well, so... Clueless. Absolutely clueless. She won't talk, won't interact. I don't know if there's a way in for me.' She smiled sadly up at Bobby. 'For us.'

'There's no way you can force it. The poor child has no grounding. No understanding. She feels completely alone. Abandoned. All you can do is let her know that she's safe. That you're here for her when she's ready to let you in.'

Jasmine sighed theatrically. 'It's so hard.'

'Of course, of course. When did you last see her?'

A laugh that wasn't a laugh. A grimace. A shrinking of her body. 'Not since she was a toddler.'

The woman looked down at the file on her lap. 'Of course, yes. It's all here, but we have to check and double

163

check.' She smiled. 'Tick all of the boxes.'

'I know I can never make it right for her, and she's been through hell, but I need something to give, you know?'

'Time. Nothing else. Just time. She'll come round when she's ready.'

'Should we even be sending her off to school? I mean, with everything?'

'Yes. Definitely! It's important to keep things as normal as possible. Give her something else to focus on. Some semblance of normality. Of stability.'

'Sure. Keep it normal. Keep it real. But how can any of this be normal to her? I worry for her, you know?'

Oh, like you worried for me for all of my life so far? Like you ever even cared! Hypocrite!

The woman checked her watch. Smiled. Closed her file. 'Right then. You've got my number. If you need to talk, give us a call.'

They watched her walk up the towpath.

'That's it?' Jasmine asked.

'I guess so. For the best in my book. Social Services. Yeah right!'

'Maybe we've made this huge mistake. Maybe we should just have let it be. Said no. I mean, such a fucked-up situation.'

'Hey now. You know it'll all work out. Things just do.'

'I guess.'

'And she is your flesh and blood after all.'

'I know, I know, and I want to make it right. I really do. But...'

Charlotte curled herself into a ball, squeezed the pillow

over her head. Too much. Too much. She didn't want to be any more. She could just slip into the canal, breathe in the water, and that would be it. She would be free. Through the porthole the water sat glaring at her, calling to her. Slow and thick. She pictured her body sinking through the murk, settling on the bed before slowly slipping back up. Released. Dead. Nothing.

Chapter 36

Tommy's priority now was his horses. Despite the pain he was in, they had to be found, made safe. He ran in the direction he had seen them bolting to, Rona alongside him. He prayed that they would have stayed close. Known that he would come and find them. The darkness would cover the land completely very soon. The sky was thick with cloud, no stars, no moon to help guide their way.

He stopped and listened, hoping for a familiar snuffle, or whinny. His ears brought him the rustle of leaves, the flap of wing. Velvet like the night-callers. No hoof, nothing of horse. His head was buzzing, both from pain and distress, making thought even more difficult. He lowered himself to the ground, resting on his haunches, and tried to think logically. What would the horses do? That would depend on how scared they were; what had been done to them to cause them to bolt like that.

He decided that the best thing to do was to return to the camp. They knew it well and would find it again easier than he would find them stumbling about in the dark. And if they were to return and come across nothing but charred remains and the blanket of anger that had been lain across the ground they might well carry on. Leave completely, never to return.

His shoulders slouched as he headed back, feeling empty, useless, a failure. He was nothing now. Nothing. As if sensing his state Rona jumped up at him and barked. 'Aye, I've got you right enough, wee one. I've got you.'

He sat bolt upright throughout the night, tuned in to all of the sounds that crept over the land when most were asleep. Dawn broke. Still nothing. With the weak light of the early morning he began to pick through what was left amongst the charred ruins and ash. The tent was gone bar the odd tatter of damp canvas that had managed to fight off the flames and cling on. He kicked at the ash, swinging his foot from side to side, uncovering what was left beneath. His plate, the pot, the animals' bowls, those things that were indestructible had clung on, blackened but still there, but clothing, bedding, everything soft had gone.

At least he had his money-belt on him, like always. Nothing that had burned couldn't be replaced. It would mean venturing into a town, into shops, which he was loathe to do, but there was little choice now. He would have to confront the world.

He blew out a heavy breath as he watched the mist rise from the grass with the swelling warmth of the sun. There! A shadow. In the clearing mist, a shadow. Indistinct. Blurry. He rubbed his eyes. Honed in on the shape. Was this his imagination? No. It was real. As real as he was breathing. There standing at a safe distance was Seil. She was alone, but she had returned. At least she had returned.

167

Tommy fought the urge to run to her. He walked, slowly, so as not to spook her, his face tear-stained, trying so hard to keep himself calm. Seil tossed her head, whinnied and trotted towards him, her tail swishing to and fro. She lowered her head for a stroke, a nuzzle. It was the very best of feelings. The return of something so deeply loved.

'Bonnie lass,' he whispered against his horse's neck. 'My brave bonnie lass.'

He hugged her, stroked her. 'Come away now.' He clicked his tongue and Seil followed, tentatively, looking around, ears pricked and twitching at the slightest sound. Tommy put his arm across Seil's back. 'You're all right now, lass. I've got you.'

He buried what would decompose, did his best to leave the land unscarred, but this hadn't been him. It wasn't his scar, and there was little he could do about what those men had done. He wanted to hold on for a day or two to see if Coll managed to find his way back, but he was fearful of those men returning; of what they might do to him, to Seil, to Rona.

Chapter 37

Unfamiliar smells drifted on the heavy, sticky air. Unfamiliar sounds thrummed through Charlotte's head. Loud. It was all so very loud. She knew she could never get used to this, feel at home, feel content to be here. To be this. She stood, terrified, at the school gates, her heart thumping, her breath catching, struggling. The vastness of the place. Voices, screams, running feet, laughter.

She stepped back. Stepped away. Her dad would want her to go. To learn. To be the best that she could be. But she couldn't. She could feel tears falling down her face, but it was like they were somebody else's. She was watching, not doing, not being.

'Oh Charlie, come here,' Jasmine said softly, quietly, stretching her arm over her shoulders, pulling her into a hug. 'You're not ready for this. Come on.'

Charlotte didn't fight it, although she wanted to. Didn't break free, although everything inside her said that she should. Every feeling, every thought, every breath. But she couldn't. There was nothing of her left. No strength. No fight. Instead she allowed her mother in. To comfort her. To be there.

They turned away, oblivious to the busy streets, the people, until they reached the canal and its calm quiet. A feeling of relative safety amongst madness. A dog barked. Another replied. Pigeons scattered and swooped, the song of their wings echoing through the air. Almost alarming. Almost. But somehow soothing.

*

'Well, that's a surprise!' Bobby said as they stepped onto the boat, a grin stretched across his oil-smeared face. 'No school today then? Can't say as I blame you. Never did like those places much myself.'

Jasmine shot him a look that said, "Don't!"

'Right. Cup of tea? Always good, right? Right. I'll just go and...yeah.' He scratched his head as he disappeared below deck. The sound of the kettle being filled. The strike of a match. The catch of the gas.

Charlotte took her usual place at the bow of the boat, staring silently out at the water.

'I'll just go and help. Won't be a minute.'

A release as Jasmine disappeared. No need to pay attention to anything now. The buzzing in her head stilling, settling.

'She's a mess,' Jasmine whispered.

'Yeah, well, but we knew that anyway, right?'

'This was worse. She just broke down. I mean completely broke down.'

'I reckon that could be a good thing. Emotions getting out, you know? There's a lot in there that needs breaking out. Getting rid. A lot of bad shit that shouldn't be kept inside.'

'Yeah. I guess so. But what do we do? I can't keep

putting her through that. She was terrified. It was...it was awful.' She sniffed. A tear slipped down her cheek.

'Aw baby. Come here.' He pulled her into him, kissed her hair. 'We'll sort this.'

'I don't know how. This is...this is so beyond me.'

'No it's not. It's new, that's all. You and me can ride through anything, right?'

She smiled. 'Yeah.'

He kissed her, caressed her, their breath getting heavy as they gravitated towards the bed.

'Uh-uh!' She fought against the urge. 'We need to sort this.'

'Ah. Shit. Yeah. Child.'

'Child.'

'She's not really though. I mean she's nearly sixteen, right? And school holidays start soon enough. We could just, you know, take off. Chill out. Slip along the canals in a different world.'

'You know, that would probably be a very good idea, but I don't know what the authorities would say. Child services and all that. I made a promise.'

'Since when did you care about what the authorities thought?'

She laughed. 'Yeah, well, there is that!'

'We could get her a medical note. Get her signed off or whatever. That should be easy enough, right?'

'Okay. Okay. Plan!'

'Cool!'

He filled the teapot, slipped three mugs onto his fingers and they went on deck. There was a light drizzle. A bit of a breeze. He looked skyward. Patches of blue. They should be fine.

Chapter 38

Tommy strapped the little he had left across Seil's back, straddled her, called Rona up onto his lap, and they rode off. As he left the shelter of the trees and headed out across open land he couldn't simply focus on the way ahead; on how to get to the nearest village. He was constantly distracted by the need to search all around for signs of Coll. Once he was confident that he was out of earshot of the men he began calling and clicking.

'Coll! Come on lad. Come to me.' A stream of clicks from his tongue. 'Coll...'

It was an awful contradiction that clawed at him. The need to get away. The desire to stay, for Coll, for home. That was his home for the high summer. It always had been and he thought it always would be. Why would he ever think otherwise? That had been the way of things for generations. The same stopping-places were bound into his life.

Perhaps it was right? Perhaps everything had to change because his world had spun out of control? He no longer was that Tommy. The son of Jeannie and Robbie. The brother of Jimmy and Donald. The other half of Charlotte.

The Tinker who stopped by the pearl-river every summer. He was someone else, but he didn't know who that might be. This new man. For now he was a sad and empty being with no purpose. With no idea. He felt broken.

Some houses appeared on the horizon. A clutch of them sitting grey amidst the green of the fields. As he drew closer he did his best to push the nerves he felt down. This was something he had to do. He was on a road now. Tarmac beneath Seil's hooves. A loud clip-clop announcing their presence. The constant whisper from Tommy. 'It's all right. You're all right.' He had to swallow down his own anxiety for the sake of his beasts. They would feel it and right now that could be very dangerous.

On the outskirts of the town there was a garage. A petrol pump. What looked like a small shop. If they had what he needed it would avoid him having to go into the town proper. It would be a good thing. He slipped off, tied Seil to a fence, called Rona, although there was no need. She stuck to his heels like a shoe.

He reached his arm out to push the door open. Caught the reflection of his face in the glass. He was filthy. His hair long and matted. His face smeared with blood and dirt. He put his finger to the gash and traced it down the whole length of his face. His eye to his mouth. The pain of it, raw and angry.

'Jesus!' he muttered, before quickly retreating and riding off again. He was called a dirty Tinker when he wasn't. His family kept themselves clean. Took pride in it. This wouldn't do. He couldn't be seen like this. There would be taunts, jeers. He would be sent on his way.

Down at the river he waded in, bringing Seil with him.

He washed himself, vigorously scraping at his skin, his hair, his clothes. Then he swam with her, stroking her, bathing her, soothing her. He knew she was hurting too. She had been with Coll her whole life. She had had two of his foals. He wondered if she knew. If she had seen what had happened to him. Where Coll had gone.

'If you could just talk to me, Seil. If you could just say,' he whispered, his forehead against hers. 'We'll be all right though, you and me and Rona. We'll be all right.' He tried his best to believe his own words.

*

The bell rang as he opened the door. An old man clad in oil-stained overalls lifted his eyes from behind the counter.

'You'll be wanting to fill the horse up, aye?' he asked.

'Um...' Tommy stared, looked totally bemused.

'Wee joke, son. Wee joke. Petrol station. Horse tied at the pumps.'

Still Tommy wasn't getting it. He stuttered. 'I-I'm looking for...Would...would you have s-some canvas? A m-muckle big piece of c-canvas.'

The man's eyes widened. 'For covering a car, like?'

'Aye, two of them. B-big.'

'Well now,' he rubbed his chin, slipped off of his stool and came to the front of the counter. 'Come back here son and let's see, aye?' He led Tommy into the workshop where a car sat under canvas. 'This type o thing ye're after, is it, aye?'

'Aye. G-grand. That would be just grand! Two of them. J-just like that.' He was pleased with himself for managing to spit the words out. To make some kind of sense and in turn to be understood.

The man left through a door at the back of the workshop and returned with two packages. 'Now then, you're in luck, see. I'd just ordered these in for myself, like. Now I'll need to be replacing them quick, aye? So it'll cost you.'

'Fine.'

'Right then.'

They agreed a price and money and goods changed hands. Tommy had no idea if it was reasonable or not but it didn't matter. He needed shelter. He needed his tent and the sense of security it offered. A semblance of home. And the feeling from this man was decent. A goodness.

'Don't take this the wrong way, son, but you're looking a wee bit the worse for wear, aye.' He pointed to the wound. 'That's...that's not looking so good.'

Tommy's hand instinctively reached up to cover his face.

'Tinker lad, aye? Been in a bit o bother, have ye?'

He didn't know what to say. What to do. All of his confidence slipped through the floor and left him on the edge. The edge wasn't a good place to be. He fought with himself. Counted in his head over and over.

'Son. I wasnae always a scaldie. Ye're all right here. Ye're all right. Why don't you just come by and have a wee sit down for yourself, aye? And we'll bring yon fine beast o yours round the back. I'm a Smith, by the by. Jamie Smith. You?'

'McPhee. T-T-Tommy McPhee.'

'Oh are ye now? There's a good bit o history to you an yours then, aye. Good bit history.'

176

Tommy smiled.

'Looking at ye now, aye, you'd be one o Robbie's?'

'Um. Aye. Robbie's.' He felt his stomach wrench. His heart thump. He didn't want to do this. To face this. But he was a man now. Things had to be stood up to. Dealt with. Wee Tommy had to become a distant memory as did his previous life.

'Fine man yer da. He'd pop in for a wee dram every year at berry time, so he would. Bit o craic an a blether. Aye. Fine man. Now. Let's be getting that cleaned up so as ye don't end up wi an infection or some such!'

Jamie fetched his first aid kit and cleaned the wound as best he could. As he worked Tommy saw his ma. Felt his ma. She had been a woman of herbs and potions who knew how to cure most ailments; who would have been burned as a witch a couple of centuries back.

'You'll be the quiet one then.' Jamie chuckled, grinned as he stepped back, appraised his attempt at nursing. He shook his head. Tutted. 'That's gonnae need a stitch or ten, son. I could do it for you. Got some o them wee paper stitch things for mysel, like. Always stabbing mysel wi something or other, so I am. And no time for hospitals and the likes. No time.'

'Aye. Aye that would be grand.'

He did his best to close the wound and seal it tight with the stitches, then he dressed it with lint, covered that with a strip of sticking plaster. 'Right now. You watch that heals proper, like, aye? There's a spare dressing for you too.' He slipped it into the bag with the canvas. 'Now you take care o yersel. An send my best to Robbie.'

Tommy stared. He should say something. But he didn't

know what. He didn't know how.

Chapter 39

Charlotte hadn't responded as they told her of their plans. Forget school. Leave the city. Slip into a quieter life. But she seemed to relax a little. Her shoulders dropped as if they had somehow been unlocked.

They left at dawn, creeping along the canal, slipping past silent warehouses, the city waking as they went. The hum of noise building, but caught by the sound of their engine, their travel, the buildings and walls of the canal, the trees and shrubs.

Jasmine and Bobby held smiles which seemed to strengthen as the days wore on. As the cityscape changed to countryside and greenery. Nods, waves and smiles at other boat-dwellers, holidaymakers. Some were known to them. Fellow water-travellers whom they had met year after year.

They pulled up and moored close to a pub. A row of canal boats moored nearby. A garden sprawling with tables and umbrellas. A buzz of human activity which they hadn't been amongst for days. Music drifting out of the building. The clatter of glasses. The clink of cutlery on plates. Loud voices. A burst of raucous laughter. Hot food carried on the air. A tang of vinegar. Chips. Chicken. Scampi.

Bobby rubbed his hands together. Grinned at Jasmine. 'I am so looking forward to this!'

Charlotte hung back. Sat at the bow watching.

'Come on Charlie! The food's great here. You'll love it!'

Oh God, enough of it. I won't and you have no idea of what I love or don't anyway.

'Charlie?'

She shook her head.

'On you go Bobby. Maybe bring us something on the boat?'

'Really?' He raised his eyebrows at her. 'Come on. She can't just stop us from doing everything. I mean, she has to start somewhere. Give a little.'

'But–'

'But nothing. You can't just pander to this. Encourage it. All you're doing is reinforcing that her behaviour, this behaviour, is somehow fine. And it's not, is it?'

'I guess.' Jasmine turned back to face Charlotte. Sighed. 'You'll be okay, right?'

No response.

'Right. Come on then.'

She didn't watch them leave. Didn't care.

The sound of revelry grew as the light faded and succumbed to the night. Neither of them had returned with food for her and she raided the cupboards instead. Some home-made bread. A hunk of cheese. It didn't really bother her. Nothing much did any more. She sat and watched as a moth batted itself against her window over

180

and over again. She turned her light off, but still it kept trying. Why would it do that? Try so hard to get into this space when the world was out there. It was free.

She felt the boat dip, as if someone were stepping on it, coming on board. Holding her breath she listened harder. Definitely steps, but only one person. That was odd. Perhaps they had realised; remembered that she had been forgotten. One of them had come back with food for her.

No lights had been turned on. That felt wrong. The glow of the pub crept into the boat, lighting up enough to cast shadows, one of which stopped at the door to her room. Breathing. Heavy breathing. The door clicked open. A crack. Wider. The click of it closing again. But the person was still here. Still inside her room. Too quiet for this to be okay. She silently, slowly, pulled her covers tight around her. Feigned sleep. That smell of oil and alcohol. The weight of him settling beside her. His hands. His breath. He wrapped his arms around her. He stroked her hair. He ran his fingers down her arm.

Her dad used to do that. Used to cuddle into her, stroke her hair, tell her he loved her, but it was good and pure and she begged for it. Prayed for it. She would give anything for it to be him. So similar but so far apart. This felt wrong and dirty. Silent tears soaked her pillow. A shiver ran through her. Her breath faltered. Threatened to stop. Her pulse raced. The buzz of a thousand insects nipped at her brain. Nothing else there. A deafening buzz. *Leave me alone. Please just leave me alone.*

A breathy whisper. 'So beautiful.' A nuzzle at her neck. His breath on her skin.

Voices drawing closer. Jasmine and somebody else. He

peeled himself away from her. Kissed her head. Quiet footsteps slipped away.

She lay there, unable to move. Unable to do anything. The door clicked closed.

'You were taking so long we thought we'd better come get you before you smoked it all!'

He laughed. 'As if! Just checking in on her.' He jerked his head back in the direction of Charlotte's room. 'Fast asleep. I told you she'd be fine. Right then. Time for that joint, yeah?'

Through the wall she could hear a hum of muffled voices, laughter. She didn't try and listen. Didn't want to hear. Didn't want to be. Something dark and dangerous had visited her. It left her cold. Confused. She didn't understand what had just happened. Couldn't process it. She stretched up and opened the porthole. A different sound now; gentle lapping of the water; breeze fed rustle of the trees. The song of a night-singer. Two. More. She called them in; drifted away with them.

Chapter 40

Tommy had gone as far into the world of people as he wanted to. Stares cast at him and his animals. Him and his bandaged face. Him and his dishevelled appearance. He'd tied Seil to a lamppost, tucked Rona under his arm, ducked into a couple of shops. Constant glances over his shoulder, checking on Seil. Checking on Seil.

Stares from the shopkeepers. Thoughts of protesting "No dogs!" but thinking better of it. The Tinker looked wild. Frightening. Maybe call the police? No time for that. Best get it over and done with. Get shot of the man.

He picked up some clothes, some blankets for him and his animals; enough to see him through for a while. It had been hell, but he'd done it. He'd ignored everyone, everything, tuned out the comments, the nudges, held his head high above it all. Been someone else.

As he rode back out of town he fought away the urge to gallop, to get out of there as quickly as he could. *No. Take your time. Slow and easy. Slow and easy.* Inside he felt like shrinking into invisibility. *Focus on something else. Think of something else.* Thoughts trickled in of where to go. What to do. Pictures of the river. *Yes, focus on that.*

He could go to the side of the big house? Charlotte's side? He'd seldom seen anyone there other than Charlotte herself. If he pitched deep enough into the woods, out of sight, he might be safe. He was quite sure the wicked men weren't from that side and he could keep an eye out for Coll. They'd smell each other – the horses. Smart beasts with memories longer than time. Coll might just come back this way if he could. If he was free. And they would find each other again.

His mind now set with an idea that felt hopeful made him straighten up. Sit high on his horse like a proud Tinker. A part of this world, but not caged by it. Not ruled by it. He smiled at wee Rona who seemed to feel it too; her head high as she stood on the horse's back as if balancing like this was what she was made for.

The men had returned. Multiplied. They had brought chainsaws and violence, cutting the forest back. Slashing it to the ground. Crows and their allies swirled and screeched. This new threat wouldn't be harried away. Chased off. No matter how many, no matter how strong an attack the birds could mount. Swoop and retreat. Swoop and retreat. Retreat. Retreat. Survival. That was all that was left. Stripped back survival in a place of destruction.

The fall of each tree cut him. He fought for breath. Thoughts scrambled. Blank. Dirty. Foul. No sense to them. Nothing coherent. His life bled with the sap of the trees. His fingers curled with the fear of the leaves. Other eyes stared like his in terrified disbelief as nests tumbled and splintered. Scuttlers scurried and flew. Cawers circled and screeched. Swooping and diving. Not at the threat of a great-sky-dweller. At man.

184

Tommy had to turn his back on it all. He looked away, skirted far around the field, far away from the men and their chainsaws and their threat. He waded through the river and made his way along the bank, eventually reaching the pearl-pool. He jumped down at the little beach where he had spent so much time with Charlotte. It felt wrong, different, without her there. He closed his eyes, trying to push empty thoughts away. There was a pang like hunger, but he had no need for food.

All three of them had a drink of the cool, clear water. They wouldn't stop for long though, despite wanting to. Despite this being one of his special places, he couldn't linger. Fingers with a hint of dusk began to whisper to the sky and he wanted to have found his piece of seclusion before nightfall. Evensong was building in the trees as he walked slowly through the woods. He breathed it. The sound filling him. Comforting him.

The forest thickened and they carried on through places where no sign of human presence dented the grass, made tracks. The going was slow because this was difficult for Seil. No easy track for her hooves. The danger of slipping, stumbling on the steepening slope of dense undergrowth. Tommy knew that deep in the forest there was a small clearing with grass for Seil and a place for his camp. There might not be time enough to pitch his tent and settle, but a night under the stars when the sky was cloudless, like this, would have been his choice anyway.

He found the clearing just as dusk tinged the canopy with a soft, golden hue, trickles of fading sunlight crept through to the ground. Still no sign of another human having been here. The sense of solitude as he stepped into the little circle. It felt like it had been made just for him, just for this time.

He freed Seil of her load and set his few possessions on the soft, sweet, mossy grass. His fingers pushed their way through it. A fine bed it would make. He fed his animals and himself before settling down for the night. There wasn't a feeling of security because he wasn't quite sure of anything any more. Destruction lay just across the water and he could feel it creeping from cell to cell beneath the bark of the trees, whispering through their roots. *Danger. Danger.* A sickness that threatened all who rested here. All who had stood strong and proud for decades, for centuries. He worried about what he might wake to. Not just tomorrow but the days, weeks, and years ahead. Until dawn though, they would be safe enough.

'Come find us Coll,' he called softly. 'Come find us.'

With each day that passed he felt more at ease with this new stopping-place. The woods were heavy with foliage now, wild berries swelled, the river likewise with fish. There was ample to keep him and his animals satisfied for the summer months.

His tent was completed, strong and secure, camouflaged with a layer of foliage, moss and branches. Fires were kept unlit until dusk and beyond, which was a challenge in high summer when night didn't show itself until nigh on midnight. He climbed far up a tall pine every evening to scan the land around, checking for those men and how far their trail of destruction had crept up the hillside. The scarring hurt him, but he was thankful that they were keeping to the other side of the river, a mile or so between them. He watched too for the gamekeeper, strangers, anything out of the ordinary, but most of all for Coll.

He didn't feel like the horse had truly gone. One day he would find his way back to them. He had to. He was the only living link with his ma. She had loved that horse as much as a human, as her own child, as family.

As dusk began to wrap itself across the land he would walk down to the river and they would paddle along the shallows of the water; trees and the hill on one side, fields and shrinking forest on the other. His ears kept guard of the woods, his eyes the fields, although he could hear little above the flow of the river, the splash of hooves, the rustle of leaves. Rona would be the one to pick out anything untoward. Despite her natural instinct to hunt she knew that this wasn't the time. She had a job to do and it was protection. It was all so very beautiful, so close to perfect, if only his heart didn't ache with the weight of so much loss.

Chapter 41

Dougie was looking forward to getting back to work. He'd been away for a couple of weeks on a course about land-management and rewilding. The two working hand in hand. It had been good. Interesting. And he would be able to put a lot of what he had learned into practise. Build for the future. He had picked up Gypsy from the kennels – not really kennels as such, but a farmer who was happy to take his dog in when the need arose.

'Aye, I'll take that one off your hands any time. Great wee dug, so he is. Just you say the word and he can join my lot.'

'Surprised at you still asking, Jock. He's so not for sale. I'd sooner give you my wife, if I had one.'

A shared laugh and a friendly handshake.

He was enjoying the slow walk across the brow of the hill. Gypsy bounding ahead excited to be back on home territory, circling back to check his master was there, and off again. Smells. Dougie found himself wondering what that must be like. Your world filled with knowledge and understanding by what was carried on the breeze, trailed in the undergrowth. He smiled at the sheer enjoyment of it all. Nose down, nose up, tail beating, tongue lolling, breath panting. Gypsy came back and clung to his heels, looking timid. Nervous. That was peculiar.

'What is it boy?' He ruffled the dog's neck. Lifted his own head high to the breeze. A whiff of something bitter mixed with the pine, the forest. Unpleasant. A trace of smoke that didn't smell like a camp-fire. There was more to it than that. It carried petrol, rubber, and there was the high drone of machinery.

He whistled softly to Gypsy and they headed down the hill to investigate further. He walked up-river to where the water narrowed and deepened and the little wooden bridge stretched over it. As he crossed into Craigdour land he reminded himself of the need to replace this. The wood was crumbling. Dangerous.

He stared in disbelief. There, in front of him, the scar on the hill. The felling of trees, but not just trees. Ancient woodland that had stood for centuries. Irreplaceable. And in the place of the Tinker camp that had been there every summer for as long as he could remember was a stain. Scorched land. Something monumental was happening and it felt so very wrong. He toyed with the idea of striding up to the Craigdour estate office. Demanding an explanation. No. Better to go forewarned. The laird. He would know.

He knocked on the door of the Manor. Muffled noises grew clearer. The familiar footsteps of the laird, slower now, accompanied by the click of a walking stick, but recognizable nonetheless. He would open the door, as always, dressed in his tweed plus-fours and matching jacket, highly polished brogues, a smile hiding behind his waxed white moustache, a twinkle in his grey eyes. He was such a dichotomy. His looks shouting hunting and arrogance, his nature so far from that. "Just like the ruddy clothes, man! No time for the rest of it, let me tell you!"

Gypsy wagged his tail, circled both Dougie and the laird, before trotting in to the house, his claws clacking on the old stone floor. Both men laughed as they watched the dog sniff his way around the hallway.

'Ah, Dougie man! How the devil are you? Good course?'

'Aye, it was grand. Interesting stuff. I'll have a lot to swing by you, but that's not why I'm here.'

'Come away in.'

The heavy door clunked closed behind them and they walked across ancient stone floors, past walls hung with ancestral portraits, the grand stairway twisting its way lavishly up to the second floor and beyond.

They sat in the drawing room, as big as Dougie's cottage. Vast windows overlooking the estate. Leather chairs that bore the scratch of time but held on to their stateliness. More original artwork on the walls flickering with orange and red light cast by the flames emanating from the great stone fireplace.

'Ruddy place always cold irrespective of the time of year!' Alexander said with an ironic laugh.

'Aye.' Dougie replied, his thoughts elsewhere, his gaze taken by the windows that looked out onto the hills. An image that was now changing, scarring, a tangible sadness creeping up the hill like a mythical beast.

Alexander followed Dougie's gaze. 'Ah.' He shook his head sadly. 'Such a blight on this beautiful place. It's breaking my heart. And the wife's.' He smiled weakly across at Katherine.

'Aye. Mine too. I'll cut to the chase. That was what I wanted to talk to you about.'

Alexander held his hand up. 'By God, we've tried, haven't we, my love?' He turned to Katherine and they exchanged soft smiles. 'It was the day you left. Right out of the blue. Went straight across. Had it out with them. Ruddy man wouldn't budge an inch. Great for the local economy. The jobs, the tourism, blah, blah, blah, balderdash. Couldn't even find out who the actual owner is. Some foreigner. Just talked to the factor chap. Not a pleasant man, let me tell you. Of course we always worried it would come to this. So many estates going the way of the hunting-lodge. Money to be made. Money indeed. The offers we've had for this place. Formidable, let me tell you!'

'Yes, I thought as much, but Durnoch? You wouldn't...I mean...you wouldn't sell, would you?'

'Good God man, over my dead body! If I'm leaving here it will be in a coffin.'

'Alexander,' Katherine said softly.

Dougie looked from one to the other. 'So you're staying put?'

'Of course we are! I didn't send you off on that course without a purpose. Durnoch will thrive! Its land, its animals, the lot. That ruddy man can go to hell with his shooting and burning and whatever other monstrosities he decides to inflict upon the place. He is not getting an ounce of flesh from me!'

Dougie smiled. The fight this old man had in him. That

bloody-mindedness. He was such a man of principal. He would fight for what he believed in. Relentlessly! And Dougie was mighty glad of it. He took his leave and headed homewards.

Gypsy snuffled around his feet before running ahead zig-zagging on the trail of an irresistible scent. He stopped. Looked back at his master.

'On you go, lad!'

The panicked flap of grouse fleeing beat the air. Dougie whistled, called him back. It wouldn't be long now until, across the river, far too close for comfort, they would be flushed out by dogs trained for just that and shot at by men who had paid a considerable sum for the privilege of shooting them down as they fled.

He opened the door to his cottage. Smiled at the familiarity of it all. The sense of belonging.

'I'm home, Sarah. I'm home.'

Chapter 42

Charlotte waited until she had heard them get up before surfacing herself. A pot of coffee sat brewing on the stove. Jasmine was slicing thick chunks of bread, Bobby preparing a fresh fruit salad. They huddled around the little galley-kitchen table. Everything was normal. No knowing glances, warnings. Smiles and breakfast like nothing had happened last night. Perhaps she had misread it all. It was just her stepfather being concerned. Caring. They were so unlike anyone else that she had met before it was possible. This was just the way of them.

'Sorry about last night,' Jasmine said. 'Not bringing dinner back. We just, well, we got caught up with some old friends, lost track of time. You know how it is. What a blast!'

'Yeah, for sure!' Bobby smiled first at Jasmine then at Charlotte.

Was there something there? In that smile? Something other than his normal smile? No. He was always grinning at her. Trying to cheer her up. That was all it was. His knee brushed against hers. She ignored it. Crossed her legs.

'Eat up, Charlie. Some juice maybe? Water?'

She knew what was going on here. Questions that needed answering. They were relentless. Every opportunity they could find. She shook her head.

Jasmine sighed. 'I just wish you'd try, baby.'

'In your own time,' Bobby added. 'In your own time.'

A gentle tap on the boat. 'Hello! You guys surfaced then?'

'Debs! Come away in. Quite a night, eh?'

'Sure was. Look, you were serious, right? About the...you know. The little surprise?' She nodded towards Charlotte.

'Shit, yeah, sorry. Charlie, this is Debs. Debs, Charlie.'

'You were right. She is your double and no mistaking! Reminds me of when we were at school. Christ we had a laugh, didn't we?'

'Yeah. The terrible twosome. Not so sure the teachers did much laughing though. So bad!'

'Straight A's in badness!'

'Now see, if they'd only appreciated us, it would all have been fine. I guess you really don't want to go there right now though.' She nudged Jasmine, eyebrows raised, giggles. 'Anyway, look, I won't disturb you, but it's out there, in a box. Enjoy!'

Bobby leapt up. 'Cool, cool, cool. You're a star!'

'I try.'

Bobby came back with a small cardboard box in his hands. He held it out to Charlotte. 'Here you are, baby girl. Just for you.'

She glared. The distaste dripping off her. *Baby girl? Seriously?*

194

'Come on! Open it!'

Reluctantly she peeled the top open. A kitten mewled at her, its eyes staring. Pleading. It was the double of Kittie. She whimpered. Felt her body crawl in on itself. Her knees hugged tight to her chest.

'Charlie?' Jasmine reached out. Charlotte pulled herself tighter. 'Sweetheart, I.' Her fingertips brushed Charlotte's knees, wanting to touch, but unsure.

Charlotte pushed her aside and escaped to her room.

'There's just nothing that works. Every damned time we try we fall flat on our faces. Shit!' Jasmine said.

'At least she made a noise. That's gotta be some kind of progress. Yeah?'

'Maybe.' Jasmine's head dropped. 'So out of my depth.'

He put his arms around her. 'We'll sort this.'

'So what do we do now? Go after her?'

'I reckon leave her be.'

Chapter 43

Summer had slipped away, tinges of red, orange and yellow lit up the leaves, a light carpet lay on the ground, signalling that it was time to move on. It had always been a time to move, back then with his family, for work, different crops, different stopping-places; for him now it was about safety. His camp would be revealed soon enough with the fall of the leaves.

For the first time in his life he didn't want to travel on even though the need pulsed through his veins. The call was there but the desire wasn't. He wanted to stay in the place of Charlotte, in the place of Coll. Reluctantly he packed up, checked the ground carefully for any signs of him having been here. That was a part of him, of his father, of his people.

"The folk won't remember yer smile or yer song or yer kindness, they'll remember any mess ye left behind."

They walked slowly away, not looking back. Always forwards, always forwards.

He had decided that he would follow the river up through the valley and veer off into the hills and mountains beyond. They had only travelled a few miles when Rona pricked her ears. Her hackles stood up tall and straight. She barked and barked, not letting up.

'Wheesht lass. I can't hear what you're barking at. Wheesht!' he whispered urgently.

Rona quietened, but her body remained rigid, ready, her eyes staring through the gloaming. Seil shivered, stamped on the ground. Something was up with both of them.

At first there was nothing obvious, but as Tommy's ears focussed he heard it too. The whinnying of a horse in distress. Not just any horse. That was Coll and he was hurting!

Tommy slipped off Seil, scooped Rona up, and they crept over a field of harvested crops. Bales of hay stood waiting for collection. Mice scampered through the stubble. Beyond the field there was a line of trees and through them he could make out a building. Buildings.

He crept forward to the trees and stood watching from their shelter. Coll was in a paddock, two men wrestling with him, each holding a rope that was tied around his neck. He was bucking, resisting. Hooves scrambling at the air as he stood on hind legs.

'I'll break you if it's the last damned thing I do!' one of the men shouted.

'Enough for today. We'll get nothing out of him until he calms himself down. Tomorrow. We'll get him sorted tomorrow.'

They left for the house, muttering curses and shaking their heads. 'Bloody Tinkers! Their horses are as bad as they are!'

'Aye. They are that. Beautiful beast but wild. So wild!'

197

'I tell you, if he's not broken by the end of the week he's for the knacker's yard.'

Tommy was desperate to bolt across and comfort Coll, rescue him, but he knew these men. He knew what they were capable of. He had to bide his time. Wait for the lights to go out. For human interference to slip from the land. It was killing him. Seil too. She was acting up even more. Pawing at the ground. Snorting her displeasure. Her anxiety.

'Hush now,' Tommy whispered, stroking her flank, calming her. 'Hush now.' The words, the feeling, meant for him as well as his horse.

At last the house stood in darkness. An owl called. Bats flitted through the air. The creatures of the night took precedence once more. Tommy waited for as long as he could bear. He had to be absolutely sure. This had to work. No second chance. No room for mistakes. The air crackled with tension, with apprehension, with fear, with all of the things he didn't need. They had to do this together. Him and his beasts had to be like one. He set Rona to heel and led Seil close by his side, their bodies touching. *Stay calm, stay calm. Stay calm.*

Coll had sensed them, smelled them, seen them. This was the most dangerous part. He had to stay quiet. There was a snuffle, a shake of the head, a toss of the mane.

'Quietly now, Coll. Quietly now. Good lad,' Tommy whispered over and over as they inched forward, his hand outstretched in both greeting and command. 'Good lad.'

His hand had just reached the latch of the gate when a low growl crept out of one of the barns. Hunting dogs. He should have guessed. Been ready. *Shit*! Too late now. He slipped the cold metal latch up and over, swung the gate open. A squeak of hinges. Growls growing into barks. Coll was still agitated, unsettled. Tommy knew there was no way to get a hold of him now. He had to trust the horse would do what was needed. What was right.

'Come on, Coll lad. It's us. You're all right now. Come on.'

Coll sniffed at the night air.

Tommy leapt onto Seil and called in an urgent whisper. 'Come on, Coll. Come on!'

This was it. He had to understand. He had to follow old orders. Old ways.

Tommy clenched his knees around Seil. 'Go!'

She ran, hooves softened by the damp grass. A whinny.

Tommy's eyes were on Coll. His face broke into a smile. The horse was galloping after them. Tommy wanted to call out, wanted to whoop! He kept it inside as they galloped on without pause until they were far, far away. Then he cried out.

'You beauty! You fucking beauty!' He didn't know where that word had come from. He didn't swear. Never had. But that felt so right.

He stretched across and patted Coll's neck. 'Hello boy.'

He didn't like reins. His horses didn't need them, but for tonight he held on to the ropes that bound Coll. Just until he was sure that the horse understood. He was safe now. He was home again. They were high in the hills far away from people, from farms, from anywhere. He was home.

They would follow the stars until they found their winter place once more. They would stay hidden and quiet and safe until spring opened up the world again. Then what? It didn't matter for now, he convinced himself. They were together again. There was nothing else.

Chapter 44

Dougie was walking the boundary of the estate, checking on the woods, the river. He would make a slow ten mile walk every day. Other managers, factors, drove jeeps, quad-bikes. The whine of them breaking through the natural orchestra like an out of place horn section. Brash, loud and disrespectful. That aside – the distraction of them – how could you know what was truly happening without feeling the land under your feet? Without breathing the air slow and steady? Some scorned, mocked him for it, but nonetheless he was respected. None could doubt his knowledge of the land. His feel for it.

He had reintroduced beaver and took great pleasure in watching signs of their settlement scattering the riverbank. Fallen trees, a mass of branches and twigs, a new swell of quiet water. There. The splash. The streak of brown flashing through the water. Silver bubbles trailing behind them. He smiled. At least on this side of the river the wildlife would be allowed to flourish.

He had dreams of more, ones which the laird shared. One day lynx, perhaps even wolf might stroll through here. The closer this land was to how nature intended, the better. But that was for the future. Nothing more than a dream perhaps. The worry now was how to encourage the beavers to stay on Durnoch territory and not drift over to what used to be Campbell land. Craigdour. Fences would feel wrong, but now, perhaps, they had become a necessity. He would wait and see.

He'd taken to spending a few hours on a Saturday night at the village pub; a small, simple place that was tacked on to the hotel. Rustic wooden tables and chairs nestled on the stone floor, black and white pictures of times gone by hung on the whitewashed walls. In the summer there would be tourists, foreign chatter even, but for the rest of the year it was the domain of locals. Farmhands, gamekeepers, groundsmen, ghillies, would gather and share stories of things done, people seen, local gossip.

Dougie was sitting at the bar, not feeling like company, nursing a single malt. He was watching Gypsy happily visiting all of the tables, accepting strokes and smiles, his tail gently swishing. He would do the rounds then come back and sit at his master's feet, like always.

Dougie's ears pricked at a conversation from the table behind him.

'Aye, polis the lot. But no a sign o the horse anywhere. Just vanished, so it says.' He flicked the newspaper in their direction to reinforce the point.

'I heard something of the like myself. The new folk at Craigdour?'

'Aye. I heard an aw, frae ma cousin, ye ken big Archie. Constable, like. An he says that he reckons they were just careless. Left the gate unlatched. But they're swearing, naw. It was locked, as always.'

'Smart beasts, horses. Could easy flick a latch that wasnae closed right.'

'Now, see, that's what I reckon, but I'm that wee bit more careful now. You never know these days, do ye?'

'Aye, well, it's no like it was, that's for sure.'

'Aye, right, cos when you were young there was none o that eh? Folk were all honest and friendly and the lassies were bonnier and the laddies –'

'Enough o that ye cheeky wee rascal!'

A hand was raised in mock aggression. The young man ducked. Laughter erupted.

Dougie grinned. Not so much at the situation, the banter, but at the new owners getting a bit of karma.

'And then there was that murder down by. Maybe the same thief.'

'Aye. Shocking that one. A young lassie left wi'out her father. Polis no got a clue. Still asking for witnesses, it says. Bonnie wee thing too.'

The barmaid reached for Dougie's empty glass. 'Another one, Dougie?'

'Ah, go on then.'

'You not joining them tonight, then?' she asked as she placed a large Glenmorangie in front of him.

'If I did that I'd be here all night and I'm not feeling like a lock-in.'

'Now that's a shame.' She smiled, stroked his hand discreetly. 'That's a shame. You know they're also saying the Tinkers have been moved on. Camped in Craigdour land for years, so they have. Wouldn't surprise me if they took a wee bit of revenge. Them being Tinkers and all that. Who knows? Maybe the break-in too?'

'Aye, wouldnae put it past them,' was added from a ghillie leaning against the bar, his empty glass raised and shaken. 'One more when you're ready, gorgeous.'

Dougie shook his head at them. 'Decent folk, that lot, and I for one am sad to see them gone,' he announced to the bar.

Enough said. He knew that deep down the stories held. Tinkers were not to be trusted, and there was barely a person here who felt differently. They'd employ them soon enough. Work with them. Hard grafters who knew their jobs and did them well. But that would be the sum of it.

His mood had soured even more and he downed his whisky and got up to leave. They were such a unique family, that one. The last of a kind. And that boy, the pearl-fisher, what of him? He had seemed like such a gentle soul. It was a very sad thing to hear of their departure. People could be such fools.

It dawned on him that it had been a while since he'd seen Charlotte too. The thought grabbed him. Surely not. 'Can I get a look at that paper?'

'Aye, on ye go.'

His heart sank as he read the article, looked at the picture. It was her all right. What an awful thing. He let out an unintentional sigh.

'Did ye know her then?'

'Aye. Aye I did. Nice wee thing. She used to come by the estate quite often.'

'You wouldnae credit it. Murder? Up here?'

'Take care, lads,' he called, as he reached to take his jacket off the peg. He wouldn't leave a sour taste in his wake. Best to keep in with the locals, many of whom had been friends of his since he first arrived. Differences perhaps, but friends all the same.

'Aye, you too, Dougie man. You too.'

As he made to leave, the door opened. All eyes turned to see who was arriving. Gypsy bared his teeth. Growled softly. Approached slowly. Tail tucked tight between his legs.

The man stopped, stamped his foot. 'That dog should be on a lead,' he snarled.

'My dog only growls for a reason and I'm guessing you're it.' Dougie snapped. He knew the man by sight. Had seen him striding around Craigdour, checking on the felling of trees. He leaned down, patted Gypsy. 'Good boy.' Gypsy relaxed, wagged his tail as they brushed past and into the ominous breeze of an early autumn evening.

Chapter 45

Tommy rode on, following the stars when they were out, judging direction by the sun when they weren't, fixing a distant point to focus on when the sky was no friend and heavy with cloud. He began to realise just how little he knew of the world around him. The paths his family had followed, their stopping-places, the farms they worked at, were firmly imprinted in his brain. But breaking that route; that tradition, had left him blind. He had been keeping high up the hillsides, avoiding habitation; the lochs with their twisting roads and pretty wee villages. Now perhaps it was time to venture down. At least to find out where he was.

As he played it all over in his head he knew that he had done nothing wrong. Coll was his. And anyway, all he had done was open a gate and the horse had followed. It would be easy enough for those men to think they had left the gate unlocked. They were angry and in a hurry. Surely they would blame themselves. That was what he clung to.

He paused as they reached a wee single-track road that twisted around the loch. It was quiet enough. Barely a car to be seen. He slipped off Seil and led his horses across the road and down to the water's edge. The loch was clear; the water pure and inviting.

Tommy and the horses walked across the smooth pebbles and into the water. It was cool and crisp and life-giving. He scooped water in his hands and let it fall over his head, his face, his shoulders. The horses drank, tossed their heads, whinnied. Rona stood tentatively at the water's edge, allowing her paws to touch the water as she lapped.

'Come on, lass. Come away in. You'll like it,' Tommy called, clapping his hands in gentle encouragement.

She looked at her master as if sizing him up, checking if she could trust him in this, before inching in.

'Good girl! Come on then. A wee swim. You can do it!'

Finally she was out of her depth, her little legs beating against the water, propelling her towards Tommy.

'Well, look at you now! Swimming away!'

It seemed she was enjoying it as she swam around and around him before heading back to the safety of the shore.

'Is that a wee swimming-girl I've got now then? Grand!' he said, as he rubbed her head in congratulation.

Tommy sat in the autumn sun, a chill to it now, but still a hint of warmth. He gazed out at the loch; its waters so still that everything was reflected in the glistening mirror. The multicoloured woods in every shade of orange, red, and green. The hills clad with heather, its blossom almost gone now, but still that hue of purple and white.

The stark peaks of the mountains were already playing host to the first snows. At the far end of the loch a small collection of houses nestled together, most a brilliant white, others grey, pink. It looked welcoming, friendly, but he knew from experience that, for him, places of people were often far from that.

He had cleaned himself up as best he could but he knew his hair was long and unkempt, his face scarred and unshaven. The horses were tied up at the edge of the village as he and Rona made their way towards the only shop. It was just a cottage itself, with a sign declaring it to also be the post office. He took a deep breath, pulled his shoulders back like his father had taught him. *"Stand tall, lad. Stand tall. Look them in the eye and be proud of who you are; who we are. Always!"*

It wasn't so easy without his family there beside him, behind him, just knowing that he was completely alone. There was only him in this world and it ached. As if she had read his mind, his feelings, Rona jumped up and pawed at his legs, making the cutest little whimpers.

'Aren't you just the best, wee one,' he whispered down to her. He could do this. He had to do this.

A bell tinkled softly as he pushed the door open. The girl behind the counter stood, open mouthed and silent. His courage fell through his boots and he turned to leave.

'What is it you'd be wanting then?' she called after him, her voice soft and friendly with a hint of curiosity about it.

He stopped. Turned back around. 'I-I'm a bit lost,' he stammered out. 'I n-need a map. Would you have one? A map?'

'Aye. Aye, we've got maps, right enough. Where is it you're heading to, like?'

'Um...I...um.'

'Not big on words, then?'

He felt himself turn red, switched his gaze to the floor.

'The whole of Scotland, the Highlands, just the county? What is it y'er after?'

'All three, aye.'

'Right...' she said slowly as she spun a display rack around and pulled out three maps. She placed them on the counter and smiled expectantly. 'Anything else?'

'Could you maybe show me where we are?'

'You're having me on?'

'No. I got myself a b-bit lost a while back. A b-bit lost.'

'Is that right, aye?'

'Aye.'

'Okay, the customer is always right, or so my ma says, so...' She smiled as she opened up the map of Argyll, flattened it out and pointed. 'Right there.'

'Could you m-mark it for me? A c-circle around it.'

'If you pay for it first. Can't be selling on a defaced map now, can I?'

The money was still in his da's belt. Should he turn his back? Of course he should. It was a secret thing in a secret place. He trembled as he untucked his shirt and fumbled at the clip.

'Hey! No funny business, right!'

'It's j-just. N-no I'm. Oh Christ!' He managed to peel out some notes – much more than he needed – before turning back around and laying them on the counter, his hands still shaking.

'My da's out the back, my brother too. Just so you know!' No friendliness now.

He snatched at the maps and hurried out. That was hell. Nothing less than hell! He and Rona ran back to the horses and they rode off. He should have bought some supplies. He should have done better. He should have been normal. But there it was. He wasn't. Never had been, and that was fine. Back then it was fine. Now all that he could do was doubt himself. Stay away. Hide.

He took the road out of the village, pausing at the sign declaring its name, whispering it over and over, fixing it to his mind. The wee road, dotted with passing places, sucked its way around the loch then veered off into nothingness. As it did so his anxiety began to slip away; desolation was comfort, the trees that flanked one side friends, the bleak moorland that stretched up the sides of the mountain likewise. He knew this. He could breathe here.

They walked across the moor, up and over the hills, ducking down again into another valley. They came upon a narrow gulley that housed a fast-flowing burn. Dense moss covered the sides of the rock-face on either side of him. He could almost touch both sides and the horses hesitated, pulled back. A tight fit for them.

'It's okay. On you come now.'

They stepped cautiously as they made their way through the dripping overhang, the tumbling water. When at last the way widened it was as if they had stepped into another world. A small green valley encircled by high heather-clad hills. A sprinkling of trees. He looked around. Nothing. This was secure.

He let the horses wander, grazing as they did so. Rona sniffed around, chasing smells of wild things known only to her. He spread the map of Argyll out on the mossy ground, trying to bring back the image of the girl pointing.

It was normally something he could do with ease, but his anxiety had been such that the memory was blurred, indistinct.

As he stared at the map he found himself back with his ma. They had spent hour upon hour poring over their maps. It was something special to her. Seeing the land on paper. Learning more about the lie of it. Her finger trailing the edges of a loch, following a river, skipping around a mountain range. Islands had been chosen for the names of their animals. Wee places with a call that touched them. A feel to them. She had talked about places she had been, things she had seen; the quartz heart where she had married his pa. *"I'll take you there one day, son. The most beautiful wee place, so it is. And what a day it was! The rain bucketed down, and no mistaking! Drenched through, we were. Drenched through!"* She had laughed at the memory. *"But it didn't matter. It was just me and him in this beautiful wee place, telling the world that we loved each other. Aye."*

He could see that picture as clear as a lochan on a crisp winter's day. Her finger pointing to the spot. Her smile for the memory. The wee tear that snuck down her cheek at the joy it brought. The life Robbie had led her on wasn't for everyone, but for her it was perfect. *"May you be as blessed, lad. Aye, may you be as blessed."*

For the past year he had tried not to think about his loss. It hurt too much. But now it felt like he could, he should. Memories like that couldn't be allowed to fade. He had no one to tell stories to. No one to share the family history with. Such an integral part of his life – of their lives – had been snatched from him. It was a part of his soul. Sharing in stories, huddling around a campfire, listening to the soft sounds of his parents' voices, the laughter of his brothers, the singing of their songs. If the mood took him his pa would sometimes sing bits of the stories themselves, his ma making harmonies. That was magic. Just pure magic.

He scoured the map and found the name of the village soon enough. A place scant of settlements. Scant of names. He worked his finger back over what he thought was the route they had taken. The burn they had followed, the twist of the hills and finally the valley where he now sat. Content that he now knew where he was – he had a foundation to work from – he whistled his animals to him, set up a camp and built a fire.

As the light faded, taking all of the world with it, until there was nothing but the glow of the fire, the flicker of the flames, he began to whisper. This time it was him telling his stories, sharing his memories. It didn't matter that there was no person to hear them. It mattered that he was telling them.

Sleep came soft and gentle.

Chapter 46

The next morning Charlotte hadn't shown herself. That was no surprise. But a soft giggle slipped out of her room. Jasmine looked around. The box had gone. She smiled at Bobby. Squeezed his arm.

'I think, maybe, you're a genius,' she whispered.

'Just maybe?'

She laughed. 'Okay. Full creds for this one. You are a genius, and I love you.' She kissed his cheek.

They stood silently listening. Was she chatting to the kitten? Actual words? They tiptoed closer. A creak. Retreated.

'Best leave her be, yeah?'

'Yeah.'

Charlotte lay on her bed, the kitten clambering across her, pouncing on her. It stopped, stared, mewled at her. She stroked it. Its little tail quivered in delight. She would have been happy to stay locked away in her room forever, but the kitten needed fed, as did she. She swung her legs off the bed and tuned in to the sounds from beyond. Whispers from on deck. Good. They were outside. She could creep out, grab some food and sneak back in again with no confrontation. Questions.

She opened the door and tiptoed out. The kitten followed, prancing at shadows. The kitchen window sat ajar, the door open. She poured a bowl of muesli, shared the last of the milk between herself and the kitten, filled a saucer full of cat food. As she turned to retreat to the safety of her room footsteps moved across the roof of the boat. She stared in panic. Too many things to carry all at once.

The kitten was running towards the door. *No!* Bobby jumped down, a grin on his face. He snatched the kitten up and moved towards her. Too close. So close that she could feel his breath on her face. His look serious now.

'Best be taking care of this little thing. Can't have it falling off and drowning itself, now can we?'

She stepped back, held her arms out for the kitten.

'Why don't you take that?' He nodded at the food. 'And I'll get this little thing safely back in your room. On you go.'

Her hands were shaking as she picked up the bowl and saucers. *Stop it! Stop it! Stop it!* She was sure that she saw him smile at the shake.

He sat on her bed, put the kitten beside him, trailed his fingers across the cover. 'Come on then pussy cat. Catch me if you can.' He laughed as the kitten pounced again and again and again.

Can you please go? Can you please just get up and go?

'Best sit down and eat that before it gets all soggy,' he said, nodding towards the bowl of muesli.

There was nowhere to sit other than the bed. That was

all her room was. A bed, a couple of cupboards high on the wall and about a metre of floorspace.

It'll be all right. She's up there. He won't do anything when she's up there.

She sat down as far away from him as she could and tried to eat, but her mouth was too dry. The food got stuck in her throat. She couldn't swallow.

Leave. Leave. Leave.

He sidled along the bed towards her. Put his arm around her waist. Squeezed.

'There now, see? I don't bite.'

A lecherous grin.

Chapter 47

Dougie took a drive down to Charlotte's house. Police tape fluttered across the gate, the door. A swathe of sadness slithered over everything. He jumped out of his jeep and walked along the track to the back of the house. Charlotte's bike no longer stood propped against the garden shed. A sense of abandonment clung to everything. Grass and weeds run wild were attempting to stake their claim.

'Is there something you're after?' Martha called across at him, a heavy, threatening frown. Brown eyes narrowed, glaring.

Dougie wasn't sure how to respond. What to say. Did he even have a right to ask anything? Yes, of course he did. 'Young Charlotte. I knew her quite well. I thought I'd ask after her.'

'Is that so? Well, I can't say as I've seen you hereabouts, so I can't imagine you knew her that well. There's been a lot of nosy folk poking around here, where they've no business. The scene of the crime, eh? Is that what you're after? A wee look? A shameful wee thrill? I'm sick of it. Sick of the lot of you. Now off with you before I call the police out. Again!'

He put his hands up. 'I'm sorry. It's nothing like that. The name's Dougie. Dougie Jamieson. I'm manager up at the Durnoch estate. Young Charlotte used to come up on her bike and sit by the river. We'd chat sometimes. She took an interest in the place. The wildlife. Nice wee thing. I was concerned, that was all.'

'Is that right, aye? Next you'll be taking out a notebook and telling me you're not a journalist. The damned cheek of you all.'

'I'm so sorry. I didn't mean to intrude.'

She looked from man to jeep. The dog sitting in the passenger seat. The mud on the tyres. The look of him. His story rang true. 'Come away in then.'

'If you're sure?'

'You'd best hurry before I change my mind!'

He smiled, followed her inside. Accepted a cup of tea. His eyes trailed across the photographs that lay on the table.

She gathered them up. 'Sorry about the mess. My job.'

'Oh, so you're a photographer?'

'I am that. Mostly weddings and the likes, but my passion's with nature. Wildlife. You know. And this place. Well. It's paradise for me.'

He nodded. 'Aye. Me too. Do you mind if I have a look?'

'No, not at all. Not at all.'

She was good. The way she caught the light. The shadows. The essence of this place.

He sighed. 'Well, that's me put to shame.'

She laughed.

'So, Durnoch eh? That was her wee secret place? Her dad and I wondered. He trusted her though, and that was good enough for me. If it had been my daughter, well, that would have been a different story. But it's not my place to interfere, although I did help out a fair bit. He was sick, you know, before all of this. Poor family. What a thing to happen. You know, you see these things on the telly all the time, but when it's this close to home. Well...' She tutted. Shook her head.

'A terrible thing, so it is. And Charlotte was there, saw it all?'

'Well now, they don't know for sure. The poor girl hasn't spoken since, last I heard. You know, I offered to let her stay here, but they said no. Took her off to some stranger's house. That's social services for you. Think they know better than those that know. Aye, that's for sure.'

'Do you know where she is now?'

'Well, as I'm not family, they wouldn't keep me informed, but you know what it's like up here. Everyone is somebody's cousin. And one of mine told me that she was with her mother. London apparently. Can you imagine that? From this to London, with as good as a stranger!'

Dougie sighed, shook his head. 'You wouldn't have an address would you? I was thinking a wee note, some pictures. Something to let her know I care.'

'That I don't. My cousin said that he'll let me know as soon as he can find out. Anyway, if I hear anything I'll let you know. Durnoch you said?'

'Aye. That's mighty kind of you.'

He tipped his cap as he left. Glanced back at

Charlotte's empty house. A shiver ran through him.

Chapter 48

Autumn had fully come, wild and wanton and there was work to be done. Tommy had found his way back to the tumbledown building of the year before and was able to ready himself for the oncoming winter well enough. The place had survived and there was little repair needed but he built it better, more securely. He knew what to do as he had helped his da make secure their winter resting place of old.

Other Travellers wintered in houses or caravans in towns, secure and protected from the cold. His family didn't want that. This life of little, of freedom, of belonging only to the land, was precious to his parents. Change might have been coming soon enough, though. He had heard conversations. Picked up on a different mood.

'We're getting on Robbie. These old bones maybe needing a wee rest, aye? And the laddies? It's no fair on them. Besides which, I reckon one or both will be off with girlfriends soon enough, their own families to make.'

Robbie shook his head slowly, met her eyes with his. That look in them that she knew so well. 'It'd kill me, so it would.'

'Maybe this'll kill you sooner?'

'Better that than the other.'

She smiled. This wasn't a new conversation. The next line was always the same.

'When nature wants me back, I'm hers.'

She agreed. Deep down she agreed. She loved their way of life. She loved him for his dogged determination to carry on like this. Just them. No masters. No chains. But sometimes, when the wind bit hard and the rain stung, and her breath caught unexpectedly, and another pain struck at her, and her boys looked to far away places. Then she wondered. The doubt didn't last. A fire would be lit. The family would gather. Story and song would strike up. And of course there was Tommy. Nothing else would do for him, of that she was quite sure. No. There was nothing else.

*

By the first fall of snow he had made good and prepared his dwelling place for the season ahead. There was shelter for his horses, a tight little space for him and Rona to sleep in, canvas secured inside four ancient walls, just big enough for comfort, small enough for warmth. He had cut and piled high logs; scythed, tied and stacked grass, and laid out reeds that he had harvested for basket making.

The pelts of the rabbits that Rona had caught were cleaned, dried and set aside. She had ratted at them to begin with, tried to kill them all over again. And despite his best intentions, Tommy had laughed at her, which only made things worse.

'What am I going to do with you, eh? You wee rascal!'

He stitched one of the skins up with a needle made of rabbit bones, thread made of hair. He stuffed it with dried grasses and stitched up the last remaining opening.

'Right wee one. This here is for you! The others you leave alone, aye?'

He threw it for her and she tossed it about before dropping it at his feet, over and over again. Endless amusement for both of them. When she wasn't playing with it she slept on it.

The days were short and the light low as he sat twisting and weaving the dried reeds, making them into baskets like his ma had taught him. Strong sensible ones that folk would need. Folk that knew him. His fingers worked with little instruction, knowing what to do with each piece of reed.

With the finest reeds he crafted a small intricate basket for Charlotte. She had gone. He didn't know why, or where, or if she would ever return, but if she did she would find his gifts, like every year before her disappearance.

As he twisted the reeds he could see her smile, the twinkle of her eyes, hear her laughter, loud and boisterous, more like a man's than a wisp of a thing like her. It took him to a different place, a different world and he felt content, clinging to the knowledge that one day they would share a breath again.

He rose with the daylight and rode the horses through the early morning mist that curled around the hills, twisted through the trees, and drifted across the water as if it were its breath. A time of magic, of impossible beauty. The horses' hooves created a small track around the lochan that was theirs and theirs alone. Beneath the surface of the water there were still fish aplenty, and they bit quickly and regularly. Ice crept from the edges, fragile and lace-like, crunching underfoot as he chose his spot to fish from. By mid-morning the smell of frying fish would mingle with smoke and fire and the earthiness of the ground, deep and musty.

He would keep to the same routine every day. A grounding. A predictability. A passage of time. The days would keep shrinking; the sun, when it chose to show itself, lying so low it was barely there at all. Harsh and glaring. Blinding. Then gone again. Shadows then darkness. He would hunker down, stay safe here until he could smell that change in the air. The softening of spring like the whisper of a mother's breath on a fevered brow.

Suddenly, Rona lifted her snout, focused on the distance. Alert.

'What is it, lass?'

He followed her gaze and saw nothing untoward. Perhaps she had picked up the scent of something wild. Fox, mountain hare, deer, a sea eagle swooping in for its kill. The light was slipping away now. Darkness would wash over them soon enough.

'Come on. Away in and we'll settle for the night.'

He clicked his fingers and Rona followed him inside, taking one last glance behind her before the walls shut the world out.

'Best get the fire lit, eh? A wee bit warmth before bed.'

He built a pyramid of sticks as kindling and layered logs around it, struck the flints against each other. That feeling of belonging to the earth as spark flitted to flame. Once the wood had taken he carefully placed more logs on the flames and sat back on his haunches to watch them lick their way through the wood.

Still Rona wouldn't settle. This wasn't normal behaviour from her. She knew the routine as well as he did and would enjoy settling down in the soft glow of the flames, dozing before retreating into the canvas lean-to at bed-time. But no. She paced up and down, sniffing at the cold air that crept in.

Her hackles went up and she burst into a fit of furious barking. He hadn't seen her like this since that day back at the summer stopping-place. Since those men.

'Wheesht now,' he whispered sternly. 'Let me hear.'

She growled softly, not taking her eyes off the entrance.

Voices. Footsteps. 'I told you. Someone's settling in.'

'Aye, well, we'll soon see about that!'

The door flew open and there was no calming her now. She lunged at the feet of the intruders, barking and snarling, barking and snarling.

Standing in the opening two men. An air to them. 'What the devil?' A kick aimed. A yelp.

Rona ran to her master. Tommy gathered her to him, stared, frozen, unable to speak. A torchlight glared in his eyes, blinding him, scanned across his canvas, his possessions, before settling on him again.

'This here's private property. You'll need to leave. Now! Pack your things and move on.'

Tommy wanted to protest. Wanted to ask for a bit of kindness. At least for them to let him stay until morning.

But he couldn't. All he felt from them was anger and danger. They stood and watched as he did his best to pack up in the near dark. The flicker of the fire, the flash of the torch a distraction, not a help.

'Get a move on. We haven't got all night.'

He had his canvas and, he hoped, his essentials, but his mind was muddled, blacked out by fear. The horses whinnied. He closed his eyes. Prayed.

'Horses too, eh? Payment perhaps. Rent due?'

Tommy charged, pushing through them. The men staggered, stumbled. He threw the canvas and his bag on Coll's back. Leapt up onto Seil. Rona too. And they galloped off into the darkness. Shouts and curses following them.

He headed blindly up, deeper into the hills. Men like that would have transport. A Land Rover or something similar. He didn't hear anything following him and the terrain would have been too difficult anyway. They must have parked further downhill. By the time they got back to their transport he and his beasts would be well gone.

As the terrain steepened and hardened he walked in front of the horses for fear of them losing their footing on the frosty ground, falling, getting injured.

The men wouldn't follow. Not all the way up here. Not in this weather. Snow swirling. Wind whipping through the hills. Becoming lost, disorientated, was a strong possibility. But he felt safe now. Not safe enough to stop though. Movement. Travelling. In that there was safety.

Assuming that he had read his map correctly, on the other side of the hills he would reach the spring of a burn that trickled its way down to another valley. No buildings were marked. No places of habitation. He might be able to rest there, to settle for an hour or two, to gather his thoughts.

Chapter 49

'So, what have we got?' DCI Graham asked.

PC Jamieson pulled a face. 'Next to nothing, sir. There's a few sets of prints that aren't the victim's or the girl's, but no matches.'

'And the broken window?'

'That's the best lead we've got. Prints on the sill, DNA, but, again, no matches.'

'And no word from the girl's mother about the child speaking again? Have our colleagues down south been pushing it?'

'Well,' PC Jamieson shuffled. This was going to go down like a tonne of lead. He braced himself. 'The thing is, she's one of those transient types. Lives on a boat.'

'Yes, yes. I know that. And?'

'And she's sort of moved off.'

He thumped his desk. The air crackled. 'Moved off where, for fuck's sake?'

'They don't know. The girl never showed at school and, well, they disappeared.'

'The deal was–! Christ! So, let me get this straight. The Met have let our one and only witness to a homicide just disappear!'

'Yes, sir. Seems that way.'

'And meanwhile there's some fucking murderer zipping about free as a bird.'

'Yes, sir.'

'Get on it. Get on them. Tell them they're a bunch of useless bastards. Get appeals out. Get squad cars cruising. Get everything. EVERYTHING on this. Am I making myself clear?'

'Yes, sir.'

'Well don't just stand there. Do as you're bloody told. And don't say "Yes sir!"'

'Sir!'

'I'm surrounded by fucking idiots.'

Chapter 50

Jasmine, Bobby, and Charlotte kept moving, their boat leading them along a trail of canals. Towns and cities slid past, strangely distant, as if they were travelling through an alternative reality.

'I'm thinking we should just keep going on the canals. I mean, school's kind of a no-brainer for her, isn't it?' Bobby said.

'Yeah. I was thinking something similar. Life's better for her out here, you know? The freedom. The fresh air. We might even get her to say something by Christmas!'

'You reckon?'

Jasmine shrugged.

'I can't get my head around it. I mean she seems okay to chat away to that little cat, but us? Weird. Just weird.'

She sighed. 'I know, baby. But it'll come. When she's ready it'll come. She just has to trust us.'

'Yeah, right, s'pose.'

Her first attempt at communication with them had been when she wrote the kitten's name on a piece of paper and slid it over to Jasmine. *Tinker* it read.

'Oh baby, that's such a cute name!' Jasmine skipped on

deck to find Bobby. 'Look Bobby. Words!'

'A word.'

'Still. It's something.'

'S'pose.'

She grinned, hugged him. 'Yeah, it's something. It's all gonna be all right.'

'If you say so.'

'I do.'

Charlotte had taken the paper back, sketched a harness, slipped it across the table to Jasmine.

'Yeah, for sure. We can do that.'

*

Charlotte watched how they manoeuvred their way through a succession of locks. Him pushing the levers, spinning the wheels. Jumping on and off. Her standing at the helm, tall and proud, like she was posing for an artist. That's what she looked like. A model. Someone from a fantasy world, all flowing hair and flowing clothes and otherworldliness.

The thrill of the rush of water lifting the boat from dark depths up to the next level held Charlotte in its grip. The fear of the swell. Its power. She imagined the ease with which it could take a life. Part of her wanted to be on land, watching from a safe distance. The other part was hooked on this adrenaline rush. This danger. The roar of the water so loud that nothing else could be heard above it. Dark black walls, high and insurmountable, on either side.

'Why don't you come and help with the next one?' Bobby called.

She shook her head. Turned away.

*

The next day Bobby appeared with a blue velveteen harness and lead that were jangled in front of her. She beamed, snatched them, retreated to her room.

'I dunno. Thanks maybe?' Bobby muttered under his breath.

Tinker held his body close to the ground as if the weight of the harness might break his back. Charlotte giggled. A few hours later the lead was clipped on. Soon they were happily walking up and down the boat. That Sunday she scooped Tinker up and stepped tentatively along the edge of the boat and onto the towpath.

Jasmine and Bobby watched, holding hands, hardly daring to move, to draw their eyes away, in case the vision might disappear if they weren't holding it in place. This was the first time since that fateful trip to school that Charlotte had left the boat. Little things all joined together were becoming very significant.

'Shall we stop at the Dog and Duck for the night? A celebration?'

'Oh, I reckon we deserve it!'

Again, he visited her room. Again nothing really happened. Again she felt like something had. Dirty. Used.

She could read it now. Every time they stopped at a pub for the night he would visit her. She wondered what excuse he made to Jasmine. Just going to check on her. Just getting some air. Just... This time he was different. This time she felt his hand push her face into her pillow. This time she heard his zip. This time he spread her legs and forced his way in. He grunted and thrust and tore. And she did nothing because there was nothing she could do.

'Hush now. Just our little secret.'

He kissed her head before he left.

*

That night she waited for the sounds of sleep to fill the air; soft snoring, heavy breath, mingled with the night noises. The soft lap of water. The creak of the boat, as if it were alive, breathing.

She stretched her fingers deep into the furthest corner under her bed and pulled out the bag of her old clothes. Dressed in what she had arrived in she felt stronger. A new layer settled upon her. Her choice. Her things. Jeans and a sweatshirt. Hers!

She stuffed her sleeping bag into a holdall, placed Tinker on top. He pawed at the soft material, curled up and settled down as if this were the most normal thing to be happening. *Good cat!* It would be a challenge to get through the barge and off it without making a sound. Without waking someone.

She knew the layout well enough now, but it was cramped, narrow. She had to remember where the table edged out, where the bench lingered, where the handle of the wood-burning stove jutted out, where the basket of wood sat, where the spare water container stood, where the flowerpot overflowed with trails and tangles of leaves.

It was about taking her time. Not panicking. Not rushing. A heavy stench of alcohol and weed hung in the air, stretched across the furniture, clung to the walls. That was good. A heavier sleep. A greater distance between them and her. Each step closer to escape. A creak. She froze. Closed her eyes. Held her breath. A soft mumble. A cough. She waited, minutes disguising themselves as hours, until finally the silence was heavy and deep and smothering once more.

The door. Nearly there. No wait! She could dip her hand in Jasmine's bag. There was money in there. Always money in there. It was so close, hanging on the hook next to the sink. Two steps back. No more. She hesitated. Stepped back. One. Two. Fumbled for the bag. One of those big, deep fabric ones. Patchwork. Hippie. All curled up and twisted. Where the hell was the opening? Her hands shaking. Her breath quickening. A pain screaming from deep inside her. *Bastard!* Okay. Got it. Fingers pushing through, down. The money-bag. Velvet. Tied up. She clasped her fingers around it. Inch by inch. Up and out. Almost a sigh of relief. Held back. Swallowed.

A knife. While she was here she should take a knife. She stretched out past the sink. The cold of the steel against her skin. A fumble. A clatter of steel on steel. *Fuck!* Freeze. Peel through the whispers of the night. Nothing. It was okay. Move. One. Two. The door again. Slip a jacket off the peg. It didn't matter whose. Not now. Just warmth. That was all she needed. A gentle push. A silent opening. No squeak. No betrayal. Slip through. Night air. Cold now. Winter calling.

She crept across the towpath towards the grassy verge. Paused. Crouched down. Glanced back. A shadow. His shadow.

'Going somewhere?'

She stood up, ready to take flight. Stumbled. A hand clasped her throat. She tried to wrestle free. Kicked at his shins, bit his hand. The taste of blood.

'Fucking bitch!' he spat. Lunged at her.

She ducked away. The water black and silent behind.

He lunged again. A grunt. A splash. Silence.

She didn't wait to see. Didn't dare. Didn't care. She ran, ducked through the trees and bushes, didn't pause to look back until she was sure that she had escaped. They had escaped. The sky above black. The earth black. Far in the distance ahead, a glow. A town. She had no idea of where she was, what part of the country. Nothing. Life had slipped by her. Her world that boat. Behind her she could see nothing but shadow now. Hear nothing but the wind in the trees. It didn't matter where she was going. Just away.

Chapter 51

Tommy vowed to keep moving. No more than seven suns in any one place. It made life more difficult, but it felt safer. To be moved on from a place of short-lived expectancy was not such a hardship. He set up his temporary camps in the shelter of trees, in a cave, hidden behind an outcrop of boulders, places that didn't belong. Places that were wild and desolate and unbound. So far he had been left undisturbed.

He had proven that he knew how to survive on his own well enough. No need for people, their ways, or their places. The one thing he was sure of, he would return to the land of the little beach by the river every summer when it was the time of the berries, when the air would be sweet with the scent of new life. He relished that time of year. The ease it brought to survival. A warmth in his bones. Food would be all around for him and his animals, the days long and gentle. Expectations high.

Later though. Later. For now he had to get through another winter, and it was so tiring like this. Always moving. No pattern. No routine. The fear that those men had settled on him wouldn't shift. Not just them. The men at Craigdour as well. As hard as he tried, even the wildness couldn't shift it. The whistle of the trees. The swoop of an eagle. The cawing of the crows. They brought a smile to his face. A whisper of joy. But crouching there in the depth, always that fear.

He hated them for it. It was a new thing. This hate. The men at the summer stopping-place. Now these men. How much had his family sheltered him from? Or was it just that his world had slipped? The tilt of its axis opening the door for evil. For hate. It was a dangerous intruder for him and he wanted it gone, but he didn't know how to do that.

He stood high on a snow-covered hill, the wind whipping at his face. His eyes squinting against it. Ahead, bare moorland. Open. Exposed. Nothing. To the east, pine forest. Ordered. Made by man. Dangerous. To the south, the hills rolling into something softer. Sheep. Farmland. People. Nothing for him but warning signs. Westward, patches of untamed, ancient forest held fast. Almost bare of leaves now but dense. Twists of trunks and branches. Hollows carved in the earth by beast and root and weather.

Tommy decided on the westward option. Ancient woodland. A wise old friend. There he found the right trees to make a new frame. The right places to forage. A burn churning through the peaty ground.

As he worked away more of that ancient story came to his mind. More of his da's words.

*

"Aye, when the men came on their horses wi their bits o paper that meant nothing but took everything, those that couldnae run or leave, for whatever reason, for sickness. for legs too old to bear that, for a binding so tight to this

land that wouldnae break. They hid.

"They hid in hollows in the ground dug out far enough to hide a body or two. They hid as the cries grew distant. The hills grew quiet but for the shouts o the factor's men. 'Make sure every last one of them is gone!'

"Every building was set alight. Burned out. Everything. Centuries. Gone.

"The hills grew quiet. Too quiet. Like the very life had been sucked right out o them. Like the place they had loved as a daughter had turned dirty and wicked and evil. They hid out in their hollows. Sickness, hunger and cold hiding wi them. Awfie bedfellows. They watched as their flesh crawled back into their bones; as their skin lay like paper covering the dead.

"Now the following spring our Mary came back. Her and her family. Of course they had seen it the year afore. Other Tinkers had told their stories too. Nothing left in the wee places that used to hold lives. Mary wanted to see it for herself though. What had become of it. To make sure that there really was nothing; there was no one left. More important to her, no one had returned. For there was always that hope.

"That chance.

"Her Jack.

"He was a good man, see? A strong man. If anyone could make it back it would be him. And she wasnae one to be ignored. Naw! No our Mary.

"But oh how she cried when she saw it all. 'What have they done?' But there was a feeling. Like they were being watched. Eyes on them. They searched, though it was hard. That smell o death and hurt. Aye, it was everywhere.

237

But there, in amongst the trees, in a wee cavern they'd dug out for themselves, there was an auld man and woman, clinging to each other, looking like death, but hanging on. God alone knows how, but they had clung on. It wasnae their time, see? It wasnae their time."

Chapter 52

Dougie walked up the hill from the river, his eyes drifting across to the decimation that stood on the hill opposite. Trees cleared half way up the hill. A landscape that already looked alien, but would seem more-so by the time they had finished. He had already raised objections to the creation of yet another grouse moor. Ignored. Objection to the impact on his employer's land. Ignored. The laird had already tried and failed. He knew that his voice was less powerful, would have little effect, but he had to do his best. Fight on. It infuriated him. This situation cut him as if he'd been struck by a knife. The place ran through his veins. He loved it and it was disappearing. The least he could do was put up a fight. Any fight.

He went back to his cottage, cleaned himself up. A quick shave, a comb through his hair. Grey creeping through the brown. A splash of aftershave – the good stuff that had sat there for years. He slipped his one and only white shirt on and tucked it into clean jeans. No tie. That would be too much. Too unnatural. His tweed jacket – given to him by the laird many moons ago and seldom worn, but appreciated nevertheless – finished the look. He checked himself in the mirror. Nodded at his reflection. Smart but casual. Serious but friendly. That was what he was going for.

He called Gypsy into the jeep and the dog gleefully took his place on the passenger seat. Eyes alert as they headed into town.

He would speak to them face to face. Hold their eyes with his. Tell them what he saw. But there was no getting past even a secretary.

'I'm sorry, sir. You have to make an appointment.'

'Aye. I've tried that too. None to be had. Look, all I need is a few minutes. Just to explain.'

'I'm sorry.' She shook her head, smiled so falsely, so weakly, that it wasn't a smile at all.

He could feel anger burning its way up from his gut. Losing his temper would do no good. He knew that, but God how he wanted to shout. To tell them they were all bloody fools. He leaned the flat of his hand against the counter, leaned in close

'Do you not even care?' he whispered.

'Sir!'

'I guess not.'

He turned and left.

'Right Gyp lad, let's try the town records.'

Gypsy wagged his tail, stared out of the windscreen as if he understood.

He took Gypsy in with him, walking through the doors with a smile on his face and carrying a sense of entitlement. The receptionist smiled, leaned across, patted Gypsy.

'The plans for Durnoch and?'

'Craigdour.'

'Right. Just you wait there and I'll see what I can do for you.' She grinned, stroked Gypsy again, before disappearing into the office behind her.

'I should take you to meet officialdom more often Gyp, my lad.'

He spread the plans out on the table, traced his finger along the boundaries. 'Well, well, well,' he whispered.

'I hate to ask, but can you make copies of these for me?'

'That would be my pleasure! I'll have to charge you though. Is that okay?'

'Aye. Of course!'

He hurried back to Durnoch. 'You're not going to believe what I've just learned!'

'Come away in, man. Come away in!'

Chapter 53

Charlotte knew one thing. She wanted to travel north. It didn't matter how she got there, as long as she did. Durnoch. Her memory was patchy, people weren't showing themselves properly to her, but this place? This place held true and strong and she could feel it. Such a powerful calling.

The urgency to get as far away as possible kept her fighting against the fatigue that seemed to come in waves, wrapping itself around her, tangling her legs. A stumble, a pause to catch her breath, and she would feel okay again.

At last the blur of distant buildings began to take form. A motorway built on concrete stilts, streaked around the outskirts of whatever town this was. Loud and intrusive. She stared up. Who were they, these travellers? Where were they all going? So many lives. So disconnected. She ran under and kept running until it was a far-off hum.

She sat down under an oak tree, breathed, picked Tinker up and put him on the ground. He sniffed warily, picking his paws up high with each step. Hunkering down low at the swoop of a crow. A peculiar mewl. Wild. Hungry. Charlotte stroked him.

'We need to get some food, don't we?'

She checked the contents of Jasmine's purse. Coins! Nothing but a few measly coins! Disappointment slapped her. How were they going to survive now? She wanted to cry. Her eyes suddenly felt heavy and she could feel sleep creeping up on her. Not here. This was too open.

'Come on Tink, let's go.'

She smiled as he ran on ahead, halted at the tug of the lead, waited, and did it all again. Eventually he realised he should just walk. When they reached the town, pavements, roads, she picked him up and put him in the bag. Within seconds he had jumped out again.

She sighed.'Okay, you win.'

People would notice them now. A girl walking a cat. Did it matter? Would anyone even be looking for her? She doubted it. For now she needed sleep. A desolate car park. An abandoned car. She clambered in, curled up, tried to shut everything out.

*

Jasmine woke up with a feeling that something wasn't right. She stretched her hand out. No Bobby. She twisted her hungover body out of bed, pulled her kimono on, tied the belt, walked through to the kitchen, her head heavy. No one there. 'Bobby?' Her voice croaky and tired. Had they had a fight? No. She would remember. Blank spots were blank spots but fights always broke through. Maybe he had just got up early, gone to work on his plants, or the engine, or something.

Her head was thumping. 'Oh God, never again!'

She poured herself a glass of water, forced it down with a couple of Aspirin. Made a dash for the toilet. Tried to gather her thoughts. Gather herself. Force it back to last night. He had come to bed with her. Definitely. They had fucked so hard. No. It had all been good.

She checked in on Charlie. An empty bed. No cat. Her holdall gone. Her sleeping bag too. Up on deck. No one there. 'Bobby! Come on man, where are you?'

She stepped onto the towpath, eyes scanning. She screamed. Screamed and screamed like a mad woman. People from the neighbouring boats came running. Followed her stare. The body of Bobby trapped between the boat and the canal wall.

Chapter 54

Tommy lay in his bender, turning things over in his mind. The wind was whistling at him, tugging at the canvas. The horses were restless, unsettled. This had been a bad idea. The exposure. The trees were offering scant shelter. He chastised himself. Lack of thought. Lack of awareness. If they were to survive through the winter it wouldn't do. Annoyed at himself he packed up and moved on.

Over the next hill he came upon forested land. Row upon row of pine trees. Perhaps there would be a hut like the one old Sandy had been in. That would do just fine. He kept his eyes peeled, remembering just how well camouflaged the last hut had been, staring beyond trunks, through pine needles. He followed the tracks made by machines, rutted muddy trails churned deep by heavy tyres, before veering off onto a smaller, quieter track. With each heavy footstep he cursed himself for his poor decision making.

Yes, he had been lost, and scared, and the world had seemed so black, so forbidding. But if he had managed to make his way back to land he knew, land his family had stopped on, he would be fine. The old crofter would have welcomed him back, invited him in for a blether and a cup of tea. He would have found safety at the abandoned village, their lochan. Their stopping-place. But it would also have meant confronting the past. Admitting it all to the old man, to himself. It would have been the right thing to do if he had been someone else, been stronger. A better man.

He turned off the track and deeper into the rows of trees. Row upon row upon row. Nature, but not as nature intended. Crows and rooks and jackdaws swirled and cawed overhead. He stopped and watched their black shadows flying across the darkening sky, flitting from tree to tree. He listened to the caws and the shrieks and the beat of wing, the flutter of feather. At least there was that. Some wildness.

He drew his attention back to the ground, the way ahead. Light was disappearing. The sky slipping into navy-blue with swirls of black where the clouds were massing, swelling. They held something. Rain or snow. As the forest succumbed to darkness he had to stop, shelter or not. He tied his horses to one of the trees.

'We'll settle soon enough, just bide here for the night,' he said, stroking their necks, patting their backs. 'Aye, soon enough.'

He set his frame, cast his canvas over it, crawled in. Rona barked and scratched at the ground outside, digging and spinning. 'Calm down you. In you come now.' She stared, cocked her head, accepted defeat – he wasn't going to play with her – and crawled in beside her master. She curled at his head with a sigh. A simple thing that held him together, softened the world. 'Good girl,' he whispered.

In the morning he moved off again. With each day that passed he felt more secure here. No vehicle had been heard, no person sighted. Perhaps these forests were left untended for winter. Yes, that would be it. But still there was no decent shelter.

The rows of pine had switched back to oak and rowan and ash. No path to follow. He preferred it like this, albeit an easier place to get lost in, it was also more difficult to be found. The trees were bare, but dense. Tangles of thick ivy snaked over everything making the going difficult, the way slow, but safe. Heavy stones made him stumble.

'You wait here now,' he said to the horses, calling Rona to his heels.

He pulled the ivy aside. More. A peculiarly green scent of life, but musty, as if nothing had disturbed it for many a year. All around the rest of the plant life had died back, sleeping through the long cold months ahead. More rocks revealed themselves, this time holding shape. A wall, thick with spider's webs. Dead insects. A scurry underfoot. A bark from Rona.

'You stay by me. No time for that yet.'

Reluctantly she obeyed. They clambered over the wall. An old abandoned house stood there, completely hidden from view. A square of garden heavy with tall grass that had turned to hay, most of it flattened by the weather. More garden to the side, too overgrown to explore for now.

A sagging slate roof, once grey, now green. Windows of broken glass. An old wooden door, still standing; still holding true. He walked slowly through, senses on high alert. Inside the floorboards creaked and groaned as if protesting at his interference.

He stood quietly looking around, listening, breathing the place in. No threat to be felt. Nothing from Rona either as she happily trotted through, sniffing at all of the new smells. At the back of the house there was a kitchen. An ancient iron stove with a metal pan still sitting there, cobwebs securing it in place. Trails of mice droppings. A square sink. He turned the tap more out of curiosity than expectation. A gurgle from somewhere deep. A trickle of brown water, the smell of something fetid, rust, unpleasant, then clear. Clear water! That was something.

Here the window still held glass, the covering of dust on the inside and dirt on the outside so heavy that it couldn't be seen through. He rubbed at it with his sleeve. Another garden that had once been cultivated. Some old apple trees. Cabbage grown as tall as a man. Wild and sprouted but surely edible. What he thought was onion of some kind. Herbs perhaps. This was too good to be true.

He pushed at the walls, the ceiling, checking that they were safe. They held.

'Right, let's get the horses in, aye?'

Chapter 55

Dougie could simply have marched across and started building a fence, but there was so much more satisfaction in going up to Craigdour with the laird, showing them the maps. The legal boundaries. The letter lodged in 1835 explaining the permission for Craigdour to use the meadow by the river. They had been friends. The two estates worked closely together. The river just seemed like a natural boundary. But it wasn't the legal one.

A fire could have been lit by the flaming face of the factor. 'I'll see you in court!'

'On you go, old fellow. All been checked. All legally binding, but be my guest.'

'Arsehole!'

'Oh my dear man, there's no need for that now, is there!' He turned to Dougie, a twinkle in his eyes. 'Breeding. It always comes out in the end. Chap obviously has none!'

Dougie laughed.

Chapter 56

Charlotte woke with a start. Someone was prodding her with a stick. Shouting at her.

'My place! Get the fuck out of my place!' A child's voice. 'Out! You deaf or something?'

The stick clattered around the empty space where the car's window had once stood, spooking Tinker. The tug of his lead on Charlotte's wrist. She lunged for him. Pulled him close.

'What you got? What you hiding there, all sneaky like?' The child flicked a lighter on. Held it at arm's length. Stared.

Charlotte backed away, squeezing as far as she could into the corner of the back seat. Slashes in the upholstery. Empty takeaway containers, juice cartons, an old plastic cider bottle. A stale smell. Not nice to breathe. She had been so tired when she had crawled in here she hadn't even noticed. It had just seemed safe, quiet, abandoned in the disused car-park of a derelict block of flats. Nothing but emptiness all around.

'A cat! Got your tongue, has it?' The child giggled. 'Get it?' Giggled again. 'Ouch!' Burned fingers. She dropped the lighter. 'Shit!'

Charlotte couldn't make out whether it was a boy or a girl. An androgynous look. Really young. Maybe eight or nine. Too young to be out here on their own at night. Hair unkempt. Hacked at. Spiky. Trying hard to be punk, but failing. Instead looking sad and forgotten. Maybe there were others. Maybe she was about to be set upon by some gang. A Fagin type.

The child tugged the door open – a rusty squeal and squeak that crawled uncomfortably across skin like nails on a chalk board – clambered in. Fumbled around on the floor for the lighter. Found it. Flicked it on again. Held it close to Charlotte's face. Stared. Poked and prodded at Tinker's neck. He hissed, spat, swiped his claws.

'Best watch it. There's folk here would skin it and eat it as soon as look at it, so they would.' The child turned and spat out of the open door. 'So, you moving, or what? Fuck's sake. Need my kip, so I do. Like I said. My place!'

'I'm sorry,' Charlotte whispered. 'I didn't know.' Words felt and sounded peculiar. Words that she was making and sending to another human.

'What you got in that there bag? Might make a deal. Let you stay the night.'

'Nothing.' Charlotte tightened her hold on the bag, clenched her fingers around the handle, pulled it tightly to her chest.

'Nothing is it? Let's see what nothing looks like then. Fucking lighter!' An exaggerated blow on singed fingers. 'Should be a candle. Right there, behind you.'

Charlotte turned, felt behind her. No candle.

'Not there! Up on the shelf thingy. Proper behind you.

251

Jeez!'

Charlotte loosened her grip slightly as she stretched across to the shelf. The bag was snatched away before she could react.

'Not been on the streets long then? Don't see you lasting much longer. Gotta wisen up girl. Wisen up.'

The purse. All that she had. Little though it was, it would have fed her for a few days. Some respite. Some safety net.

The child reached through to the glove compartment. Lit a candle. Grinned at Charlotte. Rummaged through her bag. 'Well, looky here!' Pulled out the purse with a smile and a triumphant expression. 'The purse? Nothing dodgy? Needles and drugs and shit?'

'I...I honestly don't know. It's not mine.'

'Stole it eh?'

'Not really. Sort of. It was my mother's. I felt like I deserved it.'

The purse was untied, tipped upside down, the coins spilling on to the seat. 'That it then? That all you've got?'

'I guess so.'

'Well, you're a right waste of space.'

The coins were gathered, slipped into a pocket in her hoodie with an exaggerated *pff* of distaste. The purse was unceremoniously thrown back at Charlotte.

'Budge over or move on. Your choice. I'm going to sleep. And if you're staying you share that sleeping bag. Cold as anything, so it is!'

Charlotte didn't know what to do. But she was tired and despite the attempt at bravado, the child didn't seem to be much of a threat. She didn't know anything about

252

life on the streets but imagined any backup would have shown themselves by now. Just as she began to feel okay with this. A noise. Reverberations of heavy footfall. The beam of a powerful torch.

'Fucking pigs! Shit!' the child whispered, tugging Charlotte down onto the floor of the car, pulling the sleeping bag over them. Tossing some of the rubbish on top. 'Don't move! Don't breathe.'

The stench. Thick dirty air that was hard to inhale. Hard not to retch at.

A beam of light swept across the concrete, picked out the car. Held it. Footsteps right up close now. A pause as the light caught the interior, swept over them.

'Nothing here.'

They waited as the footsteps slipped away again. Waited some more until they couldn't hear anything.

'They looking for you?' the child asked.

'Maybe. I don't know.'

'You done something?'

'Maybe.'

'What? You don't know I s'pose.'

Charlotte pulled a grimace. Shrugged. 'How about you? Are they after you?'

'Maybe.'

They both laughed, just quietly, carefully, but it felt very good.

'Right then. Sleep now. They ain't coming back.'

'I don't think I can.'

'Well, you can't go out there. Girl with a cat walking about in the middle of the night. Make folk notice for sure. In the daytime? Maybe not. Well, actually, yeah, but

253

maybe not so much.'

'I don't know your name.'

'Cos I ain't told you. Best keep it that way.'

Despite her heart pumping too fast and her thoughts zipping around and this being something that should set her on edge, she felt safer than she had for a very long time. She slept.

'Ew. That's vicious. Your cat's only gone and taken a shit.'

'Oh, sorry, Tinker.'

'Sorry Tinker? How about sorry Em?'

Charlotte laughed softly. 'So, is that Em for Emily?'

Em looked horrified, sighed. 'Nope. Em for mind your own business. Jeez!'

In the light of day it seemed that Em was a girl. Her dark eyes, sunken into pale, pallid skin, looked too big for her face. One of her teeth was chipped, her cupid bow mouth swollen and split above where the damaged tooth sat.

'What you staring at?'

'Nothing. Sorry, it looks sore. Your lip.'

Em shrugged. 'Ain't nothing. Should see the other guy!' She stretched as she stepped out onto the tarmac. Put her hands on her hips, breathed in the morning air. 'That's better. Stinky little cat!'

Em was heading for a McDonald's, its arches shouting its presence from not too far in the distance. 'Best place for a free scran,' she called over her shoulder. 'You coming or what?'

'I...I guess.'

Em hovered behind a hedge as she scoured the tables

outside. She watched a family stand up, leaving the remains of a Happy Meal in their wake. She sat down and started eating. 'Hungry? Still warm.'

'No, you're all right.[1]

Em shrugged. 'Your loss.'

The speed with which she shovelled the food into her mouth made Charlotte wonder when she had last eaten. She felt uncomfortable with all of this.

'Right, um. I'll be off then.'

Em stuffed the remains of the burger into her mouth. Scooped up the last handful of fries, ketchup dripping from them. Trailed behind Charlotte. 'Can't be sharing my space and just leaving. Rules of the street, you know. Where you going, anyway?'

'North.'

'Right, north's good. I like north, me.'

Chapter 57

Dougie had become unusually restless. He wanted a barrier of some sort secure and ready. More of the forest in Craigdour was being cleared. More burning. More wildlife in distress. A fence would keep his side safe, but what of the others? It broke his heart to imagine the flight of panicked deer being blocked by him and his actions. No. He had a better idea.

He put his suggestion to the laird. Wait until Craigdour had cleared further uphill. Until those that needed to flee had done so. Then the fence. Then the creation of a new native woodland. Something wild. Something to make a dent in the damage done. It couldn't be replaced, a forest like that, but something new could be begun. Something good.

'Dougie, my man, I have the utmost faith in whatever it is you decide to do. Treat the place as if it were yours.'

'That's appreciated. Thank you.'

'I have been meaning to have a proper chat with you anyway. Serious business. Man to man.' He winked, slapped Dougie on the back, ushered him in.

'Katherine, be an angel would you? A couple of glasses

of the good stuff.'

Katherine smiled. 'Dougie. Always a pleasure.' She walked over to her husband, squeezed his hand. 'So this is the great reckoning, is it?'

'Yes, my dear. I believe that now is the time.'

Dougie swallowed hard. He sat in the old leather Chesterfield, remembering many a pleasant evening spent here. He had been so lucky to be taken on all those years ago. Sixteen and fresh out of school. He had come up here with a couple of mates and a tent. No plan, just a bit of a laugh and an escape from gloomy grey tenements.

They had left Edinburgh on the ten o'clock train and an hour and a bit later stepped out into a different world. They had explored for a week, moving a bit further north each day. A bit further away from their reality. On what should have been their last day they were in the village. A wee shop with a sign in its window. Seasonal workers required. And just like that Dougie's life changed. His friends were heading back. He wasn't.

'Are you sure about this, Dougie mate?'

'Aye. Aye, I am.'

His love for the place was apparent and when the season ended he was offered full-time work. Labouring to begin with, a farmhand, then assistant groundsman. Finally he had no boss other than the laird himself. The job came with its own cottage. Life had turned into something quite wonderful.

The estate was magnificent and to work here was privilege enough, but to have an employer like this. Friends, despite their hugely differing situations, disparate backgrounds. He knew that few were as lucky as him and it would break his heart to lose any of it. Of course the laird and his wife were old. It would all have to come to an end one day. But not now. Please, not now.

They sat quietly, a peculiar air had settled on the room. Dougie dreaded the words that he felt were coming. The clink of ice on crystal sounded sharp and loud as Katherine handed each man a glass and sat next to her husband, cradling one of her own. She smiled, first at her husband, then at Dougie.

'Right then! I...' The laird paused, swallowed hard. Took a deep breath.

Dougie felt his heart stutter.

'Well, the thing is, old chap, Katherine and I have decided that, well, our bodies, and indeed minds!' He chuckled at Katherine. 'They're not quite what they used to be. Not exactly up to par, one might say.'

Dougie's thoughts had already sunk into a very dark place. Where would he go? What would he do? Would the new owners allow him to stay on? If so, he doubted it would be in the same capacity. Some menial job probably. A move to another estate? Perhaps a gamekeeper, but that was so far from his planned future. So far from what he wanted to do with the rest of this life. He suddenly realised his thoughts had drifted off. Words were being said and he hadn't heard any of them.

'Dougie? I must say I was expecting a rather different reaction.'

'I'm sorry. What? I...I lost myself for a moment there.'

Katherine rose, walked across to the writing bureau, pulled the hidden drawer open, handed a large brown envelope to him. 'It's all in there,' she said, smiling.

'Sometimes the brain can't quite process things correctly until they are seen in black and white.' She patted Gypsy's head as she returned to sit beside her husband. Gypsy's tail swished in pleasure.

Dougie turned the envelope over and over again. His fingers trembled as he fumbled his way under the flap. A severance package? A reference? He stared at the papers lying on his lap.

'Well, read it man!'

As he read he let out a succession of peculiar sounds, more than sighs, less than screams. Gypsy was staring at him in concern. Katherine and the laird in expectation.

'I...what can I say? This is. This is so much more than generous.' He downed the rest of his whisky. Enjoyed the burn, the tingle.

'Another?'

'Aye. Aye, I reckon I need one or two to help this sink in.' He took a deep breath. 'So, what you're saying is that you're handing the running of all of this over to me until such time as you, ahem, die.'

He looked from one to the other, their smiles fixed, their fingers linked like two young lovers.

'And when that happens, you're leaving it all to me. The whole estate. Am I getting this right?'

'Indeed you are, my man. There really wasn't much discussion needed, was there?'

Katherine shook her head. 'Such an easy decision. We were never blessed with children, and, well, you're the closest thing we have. It makes absolute sense.'

'I can't. It's too much. Too generous.'

'Nonsense, man. Sign the damned papers and be done

259

with it! You're not leaving here until you do! Katherine, lock the doors, bar the windows.'

They laughed.

As Dougie signed he felt the weight of what had been placed on his shoulders. But what a magnificent weight!

Chapter 58

There was an upstairs too. Tommy stood at the bottom of the steps. Looked up. Decided against it. What he had down here was more than enough. He thought the kitchen would be best for his living quarters. It would be easiest to keep warm when necessary and there was the back door to open wide when he needed the air, the wind, the sounds of the outside.

His horses were happily nibbling on the grass in the back garden as he and Rona set off to gather small branches of pine and spruce to use as a mattress. A bit of insulation between his bones and the cold, hard ground. He lay them on the kitchen floor, covered them with his one remaining blanket. Cursed at the loss of his rabbit pelts. They would manage though. He would gather and build and make himself and his animals safe and warm enough to get through another winter. Before he settled down he jammed the back door open to keep that connection. To bring the fresh air into the staleness. To feel safe.

He woke to the early morning. Pale light. The hint of a sunrise breaking through grey cloud. Something was wrong. Noises. Upstairs. He focussed. This couldn't be. There was no way another human being had set foot in this place for a very long time. You could tell such things. Feel them.

He looked around for Rona. A panic. She was always there. Wee Rona was always there! He whispered her name. Nothing. Called her. The click-clack of her paws trotting across the concrete of the kitchen floor. Relief. It had just been Rona snuffling around.

'What have you been up to, wee one?'

She wagged her tail at him.

But there was still a sound coming from upstairs. Something he couldn't identify. A dragging, scratching sound. He didn't like this one bit. If he had been outside in his tent he would know, but here in a house, a place such as this, a place of strangeness, that was a different thing altogether.

He peered out of the back door, checked on his horses. Both there. Both fine. He was about to go back inside, confront whatever or whoever was there, then he remembered old Sandy and his branch held high in defence, or attack, and the terror that it had sent through him. An old man like that who had lived his whole life with nothing and no one. He knew how to survive. Tommy would copy.

He found a piece of tree lying, dead, across the wall of the garden. He tugged at it, pulled it free of the ivy that bound it, jumped on it. A loud crack echoed through the air, off into the trees, the forest. He grabbed a piece that was about half the size of him and returned to the house. Rona was barking, but softly, like she wasn't too alarmed, just warning of something not normal.

'Hush now.'

Should he tiptoe or be bold and noisy? He decided on the latter and strode across the kitchen, the creaking floorboards of the sitting room. The stairs rose from behind a door which sat ajar. Now he was more careful, testing each step before putting his full weight on it. He had never set foot on a staircase like this before. Not in a house. A scaldie house.

The darkness of the stairwell was now broken by a shaft of sunlight. Dust motes drifting. Around a corner. Three doors. Two closed, one open. He decided on the open one. Stepped in, branch held high above his head. A smell. Something living. Something wild. He relaxed. The flap of wing. A screech of fear.

'What have we got here then?' He edged closer, crouched lower. 'It's all right. I'll not harm you. It's all right.' He sat down in the middle of the room. 'You too wee one,' he whispered to Rona, pointed to the floor. She sat, confused. This wasn't prey. More likely she was. She shuffled towards her master on her stomach and attached herself to his thigh. And they waited.

The bird screeched and flapped some more, then settled down.

'That's it. That's it.'

As the sun rose higher, pushing more clouds aside, a shaft of light stroked the floor, stretching across to the corner of the room. There, huddled, staring, he could clearly make out a buzzard, one wing limp, trailing, its eyes wide in fear, its beak open. Perhaps it had sought shelter here after injuring itself. Perhaps it was the building that had caused the injury. Whatever, the beast needed feeding.

They backed out quietly and retreated down the stairs. 'Right, wee one. Something for the pot.'

She knew full well what that meant and was off streaking into the woods, snuffling and yelping. Her return was quick. The limp body of a rabbit dangling from clenched jaws.

'Drop. Good girl. Now away and get some more. Something for the pot!'

A second hunt wasn't the norm but she didn't care. It was a source of great joy for her, bettered only by her master's praise.

Tommy crept back upstairs, slow and steady. He sat again, not looking at the buzzard, not threatening it, and slid the rabbit across the floor. The bird didn't hesitate, her hunger greater than her fear of this human. He waited until he heard Rona return before leaving the bird in peace.

Days were spent going through the garden, pulling grass to dry inside for the coming snows, for come they would. He harvested what food he needed for himself, leaving what he knew would survive through the frost and the snow. He visited the buzzard regularly through the day so that she would get used to him. Trust him. He wanted to get close enough to check on that injury. It might be something he could fix. Something stuck. A piece of wire. A splinter of wood, or even glass.

The joy he felt when she finally allowed him to reach out and touch her. A stroke of the head. Just lightly. Just for a second. But it was so special. Soon he reached for her back, slowly, slowly. Her beak was a weapon, as were her talons. She could turn and rip his flesh in an instant. He kept those thoughts away thinking only of help, of care.

After a week she had hopped across to him, pecked at the food on offer, stayed close by as she ate. Once finished she stayed there by his side.

'Look at you, my beauty. Aren't you just something.'

He reached out, stroked her back, let his fingers linger over the damaged wing. She turned her head. Stared at his hand. No peck. No attack. Just watching.

'Aye, I'm just helping you. Just helping you, is all.'

There, wrapped around her wing where it met her body, a length of fishing line.

'Now we need to get that off of you. You just hold still now. Hold still.'

He reached for his pocket-knife and slipped it, slowly, slowly, in between line and feather and snipped. And again. And again. She was free of it and his hand was still in one piece!

'We'll soon have you right as rain.'

His heart swelled with the success of this, with the connection he had made.

Chapter 59

Charlotte had no intention of pairing up with Em, with anyone, but the girl was relentless. She had tried to say goodbye at McDonald's, again as they walked along busier streets, the feel of a town centre drawing close. A crossroads.

'Right, I'm going this way. Bye.'

But Em wasn't having any of it. When Charlotte picked up her pace, Em ran to catch up, tugged at her jacket to pull her back. All the while chattering away.

'So, what you on the run from? Law, is it? Done something bad? Shitty parents? A lot of us had shitty parents. A lot of us on the run from the law too. Filthy pigs! Nothing better to do than make trouble for us. There's bad stuff going on out there. Really bad people doing really bad stuff and they come after us. Tch!'

'And you? How come you ended up like this?'

'Oh right. Think I'll fall for that? Turn it round on me? Huh! Come on. Spill!'

Charlotte sighed. 'Yes. Shitty parents.'

She felt bad saying it. Parents meant her dad as well, and there was nothing shitty about him. A sudden flashback to that night. To that feeling. She closed her eyes. Tossed it away. No point now. No point at all.

'Thought so.'

'What?'

'Shitty parents!'

'Oh, right. Yes.'

'So did you kill them then? They were so mean and cruel and horrible that you killed them.'

'No! No, of course not!'

'Wouldn't blame you. Know someone that did. Poison. It's true. Poisoned her parents. The both of them. Just like that. Dead! Said it was the best thing she'd ever done. Said it made her feel right good.'

'You talk a lot, don't you?'

'Dunno. S'pose. Got a problem, like?'

'Maybe.'

'For real?'

'Yes. It's a bad idea. You and me.'

Em's shoulders dropped, a deep sigh escaped. She started to cry. Dropped back a pace or two.

Charlotte didn't really know what to do. This is what she'd been wanting from when they woke up this morning. To be left alone. A kid like Em tagging along could only cause problems, slow her down, get her noticed. She didn't know if she could cope with this. With her. Something tugged at her. She stopped, looked back.

'Look, I'm sorry, okay? Just...just pipe down a bit, all right?'

Em dashed forward. Took Charlotte's hand. Thought better of it. Held onto her sleeve instead. Kept her face to the ground. They walked on in silence until they reached the city centre. Em stopped, tugged at Charlotte's sleeve.

'It's you! Look!'

A photo of her stared out of a television set in the window of an electronics store. A news story. Next a photo of Bobby; a dead body lying by the canal. *Police appealing for witnesses in local death* scrolled along the bottom of the screen. *Search for missing teenager* followed.

Em gawped, a soft whistle. 'You did! You only went and killed him. Ha!'

Charlotte pulled her away. 'Shut up. I did no such thing. We had a fight, all right? Just a fight.'

She glanced around. Had anyone noticed? A man and a woman, arm in arm, looking in the window. *Shit!* She turned her back to them. People everywhere. Her heart thumping. Mouth dry.

'And now he's dead, and the police are after you, and you're a real live criminal, and you're my friend!'

She dragged Em on. Pulled her close. Whispered. 'Not if you don't shut up, I'm not!'

She slipped up a side-alley, strode on. Em running to keep pace.

'How well do you know this place?'

'Really super well!'

'We need to get out of here. To leave. Get far away. Can you do that? Get us far away?'

'Course I can! Like a magician, me. When I need to be.' She grinned.

Charlotte imagined her face staring out of TV screens all over the place. In people's front rooms. In their bedrooms. In shops. In bars. People looking for her. Police

268

looking for her. And Bobby dead. Did she do that? Cause that? Did she kill him? No time to think back on it. To do anything apart from get the hell away.

At least there was no mention of Em. Of course there wasn't. Why would there be? She had slipped from being a liability to a godsend.

Em had been true to her word. She led the way through side-streets and alleyways, housing schemes and affluent detached houses with sweeping gardens and high walls.

'Robbed that one once,' she declared proudly, nodding towards a sprawling white property sitting on the edge of town. 'Not inside, like. Just the greenhouse, but still! Were a laugh, weren't it. Me living off of fruits and vegetables for a few days. Body didn't know what was going on. Had the skitters something awful.' She laughed, nudged Charlotte. 'Know my way around. You hungry?'

'Yes, but not so much that I'd go to jail for it.'

'Chicken!'

'Law-abiding!'

'Oh right. Picture on the telly. The pigs after you. That kind of law-ab...whatever. That thing you said.'

'Abiding.'

'Yeah, that. Getting dark. Wait a bit. Sneak in. Fill your bag. Sneak out. Easy peasy! Might even get a fish from the pond for little cat-face.' She reached down, stroked Tinker's head, enjoyed the purr in return. 'See, cat likes the idea. Ain't that right, Kitty-cat?'

'I don't know.'

'Aw, come on. They won't even know we paid them a visit.'

They walked around nearby but not too close, until it

was dark, so intent on keeping an eye on the seemingly empty house that Em bumped into a woman.

'Sorry missus!' Em called.

'No harm done,' the woman replied, although her scowl said otherwise. She unlocked her car, climbed in, and drove off.

Once the sound of the engine had slipped into the night, all was quiet again. Eyes trained on the target house. No cars pulled in, no lights flicked on. Promising.

'Right. Super quiet now,' Em whispered, pulling her finger to her lips.

Charlotte held back. 'Look, I'm not okay with this. I'll wait here. Be look-out.'

'Chicken!'

Em leaned against the gate, slipped her hand through the wrought-iron flowers, felt the latch, took a deep breath, pressed the latch down. The gate swung open. Not a creak, not a clunk. She turned and grinned at Charlotte before running in. Charlotte scanned the street. Quiet. Looked back to see Em bent over, keeping as low to the ground as she could.

A gravel track led to the back of the property. Impossible to keep quiet on that. The sound of Em's steps bouncing back at her filled the cold night air. The bark of a dog. Loud, fierce, alarmed.

'Fuck!' Em whispered. 'Dog! That's new.'

A light cascaded out of the windows. She froze, eyes wide.

'Run!' Charlotte called, louder than she had meant to; louder than she should have.

Em bolted back along the track, across the lawn, and

out. She grabbed Charlotte's hand and they ran, not slowing until they had left the city limits what felt like a safe distance behind them.

'Any more bright ideas?'

'Least I had one. Not so much from you!'

'Look, shouldn't you go back? I mean back there is where you belong. Not tagging along with me.'

Em hung back again, started to cry again, the figure of Charlotte walking away blurring through her tears. She dried her face with her sleeve, sniffed, ran after Charlotte. She caught up. Stayed just behind.

'Please? Hate it there. It's all really, really shitty and scary and I don't...I don't want it no more.'

Charlotte slipped Tinker out from under her jacket and set him on the ground. He sniffed and mewled. Unsure.

Em reached her hand out. Tinker nudged it, rubbed against her arm, her legs. Purred. 'See? Kitty-cat wants me to come. We're super friends, ain't that right Kitty-cat?'

Charlotte shook her head. 'His name's Tinker. He's my cat.' She held the lead out. 'You can walk him for a bit though. Keep your hand tight through the loop and no messing about, okay?'

'Okay, okay, okay. Promise!'

They walked along the kerbside, stepping back into the grass and ducking down at the sound of any approaching vehicles. The odd car, a truck or two. Hardly anything.

'Any idea where we are? Where we're heading?'

'Uh-uh. Only know the city. This place? Dunno. Some countryside place.'

'Right, so you're useless then?'

'Nu-uh. Can still do stuff, like, like got your back. And!' She grinned.

'And what?'

She pulled a purse out of the pocket of her hoodie, held it up high.

'Where did you get that from?'

'That woman. Back there.'

'The one you bumped in to?'

'Yep!'

'So that was all an act?'

'Yep!'

'Unbelievable! And you didn't think to tell me before. I mean, she could have called the police on us.'

'But she didn't. And...' She undid the zip. A decent wad of notes. She whistled. 'Looky here!'

Charlotte snatched the purse, wiped it clean, tossed it far into the trees. She shook her head and held her hand out. 'Money,' she demanded.

'Uh-uh. Mine.'

'Give me the money or I leave you. Got it?'

'So unfair. You're just mean.'

'Really?'

'No. Just.' She sighed. 'Go and let me keep a bit. For emergencies, like?'

'Okay, okay.'

'Should've taken the cards too. Rich folk like that. Loads of cards and stuff. Could've bought new stuff, nice stuff. Loads of it.'

'Could end up in jail. Years of it.'

Em laughed. Charlotte shook her head.

The heavier night fell, the quieter it became until it felt

like it was just them in this world. Charlotte had taken Tinker back and he slept happily in the warmth of her body.

Strange noises. The hoot of an owl, the rustle of its prey running for cover. A shriek that pierced the night.

Em grabbed on to Charlotte's sleeve. 'What's that? You hear it?'

'A night-caller. Nothing to worry about.'

'A night-caller. You what? Call that nothing. Fucking creepy, that is!'

'You'd better get used to it. Night-time will be our friend for a good while.'

'You're weird!'

Chapter 60

PC Jamieson knocked on the door, checked his uniform, picked off a hair.

'Well?'

'They found the mother, sir. Nottinghamshire.'

'And?'

'Her partner died under suspicious circumstances.'

'And this was when?'

'A week past, sir.'

'The girl?'

'Ah, well, you see, sir, she's...' He looked at his feet, cleared his throat. 'She wasn't there.' He held his breath, glanced out of the window. Heavy grey skies. Roofs slick with rain. The last few leaves being torn from their branches, tossed along the empty streets. Bleakness everywhere.

The reply was almost whispered, which was far worse than a shout. 'Can this get any worse?'

'She's wanted. A witness, maybe a suspect. Anyway, APB's in all forces. An appeal's been made. Posters up.'

'And there's a reason why we weren't informed of all of this when it happened? Why we're the last to know? Do they even know that A is followed by B?'

Jamieson laughed nervously.

'That wasn't a joke, constable. None of this is a bloody joke. We've got a damned murder to solve.'

'Yes, sir. Sorry sir. Sightings being called in.'

'Any of them any use whatsoever?'

'Perhaps. They were seen in the city, in Nottingham, by all accounts.'

'They?'

'According to some of the calls she's travelling with a much younger child. Um, and a cat, sir.'

'Is that right?' His eyebrows raised, he looked skyward, blew out a long, slow breath.

Chapter 61

Tommy wasn't comfortable. The house felt hollow and wrong. It would be easier to keep a bender warm than this bleak place with its windows and doors and cracks and holes. He couldn't settle here at all. Further up the hill, deep in the trees, he had found an overhang of rock and hidden beneath it, a cave. It was just about the perfect size for his horses. Nature's stable. A place of shelter for them if the weather turned too wild.

A shelf of grassy land stood fifty metres or so further down the incline. Trees all around. A burn cascading to his left, steep hills to the right. The sound of water and wind and wildness. By early afternoon he had pitched his bender, small and compact, but big enough for him and Rona. He walked the horses around the new territory, showing them their boundaries. Helping them settle.

The last thing to do was bring the buzzard. She couldn't fly yet and would no doubt die soon enough left to her own devices. He pondered leaving her in the house and going in every day to feed her and sit with her, but he was quite sure that that place must feel as alien and uncomfortable to her as it did to him. No, he would bring her to his new camp. He created another shelter for her made of pine branches and bracken, moss and twigs. It was secured into the ground next to his tent and held steady with rocks.

As he walked in through the back door of the abandoned house he was relieved that it would be for the last time. He climbed the stairs, walked in to the bird's room and was met with a squawk as she hopped towards him. He smiled.

'Right now, let's see, shall we? Tch tch, on you come.'

He covered his right arm with a piece of folded canvas, held it out towards her, his other hand dangling some fresh rabbit meat above it.

'Come on now.'

She cocked her head from side to side, skipped a little bit closer, cocked her head again, stretched her neck forward. He moved the meat further up his arm. She paused, stared and jumped up. It was the hardest thing not to react, not to celebrate. He did so inside.

He stood up, slowly, slowly, and moved towards the door. She stayed put. Down the stairs, into the kitchen. Another piece of meat. Out into the woods. Did she know that she couldn't fly? Did she understand? He held his arm as still as he could, the weight of her and the awkward angle making it difficult. Rona was at his feet, her eyes fixed on the bird, until a smell took her and she was off. As they twisted through the trees he could feel her talons tighten. At last, their camp. It wasn't far at all, but the worry, the care required, had made their journey seem so much longer.

He sat down on the grass. Still she clung on tight,

taking it all in, looking around.

'You can go for a wee wander.'

He reached into his pocket and pulled another piece of meat out, threw it to the ground just in front of the entrance to her shelter.

'On you go, now.'

She paused, looked from the meat to Tommy and back again.

'Go!'

And she jumped off. Titbits trailed into the shelter itself and by nightfall she was there, settling herself down in its cover. Tommy climbed into his tent with Rona and the world felt very good.

The bird's shrill cries woke him in the morning, pealing through the dawn. Tommy flicked the canvas open and there she was, standing staring, as if waiting for breakfast.

'Let's be giving you a name, aye? How about Mona? A bonnie name for a bonnie bird!'

He fed Rona first just so that she knew the pecking order here. Rona would always be boss. Mona second.

The days had shrunk right back and winter settled itself on them. Days of darkness. But still this all felt good and safe. The bender held against the fiercest of storms, the horses took their shelter in the cave, and Mona stayed. Her wing had healed up and she flapped it about as she strutted across the ground. A jump and a small flight. A few metres. Another day, another jump, a few metres more. Soon enough she was swirling above them in great joyous circles, mewing at Tommy far below. *Peeee-uu, Peeee-uu.* He had learned to imitate her call and replied.

Still she stayed close. Still she settled for the night in her shelter. He was sure that one day she would take off and fly far away. It would be a wonderful thing to see her free and wild again, doing what she was put here to do, but he would miss her. She had become a part of his family and he loved her as such.

He knew now that they would be safe here until spring arrived. She would announce herself with a new song. The birds, like him, heralding her arrival. The days would stretch along with the animals coming out of their winter resting places and life would become that bit easier. They would move on with the season, hunt, and forage, and feed on the new growth. Would Mona follow from the sky? He hoped so.

Chapter 62

Em and Charlotte had been walking all night. Soft hills and heavy forest caressed the road they followed. Em was dragging her feet, grumbling. 'Really, really tired. Could sleep...could sleep in that puddle right there.'

Charlotte laughed. 'I doubt that, but okay, it's probably best to stop and find somewhere to sleep.'

'What you thinking?'

'An old shed, a barn, something like that.'

'But we've got money. *My* money!'

'Right, your *stolen* money. And you think we should blow it all on a night in a hotel, or something, because, of course, they'd happily let us stay. Or we could be smart and keep it for food and important things like, oh, staying alive maybe.'

'Snarky when you're tired then?'

'Where are we anyway?'

'Told you. Dunno.'

'No, I mean whereabouts? North, south, east, west, kind of thing. What city was that we were in?'

'Wow! You just got out of a funny farm or something?'

Charlotte's stare said enough.

'Nottingham. Wicked Sheriff and Robin Hood and his merry men and stuff.'

'Oh right, that fits. You and your thieving.'

'Yeah. In my genes and stuff.' She laughed a soft easy laugh that made Charlotte think of just how young she probably was. Sad how life can force age on you when it really shouldn't.

They took a narrow turning through the trees. Tractor marks had gouged their way along the mud. With a bit of luck it would lead to somewhere they could rest. Shelter. Within a few minutes they had come upon a field dotted with small huts.

'Stinks! Christ! What is this place?'

'Countryside. Nature. Smells like a pig farm.'

'Smells like shit you mean!'

They walked through the snuffling and grunting of pigs. Beyond the field, a barn stacked high with bales of straw.

'Perfect.'

They pulled the door to behind them. A loud squeak, but they didn't think there would be anyone around to hear it. They clambered up, cleared a space and settled down. Tinker was sniffing at everything. Smells of mice and spiders and a host of other tasty cat-snacks. He miaowed as if asking to be let off the lead.

'Sorry Tinker. It's just not safe.'

'That's cruel. Poor little Kitty-cat. Probably starving hungry and there's all this food and you won't let him go catch any of it.'

'Maybe you're right. Okay Tinker.' She unclipped the lead. 'You stay close, now.'

'Cos Kitty-cat speaks, right?'

A shared quiet chuckle.

They huddled under the sleeping bag.

'Something's biting me!' Em grumbled. 'Creepy-crawlies all over me. Hate the country.'

Charlotte laughed. 'Says the girl who was living in a stinky car in a disused car-park.'

'Yeah, well, knew that stink. My stink! Wasn't crawling with disgusting crawly things that wanted my blood.'

'How did you end up there anyway? I mean, you're too young to be on the streets like that.'

'I'm fourteen!'

'No you're not.'

'Okay then, twelve!'

'Right, so, I'm going with ten, at a push. Like I said, too young.'

'Mum and Dad were junkies. Social services took me away. Foster mum was a bitch. Foster dad stuck his dick in me. I scarpered.'

'Oh Em, I'm sorry.'

'S'all right. Least I didn't kill him! Probs would have if I'd stayed, you know?'

'I didn't...it wasn't like that.'

'But he was a perv, right?'

'Yes. Yes he was.'

'And now he's dead.'

'Seems that way.'

'And you're a fugitive. And now I'm your accomplice, like Bonnie and Clyde, or the bold Robin and what's his name? Yeah, Friar whatshisname, or dunno who else, but we're a team. You and me. On the run from the pigs. Ha-ha...not those pigs out there. Uniform pigs. Police and dirty rotten bastard paedos and that's cool.'

'If you say so.'

'Just did!'

'Go to sleep will you?'

'Try.' She closed her eyes. Began to drift off with her thoughts. She shrieked. Laughed. 'Cat attack!'

Soon enough all three were curled up together. An island in a sea of straw.

Chapter 63

'Anything since that sighting in Nottingham?' DCI Graham asked.

'Nothing, sir.'

'Wonderful! So they've   just...' He stared at the window. 'Vanished.'

'Seems so, sir.'

'They can't have simply disappeared. Christ! Two girls, on their own just vanish?'

'Aye, well, it wouldn't be a first, now would it?'

He sighed. 'No, no it wouldn't. But really? These two girls?' He leaned back in his seat, scratched his head, swivelled, glanced out of the window. 'We're missing something here. Someone other than the daughter must have seen something. Heard something. It's a small place. Everyone knows everyone else, and yet we have nothing.'

'There's the neighbour.'

'Right. Right. Two shadowy figures...' He looked skyward, sighed. 'Go back there. Question her again. Question everyone again. The whole bloody village, and beyond.'

'Yes sir.'

'Migrant workers, Travellers, they come up here for seasonal work, no? Berry picking, or whatever it is they do. Did you check all of them?'

'Aye, well, we did our best, but you know what they're like. Thick as thieves, that lot, and working on the black. It's a devil to trace them all, let alone get anything from them.'

'Do we have any local sympathisers? Anyone who might be able to find a way in?'

'Well, there's the folk over at Craigdour. They've let them camp on their land for as long as I can remember. But they sold up last year. The new owners aren't sympathetic. Cleared the Tinkers off, so I heard. And there's Douglas Jamieson, manager over at Durnoch. He can be heard sticking up for them more often than not. Even married one, so they say.'

'And has he been questioned?'

'I, em, I assume so.'

He stared in disbelief. 'You assume? Get on it constable!'

Chapter 64

Tommy inhaled the weather. The snows had crept away, further up the mountains. The valleys and lowlands were bursting with signs of spring. Rivers in full spate, lochs deep and heavy. New life was unfurling all around. His senses were set alight by it all. The camp had been packed up, everything as it should be. He stood, hands on hips, looking all around. Remembering. This had been a special place. A safe place. He would return. Of that he was sure. There was almost a sadness to their leaving. Almost.

He mewed to Mona, her reply, almost instant, crackled through the hills. She swooped down and landed on his outstretched arm. They had practised this all winter and he had delighted in the speed of her learning, the consistency of her answer to his call. He had made rabbit pelt coverings for his arm, for his shoulder, to protect himself. One day she would find her lifelong mate and leave, for now though she was here and he rejoiced in it. He pointed to his shoulder and she jumped up. Him astride his horse, Rona on his knee, and Mona on his shoulder. What a thing. What a very fine thing.

As the hills softened and more buildings speckled the

land, a fresh swell of emotions surged through Tommy. The tallest was excitement. Each mile travelled drew him closer to the place of Charlotte and there was always that chance. He didn't know where she had gone, nor how long for. It might just be a settled-folk's thing that he didn't know about, and it might be over, and she might be there waiting for him this summer.

Sitting just below that was fear. He knew he had to be more careful now. Not just the usual apprehension that had always come along with strangers. No. Now they were dangerous. He had made enemies and he didn't know how deeply that sat. Who might be after him. His horses, so identifiable, so beautiful. He kept his senses even more highly alert than he used to. Every sight, every sound, every scent would be caught and made sense of. At least he knew this land, and it him.

As he travelled, niggling away, a constant gnawing worry. What might greet him when he finally made it back to that river? That forest? What might be facing it now? What devastation would those men have left? He didn't like such dark thoughts. Sitting brooding on something like that could never do anyone any good. He knew that. His family had taught him that. But as he drew closer he found it more and more difficult to fill his mind with something else. He wanted Charlotte and beauty and their own special wild places. There might be nothing.

Chapter 65

Trudging through the countryside had been slow and Em was struggling. Funny how the little nuisance had become something important. Someone to care about. Both were hungry, nature not offering anything at this time of year. Nothing left of their last venture into a shop. The hum of heavy traffic crawled through the air, not too far off.

'We might find a signpost. Make sure we're still heading in the right direction.'

'Yeah.'

'And maybe a service station? I doubt anyone would even notice us.'

Em laughed. 'You reckon? Bit of a state, like.'

Charlotte glanced over Em, over herself. 'Maybe, but we just need to nip in, buy what we need, nip out again. I doubt we're even news up here anyway.' She paused. Stared. 'Are you news? Is anyone looking for you?'

'Nu-uh. Not like they are for you. Kids like me go missing all the time and no one gives a shit. I mean, it's not like I've got Mummy and Daddy making appeals on the telly. For Social Services I'm just one less headache. I mean, it's not like I killed anyone.' She grinned up at

Charlotte.

Charlotte shook her head. 'Enough, all right?'

It was already dark by the time they reached a service station. They paused in the car park. Busy. That was probably good.

'Ready?'

'Course!'

'We go in. We buy what we agreed. We pay. We leave. No thieving, right?'

'Right.'

'Tell you what, you take Tinker. Keep him safe and you occupied.'

'What, don't trust me then?'

'Nope!'

A Christmas tree twinkled, lights and tinsel sparkled.

'You reckon it's Christmas?'

'There or thereabouts.'

'Never got a proper Christmas. You know, presents and stuff, and happy people like you see on the telly.'

Charlotte didn't reply, her thoughts ran back to last Christmas. A memory out of nowhere. Her dad and her in the snow, laughing and playing. Dragging the Christmas tree in – that smell – decorating it. The joy as the lights were switched on. Presents and far too much food. Martha there with them. Her dad winking at her. She was sure he had winked at her! "Well, we can't be leaving her on her own at Christmas," he'd said. Pictures flowed in a stream. Feelings. Words. No dismissal this time. She let them stay, play in her head, connect.

A tug at her sleeve. 'Earth to Charlotte, you still here?'

'Sorry Em. What were you saying?'

'Nothing.'

They picked up enough food for a few days. A big bag of dried cat food. A couple of *No Fear* baseball caps.

'Cool huh?' Em said with a grin, modelling hers.

A smile in return. 'Cool.'

Charlotte also picked up a pair of sunglasses.

'Why don't I get a pair then?'

'Because you'd look silly, and you don't need them, okay?'

'You're mean.'

'Uh-huh.'

She took a pair anyway, slipped skilfully, discreetly, up the sleeve of her hoodie. Sometimes wearing clothes that weren't yours, clothes that were far too big, had advantages. Thieving was one of them. The hoodie itself had been stolen, well, picked up really. It was just sitting there on the back of a bench, its owner too busy making out to notice. A slight of hand, a dip into the bushes. Done! Turns out it was a decent one too. Versace in gold letters on its front.

They found a quiet, dark corner outside, under the overhang of the roof, the soft glow of a string of red Christmas lights trailing around it the only illumination. A ledge just wide enough to perch on. People walked by but no one looked their way. They hoofed down chicken sandwiches, some chocolate milk and a slice of carrot cake and Tinker devoured his Go-Cat. It felt like they were invisible. The world beyond them something else. Somewhere else. They moved towards the roar of traffic, the slip-road, and read the signposts. THE NORTH.

'Okay. We go that way,' Charlotte said, walking away

from the motorway, heading towards the rear of the car park, the outline of trees beyond.

Em tugged at Charlotte's sleeve. 'Look. We could do that.' She was pointing at some hitch-hikers. 'Look! Look! Someone's giving them a lift. What d'you reckon? A laugh, right? Better than freezing our nuts off out here.'

Charlotte didn't answer. Watched the truck pull away. A barrage of possibilities, of problems, filled her head.

Em slipped her sunglasses on. Aviators. Too grown-up, but not to her. She felt important and mysterious and cool. 'Come on. You don't look like you and no one gives a shit about me. So?'

Charlotte shrugged, pulled a "maybe" face, noticed the sunglasses. 'You!...' She shook her head.

Em grinned, clapped her hands, skipped.

'And glasses off.'

'Aw. Why?'

'Because it's dark and you look silly and this isn't a game.'

Em puffed out a disappointed breath and slipped the glasses into her pocket. 'So mean...'

They hadn't waited for long when a Jaguar slowed down, cruised by, stopped, reversed back towards them.

'Well, fuck me!' Em squealed.

Charlotte stared a warning at her.

'All right, all right.'

The passenger's window slid down. 'Where are you going, girls?'

'North!'

'We gathered that.' He turned and grinned at the driver. 'How far north?'

'Scotland.'

'Right you are then, jump in.'

'That's really kind of you.'

Charlotte whispered a warning to Em as the door opened. 'Let me do the talking, okay?'

Em stared back at her as she slid along the leather seat. Loud music pumped out of the speakers. This was unreal!

'Bit young to be out here all on your own-some, aren't you?'

'It's complicated.'

'Always is, love. Not runaways are you? Could get us in trouble, that could.'

Charlotte did her best to laugh normally. 'Of course not!'

The blast of warm air from the heaters, the softness of the leather seats. Both girls felt their eyes closing, their heads drooping. A jump awake then off again. Uncomfortable dozing, but irresistible. No fight in them.

The car lurched, travelling too quickly over a bump. Both girls woke up alarmed. Blackness all around. Nothing to see. No traffic. No lights. Nothing.

'Where are we?' Charlotte asked, a slight panic in her voice.

'Just a short-cut,' the passenger said over his shoulder, a leery grin on his face.

Everything about this felt wrong. Gut reactions screaming, *Get out.* Charlotte fumbled for the door handle. Nothing happening. *It's locked!* She mouthed at Em.

'Can you let us out please?'

'Not yet.'

'I said, let us out!' Charlotte kicked at the seat in front of her.

'Oh hey! That's not polite now, is it? Us giving you a lift an' all.'

Trees zipped past, black on black. Charlotte felt beads of sweat building on her forehead, trickling down her back. She turned to Em. Eyes wide.

Em chewed on her lip. The knife. She had the knife. The weight of it against her chest. She didn't look down, her gaze still fixed on the passenger seat. Its occupant grinning.

Her fingers slipped into her inside pocket. They crept up the handle, twisted around it. Clenched it. She exhaled as she drew it out. Slowly, slowly. She slashed at the driver's chair, splitting the leather with a satisfying zip. 'I'll fucking use it on you next,' she snarled, the knife pointing at the passenger's face.

'That'll cost you, you little bitch!' He undid his seatbelt, swiped at Em, at the knife.

She was ready and slashed at his hand as it reached for her. Blood streaming. 'Stop the fucking car!' she screamed.

'She's fucking stabbed me! Fuck!' He slumped in his seat, one hand clasping the other. Blood oozing between his fingers. The pain shouting from his face.

The click of the doors unlocking. The squeal of the brakes.

Charlotte kicked the door open and they tumbled out of the swerving car. One hand was on her bag, the other snatching at Em. Tinker's claws sunk into her neck. All that mattered was that he was still there. They were all together.

The car sped off again, its tail-lights snaking away into the distance.

The girls didn't stop. Didn't think. There was no time for that. The car could turn around any minute, come after them. A change of heart. Retribution in mind. They charged into the woods, undergrowth snapping at them. Slowing them. Still they carried on until they were quite sure that enough space had been put between them and the road. In the distance, headlights. Far away. Speeding off. Probably not even them.

They slowed to a walk. Breath calming. Heartbeats slowing.

'You can be my Bonnie any day! Brave as, well, yeah. Brilliant!' Charlotte said.

'Oh, right, so I'm Bonnie and you get to be macho tough old Clyde. Huh!'

Charlotte laughed. 'After that you can be just whoever you want to be.'

'Just yanking your chain, Clyde.'

'Are you okay to keep going?'

'Course.'

'I've no idea where we are. How far they took us. You?'

'Nu-uh. Zonked from start to finish. Must have been right knackered.'

'I guess we're lost then.'

'Guess so.'

Chapter 66

Dougie heard a car pull up. The slam of a door. Confident strong footfall. Loud insistent knocking. He glanced out of his window. A police car.

'Just a minute,' he called, a sense of trepidation, but he wasn't sure why. He opened the door wide. A smile. 'Yes?'

'I'm looking for a Douglas Jamieson.'

'That would be me. How can I help you, officer?'

'Can I come in?'

'Aye, sure.' He ordered Gypsy into her bed. 'You stay there now. No nonsense.'

'Oh, I'm just fine with the dog.'

Dougie pulled out a chair, invited the policeman to sit.

'Right, well, just a few questions about that nasty incident down at Briar Cottage. The murder of Mr Desson, back in the summer. I'm sure you've heard about it.'

'Yes, of course. Awful thing. I knew the girl, Charlotte, quite well.'

'Did you now?' He took out his notepad, started writing. 'And did you know the victim? Her father?'

'No. Not at all.'

'Bit unusual that, knowing the child but not the father, wouldn't you say?'

Dougie bristled. Didn't like the man's attitude, police or not. 'Not at all. She used to cycle up here. Spent a lot of her time in the woods, down by the river. Nice wee thing, always keen to know about the place, the wildlife.'

'Is that right? And was she here on her own? Just you and her?'

'No. She was with a friend some of the time.'

'And who was this friend?'

'Tommy.'

'And where might we find this Tommy?'

'I have no idea.'

'But you know his name. Local boy, is he?'

'Not really.'

'Not really,' he repeated slowly, as he wrote the words in his notebook, as if they were of great significance. He looked up. Smiled. 'And what exactly do you mean by not really?'

'He was only here in the summer months.'

'Can you elaborate for me, sir?'

'He and his family stopped by to pick the berries. They've been coming here for years. A decent lot.'

'A Tinker then. Is that what you're saying?'

Dougie took a deep breath. He should have kept his mouth shut.

'Yes. A Tinker family.'

'Right, well, now, we have a few questions we'd like to ask of the Tinker folk, but they can be closed. Not open to outsiders, you know. And we need to find out who was here at the time of the murder. They might have seen someone. Heard something. Is that something you could maybe help us with? It's said that you're quite friendly with them. Maybe you could ask?'

'I'm sorry, no can do. That family were moved on by the new owners at Craigdour. I haven't seen them at all.'

'So they haven't been back since the murder, then?'

'Not to my knowledge.'

'Right, right. And where exactly were you at the time?'

'At the time of the murder?'

'At the time of the murder.'

'Here. Asleep.'

'And do you have any witnesses to that?'

'I live on my own, so no. No I don't.'

'That's unfortunate, sir. Just a couple more questions, if you don't mind.'

'Actually, I do mind. I've got work to do.' He moved towards the door. Put his Barbour jacket on. Ushered the policeman out in front of him.

'Just doing my job, sir.' He flicked at his notebook. Frowned. 'Can I just ask–'

'As I said, I have nothing more to say, unless you're going to arrest me, of course.'

'Now why would I do that?'

'I have no idea.'

*

He returned to the station with a feeling of achievement. The defensiveness of the man. His attitude. There was something there all right. For once he wasn't filled with trepidation as he approached a meeting with the DCI. He was quite sure that Douglas Jamieson should be brought in for questioning.

Chapter 67

In the distance Tommy could now see the buildings belonging to the men who had stolen Coll. That night when they had found each other again. That magical night when he had felt close to whole again. The terror of it. The sheer joy of it. He could think on that. Harness that feeling.

He decided it would be smart to steer well clear of the place. He would take a detour. A long trip around the back of the hill to his right, through the pine trees that still stood, that still held their needles, still offered sanctuary. From there he would find his way to the river and back into the woods he knew. Perhaps that could become his new summer stopping-place? Perhaps he would be safe enough there?

Tommy waited for deep dusk before leaving the shelter of the woods. It was only a few miles, no more, to a place of relative safety, at least so he hoped. He had slipped ropes around the horses' necks just as a precaution. The fear of those men and what they had done. The memories would still linger, especially in Coll. He had to make sure that they stayed right by his side so that he could comfort them, hush them, keep them from bolting at a flashback, an unexpected danger. They could also pick up on his feelings. Feel any fear. He had to push it down as best he could. Call on the joy. That memory. That feeling.

A northerly began to pick up, bringing a chill on its breath that made Tommy shiver. He stopped. Held his head high in the wind. A voice carried on it. Male. Young. Another.

Tommy felt completely exposed in the centre of the valley. The white coats of his horses, their lush tails, seemed to him to glow, shouting their presence even in the dark. He couldn't decide what would be best. To keep walking, edging closer to the woods and a place of hiding, or to freeze. Stay right here and hope that they wouldn't be noticed. That whoever it was would pass by soon enough, focussing on themselves, on whatever it was that had led them to be here, in the middle of nowhere, at night.

His brain was scrambling now. Cloudy and messed up. He had no idea; even less now than he had had before. What might folk be doing? Farmhands maybe? Checking on something? Checking on him? No. That couldn't be. He had been careful enough and they sounded more like they were up to mischief or having fun. A laughter to their speech. The rustle of young leaves, the whistle of the wind through the trees. Their voices fading now. Drifting off into nothing.

He waited. Listened. Waited. He wasn't picking up anything to fear, neither were the animals. They would continue. Slowly. Quietly.

The desire to rush, to run to a safe place was biting at

him, but he swallowed it down. Counted in his head, over and over. *One, two, three, four, five...* The wash of the river as it ran over stones. The scent of it breaking through. Its spring perfume was different. Earthier. Heavier. The water brown and churning, deeper than its summer swell. He would have to be vigilant. He sat astride Seil, called Rona up, held tight onto Coll's rope, and they slowly, carefully, eased their way across the river, him whispering to them. 'On you go. That's it. Easy does it now. Easy does it.'

The water was now up to the horses' bellies. A slight panic ran through Seil's skin. Her nose flared and snorted. She sensed danger. They all did. Despite the bitter bite of the water and the hidden strength of its current, they would have to swim if they were going to reach the other side.

The pull of the current swept them further downriver, the opposite bank kept painfully distant. The switch from swimming to walking told him that, at last, they were getting there. They would make it. He allowed himself a smile, patted Seil. 'Well done. Well done my beauty,' he whispered to her.

Chapter 68

'Never walked so far in my whole life! Feel like a proper bandito. Knackered though.'

Charlotte laughed. 'Bandito! Where did you get that from?'

'Dunno. Someone, I guess. Never thought I'd be one, like. Not me. Not really.'

'Well, you're not really.'

'You think? Robbery and stabbings and hiding and being on the run. Reckon that's a Bandito, me. For sure. And accompli...accom...what is it?'

'Accomplice.'

'Yeah. That. See, that's as big as the crime itself. The accomplicing. That's you and me tied together forever, that is.' She nudged Charlotte in the ribs. Grinned up at her.

They'd been walking for weeks now, keeping to quieter places, skirting around villages, avoiding roads. It made the going much slower, more difficult, but it also felt safer. They certainly weren't about to try hitching a lift again. Buses were too much like a no-way-out kind of thing. A trap. No. This was safer. When they needed to pick up supplies Em nipped into a small local shop. A story on her lips alongside her smile.

Tinker had quite taken to this life and happily trotted along at their feet, or close by. The odd scamper after some poor little bird or rummage through the undergrowth after a rustle or a twitch. The girls would wait, watching, laughing at his antics, until the chase was done and Tinker came back. Nothing caught but a damned good try. He would master it soon enough and the humour would slip away.

They had managed to find overnight shelter in barns or sheds, even an abandoned cottage, which turned out to be creepier than anywhere else.

'Think someone died here.'

'Don't be silly.'

'Really! Can smell it, I can. Dead people.'

'And what does a dead person smell like?'

'Like this. What you think? Jeez! Dust and dead-people-smells. Gross!'

'Do you know what dust is made of?'

'Uh-uh.'

'Tiny, little pieces of dead skin.'

'What did you go and say that for?'

'Because it's true.'

'You didn't have to go and tell me right now, did you?'

Charlotte laughed. 'Go to sleep.'

'Can't. You hear that?'

'Hear what?'

'Creaks like, like footsteps.'

'Ghosts, I suppose.'

'Yeah. No. Dunno. See what you've gone and done?'

'There's no one here. There's nothing here. You're okay.'

'Don't feel okay.'

They snuggled together under the sleeping bag, Em's arm tightly around Charlotte's waist. In the daytime she was brash and cocky, throwing a finger at the world. But at night she became a scared little girl who needed to cling on like a limpet.

The landscape had become hillier, bleaker, more desolate. Villages and farms fewer and further apart. They stood on a hill, high above the world. The sun shone and a brisk wind blew. A feeling of something else in the air. Spring.

Em stared, her hands on her hips. 'Wow!' she whispered as hill after hill spread out before them, rolling into the sky. 'This is right pretty. Scary like, but pretty.'

'Why scary?'

'There ain't nothing here. Just us and nothing. Weird like.'

'Nothing is the safest place in the world.'

'You're weird!'

'So you said! Right, we need to move it if we're going to find shelter for the night. Race you down!'

They ran, laughing as they went, twisting across the hillside like slalom skiers, back and forth, back and forth, voices trailing off in the wind. Tinker ran with them, bounding ahead, pausing, letting them get in front and zooming past again, his long tail tall and erect.

'Okay. Enough,' Em called as she stopped, hands on knees, breathless. 'Legs ain't as long as yours. Gotta work harder.'

She slipped her hand in Charlotte's as they walked on down. It was a nice feeling. A safe feeling. Albeit a strange feeling.

A mist began to swirl around them, cold and wet. As wet as rain. It sneaked through their clothes. Wrapped them up in it. The wind soon brought with it rain, so heavy they could barely see.

'Shit!'

Chapter 69

A squad car was parked outside Charlotte's old house. A man and a woman stepping out. They looked officious as they strode around the property, checking windows, doors, even the garden shed.

'She's not going to show here, is she? I mean, by all accounts she's intelligent.'

'She'll also be scared and you and I know what that can do. People on the run do stupid things.'

'Well, there's no sign of her here yet.'

'The boss reckons she'll show sooner or later. Better follow orders. Check with the neighbour. Question her again.'

Martha was watching from her garden, arms folded across her chest, a scowl on her face. God alone knew what had happened to that poor girl, and the police after her like this. Well, it just felt wrong.

'Afternoon ma'am. We were just–'

'I've said before, if I see anything I'll let you know.'

Kitty twirled around her ankles as if offering support.

'It's not just that ma'am. Can we have a wee word?'

She sighed. 'I suppose so, in you come.'

'We just want to run over what you saw again. A bit of new information's come to light.'

'And what might that be?'

'I'm afraid we're not at liberty to divulge anything as yet. Now, the men you saw, definitely two of them?'

She nodded. 'No doubt about that.'

'You're absolutely sure?'

'As I said!'

'It was dark, you must have been frightened, confused. Shadows all around from the trees.' He peered out of the window, raised his eyebrows in question.

'And the light streaming out of my back door. Two men, constable. Two young men.'

'And what made you think they were young?' the WPC asked.

'I couldn't say for sure. It just felt that way. Something about the way they moved maybe. Young and strong. That was what they seemed to me.'

'Strong as in men?' She paused. 'We are talking about men here, not boys?'

'From what I could tell they were men.'

'Men that worked hard, maybe worked the land?'

'Your guess is as good as mine, constable.'

'But they looked like they could handle themselves?'

'Yes, yes they did.'

'And you're quite sure you didn't see anything beforehand? Someone hanging around perhaps? Maybe not that night. A few days before? A week or two even?'

She shook her head. 'I'd have remembered that. It's a quiet wee place and you notice folk.'

'And there was nothing about them that looked familiar

at all?'

She shook her head. 'No. Not that I could see.'

'Do you think they could have been Tinkers? Travelling folk not from these parts?'

'And how do you think I'd be able to tell that? Look, I've told you all I know. I've nothing more to add.'

'Right you are. Just doing our job, ma'am. You will let us know if anything comes to mind?'

'Yes, as I said before.' She stood, glaring, until they pulled away. As she was closing her door another car pulled up. 'Can a body not get any peace?' Her frown lifted when she saw it was Dougie.

'Good afternoon!' Dougie called. 'I was just passing. Saw the police car pulling off. Thought I'd pop in and see how you were doing. Rum business this.'

'Yes, and no mistaking. Poor wee lassie! I can't imagine how she must be feeling. On the run like that. Scared of her own shadow, I've no doubt. Well, if the authorities had just let her stay here with me things would have been a whole lot better and no mistaking. That mother! Tshh!'

Roger had confided in her. Told her all about it. The woman's fondness for drugs, for other men. For just disappearing for weeks on end, until he'd had enough. He told her not to bother coming back next time. They were better off without her. She'd smiled, shrugged her shoulders, packed a bag, and left. Not even a goodbye to her daughter.

'Have they been around a lot then?'

'Oh aye. Them and others. Them and others. There's not a day goes by when someone or other doesn't stop for

307

a poke around. First it was all the crime tourists wanting to see the murder house. Add to that the journalists and their trickery. Now we've got this! The house where she might come back to. Some folk! Come away and have a wee cup of tea, why don't you?'

'Oh, I don't want to put you to any trouble.'

'Ach, away! You're no trouble. Any friend of Charlotte's is a friend of mine. In you come, why don't you?' She made the tea, brought it through with a plate of biscuits, sat down. 'You know, the police and their forensic folk have been back. Every inch gone over, and over again.'

'Is that right? They've been at my door too, making out I was a suspect. Would you credit it? Asked me for an alibi.'

'No!'

'Aye. I know they've got their job to do and we all want whoever did this caught, but, well.'

'So would you be that new information they were on about?'

'I sincerely hope not!'

'Well, come to think of it, they were trying to get me to say that it could have been Tinkers.'

'Were they now?'

'Yes. And I don't take too kindly to that. Having thoughts put in my head. That's not the right way to go about things now, is it?'

'I think they're getting a bit desperate. That's a year now and not even an arrest. Clutching at straws, I imagine.'

'And do you have one? An alibi I mean. I wouldn't!

Just me on my own.'

'Oh I've got one and they'll get it if needs be, but a man has his private life, after all.'

She blushed.

He laughed.

Chapter 70

In his mind Tommy could see the trail through the trees that he had followed the year before. The season was different. The air different. but it was the same place. The same feeling. Something deep and ancient like he was walking with generations who had walked here before. Like he belonged. Once the track was found, he followed it, walking again, feet on the earth. He blew out a deep breath as the trees wrapped themselves around him. It wasn't far to the small clearing where they had stopped before. A safe place.

The animals felt it too, a loosening of skin, a slackening of muscles, a tossing of heads from the horses and a wag of Rona's wee tail as she scurried around picking up familiar smells, old trails. Mona kept herself perched on him. This was all new and strange to her. Finally the exact spot. The clearing.

Despite the dark, the lateness of the hour, he wanted to set up a tent right now. He slipped the baggage off Coll, found the sticks, twisted them and bent them and set them into the shape he needed. The canvas thrown over it, weighted down with stones. The same stones he had used before. It felt as if nothing had changed. No one had been here. And that was a very good thing.

Mona settled in a gnarly old oak tree. He threw blankets over his horses, whispered to them before crawling into his tent with Rona. That old feeling. That excitement. He tried to quell it. Charlotte wouldn't be here. Not for a long time yet...but maybe...just maybe? He fell asleep to the creak of ancient limbs, the song of the trees, the rustle of the night, the memory of her.

Chapter 71

It was dark and Charlotte and Em were soaked through. Both so cold that their teeth were chattering. Finally the outline of a building crept through the shadows. It was locked up. A feeling of emptiness hovered around it. Em peered through the windows. Nothing. Not the glow of anything on stand-by.

'Reckon it's been empty a while,' Em said.

'And just how did you work that one out?'

'Know stuff, me. Stuff you wouldn't expect.' She puffed her chest, stood taller before trying the front door, the back door, the windows. All locked. She rummaged through the garden, picked up a rock. Raised her arm.

'What are you doing?' Charlotte screeched.

'Dunno about you, but not wanting to die of coldness, me.'

She banged it against the window. Again, harder. This time the window smashed. Glass tinkling on the floor. She stretched her arm through, fumbled for the latch. Twisted it and slid the window open. She turned and grinned before clambering in, disappearing into the blackness.

Charlotte closed her eyes. That sound. Breaking glass.

Her father. *No!* She took a deep breath, blew it away, checked around, listening for something, but she wasn't sure what. There was nothing to see other than darkness, not even the hue of a far off habitation. The only thing she could hear was the rain.

'You coming or what?' Em whisper-shouted. 'It's Deserted! Dust everywhere. We're all right.' She shivered as the memory of what Charlotte had told her about dust leapt out. Screwed up her nose at the thought of some stranger's dead skin settling in her lungs. She slipped from room to room closing all of the curtains. The kitchen backed onto woods and a hill beyond. She decided it was safe to flick the light switch on. Nothing. 'Fuck it!' she grumbled

'That's good. It means the place is properly empty.'

'Yeah but me, I'd like a bit warmth, maybe a light.'

'There must be a mains switch somewhere.' Charlotte kicked the broken glass into a corner before unzipping her jacket and letting Tinker out. 'Sorry kitty, that wasn't so much fun for you.' More stabs to her memory. Kitty. Her dad collapsing. Blood. Blood on her hands. Staring at blood on her hands. *Don't go there now. Keep it together. Keep it together.* She focussed instead on finding the fuse box. There. Next the mains for the water.

A few minutes later the power was on, the heating ticking as it fired up.

'Quite handy you! Where did you learn that stuff?'

She shrugged, didn't want to mention her dad. There was a pack of instructions on the kitchen table. No food anywhere. No clothing. But there was a tumble drier, towels and bedlinen.

'Haven't had a bath since...dunno when.'

'How long is it since you had a home then?'

'Dunno. Two Christmases. Summit like that anyways.'

That night they had beds and comfort and warmth and, as far as they could tell, safety. Em crept into Charlotte's bed anyway. Clung on tight. Sleep swept over them like a feather. Come morning it was still grey outside. Clouds so heavy they seemed to push down on them. An extra weight to their shoulders.

Em was flicking through the instructions, chuckling to herself. 'Even tells you how to use the kettle! Jeez. Folk must be right stupid, eh?' She turned to the last page. 'Oh! Oh, oh, oh. Bikes. It says there are bikes! Looky!'

'Criminal damage. Breaking and entering. And you want to add burglary?'

'Why not? It's not like they'll EVER know it was us.'

'Our prints are everywhere. I doubt they'll report a break-in if nothing's taken, but a burglary? Sure as anything. For the insurance if nothing else.'

Em sighed heavily. 'Guess so.'

'We clean up, stick a branch through the window and hope they'll think it was just the wind.'

Em sighed again. 'Boring...'

'Sensible!'

They ran along the valley suddenly feeling vulnerable and exposed. Still nothing.

'Proper lost ain't we?'

Charlotte bit her lip. 'I guess you could say that. But I'm sure it'll be fine. We'll be fine. You'll see.' She wished that she believed what she was saying, but she wasn't sure at all.

Chapter 72

Tommy woke with the dawn. It was more exposed than he had hoped, the spring foliage small and light, but it would do. Enough limbs and trunks and gorse to keep him hidden from anyone down in the valley. Far enough from the road above for it to be an irrelevance.

Every day, late afternoon, he would secure his horses at the camp and take Rona down to the river, Mona circling above as if on guard. More likely she was keeping an eye out for prey, but that didn't matter. Her presence, circling above the world, seeing what he couldn't see, was comfort enough in itself.

He didn't feel Charlotte's presence at all, didn't believe that she was anywhere nearby, but this was a ritual that he would keep anyway. Time spent sitting in their little bay of the river kept her memory alive, her picture fresh in his mind. The picture he held of her was an old one. She would be close to a woman now. Somehow he couldn't imagine that. A grown-up Charlotte. How might she have changed? Her hair, her laugh, her body, her thoughts? He wanted her to be just as he pictured. Just the same. But he was far from that himself, a foot taller, scarred inside and out. She might be too. He hoped not. He hoped that life had been kind and gentle with her.

It was another cold day, the sun trapped behind thick banks of cloud. He wanted to build a fire, warm himself and his animals up, but it was too dangerous. Smoke twirling up from this place would be easily spotted, probably investigated. He stared across the river at the barren hill, almost completely cleared of trees. Shook his head at it. Wished it had been left alone, as was right.

It was too cold to stay still, to wait for darkness. He jumped onto Seil, called Rona up, clicked for Coll to follow, and led them up the hill. They needed to run. Get their blood flowing. Warm themselves up.

At the road he checked left and right. Nothing coming. They trotted across and through some shrubbery. An open field which seemed to be empty. Nothing overlooking it. He jumped down and ran; his animals sensing what was to be done stayed close but ran at their own speed. It felt so good that he wanted to yell. To exclaim. He did it in his head instead. Then Mona did it for him. A clear strong mew carrying high in the sky.

*

Dougie had spotted him over the past few days, had watched him from high in the woods. He was a state now. Wild and ragged with long matted hair, a straggly beard, clothes too small, too tight, stained and ripped. Trousers threadbare with holes at the knees. A stretch of what looked like rabbit-skin wrapped around his shoulders. But he was still recognisable as that young man. The way he carried himself, the gentleness about him, how he seemed to be a part of the land. Dougie wanted to speak to him, to

316

help him somehow, but he wasn't quite sure of the best way to go about it. The man was anxious, timid.

*

As Tommy returned to his camp something felt wrong. There was a smell. A different air. There was no bark from Rona, no restlessness from Coll and Seil, so no one was here, but he was sure that someone had been. He flipped open his tent and there, at the entrance, was a neat pile of clothes. He stared at them fearfully, as if they might attack, might bite.

Eventually he drew closer, picked them up between finger and thumb, still at a distance, still wary. He held them against himself, inspected them. They would fit right enough, but it meant that someone knew about him, his place, and he couldn't for the life of him figure out who that might be.

He would normally light a fire now. The darkness offering that security, but he was too anxious; too concerned about strangers. Settling down to sleep he was still on edge, alert for any sounds that shouldn't be there. He didn't like this. People. People were dangerous and if it weren't for Charlotte and his longing for her he would stay well away, in his wild places far from anyone. Perhaps he should leave, never to return? No. He couldn't bear that.

He would stay and watch as the season began to change and the birds returned and life sprung back all around. He would stay until the fledged birds flew off and the days began to shrink and the moving winds picked up. Whether Charlotte had returned or not, he would stay until the time was right.

The next morning he sharpened the tip of some sticks to make arrows, twisted a branch and some ivy to make a bow. He tested it, practised his aim. It was true. The zip as the arrow flew through the air. The soft thud as it met its target. It would serve its purpose and help keep him and Rona fed. But more than that, it helped him feel secure. He would use it if he had to.

Chapter 73

Dougie kept a discreet eye on the young man from further up the hill, deep in the woods. It seemed he seldom left his camp other than to go and sit by the river at the same time every day. It had been five days now and there was still no sign of him wearing the new clothes. Dougie thought he had chosen well. Functional hard-wearing items that he might wear himself, that would blend in with the surroundings, khaki and brown, not quite camouflage but close enough. Combat trousers, a couple of T-shirts, a fleece, a Barbour. Nothing flashy or outlandish. Perhaps he had embarrassed him? Put him on edge somehow?

He decided that today he would try and approach him out in the open, down by the river. He waited until four o'clock before heading out with his binoculars. Sure enough, there he was, sitting at that little bay, his gaze somewhere far-off.

He hadn't got far down the hill when Tommy turned round, stared up, jumped to his feet. His wee dog jumped up too. It looked like they were about to bolt.

'Wait. Please wait. I'm a friend. No threat,' he called, as he held his hands up, trying to keep a smile on his face.

'I'm...I'm a friend of Charlotte's.'

Tommy stopped, had a good look at the man, trying to sum the situation up. Of course he knew him. They had seen each other often enough, always at a distance, always hoping the other hadn't spotted him. That darkness about the man. But Charlotte had had nothing but good to say of him. Someone she cared for. She trusted. Rona sniffed at him, at his dog. Tails wagged. At least the dogs were amiable.

'Can I join you, son? Sit and chat?'

Tommy stared, stuck inside himself. He did his best to stand tall, but felt so small. His heart thumped, breath faltered. *One, two, three, four, five. One, two, three, four, five. One, two, three...*Better. Calming. But words still weren't coming. What was it she had called him? Dougie. That was it. Dougie. He didn't sense any danger from the man, just that darkness, and he could feel now that it was a sad darkness. He tried harder, forced himself. 'Aye,' he muttered.

Dougie sat down. 'Will you join me then?'

Tommy hesitated, shuffled from foot to foot, before finally sitting back down.

'You look like you've been in the wars, son. It's my job, you see? To keep an eye on things. I'd seen you and your family camped across there every summer until two years back. What happened? To you, I mean, all alone and, well, looking like this.'

'I...Those men,' he whispered, flicked his head towards the land across the river. 'Wicked men.'

'I agree with you there. Tommy isn't it? Can I call you Tommy?'

Tommy nodded.

'Dougie.' He held his hand out and they shook gingerly. 'Look, I wasn't here when it happened. What did they do? The men across there?'

Tommy bristled, shivered, as the memory swept through him. His thoughts were broken by a soft whinny slipping through the trees. He sniffed the air. Jumped up. Panicked. 'My horses. I need to – My horses!'

He bolted off, Rona at his heels, Dougie trailing behind. Tommy could move, slipping through the forest as if it weren't there at all and Dougie struggled to keep up. By the time he got to the camp it appeared that all was well.

Tommy was standing in between his horses, one hand on each back, and was nuzzling into their necks. One after the other, over and over. Soft whispers.

Dougie hung back watching, smiling, until the horses were untethered and wandered off nibbling at the straw at their feet. 'It was me who left the clothes for you. Just trying to help. No offence meant.'

'I...well...thanks.'

'You don't mind me being here?'

Tommy shook his head.

'You're safe to stay here. I'll let the hands know to steer clear. Leave you be.'

Tommy appreciated the offer, but he wasn't sure. Not yet. It would mean others knowing, but they probably would soon enough anyway.

'Aye. Right. Thanks,' he said looking at his feet, the ground, the trees, until his eyes finally settled on Dougie's. A long moment of reading, understanding.

He was bursting to find out about Charlotte, but his head flooded with so many questions, thoughts flying in a jumbled stream. *Where is she? Why did she go? Who are you to her? Is she coming back? Why do you hide in the forest and watch? Why didn't you speak, come and talk? Watching. Always watching.* He knew that his words would spill out in a stammering, incomprehensible mess unless he managed to control himself. Bring something strong to the fore. Trust.

Chapter 74

The land had levelled out. Dry stone walls skirted open fields that were dotted with sheep and cattle. They had come to a small single-track road scarred with muddy tractor tracks. They both instinctively stopped. Looked around. Farm buildings in the distance.

'What now?' Em asked. 'Could just walk along the road, all la-de-da, nothing to see here.'

'Right. Two girls and a cat, miles from anywhere, just casually walking along the road. Not in the least bit odd.'

'You worry too much, you do.' She shrugged. 'Ain't nothing to be scared of. Must be so far away from Nottingham. Bet no one's even bothered about us up here. What you reckon Kitty?'

Charlotte laughed as they scampered across the grass together.

'Kitty says this way.'

Charlotte shrugged and followed them as they drew closer to the farm.

Em stopped. Stared at the mess at her feet. 'Ew! What's that?'

'Cow pats. Meaning cows. Meaning we should maybe

get back on the road.'

Rising from behind a small slope, a cow. More. A whole bunch of cows and they were staring right at them.

'Fuck me, they be mighty big!'

Loud snorts. Feet stamping.

'Don't run. We just walk nice and calmly in the opposite direction, back the way we came.'

'Calm's gone SO far away.'

'Seriously, don't run. They might chase you and that's a very scary thing.'

'Kay. How come you know this stuff?'

'I used to live near farms.'

'That where we're going then? Farmy places?'

'Uh-huh.'

Both girls looked over their shoulders. The cows were still following, still staring at them, but not all of them, some stopping for a munch on the grass.

'See? If you don't threaten them, they won't threaten you. Usually!'

A barbed wire fence separated field from road. Charlotte pulled the top strand up with her hand and the one below it down with her foot. She gestured for Em to clamber through before twisting around and following suit.

They looked up and down the road again as if wishing it to make their minds up for them. To direct them. 'Towards the farm then?' Charlotte suggested.

'Farmers work all hours, no? They'll be off doing farmy things with their farmy animals and shit.'

They walked past the barns, the farmhouse, not looking anywhere but in front of them. A door squeaking open or closed. Footsteps. Heavy. The flap of Wellies. Ignore it. Ignore it. Ignore it. Neither girl looked back until they had rounded a corner and were out of sight.

'Safe?'

'Who knows?'

Chapter 75

As the police went from door to door, village to village, new posters were put up.

HAVE YOU SEEN THIS GIRL?

And another with a picture of Briar Cottage and Mr Desson.

APPEAL FOR INFORMATION ON LOCAL MURDER.

'Well, let's see if anything comes of this.'

'What do you reckon to the Tinker idea? They can be a bit wild, can't they?'

'They can that. Different way of life from us. A violent one at that. It wouldn't surprise me at all. The DCI's keen on that one too.'

'That woman. The neighbour. I don't know, something just felt off.'

'Aye, and that Mr Jamieson. Far too defensive for my liking. The pair of them. I said as much to DCI Graham. I told him straight. Bring them in. Question them at the station. It's amazing how that can jog a memory.'

'And what was his response?'

'He's thinking on it.'

Of course he hadn't told DCI Graham. He wouldn't dare *tell* him anything, but best to impress a young WPC. He had hinted in his report. That was close enough. Graham had picked up on it. Raised his eyebrows a couple of times. He hoped that, when the time came, he would be the one to bring them in. He deserved it after all.

*

Dougie laughed when they came to pick him up. 'You're kidding, right?'

'And why would you think that, sir? This is a murder enquiry and we need to ask you some more questions, down at the station.'

'Is that right?'

He sat in the interview room, annoyed now at the waste of time. Annoyed also at the memory. The last time he'd been sat in a place such as this he had been charged with assault. He was only a kid. Sixteen. Hanging out with a crowd. The wrong crowd. He got a suspended sentence. Probation. Life was going right down the pan. And then he came here and his life changed completely. That kid, that time, had been consigned to history so deep that in all these years it hadn't surfaced. He didn't appreciate it being dragged up.

'Not from here, are you?'

'Excuse me?'

'It's a simple enough question. This is not where you herald from, is it?'

'And?'

'I'll ask the questions if you don't mind.' He smiled one of those knowing, superior, I-could-fuck-you smiles. 'Let's try again shall we? Where are you from?'

'Durnoch.'

'Less of the smart-arse comments. I know where you work. Before you came here, where did you live?'

'Edinburgh.'

'Right. That wasn't so hard now, was it? Now, a little bird tells me that you got into a spot of bother down there. Isn't that right?'

Dougie stared, part of him wanting to get into something with this annoying specimen, the other part, the stronger part, biding his time. Keeping quiet.

'I'm saying absolutely nothing without my lawyer present.'

'Oh, it's your lawyer is it now?'

A phone call to the laird, a prompt visit from his lawyer, and he was released.

DCI Graham was annoyed with himself. He'd gone about that all the wrong way. Although, to be fair to himself he hadn't expected that calibre of lawyer. That support. What he had really wanted was to probe the man's connection with the Tinkers. To get an in. Instead he got a mouthful from an uppity lawyer; a lesson in law. Christ, he'd ballsed that one up all right.

Chapter 76

The man, Dougie, had been kind. He had cut Tommy's hair for him, given him a razor. They had shared quiet evenings by the camp-fire. This man didn't need to talk like most folk did. He was quiet and listened to the sounds of the wild. They would identify the calls of birds, guess at the scurry through the undergrowth or the clamber up trees. Sit still and silent as deer approached, both delighting in the closeness, that trust between man and beast.

'What are your plans?' Dougie asked. 'You're not usually here at this time of year, are you?'

'No. Things...well, things have sort of changed.' He took a deep breath, blew it out slowly.

'You know, you could stay. There's a wee but-and-ben you could have, just up yonder. A safe place for you. A place for your horses. Even a job, if you want it. Paid work.'

It was tempting. But being in a place of stone and walls and borders with a job and a boss. Tied. Could he cope with it? Here, in this place where he had always camped wild in that same spot. Always. But now he was hiding from it all. Scared to be seen. This would make him sort of like someone else. Like one of them. A right to be here. And through it all there would still be that pull. He had never stayed put through the seasons and he wasn't sure he knew how.

Dougie could read it. He had seen the same with Sarah. That longing. We would call it itchy feet, but that wasn't anywhere near a strong enough description. It was so much more. A thread with the earth that ran through your soul and pulled. Onward. Onward. If Sarah had found it too difficult to stay he would have travelled on with her. Given it all up for her. Nothing else mattered.

'No pressure, Tommy. It's there if you want it.'

'You know the ways, don't you?'

Dougie smiled. 'I do. My wife, Sarah, was a Tinker, just like you. Proud and bound to the land.'

'What happened?'

'History, Tommy, and that's where it stays now.'

Tommy didn't question further. He knew that feeling. Some things just weren't for the sharing. His head was advising him to go against the grain, take a chance on something new, something very different. He could always change his mind, move on again, if he felt the need. Nothing was permanent. The road was always there and if the calling came she would welcome him back. For now though, he chose safety and security. And more than that, Seil was with foal. This would be a wise choice for her.

Dougie smiled at Tommy's decision as he shook his hand in agreement. Smiled harder at the sight of him pitching his canvas right against the exterior wall, setting

330

up the place for his fire, his chittle. Part camp, part building. Canvas and the open air would always call to him. Perhaps this was a good compromise.

Dougie gave him the job of assistant. An odd-job man, the wild parts of the estate his to look after, to protect, to help flourish. There was little that could better this, and the grin on Tommy's face as he went about his work stood as evidence. There wasn't much for him to learn, such was his expertise in the area, the flora and fauna. Indeed, it was often him teaching Dougie, sharing his insights, his understanding.

They rode the periphery of the estate together, Tommy on Seil, Dougie on Coll. No hiding. Out there for all to see. Side by side. These were his horses. It took a good deal of courage for Tommy to agree, of course. Coll was his mother's. Precious. But Dougie's argument had made sense. Stand proud. Stand tall. Take ownership. It's what his da had taught him and now he would make good on that lesson.

Eyebrows were raised in the village. Gossip spinning around the local shop, the pub, from kitchen to kitchen. It would pass.

Chapter 77

Em had never really thought about much other than survival. It was all about how to stay safe for another day. Where to get enough food to keep her stomach settled. How to keep below the radar of the authorities, the police. What they were doing now was all normal to her, except she was with someone. Properly *with*, like a best friend or a sister. Not someone like her, not like anyone she'd ever known. And they were out here in the countryside. And the air was clean. And that was all new too. It wasn't strange any more. And she liked it. And she thought about things.

She thought about how different her world was now. There were things to care about. Good things. Kitty-cat and Charlotte. It was like they were tied up and it was special, and super scary all at the same time. And that was confusing. She didn't know what she would do if it all got taken from her. It would be cold and horrible and she didn't want to go back there, ever. And she thought about where they were going. She didn't know. Charlotte did. Charlotte had a plan. A place she wanted to be, and Em wondered about what that must feel like.

When she first ran away from the foster parents she headed back to where her home used to be. It was far away but she thought she remembered how to get there from the city centre. She slinked along streets she used to see from the bus window, closer, that she used to walk on. To live near. Now she was hiding.

She just wanted to see them. Her mum and dad. It wasn't good when she had lived there. She was looking after herself most of the time. Staying out of their way. Strangers eyeing her. Poking fun at her. "Get to your room, doll!" But time away can soften things and people can change and she just wanted to see, for herself, one more time.

Trouble was they lived in a big grey council scheme. Tower blocks and concrete and shouty teenagers and lots of empty flats and broken windows and no good hiding places that weren't already owned by junkies and drunks, cat-piss and dog-shit. She did her best to stay in the shadows in the hope that her parents would show themselves. Maybe going to the shops. Maybe thinking about her.

She'd been skulking around for ages, trying not to get noticed. Trying not to be anything unusual. It was dark and rainy and the door squeaked open and a figure came out. A woman. She was looking for someone, glancing up and down the concrete space in front of her. It looked like her mum. Her face got caught by the sweep of a car's headlights as it pulled into the car park. She pulled her arm up to shield her eyes.

Her mum. She was sure now that it was her mum. Maybe her mum knew. Maybe she could feel her. She knew she was here and she was looking for her. Em's heart raced and she wanted to call out. To run over and throw her arms around her. She stepped out of the shadows. Took a step towards her.

The woman staggered, lurched a bit, stumbled, cursed. A man stepped out of the car. Walked across to her. Slipped his arm around her waist. Words were said. He led her up the side of the building. A dark passageway. Pushed her against the wall. Em couldn't see, but she could hear. Noises that she knew well. When he had finished he slipped something into her hand and strode away. She slid down the wall. Took her works out and was gone into that world of oblivion.

Em kept staring, quiet, wide-eyed, like she used to from behind the door, not understanding why other men were hurting her mum and her dad wasn't doing anything about it. She didn't understand what was happening back then. Now she did. Now she knew.

A few minutes later her dad came out of the door. Looked around. 'Jules? Where the fuck are you?' He found the passageway. Found his wife. Found the works. Joined her. Em turned and left. People weren't worth shit. Weren't worth trusting or caring about or hooking up with.

But Charlotte and Kittie-cat and her, that was a different thing. They were a team. And it had to stay that way or she would die.

Chapter 78

Dougie and Tommy were riding up to the village to collect some supplies. It had started raining and the Land Rover would have been the choice of most, but they enjoyed the weather. All of it. The feel of it. The patter of the drops on their hats, their jackets. Earth music.

'Wait here with the horses. I'll be two minutes,' Dougie said, as he jumped down, patted Coll, and headed towards the local shop.

As Tommy followed Dougie's route his gaze was drawn by two men jumping out of their Land Rover. His heart stopped. It was them all right. There was no mistaking that aura, that memory. He instinctively pulled his hand to his face and ran the trace of his scar. Rona growled, Coll stamped. This was the first time they had run into them since the day of the attack.

Dougie had drilled him for this very thing. It was bound to happen one day. A chance meeting. A confrontation of some sort. He tried to calm himself. It would be fine. He had done nothing wrong. But Dougie wasn't here and the vulnerability he felt was too strong. He couldn't just stay here and wait. It was too dangerous.

Men like that. *One, two, three, four, five. One, two, three, four, five.* Breathe. Hold it. Control yourself. No. Run. Get away.

He tried to be normal, clicked his tongue, guided the horses away and up a side street. *Don't look back. Don't look back.* A row of cottages. Small gardens. A narrow pavement. A twisting road. The woods. Into the woods. Now he looked back. No sign. The thumping of his heart, the rain on the leaves. Listen to the rain on the leaves. Calming now. Calming.

A woman walking up the hill. Close. Too close. The weight of the panic. He should creep back, further into the safety of the trees. He couldn't move. Like lead. His heart, his head, his body. Like lead. Instead he squealed to himself. But it wasn't to himself. It was loud, out there on the wind. The woman stopped, turned, glanced at him, frowned and strode on, quickening her pace.

He looked up at the trees, the sky beyond. Calm down. He shouldn't be doing this. Hiding. Drawing attention to himself like this. *Come on Tommy.* He pushed himself on and guided the horses back to the junction with the main road. No one there. Not the men. Not Dougie. No strangers. Breathing slipping back to normal.

*

Dougie settled his basket on the counter by the till.

'Dougie. It's yersel. And how are you keeping?'

'Oh, I'm just fine, Kirsty. And yourself?'

'Och, cannae complain. When you get to my age, well...'

Dougie laughed. 'Plenty years left in you yet.'

'Aye, aye, that's as maybe.' She pointed behind the till.

'Oh and I'll be having one of those please, Ellie?'

'That's me down to my last one. Everyone wants to read about that poor lassie, Charlotte,' Ellie replied. 'On the run now. Hard to believe. There was polis up just the other day, putting up posters all over, asking away. Has she been seen? Keep an eye out. Let them know. Oh, and I'd clean forgotten about this!'

She stretched her hand to the table behind her. Picked up the poster of Charlotte. Flattened it out. Stretched tape across its corners. Placed it carefully in the middle of the window, alongside the one of Charlotte's dad.

'Would you believe it? You know, she used to come up here on her bike. Saw her a few times myself, so I did. Anyway, poor soul. I imagine you'll have seen her too Dougie? Seems she liked the estate. So they said, anyway.'

'Is that right?' Kirsty asked.

'Aye. I saw her a few times. Nice wee lassie,' Dougie replied.

'Not so wee now, by the looks of her.'

'Time flies, so it does. I was just saying that to Mrs Blair. How time flies. Right you are then. Just let me ring up this lot and I'll be with you, Dougie.'

'No rush. You ladies take your time.'

'Oh, and did you hear about the McLarens? Getting divorced, so they are.'

'Quite a shock that one. I mean, good church-going folk. Who'd have thought it?'

'Aye, well, some men just cannae...' she looked at Dougie. 'No offence son. Why don't I just take you first eh? Then Kirsty and I can have a right blether!'

337

'If you're sure?'

'Oh aye, on you come.'

He was glad of the option. Sometimes the gossip here went on and on, like a freight train that had lost control. No stopping it. He was quite sure that he had been the topic often enough and he probably would be again as soon as the door closed behind him.

'And that was your last copy of the Courier? Will you be getting any more in?'

'Well now, let me see, as it's you, Dougie.' She winked, reached under the counter. 'I was keeping this one by for myself, but I can get one off the next delivery.' She slipped the paper into his bag. Smiled.

'That's very kind of you, Ellie. I owe you one!' He waved as he left.

'Do you know of his story?' Ellie whispered once the bell had jingled, the door had closed. 'Before your time, wasn't it? But, well...awfie tragedy, so it was. Young wife, died in childbirth. Tinker lassie, so she was.'

'Is that so?'

'Aye. No good comes from that. You can't be mixing Tinker folk and proper folk. That's what I've always said, and there's the proof. Nice man though. Aye. Nice man.'

'Seems so.'

'Oh, but you know, they had him at the polis station?'

'No!'

'Aye!'

'Helping them with their enquiries, was it?'

'So I heard.'

*

Dougie hurried across to where the waiting horses

should have been, but they weren't there.

A whisper. 'Dougie?'

He glanced around. A wave. Tommy poking out from the road-end. Something had happened.

Tommy felt stupid. He'd gone against everything he and Dougie had talked about. The chances of them bumping into the men from Craigdour were high. He knew that, but he'd run, hidden, like he'd done wrong. Like they were in the right. Stupid. Stupid. Stupid!

Dougie mounted Coll, turned back towards the shop, the Land Rover, the men. 'Head high, son.'

Tommy did his best to keep his back straight, his head high, as they rode through, side by side, displaying their right, no, their belonging to this place. He could feel the men stare.

Dougie patted Coll, smiled at the men. 'Fine beasts, are they not?'

Tommy copied. 'Fine beasts.'

'Damned Tinkers!' was muttered in their wake.

'That older one there, he's not a Tinker. Manager at Durnoch, he is.'

'Thought I recognised him! The uppity bunch who kept complaining. The lot that stole our meadow.'

'That's them. Lord and Lady whatever.'

'Yeah. I remember him, right enough. Well, as far as I'm concerned, in the company of a Tinker, riding a Tinker horse, is a Tinker.'

The men stared after Tommy and Dougie, distaste wafting through the air around them.

'I wonder...' the driver said, a smile creeping across his face.

Chapter 79

At last, a decent lead. A witness had come forward and he didn't seem like some random nut-job. This looked and felt genuine.

'Your name, sir?'

'Harry Townsend, factor at Craigdour.'

'Can you come in to the station and make a statement confirming what you've just told me?'

'My pleasure.'

He was there and spilling his story that afternoon. *This'll teach the little fucker!*

'As I told PC?'

'Jamieson.'

'Right. As I told PC Jamieson, I was just driving by that night and I caught him in my headlights. I didn't think much of it at the time other than it was odd, someone being out, walking about, at that time of night. Then I saw the posters up in the village today. And I saw him. Two and two made four all right. It was the same man, sure as I'm standing here. Ugly scar on his face. There's no mistaking that one!'

'And the date? You have no doubt about the date of the

sighting?'

'None whatsoever. The night of the 27th April.'

*

The flash of blue lights. The screech of sirens. Tommy in handcuffs. Dougie trying to protest.

'Stand aside, sir.'

Tommy wide-eyed, staring at Dougie. Pleading with everything but words.

'Well, would you look at this? Offensive weapons if ever I saw them.' The policeman was holding Tommy's bow and arrows aloft.

'That'll do nicely.'

And then his knife.

'Right. I am arresting you on suspicion of the murder of...'

Tommy's world went black. Everything switched off. The journey in the back seat of the squad car was happening to someone else. Nothing they said made any sense. In the station there was laughter, congratulations, back slapping. And he was in a cell. Cold hard walls, bars across the small high window. It smothered him. Squeezed the life out of him.

They took him to the interview room for questioning. On and on and on.

'It's an easy enough question. Where exactly were you on the night of 27th April last year?'

He couldn't answer. The buzzing in his head took everything else away. Words wouldn't come and even if they could, he didn't know. Settled folks' days and dates? He didn't know. He forced it out. 'I-I d-don't know.' Still, his head bowed, his eyes to the floor.

'Let's make this easy for you, shall we? We have a witness, placing you at the scene. Why did you do it Tommy?'

'I don't know.'

'Right. Now we're getting somewhere.' He smiled across at his colleague. 'So, you're admitting you did it, but you don't know why.'

'No. I...' He shook his head, lifted his gaze from one officer to the other. 'I just...I don't know.'

'You were just robbing the place, right? But it all went wrong and there was a knife and you used it. That's what happened, isn't it?'

'Come on laddie. The quicker you own up, the easier it'll be on you. You were surprised by Mr Desson. You panicked. You grabbed the knife. You stabbed him. You ran.'

He could taste their breath. It sucked the oxygen out of him. His breathing faltered. Short pants as if he had been running. His body slumped forward. His head between his knees. He whimpered like a wounded animal.

'You reckon he's touched, Sarge?'

'I'll put my money on a damned good actor going for an incompetence plea. A night in the cells might loosen his tongue. Make him see sense.'

Chapter 80

Neither knew how long they'd been on the move for. It felt like forever, and yesterday, since they had passed that farmhouse. Woods and hills. Tracks and complete wildness. Both girls felt something changing. A difference in the air.

A copse stood tantalisingly at the foot of the hill they were standing on.

'Are you okay to sleep there for a while?'

'So tired, could sleep any place you say.'

Charlotte knew these trees. Ash. She smiled at Em. 'Give me that knife.'

She hacked off some branches.

'What you doing?'

'You'll see!'

She remembered how to bend them and twist them and secure them into the ground. She set Em to gather bracken then showed her how to weave it into the skeleton of the bender. It was nowhere near as good as Tommy's and they had no canvas, but it was shelter, of a sort.

'Wow! Ain't you the smarty pants? Super cool and no mistaking!' Em crawled in, ran her fingers over the structure they had made, feeling very proud of herself. Proficient. Capable. 'Only gone and made ourselves a real, proper tent out of nothing! Jeez!' She laughed. 'How d'you know this stuff?'

'Someone taught me a long time ago.'

'Could've done this ages ago, like way back in that very first forest.'

'Sorry. I forgot. I forgot about a lot of things.'

'You got that forgetting sickness, then?'

'I guess. Sort of.'

Floodgates opened now and there was nothing she could do to hold her memories back. Tommy. All that time spent with Tommy. All that he had taught her. She felt her body swell with it. She dreamt about it.

When they woke up to the dawn chorus it was time to move on.

'Can't we stay?' Em asked. 'Just for some resting days. It's so cool and I love it here and I want to stay.'

'Okay. A few days, then we're off, right?'

'Yes, Capitano!' Em grinned. Saluted.

Charlotte laughed. It would be nice to stay put in a safe place. To forget why they were hiding. To remember. She wanted time to remember.

Chapter 81

Tommy was taken to a prison. He didn't know where. Far away. A smell he didn't know. Sounds he couldn't identify. He wanted to scream. Instead he banged his fists against the wall until they bled. He smeared his face with the blood, not knowing why. Not understanding anything.

Dougie had gone to see the laird, explained everything.

'And you're absolutely convinced of his innocence?'

'There isn't an ounce of badness in the lad. Yes I am.'

'Right you are then. You leave it with me, Dougie, my man. I'll get on to... Blasted memory! What's that lawyer's name again, Katherine, my dear?'

'Andrew. Andrew McLennan,' Katherine replied.

'That's the chap. Now don't you worry. He'll get your lad out if anyone can.'

Dougie had done all that he could. But it wasn't enough. He felt impotent. Frustrated. For now all he could do was look after what Tommy had left behind. He decided that the best option was for him to stay in the but-and-ben. Keep things as normal for the animals as he could. The horses were fine. Rona paced and whined but she had Gypsy for company and Dougie was no stranger to her. She was eating. That was the main thing.

The buzzard was a different matter altogether. He heard her mew, saw her spinning in the sky above the little dwelling, eyes trained on what was happening on the ground. He had watched in awe as Tommy had walked around with her on his shoulder. As he had set her to fly and called her back. It was a beautiful thing. The trust between the two of them. He had tried to copy. To stand with his arm outstretched. To tempt her with rabbit. She was having none of it. He left meat for her on the roof and hoped that it had been her who had taken it.

*

'Yon laddie wi the scar, the gaffer's sidekick, what d'you make of him getting arrested?'

'Seemed decent enough. Quiet. Hard worker. But you never know.'

'Aye, well, he's a Tinker after all. Got chased off of here a while back, so I heard. Whole family disappeared. Queer folk.'

'What, Tinkers?'

'Aye.'

'All of them?'

'Aye. His lot especially, living in a tent like that. Thieving and the likes.'

'Is that what they say?'

'Aye. It is. And now there's this murder. Well...'

Everyone had an opinion on this, a story about something the Tinkers had done, had said. Rumours flew and multiplied. Dougie did his best to ignore it all. Keep himself to himself. He could stop and correct them. He could let his feelings be known, but for now he hadn't the will.

He walked across the field to the riverbank. Once there he crept along quietly, slowly, close enough to see but far enough not to threaten. He'd come to have a look at the beaver dam. To check on it. There it was, growing as an organic village. The flow of the water had slowed, as it drifted aside, creating a new pond. A new quiet place.

'Quite the thing, isn't it, Tommy?'

'Aye,' he would have replied with a soft smile to his face.

He watched the industrious architects gnawing and fetching, building and weaving, silently, instinctively. For now, at least, they were staying put and if he was lucky there would be kits soon enough. Dougie felt the joy of this; his heart swelled by the image, but behind it, a deep sadness. Tommy. He could picture him in a cell having the life drawn out of him. He had arranged a visit for the following week. He was dreading it.

Chapter 82

Tommy's days were unbearable. Noise and fear and everything heavy and bad. At night at least the noises lessened and when he finally drifted off he was far away. Sitting by the river. Waiting for her. But sleep was always broken. Dreams fleeting. Slipping away too soon.

Dougie had come with the lawyer. They were sitting in a small room, waiting for him. Bare walls, no windows, strip lights, plastic chairs, no air.

'Tommy, this is Mr McLennan. He's going to represent you. Help get you out of here.'

Tommy stared, tried to hold himself up. *Out of here.* He chewed on his lip, imagining it. The air, the sky, the trees, the wild. Far, far away, the wild. It broke him and he wept.

'Come on. Sit yourself down, son. We'll sort this. I promise you, we'll sort this. You'll be out of here before the swallows come back.'

'M-my ani-animals.' He looked up. A pleading in his eyes.

'They're fine. I'm looking after them for you. We're all in the but-and-ben for now. Gypsy and Rona getting up to all kinds of mischief together, let me tell you! She's missing you, keeps looking out for you, but she's just fine. The horses are run every day. Everything is fine with them too.'

'Mona?'

'Aye, she's good too. Staying close. Taking the food I leave for her.'

McLennan cleared his throat. 'Right then. Down to business. Have they explained what's going to happen to you?'

'I don't know. I don't know anything.'

McLennan glanced to Dougie, raised his eyebrows.

'Tommy, mister McLennan is here to help. He's a friend. You can trust him, okay? There's no need to be scared. Now, can you answer him? What they said.'

Tommy nodded. 'They. They said I'm going to jail for a very long time.'

'Did they now?'

'Right.' McLennan cleared his throat again. 'You'll be up in court tomorrow. The judge will ask you for your name and for your plea. Guilty or not guilty. You say nothing else. Your name and your plea, which is not guilty. Have you got that?'

'Aye. T-Tommy M-McPhee.' He shook his head, annoyed at himself for the stammer, for the way he felt, For being weak. 'N-not guilty. Not guilty!'

'That's it. Now I'll see you tomorrow. Bail's not an option, because of, well, because of your situation, so you have to prepare yourself. You'll be in here for a while.'

'I don't understand anything. I haven't done anything.'

He settled back in his cell, drifting off with the photographs Dougie had brought of his animals, of the river, of him and Charlotte.

'Oi! Tinker! You deaf or what? Did you do it then?'

'No.'

His cellmate laughed. 'Join the club!'

*

'Are you quite sure he's up to this?' McLennan asked. 'If he's up there in the stand, being questioned, well, it's not looking good, is it? I didn't know he was, well, in such a poor way, shall we say. Intellectually challenged somewhat, no?'

'No. He's one of the wisest people I know. He's just different.'

'That's all well and good, but how he comes across in court is important. I'm thinking perhaps a deal.'

'What sort of a deal?'

'This is murder we're talking about. A life sentence if it doesn't go our way. If he were to plead diminished responsibility it would be much easier on him.'

'No way! He didn't do this.'

'If that's your decision, and I'm advising against it, but if you insist, if he insists, then there are two things we need to counter. The witness who puts him at the scene on the night in question, the prints on the girl's bike. Any suggestions?'

'The witness is lying.'

'He's an upstanding citizen. Good character, by all accounts.'

'As opposed to Tommy, you mean?'

The lawyer shrugged. 'That's the way the court will see it. An itinerant versus the factor of a renowned local estate. I'm just being honest here.'

'A factor? That's their witness? From Craigdour, is he?'

'Let me just check on that.' He rifled through his papers. 'Yes. Craigdour.'

'Well now it all makes sense. The bastard!'

'I'm sorry?'

Dougie explained the history between them. The story Tommy had finally shared. The loss of land.

'It's not just Tommy he's got it in for, it's me and the laird as well.'

'Right, right. I'm sure we can cast at least some doubt with that, but we badly need a witness, then we have the prints to explain away.'

'Aye, well, the two of them were really close. Charlotte would cycle out to see him all the time. Fingerprints on her bike aren't that hard to explain.'

'And without the presence of Charlotte to confirm this?'

'Is my word not good enough, then?'

'It's not that at all, the more we have, the better. Irrefutable concrete evidence.'

'Photos. I've got some photos of the pair of them.'

'Okay. That's something at least. And you'll be here tomorrow?'

'I'll be here.'

'You're very partial to him, aren't you?'

'Because he's a very fine person and I wish there were more like him.'

Chapter 83

Handcuffs. A room that smelled of a thousand people. Trails of misery wrapped across the seats, the walls. Tommy felt his knees begin to buckle. Felt like he was being crushed. No air. Nothing to breathe.

Tommy, son, stand up tall. Stand up tall.

'Da,' he whispered.

He did as he was told. Stood tall. Looked at them. So hard. So very hard.

'Remanded in custody until...May 3rd.'

He wanted to scream, to cry, to sink into the earth and be gone, but he stood tall.

Chapter 84

Charlotte and Em could hear the hum of traffic on a busy road. They walked far enough from the kerb not to be noticed, but close enough to read any signposts.

'Jeez, seems like everyone else knows right where they are and don't need no signs. Pff!' Em said.

'I know! There must be one soon.'

Finally, the road came to a junction. Signposts!

'Any idea?'

'Never heard of Hexham, but the other sign says Newcastle. We're really, really far north.' She hugged Em. 'Well done you!'

Em shrugged. 'For what?'

'For helping me get this far. For going into all of those little shops and being smart and getting just the right food.'

Em laughed. 'That Christmas cake was the best, right? Super cheap and lasted for ever!'

'That was inspired, Em! But not the best.'

'What was best then?'

'Being my side-captain, of course!'

A smile that could lift a mountain.

Charlotte scooped Tinker up as they walked into Newcastle. He mewled a protest at her. Trotting along beside them had become the norm. A source of amusement. Of purpose. This bag was a very poor alternative. She pulled the zip up so that just his head was poking out. After giving her a dirty look he settled down soon enough, accepting his fate.

'Okay, I need you to stay right by my side. No monkey business, no drawing attention to yourself and absolutely no thieving. Right?'

'Kay.'

'Promise?'

'Said so, didn't I!'

'No. You said *kay.*'

'Promise. Promise, promise, promise.' She grinned.

Charlotte shook her head but couldn't keep a smile from breaking out. Em could be a total pain in the neck, but funny with it. It didn't seem to matter what their situation was, she could always find a way to lighten things. Bring a smile. That was quite special, considering the cruelty life had thrown at her. Charlotte ruffled Em's hair.

'Oi!'

They nipped into a supermarket, stocked up on ready-made food and a few luxuries. Chocolates, marshmallows, Smarties.

'Pockets?' Charlotte said as they approached the checkout.

'Having a laugh, right?'

'Nope, I'm deadly serious.'

Em turned her pockets inside out, patted herself down. A disgusted look on her face. 'Uh-oh.'

'What?'

'The money. Think I've only gone and dropped the money.'

Charlotte closed her eyes. Her heart sank into her boots Without that money they were in dire straits. She imagined begging from strangers, drawing attention to themselves, the police. After everything they had got through, put up with, it could all just fade away. All be for nothing. She felt like crying.

'Ha, ha. Your face! Should've seen your face!' Em held the money out, waved it in front of Charlotte.

'I don't believe it. You're a little...' She held her tongue, let go of her anger.

'A little what?'

'Nothing. Just give me that and let's get out of here.'

At the checkout Em was full of smiles and chatter, having a laugh with the man on the tills. Drawing so much attention to themselves it was ridiculous.

Charlotte kicked her, gave her a "Shut up!" stare. As they walked through the exit she was half expecting an alarm to go off. Security guards to grab them. Haul them away to an office until the police arrived. She was pleasantly surprised when the doors hissed closed behind them and nothing happened.

'Miss?' A stranger's voice.

Ignore it. Carry on.

Again, louder 'Miss?'

Her heart pounding. She stared at Em. Questioning. A shrug of her shoulders in reply. They could make a bolt for it. Run through the car park, slip into the street. Too many people. Running footsteps behind them now. *Shit!*

'Miss? You dropped this!'

Charlotte stopped, turned around.

Em kept walking.

A young man with a smile on his face holding out a ten pound note.

More relief than she had felt for a very long time. 'Really? I didn't even notice. Thank you so much. That's really, really kind of you.'

He cocked his head, grinned, handed the note over and left with a whistle. A skip in his step.

'Em?' She looked around. No sign. 'Em?' Louder now. She checked up and down the rows of parked cars. Nothing. 'Come on, this isn't funny.' She turned onto the main road and there Em was, sitting in a bus shelter as if nothing had happened, her legs swinging back and forth. Charlotte held her arms open incredulously.

'Thought we was gonna get nabbed.'

'Did you now?'

They walked on to a small park, sat down under an oak tree and tore into the food.

'Don't think I've ever been that hungry!' She looked slyly at Charlotte as her hand crept up the back of her hoodie and pulled out a harness set for a cat. 'Well, he needed it. That one's too small and this one is much nicer and...and I got it for him so it's the best!'

'Do you know what a kleptomaniac is?'

'Nope.'

'It's you. A thieving little toe-rag. You just can't not, can you?'

356

'Guess. Sort of got in the habit, like.' She grinned, apologetic, cheeky.

'What if you'd been caught, the police called? Would you be smiling then?'

'What-ifs are silly. Can't live your life full of what-ifs now, can you? Unless, of course, they're good what-ifs, like what if...' She paused, took a deep breath. 'Nah.' She slipped the new harness around Tinker's neck and chest. 'Look, Kitty-cat likes it just fine! Don't cha, Kitty-cat?' She watched proudly as Tinker strutted around seemingly proud too. The multicoloured jewels of the harness twinkled in the sunlight.

'You know he's a boy, right?'

'You saying boys can't wear jewels? That's crass, that is. Jeez Kitty-cat, she's a bit mean.'

'And his name's Tinker.'

'Yeah, yeah.'

Chapter 85

The hum of noise. The weight of the place. As the days crawled by Tommy managed to string a few words together. A few sentences. His cellmate did most of the talking, shared his story, other people's stories. There were taunts and jibes but Tommy didn't listen. Didn't care.

'Leave him be. He's all right, this one.'

'Is that right, aye?'

It seemed his cellmate was well connected. Respected. The other inmates listened to him. Left Tommy alone for the most part.

Dougie came every week. Talked him through everything that was happening. The case, the land, his animals.

'The beavers have been out with their kits. What a sight. Something to behold, so it is. You're going to love it. The sight of them diving and swimming and fooling around. Quite the thing, aye.'

'Are the swallows back then?'

'Aye. Aye they are.' He felt like a failure. He had promised and yet, here they were. Tommy still locked up, and as for the outcome of the trial, well everything was against them. He kept it hidden as best he could. 'Not long now. You'll be walking amongst them soon enough.' He smiled through the lie convincing himself that something he so desperately wanted to happen couldn't be classed as such, but everything was against them. Most damning, the eye witness.

If Tommy could just explain where he had been. If he could trawl up an alibi, a sliver of hope would appear. Without an alibi, an explanation, it would leave the jury in no doubt. Here was a guilty man. A Tinker, a thief and a murderer.

'Tommy, you need to have a really good think. Last spring, did you meet anyone, see anyone? Anyone at all?'

He slowly lifted his head, met Dougie's eyes. 'Aye. Aye there was someone. There were a few folk. After they destroyed my camp I went into yon wee town. I had to buy stuff. Important stuff.'

'When was this?'

He shook his head. 'Spring. That's all I know. But the man at the garage. The man that fixed my face and sold me the canvas. He's one of us, like. A settled Tinker. Right nice man. Knew my dad. Jamie Smith was his name. Aye. Right nice man.'

*

Dougie drove straight over. Had a good chat with Jamie Smith. Yes, of course he remembered. He'd stitched the boy's face up. What a state he'd been in! You don't forget a thing like that. And could he put a date to it? Yes, he could. The receipt for the new canvases he'd ordered the following day. Not a doubt. The date was a hundred percent accurate.

Dougie couldn't quite grasp the relevance of this, but he felt it was important. What was he missing? It didn't give him an alibi, but there was something. Something about this. He had to get hold of McLennan. Run it by him. Talk it through. It would be late by the time he got back to Edinburgh. Well past midnight. Home was just up the road. His bed calling. His dog too. He reached the junction. Left took him home. Right took him city-bound. He indicated. Turned right. Put his foot down.

Chapter 86

The sound of traffic. People everywhere. Busy. Everyone seemed busy. Everyone had a purpose. Knew where they were going. Both girls felt it. Different. Estranged from this life. Anxiety swept through them. A vulnerability.

They ducked into the railway station. Cavernous and noise-filled but somehow safer, less personal. Hidden amongst a wash of strangers.

'Could get on one. Get to the place we're going, right?' Em said.

Charlotte smiled. Yes they could. They were far enough away from everything that had happened. It had been ages. Nobody would even notice them. This would be fine.

They checked the departures. Perth. There it was on the board. The sight of it up there in bright letters as if it were calling to her. *Come on home.* In an hour they could be on a train to Perth. Almost there. Almost home. The end of this and the beginning of something else. She didn't know what that might be, but she imagined slipping into that other world where Tommy and his family lived. They could just disappear. What was it he'd said? "You can make things un-be and un-see and it's only you in your world." Become unseen. What a thought! Charlotte grabbed Em's sleeve. 'Come on!'

They hurried to the ticket office. Stood in a queue. Anxiety zipping about, but it didn't matter. They would be on their way. The person in front of them was full of questions. A foreign tourist not quite understanding.

'You say slower?'

Em was scanning around, jiggling from one foot to the other as if she needed to pee.

Charlotte only had eyes for the counter in front of her. The woman behind it. The machine she controlled. *Come on, come on*

The tourist turned around. 'I sorry for wait.'

'No, no, you're fine,' Charlotte replied with a smile. 'No hurry.'

At last it was her turn. 'Hi! An adult and a child to Perth please?'

'Would that be return or one way?'

'One way.'

The tickets were sitting there on the counter behind a perspex shield. The fares. A panic as she checked their money. And there it was. They didn't have enough left to cover the fares. Charlotte stood there, embarrassed, a flush spreading across her cheeks. It couldn't be done.

'I'm so sorry. I thought I had enough.'

'You can pay by card.'

The woman was staring now. Too intently. A spark of recognition. No. Not here. That couldn't be. She was just being paranoid.

'I...I don't have one.' She lifted her hand in apology.

A tap on her shoulder. She froze. Didn't want to turn around. Didn't want to accept that this was happening. A middle-aged man dressed in a suit and tie, a briefcase tucked under his arm. A stranger.

'How much are you short, love?' A smile.

Her mouth was dry. Words struggling. 'Um, I'm, I'm not sure.'

'May I?' He was pointing in front of her at the teller.

She stepped aside.

'A return to Manchester, and just add theirs on, if you can do that?'

'Right you are,' the teller replied. More smiles. 'That's mighty kind of you.'

He shrugged, handed his card over, turned back and smiled at Charlotte and Em. Em was staring, open mouthed in amazement.

'Here you are, sir. You have a nice day now,' the teller said.

'Thank you. You too!'

He gave them their tickets. 'You two take care now,' he said, pointedly, seriously. 'Look after yourselves.'

'I can't believe...thank you. Thank you so much.'

He left with a wave and a swathe of kindness.

'Think he was an angel,' Em whispered. 'Folk ain't like that. Not normal folk. Not for real.'

Conversations had sprung up in the queue. 'How lovely was that?' 'What a nice man.'

Charlotte didn't feel comfortable with the eyes of so many people on them. They'd caused a scene. Drawn attention to themselves. People would remember this. Remember them. Up there, CCTV being watched by

363

security, by the police. Everyone could see her. Could see them. She tried to convince herself again that it didn't matter. Not here. No one was looking for her here. Em skipped along behind, seemingly unperturbed.

Charlotte was heading for the exit. Hanging around the station for an hour wasn't something she wanted to do. They would come back just before the train was due to leave, hop on, hopefully unnoticed.

They walked around the block a few times, hoodies up, eyes down, not wanting to go far, to lose track of time, of place, to be seen. It was exhausting. This alertness. This constant worry.

Em nudged Charlotte. 'Ooo Greggies! Love a Greggies, me! Real, proper, fresh. Not-out-of-a-bin Greggies. Can we? Can we? Nice man from back there says we can.'

'Okay.' She laughed. 'Thank you nice man.' She checked the clock on the wall. Twenty minutes. Plenty of time. The shop had one customer. They waited until he left then walked in.

Charlotte had no idea – had never been in a Greggs before – so Em ordered for them. A chicken bake each. They both enjoyed the heat of it, the steam, the grease that trickled out, the flakes of pastry that clung to their chests.

'Good right?'

'Good.' Charlotte agreed.

They walked across the station concourse, the loud speakers blaring unintelligible crackled words, the hum of movement, travel. Suitcases rattling across concrete. A plethora of voices. Excitement. Sadness. Hugs and smiles and tears.

Charlotte slipped her hand into the pocket of her jacket and pulled the tickets out with a great sense of relief. She held them up for the guard. He smiled. Ushered them through.

'On you go girls. Just in time! Hurry now!'

The doors hissed shut as they made their way along the aisle, carriage after carriage. So many strangers all ignoring each other. Em was adamant that she wanted to go right the way through the train. To see it all. Satisfied she chose a seat with a table. They sat on opposite sides, looking out of the window, looking back at each other, grinning.

'You excited then?' Em asked.

'Sort of. And sort of not.'

'So why we going if you're sort of not?'

'It's home, and it's a place I love. The most beautiful place in the whole world, for me. But something awful happened and that's what makes it sort of not.'

'Hmm. And what about me?'

'What do you mean?'

'When you get there, what about me?'

'Em, you're my side-captain. We stay together, right?'

'Kay. Just checking.' She felt herself swell at the name again. Side-captain. It was a really important thing to be. A side-captain.

The train hugged the coast. Waves crashing against high cliffs. Inaccessible sandy coves. Gulls twirling and swooping in the wind. Em was transfixed.

'Ain't never seen the sea.'

'Really? It's beautiful, isn't it?'

'Yeah. It's cool.'

'We'll go, when we get home.'

'By the sea, is it?'

'No. It's miles away.' She laughed. 'But we'll go anyway.'

'Promise?'

'Big promise.'

'So what's it like then?'

'You'll see yourself soon enough.'

'Yeah.'

Chapter 87

May 3rd. This was it. Dougie hadn't slept. He doubted Tommy had either. He sat in court anxiously awaiting Tommy's arrival. The room was full. A buzz of whispered chatter. Someone laughed. Dougie glared at them. How could they? How could people find amusement here? A man's future at stake. A gasp as Tommy appeared. Silence as they watched him being taken to the dock.

Tommy's head was down, his back stooped. He just looked guilty. Downtrodden and guilty.

'All rise.'

The Sheriff entered, gowned and wigged. Terrifying.

'Thomas McPhee, is charged that on the night of April 27th last year he did murder Mr Roger Desson at his home in Briar Cottage,' the clerk began.

The walls were sucking Tommy's breath away. No air. He swayed back and forth. The words became a string of incomprehension. He heard none of them.

'My client pleads not guilty to the indictment.'

Tommy mumbled. Fumbled. Counted in his head. Stared at the floor. Anything but this.

'Your honour, if I may have a word with my client?'

The sheriff nodded. Gestured towards Tommy.

'Tommy. We've been through this. You have to stand up straight and tall and speak in a confident clear voice. You can do this. You have to do this!'

Tommy looked up. Fifteen faces staring at him from the jury. The sheriff, stern and otherworldly. He turned to look behind. So many faces. Staring. Judging. But there. There was Dougie. *Come on son,* he mouthed. Forced a smile. An affirming nod.

'N-not g-guilty. Not guilty!' he shouted. Shocked by the force, by the sound of his own voice. His eye held on to Dougie. Nothing else. No one else.

'Counsel approach. Are we quite sure the defendant is competent to stand trial?'

'Yes, your honour. The psychiatric report confirms his ability. He just needs time to settle, to respond.'

'Very well. Proceed.'

The prosecution called the arresting officers, forensics. Defence poked and prodded, but there was little they could argue.

'The prosecution calls Harold Townsend.'

Tommy now stared at this man. This man who had tried to take everything away from him. This man who stood there telling lie upon lie.

'It's not true!' Tommy shouted. 'None of it is true! He lies. The man is a liar!'

'Silence or I'll hold you in contempt of court.'

'Lies!'

The sheriff shook her head, glanced at her watch. 'Counsel, you'd best have a strong word with your client before we resume tomorrow. Court dismissed.'

Townsend smiled as Tommy was led back down. He looked across at Dougie. Grinned.

Chapter 88

Perth. This place that had sounded magical and special wasn't really. It was just a town. People. Buildings. Roads. Nothing special. Not like Em had been expecting. She screwed her nose up, gave Charlotte a look of distaste.

'This it then? The most beautiful place in the whole world. Pff.'

Charlotte laughed. 'Not here. There's a way to go yet.'

'Oh. Could've said. Let me know, like.'

'We need to get a bus from here. The station's right there, see?'

'Flippin eck! Thought you didn't want to get on no bus.'

'I didn't, but it's either that or a few more days on foot and I don't know about you, but I'm kind of done in. I just want to get there.'

Em shrugged. 'S'pose.'

It seemed like the world was smiling at them. Their bus was sitting at the terminus, just about to leave. They jumped on, paid the driver, heads down, quiet voices. Em wanted to sit at the back but Charlotte nudged her into a seat three back from the driver. An old woman sat across the aisle from them, her purse poking out of her pocket.

'Don't even think about it,' Charlotte whispered.

'What?'

'You know what.'

Em shrugged, pulled a face.

Blairgowrie. They had to change buses. It became a journey Charlotte knew well. Perhaps too well. That other person. That girl she used to be. People she had gone to school with. People she had known. Normal people back home having dinner, watching telly, doing normal-people things. It was a life distant.

They stepped off the bus into drizzle. A quiet little town, hardly anyone about. Charlotte pulled her hoodie up, checked around. Nobody. Okay. For now they were okay. She wiped the rain off the cover of the timetable. It was blurry, hard to read. She didn't really need to check anyway. A part of her history. Twenty minutes. She didn't want to stand still. Not here. They walked on.

'Where we going, then?'

'Just to waste some time.'

Charlotte stopped suddenly, her attention snatched by a poster flapping against a lamppost. 'Shit!' she whispered. There she was. Her picture on display for all to see. Above it one of her dad, her old house. She wanted to crumple up into nothing. To disappear.

'Proper bandito stuff, this!' Em giggled.

'Shh.'

They slipped up a side road, walked in a circle, keeping their heads down. Not looking. Doubts now. Doubts about all of it. Could she risk getting on a bus here? It might

371

even be one of the drivers she used to say "hi" to as she climbed on board heading home from school. She talked it over with Em. Whatever else could be said about her, she had survived on the streets without getting caught for years. She was street-wise, despite her joking around and being silly.

They agreed to go for it. Risk the bus. Em would lead, Charlotte follow. Em was drilled on what to do. What to say. Where to put the money. Where to get the tickets from. No extra chat. No jokes. This was serious.

Back at the bus stop. Five minutes that felt like forever. At last the trundle of the bus that used to take Charlotte home. She nudged Em. 'Stick your arm out.'

'Kay.'

The bus indicated. Click, click, click. Orange flashes across the wet tarmac. The door clunked open.

'Ye'll be catching yer death oot there wee yin! Awfie, so it is.'

Em struggled to understand the strength of his accent. Hesitated. Worked it out. 'Yes,' she mumbled. Handed the money over. Took the tickets. 'Ta!'

Charlotte slunk in behind her, her eyes to the ground The pull to look up. To be normal. To smile. To look around. To check for familiar faces. No. Ignore it all. This isn't happening. She isn't here.

They both kept quiet for the entire journey. Em sensing the need. Charlotte's head filling up with old thoughts. Old Places. It was overpowering. Frightening. At last they were there. She nudged Em, stood up, rang the bell. The bus pulled up at the stop near her old house.

'Thank you,' she mumbled to the driver as she stepped

off the bus, trying so hard to keep it together. Keep it normal. The hiss of the doors closing, the surge of the engine as the bus pulled off. Disappeared around the corner.

Silence, until her senses adjusted. The air. So pure and clean that it washed her, lifted her mind, her body. That smell. Forest and farm and river and meadow. And that sound. The quiet that wasn't quiet at all. The rustling of the leaves. The flow of the river. The call of the crows. The songs of blackbird, robin, lapwing, sparrow and so many more. That choir. It felt, for a moment, as if nothing had changed. She could run home, open the back door. "It's just me, Dad!"

'So where are we then?' Em asked, tugging at her, breaking the spell.

'Home. This used to be my home.' A smile she didn't feel took hold of her face. A distant smile from somewhere else.

Chapter 89

Tommy collapsed on his bunk. He didn't want to cry, but he couldn't help it. Tears fell.

'That bad, was it?'

'Aye,' he forced out between sobs, feeling weak and useless.

'Here.' His cellmate handed him a roll-up.

'I-I don't.'

'Christ man, take it and have a smoke!'

He stretched his arm out, accepted the rollie, pulled it to his mouth, inhaled. The paper stuck to his lips, the taste was disgusting, the effect on his lungs even worse. He coughed and spluttered, banging his head as he jerked up. His cellmate laughed. Tommy couldn't help but join in.

'There now. That's better! So tell me.'

Tommy told him as best he could about the lying man, about what he'd done to him and his horses, about how he got Coll back. It all came blurting out and he didn't understand why, but there it was. His story told.

'What a right bastard, eh? Who is this eejit?'

'Harry Townsend, f-factor at Craigdour.'

'See if I get off and you don't, I'll do the bastard for

you and no mistaking. Fuck's sake. Total bastard! Cunts like that need taught a lesson.'

When Tommy closed his eyes all he could see was the leering face of Townsend. Leering as he whipped him. Leering as he left the court. He would have to face him again tomorrow. His head lost control at the thought. Tomorrow.

'Tommy, man, you need to stop that. It won't do you no good. You gotta tell yourself you're innocent, tell them you're innocent, and you'll be okay, right?'

He sniffed, wiped his nose on his sleeve. 'Right.'

But there would be more of Townsend. He would have to listen to more lies. Sit there and listen and be quiet and not respond. Only speak when he was asked to. Confident and clear. That's what the lawyer had said. Confident and clear. How was he supposed to do that?

Chapter 90

Charlotte stared as they walked past her house, sad and desolate. Paused. She was torn between her house – home, but a place where something so awful had happened – and carrying on to Durnoch, to the river. It was nearly summer now. Tommy might be there. Him and his family and that world of simplicity where everything was just...right.

Just a quick look at her old house. She had to have that. They crept along the track at the rear of the house and slipped into the back garden. Police tape fluttered against the door. A knot curled through the pit of her stomach. Doubts now. No. This was just something she had to do. Had to face. She tried the door. Locked. She hurried to the shed. Pushed the door. A squeak as the door opened. '*I'll need to fix that.*' The voice of her dad. She swallowed hard. Her eyes spun around the walls, everything as it was, but different. A stale smell like rust and decay. Her dad's busy tool shelf. The old ceramic plant pot sitting upside down on a saucer. She lifted it. Almost dropped it. Closed her eyes in relief as it settled in her hand. A coating of dust on her fingers. The spare keys sat there like always. She clutched them tightly in her hand.

Em appeared at the door. Tinker at her feet. 'Someone there!' she whispered urgently.

'Where?'

'Garden next door. Looking right this way.'

'I know you're there and if you've got any idea what's good for you, you'll be off. I've called the police. They'll be here any minute, so they will. Away with you!'

Charlotte froze. Martha! She was a friend, wasn't she? The choice was to run and have the police in pursuit, or to show herself. To trust to old friendships and fate.

'Martha, it's just me, Charlotte!'

'Well, I'll be...Oh my lord. Charlotte! Is that really you? What the devil? Come away over so as I can get a proper look at you.'

She stepped out, Em in her shadow.

'Well, I'll be! Come away in, love. Come away in.'

She ushered them through her back door and into the kitchen. Such a comforting smell of home-made food. Memories of meals made and shared. Of help when times were tough.

Martha opened her arms and hugged Charlotte so tight the breath almost got taken from her. She peeled away, held her at arms length, stared, shook her head. 'Well I'll be.'

'Have you really called the police?'

'No, no. The amount of times I've said that to nosey busy-bodies, you've no idea. Folk poking around as if it was any of their business, and now there's this court case going on. Well...'

'What court case?'

Martha pulled out one of the kitchen chairs. 'I think

you'd best sit, Charlotte love.' She pulled another. 'And you wee one. Come and sit.'

'Sorry, that's Em, my wee side-captain.'

Em grinned.

'Oh my, would you credit it? Your wee cat is just the spitting image of your Kitty.' As if on command Kitty appeared, sniffed the air cautiously before jumping on to Charlotte's lap. Kneading her legs. Taking possession. She laughed before crying. Tears falling on Kitty's fur.

Em stared. 'Right! Get it now! Kitty-cat meet Kitty.' She laughed.

'I'll just make a wee cup of tea,' Martha said. 'The world's always a better place when you've a cup of tea in front of you.'

Em cast her eyes around around the kitchen. Pine units adorned with all kinds of plates. Blue and white. Pink and white. Old-fashioned looking with pictures of horses and farms and boats and flowers. Mugs hung from hooks. Tumblers sparkled behind glass doors. Every space was filled. Where there wasn't a cupboard or a shelf there were pictures. She walked across to get a better look at the photographs. 'That's you! And is that your dad?'

Charlotte nodded.

'Sorry.' Em shrugged, cringed. 'Shouldn't have. I'm a bit, well rubbish at stuff.' She quickly took her seat again. Swung her legs back and forth.

'Right, well, here we are.' Martha set a tray with a teapot, three mugs, and a plate of biscuits, on the table. 'I'll admit to being surprised at seeing you back here, what with everything that's going on.' She cleared her throat, looked hard at Charlotte. 'There have been posters up all over. You'll have seen some, maybe.'

Charlotte nodded, biting her lip.

Em stared at this stranger.

'I've said time and again that you wouldn't come back here.' She turned her back on Em. Whispered. 'Not if you were on the run, as they say.'

'It's all right. I've got nothing to hide from Em. And I didn't do anything anyway.'

Martha glanced up at the clock. 'Would you look at the time! You two must be exhausted. You'll be needing some sleep. Away up to the spare room now and get yourselves a good night's rest. We'll talk more in the morning.'

The feeling of safety, of being cared for, was immense. Charlotte's eyes were heavy. Her body exhausted.

'You won't say anything, will you? About us?'

'I'll not be saying a word.'

Chapter 91

That night Tommy had a dream. He was at his pearl-pool, wading through the water, pushing against it, but not moving. The water was rising around him. A swell stronger and bigger than he had ever seen. So strong it came in waves, like the waves on the ocean. Formidable and unforgiving. There on the opposite bank, that man, Townsend, leering as he scooped down into the water and plucked out Tommy's pearl shells. All of them, ripped from their beds, rootless and dying. Something that had been a part of his family's life for generations would be no more. Something that he had been nurturing for so very long, gone. He knew this was it. This was the end. He could give himself to the water now. Leave it all.

Dougie called from the bank. 'Fight against it, lad. This way. This way!'

Tommy pushed harder. Lunged against the water. The leering face. He leapt at it. Gouged at it. But it laughed back at him.

'Oi! Tommy!'

He was awoken by the shaking and calling of his cellmate.

'You must have been having a right bollocks of a dream. Fuck's sake. You all right?'

It took a few minutes for him to process where he was. To push away the dream and remember. He squeezed his head, screamed quietly, inwardly.

'It's your big day. Go get the bastard. Go get him!'

The journey again. The stairs up. The dock. Strangers. So many strangers watching him. He looked around. No Dougie. A panic. He needed Dougie. One person to see belief in. To know was on his side. He was sinking again. Push it away. Townsend. The words of his cellmate. *Get the bastard,* he whispered to himself.

Chapter 92

Em was sitting on the floor playing with Kitty and Tinker, giggling at their antics as they skittered across the floor in pursuit of a ping-pong ball.

Martha wasn't quite ready to explain about Tommy. This would hurt, perhaps be too much. Instead she tried to keep the conversation to Charlotte and Em. What they had been through. As the story unfolded she punctuated it with brief comments, exclamations.

'No!'

'Oh, the beast!'

'Just the two of you, all alone?'

'Oh my dear.'

Em sat quietly now, listening to it all, feeling strangely distant. Set apart. She shuffled across to Charlotte, sat at her feet, her arm across her knees. Possession. Belonging. Charlotte was hers.

'I didn't know what to do, where to go, but I had to come back. To see the place again. To be here. I need my memory of it back. All of it.'

'Well of course you do. Of course you do.'

*

'Now, I hope you don't mind, but I took the liberty of popping next door and fetching some of your clothes. Some old ones for the youngster.' She held up a pair of jeans, a T-shirt, a sweater. Smiled at Em. 'These should fit just fine. Just as well Roger...just as well he wasn't someone to throw things out that still had a use to them.'

Charlotte swallowed, bit back her emotions. Her dad spoken of in the past tense. 'Thank you. You've been so kind.'

'Ach, away with you!'

Martha walked across to the cooker, feeling awkward, memories drifting in. Secret meetings with Roger when he crept into her bed. Hiding it all from Charlotte, even now, after his death. Hiding it all. Charlotte's memories must remain unsullied. She focussed on making breakfast. Scrambled eggs, toast, cereal. Those poor girls. She sighed. The questions would come soon enough, but she would have them eat their breakfast first.

The letterbox clattered. All three jumped at the noise.

'It'll just be the papergirl. Not to worry.'

'I'll get it for you,' Charlotte said, her chair scraping across the stone floor as she stood up.

'No, no. I'll...'

But it was too late. The look on Charlotte's face as she glanced at the headline. The photograph of the accused. Tommy. So much older. His face scarred and full of fear. Barely recognisable as that boy who had changed her life. Who had completely stolen her heart. Her face drained of all colour. She felt sick. Her legs began to buckle. She swooned, stretched her arm out to the wall for support. Martha ran across to catch her. She let her slip slowly to the floor. A crumpled heap of nothing.

'Tommy...' she mumbled.

'What's going on? Don't understand none of this. What's going on? What's wrong with her?' Em crouched down beside her. 'Come on, Clyde. Come on.'

'Fetch Charlotte a glass of water, can you, Em?'

She wanted to be called Bonnie, or Side-captain. She wanted this to be different.

Chapter 93

Dougie had tossed and turned all night. Sleep didn't come easy to him in the city anyway. Not enough air. Too much noise. No darkness. Not real darkness. That was without the enormity of the court case refusing to loosen its grip on his head. Whatever he was feeling, he knew that Tommy was going through a hell far worse than his. Finally, as dawn broke, his brain switched off and he dozed. The doze turned into a deep sleep which even the alarm hadn't woken him from.

He threw his bedclothes off in a panic. Checked the time. 'Jesus!' Jumped out of bed. Leapt in the shower. Dressed and ran.

'Sir?' the receptionist called. 'A message!'

'No time!'

He was quite sure it would be McLennan asking why he hadn't shown. Nothing had ever made him feel this low. This shitty. How could he? With everything that was at stake, how could he? Tommy left without support, facing that man. What he might say. What he might do. *Please God let nothing have happened.*

He barged through the hotel's doors and hoofed it

along the cobbled streets of the Royal Mile. Horns blared as he dipped through the traffic. The squeal of brakes. A near miss. 'You fucking idiot!' screeched through the window. Dougie's hands held up in some attempt at apology.

Too many people. Too many cars. Finally there.

Chapter 94

Charlotte fought to compose herself. To think. 'It wasn't him. I know it wasn't him, but I just can't...' She closed her eyes in frustration at the blackness that stood in front of her memory.

'I'm not convinced of it myself,' Martha said. 'And your pal, Dougie, he's not convinced either. In fact he has no doubt at all that he's innocent.'

Charlotte sat bolt upright. 'I need to go back in there. I need to stand there again and remember.'

'I'm not so sure that's wise.'

'I am!'

She snatched the keys and leapt over the garden wall. Her fingers were shaking as she tried to put the keys in the lock.

'Here. Let me,' Em said, pushing her aside.

The lock clicked. The door swung open. The wrong smell. Not her house. Not her dad. Everything wrong. She stepped into the living room. The stain of her dad's blood still there.

'I'm sorry...I...they wouldn't let me,' Martha said.

She shook it away, ran up the stairs. Looked down. 'I

need you two to go.'

Em and Martha backed out of the room, worried glances from one to the other.

Charlotte went back into her bedroom. Tried to remember that night. What exactly had happened that night? She had been asleep. She tried to bring it back by lying on the bed. First there had been that sound. Breaking glass. She had leapt out of bed, run to the top of the stairs. Saw a scuffle. Called the police. From where? Her dad's room. She pushed at the door to her dad's room. *Don't look at anything. Don't feel anything. Just remember.* She picked up the phone. Repeated those words.

'Help. Help us.'

'I can't hear you, love. What's the emergency?'

'Briar Cottage. A man attacking my dad.'

Back out to the top of the stairs. She had stretched her arm to the wall, fumbled for the light-switch. Flicked it on.

'Charlotte no!'

She remembered the peculiar stillness. A moment when time stopped. Then the tussle. The man and her dad on the floor. That sound. Soft. Thick. Sickening. That grunt. She remembered it all. Felt it all.

The man had jumped back up. Stared from the body at his feet to Charlotte. He had turned and fled.

Charlotte ran down the stairs. 'What time is it?'

'Are you all right?'

'Yes! What time is it?'

'Early. Eight.'

'Can you drive us?'

'Of course. Where to?'

'The court. I need to get to the court.'

'But it's away down in Edinburgh. Could we not just call someone? The police? I mean, if you've remembered. I'm guessing that's what's happened.'

'I can't go to the police. They're after me.'

'Yeah. They want her. The pigs. Banditoes me and her! Proper banditoes!'

'Em! Really?'

'Sorry, but it's proper exciting.' She paused. 'But there's pigs crawling all over courts, right? They'll get you. You and me been ducking and diving all over the place keeping away from them and now you're gonna walk right in there to fucking pig central?'

'Em, they've got him, and I can help him.'

'They only wanted you as a witness, didn't they?' Martha asked.

'For this, yes. For what happened down there? I don't know.'

'Oh Charlotte, are you sure about this?'

'I have never been more sure of anything in my life.'

'Clyde, remember? That's us. Bonnie and Clyde. You and me till we die.'

'Em, that was a game. That was make believe.'

'Weren't no game.' She pulled herself into the corner of the back seat squeezing her hands so tight together that it hurt. She hated crying. Never got anything done ever, unless it was fake. This wasn't fake and she hated it.

Chapter 95

The first day had been torture enough, but at least he'd had Dougie to focus on. To keep him grounded. Now there was nothing, no one. No one that understood. That believed him. That lawyer, he said things, but he was lying. The feeling was wrong. No connection. No belief. Not really. Just words. So many words. Big words that had no place in real life. Big words from his lawyer, from the other lawyer, from all of them. Big words that could twist and turn and make you forget everything. Make you say anything.

He found himself looking at the ground again. Looking at his shoes. He knew that he shouldn't, but there was such a weight pushing down on him he couldn't resist. He couldn't fight against it. Not on his own. But there, on his shoe, caught between sole and upper, a tiny feather. White and pure and beautiful. He bent down, slipped it free. Ran his fingers along its perfect edge. The gift of flight. He was taken away, flying up there above the trees, the forest, along the line of the river, the bay. He looked down and saw her sitting there. Waiting. He smiled. *Get the bastard.*

He looked up, looked across at the sheriff, the jury. The

lying man was saying things. A buzz of words. His lawyer was asking questions. Noise. All just noise. His hands gripped the rail in front of him. He stood up. 'Get the bastard!' he shouted.

'I beg you pardon?'

Silence. Heavy and cold. A smirk. A murmur of whispers.

Tommy stared at Townsend. Their eyes locked.

Chapter 96

Charlotte glanced at the speedometer. It felt so slow, but it wasn't. They were driving at exactly the speed limit.

'Can't we go any faster?'

'You'll not be wanting to get us stopped for speeding. More time taken.'

'Oh Christ. This is killing me!'

Finally the Forth Road Bridge. A queue at the toll. Some idiot taking too long. Fumbling for change. Dropping it. Laughing. Getting out of the car to pick it up. More laughter. An exchange of pointless meaningless words. Pleasantries that belonged in a different world.

'Come on, come on, come on.'

Money paid. Barrier lifted. And through. Edinburgh. Chock a block with traffic. Bus lanes. Traffic lights. Everything seemed to be against them.

'Why the big rush? I mean, you'll get there today and that's fine, isn't it?' Em asked.

'You don't understand. He struggles with things that most folk don't. He might do something really stupid.'

'Jeez!'

'And Martha, when we get there I need you to take Em

away somewhere. Keep her safe. Can you do that for me?'

'Of course.'

'Staying with you!'

'You can't, Em. I want you to be safe. Just stay put.'

Princes street. Traffic crawling.

Em stared up at the castle. The gardens, the castle rock. Magical. Taken away for a few precious minutes. 'Wow.'

They turned up the steep incline of The Mound, twisted in between ancient blackened tenements on one side, classic elegance on the other. Arches, pillars, and grandeur. A wait at the crossroads, left into Lawnmarket. At last, the High Court. Martha pulled up. Charlotte leapt out.

'Watch her cos she'll try and run.' She called back at them.

Em let out a heavy sigh as she watched her disappear. 'What if they catch her? Drag her off to jail? What then?'

Chapter 97

Guards, police, people watching. Everywhere people. Head down. Walk on through. No! Head up. Look ahead. Straight ahead. Through security. The metal detector. The beep. Her brain sparking off. Did she have anything she shouldn't? The knife? Oh my God, the knife! No. No, she didn't have it. Probably just her keys or her jacket or her belt...

'Over here, miss?'

She was patted down, her pockets checked. 'You're all right. Where is it you're going?'

'The McPhee trial.'

'Packed out, that one. 1 doubt you'll get in. Just along there, to your right.'

'Thank you.'

Her way was barred. 'Sorry miss. I can't let you in. It's full.'

'But I need to! Can't you just squeeze me in? Please?'

He looked more closely at her. A twinge of familiarity. 'Don't I recognise you from somewhere?'

She turned around, panicked. There had to be another way. Footsteps hurrying towards her. She didn't know what to do. To run? To ignore? To plead once more?

'Charlotte? Is that really you?'

She turned. The weight slipped off her. 'Dougie,' she whispered.

He put his arms around her, pulled her close. 'Well, I never.'

'With you is she, sir?'

'Yes. Yes she is.'

'I was just saying to the lass, chock full today. Not a chance.'

She saw one and took it. Dodged past him. Pulled the door open. Ran in. 'Tommy!'

He looked up. His face split into something else. A smile the likes of which he hadn't felt since he had last seen her. So long ago. 'Charlotte,' he called.

'What on earth? Young lady, kindly control yourself and leave this court immediately.'

Strong hands grabbed her arms, pulled her back out of the court. 'No! I'm his daughter. Mr Desson's daughter,' she called. 'It wasn't Tommy! I know it wasn't him!'

Tommy's lawyer looked to Charlotte, to the Sheriff. 'Your honour, we obviously have a new witness here. Defence is calling for an adjournment.'

The sheriff pulled a face of exasperation. Slammed her gavel against its wooden block. 'Court adjourned.'

Townsend's leer fell to the floor.

Tommy kept his eyes on Charlotte for as long as he could as he was led away again.

Chapter 98

The next day Townsend confirmed his sighting, confirmed the scar being the most obvious means of identifying the suspect.

'And you are quite sure about the scar?' McLennan asked yet again. 'No doubt in your mind?'

'Not a shred of doubt. None at all. Picked out clear as day by my headlights.' He turned and smiled at Tommy. 'No doubt!'

'The defence calls Mr James Smith.'

He was sworn in, asked a few succinct questions. The most significant two being the date of his meeting with Tommy and the freshness of the wound.

'Oh, aye. Stitched it up myself, so I did.' He winked across at Tommy. 'Now you can't be doing that on an old wound, can you?'

Cross examination was brief. The prosecution tasting defeat. Next up, Charlotte. She had given a detailed description of the suspect to the police. A photofit had been created. There was no doubt that it wasn't Tommy. She confirmed that they were friends, that he had pushed her bike along the road for her, that he was innocent.

'Case dismissed! Mr McPhee you are free to go.'

*

New posters were put up of the photofit. A new round of door to door, questions, hoping for the best. Finally an arrest in Glasgow. A series of break-ins. The photofit looked good. The prints and DNA sealed it. They had their perpetrator. He didn't deny it. There was little point. He pleaded manslaughter. There had been no intention. An accident. That was all. One pointless, senseless act that had changed so many lives.

A witness had come forward last year saying that she had seen what had happened between Charlotte and Bobby. An accident. Nothing more. They hadn't been after her at all. One police force not communicating with the other. All that running and hiding. But she wouldn't change it. Any of it.

One year later

Dougie stood high in the forest watching the scene below. Three figures now sat in that little bay of the river as dusk fell and settled its gentle hue across the land. Laughter trickled amongst the birdsong. He could go and join them but this was how it had all begun, all those years ago, only now there was one more. Wee Em. She had slotted into it all as if it were meant to be. The hardness slipping off her with every day that she spent out in this place of wild beauty.

It was all the better for losing Townsend. Sent down for his lies. Perjury. Two years and a fine. He won't be smiling for a while.

*

'Your name's Townsend, is it? From Craigdour? Well, well, well. This one's for you, Tommy lad.'

*

Of course there was a new factor over at Craigdour now. That couldn't be stopped. Always one more. Another fight. One day, perhaps, a dialogue would be struck up between the estates. An agreement made to better the land. Let her be. Forests connecting and spreading. The hills breathing again. Maybe it was just a dream. He hoped not. And he would never stop trying.

He had met others at that rewilding course. Like-minded people who wanted to do better for their environment. Their planet. The belief that, left to herself, nature would sort it all out. No culling. No need for human intervention. Wolves and lynx and wild-cats keeping a handle on it all. They kept in touch, shared ideas, took encouragement from one another.

From where he stood he could see the new woods that had been planted under Tommy's guidance. Birch, aspen alder, hazel, rowan and willow. Nothing structured. Nothing through the eyes of man. The beginnings of another place of wildness to connect with that which climbs up from the river and beyond. A special place.

*

Footsteps crept up behind Dougie. Soft and gentle. Arms slipped around his waist.

'Well, Douglas, are you not going to join them then?'

'No Martha, love. That's their place. I'll let them be.'

'And do you think they'll stay? Tommy's travelling days are really over?'

'I don't know. There might always be that calling. It's in his soul. A part of him. But then so is this place now. He's started something special here and it'll be years in the making. Generations even. Durnoch needs him if the dream is to hold.'

'The dream of lynx and wolf?'

'Aye. That!'

'We need to call Em in for her tea, though. School tomorrow!'

Dougie laughed. 'Rather you than me.'

'Aye, well...But she's changed a lot, hasn't she? Being out here, amongst all of this. It's like it's softened all of the hard bits. Taken the edge off of her.'

'Aye, it has a way of doing that, right enough.'

'Yourself?'

'Aye! Nothing good was coming my way before I found this.' He took a deep breath, inhaled the place and her beauty and her magic.

'And look at you now.'

He kissed her hand, slipped his finger across her wedding band. Held her eyes. 'No regrets, then?'

'Now what would I be regretting?'

'Moving in with me. Adopting Em. It's quite a lot to take on.'

'It's the best lot, and I love all of it.' She pulled him close. The feel of him. Strength and goodness.

He kissed her head, whispered in her ear. 'Likewise.'

She stared past him, through the trees. A streak of something. 'What was that?'

'Lynx?' he grinned.

'You didn't?'

He shrugged. 'Maybe.'

*

Tommy and Charlotte sat still and silent, back to back, heads resting on each other's shoulders, eyes skyward. Rona was stretched out beside them. Contented snuffles and twitches escaped as she slept. They listened as footsteps became muted and voices trailed off into the trees, Em grumbling, albeit half-heartedly, Dougie and Martha chuckling softly, until sound slipped into birdsong, both plaintive and joyous, settling into silence. The caw of the last crows quieting as they roosted, rested. The sigh of the water that flowed downstream, dancing around rocks soon to be covered by the surge of autumn currents. The whisper of the trees in the late summer breeze, bringing with it a slight chill now. The confirmation that the seasons were changing. That ancient calling.

Tommy reached for Charlotte's hand and slipped his fingers through hers. She felt his smile. There, above them, circling and mewling, Mona. Her goodnight display against the darkening sky. Cornflower blue, to deep turquoise, to navy. The tiniest of stars becoming a multitude. There was no need for words. Each could read the other's thoughts. They could climb back up the hill and spend the night in the bothy. But no. This, like many before and a lifetime ahead, would be a night under the stars.

THE END

If you enjoyed this story you can help other people find it by writing a review on the site where you bought it from. It doesn't have to be much. Just a few words can really help spread the word and make a big difference to its visibility. Thank you!

Acknowledgements

I am truly grateful to my loyal band of supporters. To Jude Mondragon for the eagle eye that she lends to all of my manuscripts, to Shona Grieve for her enthusiasm, support, and appreciation of my work, to Morag Brownlie for listening, suggesting and guiding. And to all of you, dear readers, without whom this magical journey would never have taken place!

Much love. X

About The Author

Fiona worked as an international school teacher for fifteen years, predominantly in eastern Europe. She now lives in East Lothian, Scotland, where her days are spent walking her dog in beautiful places and writing. Before the Swallows Come Back is her fifth novel.

Also by this author writing as F J Curlew

THE UNRAVELLING OF MARIA

Lovers separated by the Iron Curtain.
Two women whose paths should never have crossed.
A remarkable journey that changes all of their lives.

Maria's history is a lie. Washed up on the shores of Sweden in 1944, with no memory, she was forced to create her own. Nearly half a century later she still has no idea of her true identity.

Jaak fights for Estonia's independence, refusing to accept the death of his fiancée Maarja, whose ship was sunk as she fled across the Baltic Sea to escape the Soviet invasion.

Angie knows exactly who she is. A drug addict. A waste of space. Life is just about getting by.

A chance meeting in Edinburgh's Cancer Centre is the catalyst for something very different.

DON'T GET INVOLVED
Ukraine 2001
Three street-kids
A Mafia hitman
A deadly chase

Dima, Alyona and Sasha, three street-kids with nothing but each other, stumble on a holdall full of cocaine belonging to the Mafia. This could be it. A way out.

Leonid, a Mafia hitman who will stop at nothing to achieve his goals, is sent to retrieve the cocaine and dispose of the children. They won't get far. Failure isn't an option.

Nadia, a naive expat, is looking for a new beginning. She wasn't expecting this!

As their paths get tangled up in the biting cold of a ferocious winter in Kyiv, if they are to survive, all of them will need to find more courage and strength than they ever imagined they had.

Sometimes, when you have nothing left to give, something magical happens.

DAN KNEW

A puppy born to the dangers of street life
A woman in trouble
An unbreakable bond

A Ukrainian street dog is rescued from certain death by an expat family. As he travels with them through Lithuania, Estonia, Portugal and the UK he learns how to be a people dog, but a darkness grows and he finds himself narrating more than just his story. More than a dog story. Ultimately it's a story of escape and survival but maybe not his.

The world through Wee Dan's eyes in a voice that will stay with you long after you turn that last page.

TO RETRIBUTION

He thought she was dead
She wasn't

Suze, an idealistic young journalist, is used to hiding as her cell tries to keep its online news channel open. They publish the truth about the repatriations, the corruption, and the deceit.

New Dawn, the feared security force, is closing in, yet again. Suze runs, yet again.

This time however she is pursued with a relentlessness; a brutality which seems far too extreme for her "crimes". This is more. This is personal.

When her death is finally confirmed, he is celebrating it.

Big mistake.

Retribution will be hers!